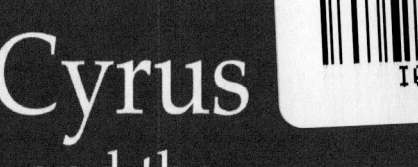

Cyrus
and the
Fighting Robot
Redemption

Joe G. Becker

Cyrus
and the
Fighting Robot
Redemption

a novel

Joe G. Becker

BBL Publishing
Los Angeles, California

Book design by Alison Becker,
artwork contributed by Stephen Morin

ISBN: 979-8-218-54850-6

Visit: joegbecker.com
BBL Publishing
Los Angeles, California

This book is dedicated to my kids,
Bradley, Brett and Lauren

Prologue

The machine was a hundred-and eighty-seven-pound creation, able to dart like a crazed fox, or more so, a crazed fox chasing a rabbit in a closed cage. It was a marvel of zipping and zagging, cast low, barely enough to clear the surface of the ground, and like most wild canines in existence, it had a reputation for ferocity, determination.

Luckily, it never once bared its sharp teeth at the teenager.

That could have really spelled trouble.

The two were locked in tandem, one an extension of the other, almost to the point where the boy felt the pulse of the machine's energy. That *its* electrical currents were *his* lifeblood. He wasn't some human who fired remote-controlled commands into a piece of hardware. No, after so much time together, the boy viewed himself as a co-conspirator in his robot's realm of destruction.

The bot had a shiny metallic veneer, rivets that stretched across its body and intersected like stitches on Frankenstein's skin. From the rear, the bot resembled a tortoise, although that was where the similarities between reptile and machine ended; where a tortoise is apt to move ploddingly on squat legs, the bot had the benefit of agile wheeled treads. Shifting from side to side, it looked like a boxer in a four-wheeled shuffle.

It measured a foot and half high; it was as wide as it was tall. Its tactical "go-to" maneuver was its upward thrusting appendage—the pneumatic flipper. A length of hardened steel that hovered above the ground less than an inch. Like the tip of a snake's tongue, it would wait in repose, then thrust at unsuspecting prey—all in the blink of an eye. This flipper extended out four inches, and with that bit of real estate the machine could do some real damage. One push of the button on the controller—Whap!—the curling uppercut would upend a rushing mechanized foe. That is, if that robot dared to come within range.

Mastering the range took some time for the boy to perfect. The optimal distance of propulsion, he concluded, was nine inches from his opponent. Nine inches to get his point across. Anything closer and he wouldn't be able to gain leverage, thus allowing the opposing robot the inside advantage. Anything farther, his opponent's machine could swing around, retreat, recompose, launch a new attack.

Above all else, one feature on the machine stood out. It was as conspicuous as a cannon perched atop a hill. If the flipper was the setup, the bot's main extremity was the death punch: a triple-jointed weapon similar to that of a human arm—shoulder socket, elbow, hand—that with a flip of a switch of the controller, it could extend at length—high, low or any variation between. Another action of the controller, the arm rotated with one hundred-and-fifty degrees of whipsawing fury.

But what made the arm so treacherous, the ultimate means of assault, was the eight-and-a-half-inch diameter, diamond-tipped saw blade mounted at its end. It could pivot, yaw, slash in any direction. At full speed, it ran eighty-one-hundred rotations per minute. A quick-twitched, deceptive, destructive weapon, like some nasty extremity on an unruly alien beast.

And all the boy had to do was guide his bot toward the target, manipulate his fingers this way and that, and sparks would fly.

And did they fly.

Wires, cogs, bolts, chains, magnets, bushings, and sprockets, everything explosively spraying out.

Only this time, they were its own.

Chapter 1

A lone light from above shone down onto the decagon floor. Its beam penetrated through the smoke and settled its attention on the discombobulated mass beyond the clear walls. Cyrus Hampstead couldn't believe his eyes: his robot chunked, jagged, twisted, mangled, its shards distorted in unnatural configurations.

Next to the remnants a fire steadily burned. The flames licked at his machine's tires, sending up wisps of dark smoke. Tendrils of wire spilled from its ravaged shell-like severed guts. To those in attendance, it must have looked like lightning had struck a cornfield barn and a super tornado had come in to finish the job.

To Cyrus Hampstead, that just as well may have been the case. Because Spiral Cyclone looked nothing like the robot he and his father had built. Not even close.

Beams of light frantically crisscrossed the arena. As the dizzying display gained momentum, the noise of the arena began to escalate inside of Cyrus' head like a gathering tsunami. The crowd's squelching cacophony seemed to go on forever. The rows, an eternity.

Finally, the spotlights settled into a single beam.

And there was Cyrus Hampstead at its center, frozen in disbelief.

A camera straddling on wires whipped over the teen's head—a

split-second flyby. But Cyrus knew the spider camera's target. There was not a doubt in the world.

As he looked up to the Jumbotron, there it was: the backside of his sandy mop of hair, expanded to ten times its normal size.

With his controller still in his hands, Cyrus turned and looked through the clear polycarbonate walls of the arena's decagon. His robot's weaponized arm had somehow Velcroed itself to one of the side walls, attached precariously by a single tooth of the sawblade. For Cyrus, the sight was incongruous, surreal; mere minutes ago the saw was spinning with an unholy force of eighty-one-hundred rotations per minute. Now it wasn't. He wondered why the arm hadn't given way to gravity, why it hadn't toppled to the floor like everything else. He wondered how a single tooth of a sawblade could stay lodged into a polycarbonate wall, keeping forty pounds of shorn metal suspended in place. He wondered how long it would stay like that. Strange thoughts for Cyrus Hampstead to have, given the circumstances.

Cyrus yanked at one of the knobs of his controller, a hopeless, desperate attempt to see if his bot still operated. Spiral Cyclone didn't hiccup. It remained there like a dead animal in the savanna, its carcass ripped and crisped and left to the world.

Totally friggen' annihilated.

Then: *How hell did this happen?*

Even though it was his inclination, this was no time for an impromptu cry out.

As the madness in the arena continued, he looked down at his controller's useless functionality. *Damn thing just seized on me!*

Cyrus stepped out from the light and straggled to a nearby table, unzipped his backpack, which was barely an audible tear over the feverish crowd, and threw the controller in with pained exasperation. The beam followed his movements and the spider cam loped behind; he turned and offered it an easy smile, a façade of unperturbed nonchalance. But there was no hiding his inner turmoil. Gazing up at the Jumbotron, with the larger-than-life Cyrus Hampstead holding center screen, he felt like the poster child of stupefied befuddlement. A stubborn teardrop tickled his left eye. He flicked it off before the spider cam caught sight of it.

Slowly, deliberately, Cyrus placed his backpack atop his wagon (a vehicle once used to transport his *once* virile robot) and folded down all four sides. There was a short wooden ramp which slid underneath, and typically Cyrus would use his foot to glide it in, but as he leveraged himself for the task, he hesitated. The thought of his opposing knee buckling and his entire body following suit crossed his mind. That, he was certain, would blow the arena's roof straight off. *As if they're not already entertained.* So, instead he opted to stand woodenly, breathe steadily, wait for the shakes to settle and the amorphous crowd to stop flogging his brain.

Eventually, he steadied himself with one hand against the wagon's side. He drew the ramp underneath with the other. *Baby steps, Cy. Slow… easy…baby steps.*

Once he flipped down the locks, two tournament officials brushed by him. They headed straight through the door and inside the decagon. Brooms in hand, they began sweeping the entrails of his fighting robot. Cyrus watched their sweeping motions, their monotonous pushing and culling of the broken cogs and rods and wires into large dust pans.

Suddenly, a scene flashed across his mind, as quick as a movie trailer: a shower of sparks, a single rotary blade, an incapacitated machine, a raging fire. Then it was all lost to some ether-world in his head.

Cyrus knew he had to focus his mind elsewhere. Think of something to take his mind away from the hell-fire squelching reverberating through the arena and his skull. He thought back to when he and his father first watched ComBot—this very event—in their den, back when Spiral Cyclone was little more than half-built creation in their basement workshop. Oh, how he loved those moments right before the action, when formalities were brushed aside and the PA announcer issued the callouts. From the high-loft rafters to decagon-side seats, the crowd would volcanically erupt in anticipation of flying sparks, colliding metal, chaos, destruction. It was blood lusting delirium. Then the decagon floor would then come alive: the fueling of the pit o' fire, the sawblade whipping out of the trap in the floor, the spiked thwacker slamming from a sidewall—obstacles to be avoided, lest a machine's demise. How he loved the insanity in this venue-packed playhouse for synthetic creatures.

He loved it all. And nothing spelled malice and ill intent more than the rabidity of those fans. The atmosphere was the main reason he wanted to compete in this twenty-seventh annual addition of ComBot. (Yes, there was the glory and the prize money, those were good reasons, too. And then there was that essential part of it he couldn't articulate, didn't quite have words for, the thing which was rooted deep within him which he was forced to answer to.) But now it all seemed…*different*. As if the same crowd he once loved was spearing its venom directly into his sixteen-year-old heart.

His legs wobbled, his hands trembled. He had the sensation of being adrift at sea during a winter squall.

As the two officials went about resetting the obstacles, his machine's arm finally detached itself from the wall. Cyrus watched as it thudded to the floor.

Instinctively, Cyrus reached for the decagon door's metallic arm bar. It was locked.

"Not yet, kid," boomed a voice from behind. A man wearing a shirt with black-and-red stripes stretched his arm across the door as if Cyrus was orchestrating a break-in. An impatient, slightly taciturn man with narrow, arching eyes and a short, snubbed nose, he appeared to have more important business to handle. *But this is his friggen' business.*

Directly behind him, Cyrus heard a howling caterwaul, some indecipherable madness in the stands. *Just let me to get Spiral Cyclone and get the hell out of here!* He imagined a cave where only the echoes of a quiet wood stretched in the distance. The kind of place where the wind whistles through rock and darkness.

His own special place. That place. The one he had all to himself.

Cyrus turned to the tournament official, disoriented, flushed.

"They gotta finish up in there," the official explained matter-of-fact-ly. "Clear the hazards. Then you can get your bot. What's left of it."

In his opponent's fighting pod, a small crowd had gathered around their robot, assessing its damage. Cyrus eyed the robot keenly, how it stood at their feet like a dutiful dog at a kennel club competition. The bot was named Doke-a-lasher and it was slightly worse for the wear, courtesy of Spiral Cyclone's sawblade. V-shaped, with a golden cursive "D" mounted on its top like some fancy hood ornament, a four-wheeled monster with two-pronged pneumatic claws in the front (minimal dam-age) and two titanium-edged rotary blades mounted on each wing, like devil-possessed weed-whackers (one really paid the price of war.) Along its perimeter was five-inch-high woven chain-link steel girder. During the fight, Cyrus remembered getting Spiral Cyclone's flipper underneath the linkage, but it had suddenly slipped out. That was early in the fight, before his mental fuzziness ran amok. Then he remembered a later part of the fight, a fight in which he moved like a harried matador—defending, countering, spinning, dodging, high tailing away from danger—when he took out one of those rotary blades. *Yes*, Spiral Cyclone had incapacitated it. *Yes*, Doke-a-lasher was on its heels. *Yes,* the tide had turned in his favor. *Yes*, he and Spiral Cyclone were riding the momentum. *Yes*, he steeled himself for the moment, slashing like mad at Doke-a-lasher's last operable rotary blade.

That's how it all went down. One blade down, on to the other!

Then, for whatever reason, fortune took a turn for the worse. His world spun out of control, his brain glaciated, his vision went from 3-D to 0-D.

And within seconds, he and his father's machine was barbequing like a whole hog on a spit.

The spotlights roamed the arena and finally cast a single beam on the victorious group, which sparked them into live-wire euphoria. The group—four men and one woman—exchanged high-fives, back slaps, photo-ops. Two of the guys initiated some weird chest-bumping maneuver, as if they were two bouncing exclamation points. To Cyrus, it seemed to go on way too long, though he had to admit, it was fitting the occasion.

Once the festivities were over the group became engulfed in a spontaneous celebratory dance. This involved them rhythmically shimmying around one of the men. He was their portly Maypole and they rollicked around him; round and round they went. As spotlights crisscrossed the reverie, the man in the middle began to spin, belly bouncing, armpits swamping, a grin a mile wide. The others took turns slapping his back. As with the chest-bumping, this all went on too long for Cyrus' liking.

Cyrus watched it all with circumspection—the fawning over the robot, the victory party, the undulations of the man's pale flesh for whom the robot was named.

It was either that or stare disappointingly through the polycarbonate wall at shrapnel being tossed into oversized buckets.

Maybe that would be better.

After all, thought Cyrus, anything would be better than watching the public adornment of the so-called legend of combat robotics, Ray Dokestout.

Chapter 2

When the official finally yanked up the door's arm lock and swung it open, Cyrus carted his wagon through. The official said something to him as he passed, something he didn't quite hear over a whistle then piercing through the arena. From the movement of the man's lips, Cyrus deciphered it as "Nice fight" or "Nice try."

"Wha?" muttered Cyrus, the word locked in his windpipe.

"Nothing. Go on," said the official brusquely.

Inside the closed decagon, the arena became a soundless, agitated beehive. Brooms in hand and tool belts strapped to their waists, the clean-up officials casually strolled over to Cyrus. *Like medics to the scene of an accident, huh?* One was a good foot shorter than the other, both bald, although the taller guy had tuffs of white hair still struggling for survival. "Boy, kid, that thing really took a beating," said the taller man.

"Smashed," chimed the shorter.

"Bashed…"

"Crashed…"

"…and trashed," they said in unison, smashing fists.

"You think?" replied Cyrus.

"Make sure you guys check the valve before you reset," the head official yelled over, pointing at the flame spitting in the corner—the pit o' fire. The very hazard that continued to produce the taste of singed metal and burnt rubber in Cyrus' mouth. The very hazard that unmercifully incinerated his fighting robot.

The shorter man nodded plainly and gave him the thumbs up. Both then padded over to the blue flame. Cyrus watched them talk animatedly, pointing here and there with their wrenches. As the taller man reached behind the valve, a burst of fire plumed out, startling the short man. Through the open door, Cyrus could hear a din of laughter, piercing whistles. The shorter official aloofly extracted a screwdriver from his toolbelt, peered into the pipe, then leisurely decided against it. Cyrus could sense an impending melee building in the stands, and along with everyone else, he wanted the two to hurry the hell up, just move on out. So he could get to his quiet place. His darkened cave. Shock still hadn't left his body, and the delay was adding little balm to his overworked nerves.

A glow in the press box above Cyrus caught his attention. Bright lights and several cameras were focused on two cowboy-hatted men. The dark-skinned commentator wore a white hat, the light-skinned man donned a black one, both beaming toothy smiles inside robust jaws. When one guy's mouth moved, the other's stopped. Cyrus guessed they were segueing into ComBot27's next battle. Then again, he thought, maybe their animated discussion was about the mop-haired kid standing like a tree stump inside the decagon.

Seconds later, the Jumbotron came alive with their images. Their voices boomed across the arena.

"Jack, what an exciting confrontation. Doke-a-lasher pulled off another one, unleashing an extraordinary show of force in that semifinal contest. A blistering, scintillating attack by the veteran, Ray Dokestout. It's what everyone in this arena expected of this champion."

"Darn right, Skip," countered the man in the white hat. "But don't forget Doke-a-lasher had a few stumbles. Ray was tested, and that's no understatement. His opponent thwarted multiple flip attempts and came on in a flurry. But look, Skip, Ray Dokestout's the current champ. He knows what it takes to recover from a few mishaps. And just in the nick of time, I might add. It was a fantastic finish when it really counted."

Skip: "That's what makes Doke-a-lasher so potent. It disabled its adversary's artillery and laid the beatdown. No doubt we'll see more these tremendous attacks on display in the championship round from the reigning champion. He's one helluva highly successful robotics engineer, this guy."

Jack: "And today his young opponent had succumbed to just that."

Skip: "I have to say, it looked as if Spiral Cyclone failed to make a coherent move at the end. It was totally immobilized. Just when it seemed the tables had turned, Doke-a-lasher completely obliterated Spiral Cyclone. And then that final send off into the goddess of fire, Jack, well, I have one word. Wow!"

Jack: "Hahaha. And an unforgiving goddess she is."

Skip: "So folks, it was a good effort by Spiral Cyclone, but in the end Ray Dokestout and Doke-a-lasher prevailed with an unbelievable semifinal victory in ComBot27. Let's watch how it all went down."

Cyrus watched as the screen transitioned from the commentators to a sequence of images, and with each transition Cyrus' stomach sunk further into a caldron. There was Ray Dokestout tensely manipulating his controls; there was Spiral Cyclone in the grips of Doke-a-lasher; there was Spiral Cyclone set ablaze; there was Ray Dokestout's proud, flashy smile; there was the back of Cyrus' head, sunk in defeat.

The man in the black hat came back on to give his final assessment: "You can see the damage it did to Spiral Cyclone. You can also see the damage it did to Cyrus Hampstead, the teenager who came into Com-Bot27 on a solo venture, making it all the way to the semifinal round. Damn impressive for a kid flying without a squadron, I'd say. Folks, don't stray too far. Next, we have the MicroBots taking the decagon at Com-Bot27, the ultimate prize in combat robotics."

The Jumbotron faded to black. Rock music filled the arena.

Cyrus would have given anything at that moment to have someone there with him. Someone (especially one person, but he knew he had to brush that quickly away) to trade loose smiles with, however unconvincing, someone who might throw out a lame wisecrack or two. Someone to remind him that not all was lost, that the crowd, the lights, the whirling cameras, and his scrabbling nerves would soon be relegated to the forgotten past.

But no matter how he wished, reality was reality. It wasn't going to happen. Not here. Not now. He had to embrace it all—the noise, his nerves, his defeat, his growing tide of insecurity, the feeling of isolation—as a sailor would the sea's unrelenting, cresting waves. Not an easy thing to do when your skull was compressing inward. Not an easy thing to do for someone with only sixteen years trailing in his wake.

Once the officials finished their adjustments, Cyrus wheeled his wagon over to the remnants of Spiral Cyclone. He could feel the radiant warmth from the triple-digit degree heat, and the acrid pungency of burnt metal gave him a jolt. Even Spiral Cyclone's logo, once a bright yellow-and-teal adornment, was a charred mess. *If that's not a sign, then what is?* Again, he tried to recall the events that had transpired. His reversal of fortune, as the commentators described it. His memory was patchwork, foggy, disjointed. Of course, there was that painful cramp in his hand, but that could hardly be called to fault.

Then what the hell happened?

The answers dissipated faster than the smoke in the arena's rafters.

The two officials slid into gloves and, with tilted heads, stood looking down at Spiral Cyclone as if the machine might be contagious. They then side-stepped tepidly around the still-hot object, found their positions, and extracted it from the extinguished pit o' fire.

Cyrus searched his ravaged robot for anything salvageable. Even Spiral Cyclone's wheels had disintegrated into a blob of tar. *Nothing worth saving here.*

"Looks like it was hit by a missile strike," said one of the men.

"The epicenter, I'd say," said the other. "But hey, there's always next year."

"Next year? Not sure about that," replied Cyrus with a hangdog expression.

"Never say never," said the diminutive man. "Hey, hold the wagon steady, kid, the natives are getting restless." The two men squatted down, took hold of the disfigured robotic hull, and set it in the wagon.

To a cascade of discordant cheers and jeers, Cyrus and the officials wheeled the wagon through the decagon's door and past the head official. His posture was erect, his eyes contemptuous, glaring. The smaller man made a tip-of-the-hat gesture to him. "All set for your dance recital, old boy."

CHAPTER 3

With legs churning, the two men pushed the wagon up the aisle's incline. Cyrus did his part by pulling the handle. Exhaustion ate at his legs, hunger at his belly, his energy all but sapped.

When they finally reached the arena's mid-concourse, the two men doubled over, collapsed their hands to their knees and huffed in large breaths of air. The taller man's sweaty head looked like a barrier island at high tide. Cyrus noticed a television monitor on the wall showing the crowd in the stands. People laughed, held signs, danced to the bass-pounding music which spilled over into the concourse.

"Been a pleasure," the shorter man wheezed. "Except for this last part."

"Oh hey, kid, if you're on the lookout for the repair room," mentioned the taller man, "it's down the corridor, second ramp on the right, down one level. Hall on the left you'll see a door that says…"

"Repair room," the shorter man bleated sarcastically. The taller man smacked his head.

Cyrus gave it a quick thought. After his quarter-final contest he left his spare gas tank and welding kit down in the repair room, just in case repairs were needed for the finals. The rest of his tools and supplies were in a slide-out compartment underneath his wagon.

"Thanks, I'll head there in minute. I…I have to pick something up first."

"Good luck, my friend," said the shorter guy with a salute.

"Which way?" the taller guy asked his partner.

"That way," the shorter guy said, thumbing to the right.

"No way."

"Yes way."

"Fairway."

"Causeway."

"Freeway."

"What the hell's a freeway?"

From his wagon's lower compartment, Cyrus pulled out a blanket imprinted with a chrome exhaust pipe crossing through a cobalt-blue "C"—the emblem of his favorite hockey team, the Kettlebridge Chromiums. He blanketed Spiral Cyclone and pressed on. When he reached the arena's upper main concourse, the unmistakable smell of warm bread and seasoned meat drew his stomach's attention. He was queasy, starving, and since breakfast that morning was but an energy bar that now swam in a concoction of stomach acid and expended nerves, he aimed for the concession stand.

"I'll have a hotdog, just ketchup, please," he said to the woman behind the counter. "No, make it two hotdogs. Both with just ketchup."

"Comin' right on up."

On the monitor above her, Ray Dokestout walked with a jocular smirk jauntily down an aisle, his crew trundling behind him. The monitor was muted and the camera angle was low, which made Ray appear grand and important, as if there was little doubt who the ultimate winner of ComBot27 would be. Fans leaned in and pumped their fists at him. Some stuck their hands out for high-fives. Ray didn't reciprocate a single shake, a slap or pump; he simply ignored the commotion and walked by. It certainly seemed to Cyrus, however, that the guy drank in the laudations. Maybe it was success in general which precluded those kinds of intimate gestures, Cyrus figured, but he wasn't quite sure. All he knew was that if he had won in the semifinals, he certainly would have slapped a lot of hands. That was a given.

"Here ya go, two dogs" the woman said, shifting her eyes between Cyrus and his wagon. Her red-dyed hair was piled high on her head and held in by a hairnet. Cyrus could see the red strands peeking through the seams. "Was watching your fight myself, right here on this television," she said, motioning with her chin behind her. She made no mention of Cyrus' pulverized bot shrouded by blanket cover.

Cyrus thanked the woman and gulped down the hotdogs as fast as a contestant in a Fourth of July eating contest. He then oriented himself to his surroundings. The arena's numbered sections were painted on the columns. Section 307 was just ahead, so he grabbed his wagon's handle and set off for the higher sections.

"Looks like they just getting underway," the woman stopped him. She pointed up to the monitor. "Little ones this time."

"MicroBots," said Cyrus, referring to the lightweight division.

"Yeah, they can cause a lot of destruction too."

"That so? Look nasty enough," she replied.

They watched as a shoe-sized bot named Purvis the Pest took on another tiny assemblage called Gadget Greer. As the contest began, it was evident to Cyrus that one or the other was going down in a hurry; they're contrasting means of attack and defense was a recipe for a short-lived fight. Purvis the Pest was shaped like a flying saucer, a hell-fire spinner on three wheels with seven sickle-like blades protruding from its circumference. At the buzzer, it spat out onto the decagon floor in a zero-to-sixty seek and destroy mission. But Gadget Greer had an answer for the violence hurtling its way. Shaped like a slice of pie turned on its side, and outfitted with a front-hinged flipper, it squared up to its opponent, shot forward, launched its flipper outward, and catapulted Purvis the Pest five feet into the air. The machine crash-landed inches from the blazing pit o' fire. It squirmed to avoid the licking flames, then bounced from one sidewall and careened into another, behaving like an out-of-control toy top. On the rebound, one of its blades caught the ground, causing it to rocket over the surging Gadget Greer. But Purvis the Pest landed true and continued its frenzied spin. Now on Gadget Greer's blindside, it went to work, tunneling deep into hardware. Gadget Greer had no chance. Yellow sparks rained down, and once vital organs were ripped into, that was the end of the line for Gadget Greer.

Purvis the Pest's victory took all but twenty seconds.

Cyrus continued watching the muted monitor as the proud operators of Purvis the Pest drank in the victory, a contained and muted celebration compared to Ray Dokestout's exhibition.

"Here ya go, son, gotcha this one here on the house," said the woman behind the counter. She handed Cyrus a frothy drink. He took a gingerly swig. "Thanks. My favorite. Root beer."

"Yep, root beer," she acknowledged.

Cyrus slung his backpack over his shoulders. As he reached for his wagon's handle to head out, the woman again stopped him.

"Hey, look, that's you," she said, "Yep, sure is. That's you alright."

A shot of Cyrus concentrating tensely appeared on the monitor. It then cut to Spiral Cyclone in tight focus. Cyrus' heart sank. His once-partner, with whom he raged alongside with a force that his own human muscles could never muster, was now but a hollow heap of nothingness slumped under his Chromiums blanket. *Ten years. Ten whole years. Practically my whole life that bot's been with me.* Another huge loss in his sixteen years. He had a hard time thinking about it, so he let it go.

"Is that what's under that blanket?" the woman asked, leaning over the counter.

"Used to be," he croaked.

With eyes glued to the soundless monitor, Cyrus watched a new scene unfold: Doke-a-lasher straddling the fire line, rocking side to side, laying into Spiral Cyclone with its last rotary blade. A savage shredding before the firestorm. He watched it rip his bot apart like a one-clawed crab picking through a limp chicken neck. Eventually, shrapnel flew east, south and west as black smoke plumed north.

Even after the benefit of two hotdogs with ketchup, he still wasn't sure how it all happened.

The monitor then showed Spiral Cyclone's arm velcroed to the polycarbonate wall, wires dangling. *Yeah, I remember that alright.*

The hotdogs in Cyrus' stomach shifted, his heart rattled inside his rib cage. He was then walloped by a realization: that in four months' time that very event would be televised throughout the country. His friends, relatives, teachers, classmates…everyone…would witness Cyrus Hempstead stuck on stupid as his robot charred to a crisp. *Fan-friggen'-tastic!*

The chatty cowboy-hatted announcers came back on the live feed. They were wide-eyed. They shook their heads. Their mouths jawed with soundless movements.

Luckily for Cyrus, he wasn't a lip reader.

CHAPTER 4

He was fading. And fast. After three wearying contests, the day was pushing hard against his troubled mind and worn-out body. And no amount of root beer or hotdogs could free him from his exhaustion.

"Thanks again," he shouted to the woman as she took another order. He dropped his cup into a trash bin, took hold of his wreck and hauled it through a cluster of fans who had emerged during the intermission. Some quietly and curiously stared at the ragged teenager dragging a blanket-covered wagon. Others passed without notice. Near his destination, Cyrus passed two guys with heavy-lidded eyes who gave him the thumbs up. "Right on Ro-bo-boy," one hoarsely yelled. He smiled and repeated the moniker to himself. *Ro-bo-boy...huh, Ro-bo-boy.*

He finally found it: Section 320. Down the perpendicular hallway he came upon a door: "Staff Only." He looked around furtively, then checked the door's handle. Unlocked, just as he'd left it. He wedged the front wheel of his wagon inside the door so that it didn't close. Just enough light seeped into the darkened room.

In the storage closet there were shelves stacked with sports equipment and supplies. Given that the only event that weekend involved fighting robots, along with the fortuitous fact that the closet seemed undisturbed, Cyrus figured it was still safe. Once again, he had the place to himself. The perfect hideout. And as of early that morning, the perfect sleeping quarters. *My own cave.*

In the rear of the closet was a small nook no bigger than a kitchen pantry. Cyrus had stacked some boxes in front of it in case anyone decided to come in and probe around. He approached the nook and slid the boxes to the side.

On the ground, untouched as he had left them, were his sleeping bag, a small travel pillow, his overnight kit, and some loose papers. *Nice, quiet, darkened cave.* A place where the noise and music from the outside world waned like a stretched-out echo.

Cyrus' eyelids began to droop; he caught himself mid-yawn. But there was no escaping it. It had been a long, tiring day. It wouldn't hurt to lay in his head for a while. No music, no crowd, just meandering thoughts travelling through a short tunnel of dreams.

Cyrus picked up the printout of his bus schedule. The next—and last—bus home that evening left in just under two hours. He set the alarm on his phone for 6:15 pm. That would give him enough time to nap, gather himself, grab his tank from the repair room, and perhaps throw down another hotdog. Then he'd head for the bus stop outside the arena.

Cyrus peeked his head out of the closet door. A couple talked animatedly as they walked past the corridor, but they seemed not to notice he or his wagon. He drew it inside. Before shutting the door, he heard the PA announcer pepper the crowd for the next bout: "Who's ready for more metal-crunching mayhem? I-i-i-it-t-t-t's ti-i-i-i-ime." Cheers rang throughout the concourse. In his head, Cyrus could imagine the cowboy-hatted commentators' peppy talk.

The door closed shut. Now pitch black, he searched for the light switch (navigating, of course, by memory) but tripped and fell and muddled around on all fours. Finally, he found the lights and fired them on. He then reassessed his path, clicked the lights back off, and settled into his sleeping bag.

Cyrus' mind was racing, racing with the fever of the event and the trauma of his defeat. Then there was all that noise…it floated across his skull like an ancient moaning of the dead. He worked down further into his sleeping bag. He drew up the zipper. Noise receded. Darkness took hold. Images fragmented. Perspectives lost shape. Suddenly, the words of one of the officials repeated itself, over and over: "Next year, next year."

How can I? he thought as he seeped into drowsiness. *How can I without him?* But he knew it was possible, somehow, someway. Because "he" was the one who told Cyrus he could. Not in so many words, that wasn't his way. It was more his prideful determination. A pride which spoke, *"If you want it, it's yours. Just find a way."* That was always his father's mindset. And the voice Cyrus heard reverberating inside his head was as resolute, uncompromising, and self-assured as if the man were laying right there next to him. It was a voice that explained the secrets of the world.

As Cyrus lay there, full of belly and hazily drifting towards sleep, his eyes moistened over. He dabbed at them with his pillow. Again, he calculated the stillness of the closet and who may disturb him. He thought he heard keys rattling. His mind was uneasy, like a soldier walking through enemy lands.

Slowly, all his musings became disjointed. However, one single image took hold—his father walking on the path behind their house with a chainsaw and a winch. Cyrus was not far behind. He was nine years old at the time. *Or younger. Eight? Maybe ten?* Regardless of the exact age, Cyrus closed his eyes.

And fell dreamily into those woods.

CHAPTER 5

The Hampstead house is a turn-of-the-twentieth-century colonial farmhouse fronting nine acres of dense woods. Beyond the backyard is a narrow slit that enters the trees, a spur that reaches only so far as a work shed set within. Beyond that, the trees and saplings and underbrush consume what decades ago had been a well-blazed trail leading to a now-defunct plot of farmland.

The woodsy thickness, however, never stopped Cyrus from exploring the woods' interior, an endless expanse of beech, sycamore, elm, and oak. About two hundred yards down the old path, a large rocky outcrop punctuates the landscape. Cyrus christened the rock "Cyrus' Stone," a spy-point for passing critters and lazy sunsets.

It was in these woods that his dream fell. It was a weekend afternoon in Autumn (a Saturday or Sunday is what he conjured, but what did it matter at that age anyhow), the time of year when temperatures begin to drop and cool winds start to move through the low, rolling hills. It was late in the day, nearing dusk. Long clouds were ushered in by northerly winds; above, the sky ashen silver; on the ground, the crickets issued their calls to the hills that the day was about done.

Cyrus had been relaxing on his back patio in an Adirondack chair, thankful for the change in weather. His fat, gray cat, Mongrel, napped on his chest, keeping him warm. Unburdened, Cyrus' only concern was if

Mongrel might roll in his sleep and scratch his chest if he began to fall.

Then, from the woods, he heard his father call out his name. The sharp voice snapped him from his rest. From the tone, Cyrus knew some type of work (not robot building, he was sure of it) was at hand. It was a tone augured by a disciplined resolve. Reluctant at first to disturb the sleeping cat (Mongrel was not accustomed to impromptu movements), Cyrus merely drew open his eyelids and waited. But not for long. No conditions or compromises would free Cyrus from a task when his father called for it. That was his nature—not overbearing, just authoritative. And always industrious.

Half a minute later, Cyrus was stepping over the dazed, yawning cat on his way to the shed. There, a chainsaw with its arm detached from the engine was sitting on a workbench. A socket wrench was nearby.

"Son, sharpen up that chain, would ya, and put it back on the saw. Make sure there's a bit a slack to it too. Not too tight. You've done it before, so you know how it goes on. We've got some work to do."

Once the chainsaw was sharpened, inspected and full of gas, his father threw on his canvas coat and helped Cyrus slide into a pair of leather boots. His father combed through the shed for the smallest pair of gloves he could find and handed them to Cyrus. "These'll work, though watch out for those holes at the tips," he told Cyrus. "Splinters will get through. I know how much you like having your mom yank those out."

"Not really. Where we headed?"

"Know that big elm?"

"Yeah."

"Contracted a disease. Saw it on the leaves this summer. Brown spotting. They've been dropping off early. It's only a matter of time for the ol' tree. Doesn't mean it can't be used as firewood though."

Together, they marched along the old path to the east section of the property as the sun headed further west.

Cyrus fell in behind his father. Yellow and red leaves pillowed lightly along the old trail, breezing away as they hiked along in silence. In his dream, Cyrus could recall the sounds their boots made as they scraped along, the rustling of the wind, the birds that were beginning to settle in for the night. Every so often a gust of wind would bring the treetops to life, and he'd watch the colorful leaves parachute down. He made a game of smacking them, an off-balancing challenge since he was holding both an ax and an iron wedge. In front of him, his father carried the chainsaw, shoulder slumped from the burden, while the other arm held a greasy old winch used to haul down stubborn lumber.

Cyrus knew the tree. It was a goliath that had bullied its way skyward past dozens of shaky saplings. Cyrus coined it "The King" because of how little light it let through. He imagined the other trees, wispy and prone to curvature, as its royal court. He knew the great elm would have to fall someday—that was the natural order of life—but he found it hard to believe "The King's" fate was now at hand.

In this dream, Cyrus could smell the spent gas as his father diligently ripped away at the elm's base, weaving deep grooves around its circumference. He could almost taste the sweetness of the sawdust as it stuck to his sweaty face. The sawing had an energy that had disturbed the peace of Autumn's silver glow, but he couldn't have been happier; a fire-wood outing with his father was a hundred times better than lazing around with that fat, lazy Mongrel.

When his father took a break from chain sawing, Cyrus grabbed the axe and had a go at the slivered sections. It was all fruitless frenzy. When he turned around, his father was kneeling down laughing, which caused a fit of laughter from Cyrus himself but didn't stop his unrelenting attack.

After an hour of work came the fall. A few sharp clicks and a thunderous crash barreled through the expanse of woods. Birds stopped chirping; crickets fell silent. Many of the royal court were wasted in the wake, buried or snapped. Cyrus watched his exhausted father collapse on the stump, wiping his sweaty forehead with a camouflaged bandana. Though his face was partly obscured by the faded twilight, Cyrus knew this was what made his father feel alive and whole. Work and the natural elements, those fed the man's soul.

Cyrus then went to work on the tree's limbs with unbridled youthfulness. His father reclined on the stump, watching Cyrus whack away with the axe until it was announced, with a finality that only a military man could, that victory was theirs. Cyrus was relieved that limb removal would be saved for another day. He knew dinner was ready. In his dream, he could smell Shepard's pie.

They placed the winch on top of the grand trunk and headed home. The darkness soaked up their rejoices of victory and the similar proclamations of conquerors who have come before.

All of this happened several years before his father was returned home, where he served overseas as an engineer in the United States Army. He came back draped by an American flag, his body inside a casket made of wood.

Cyrus was not allowed to see his father, for reasons not known to him at the time. Later, through inference and the knowledge of living, he understood why that was.

Cyrus was allowed only to see the casket. This appeared to him now, materializing slowly from a blurriness and into sharp detail: the horizonal lines of red and white; the blue box of stars; the gleam of ingrained wood; handles of brass with wing-spread eagles; the insignia of the U.S. Army on a swath of blue.

Cyrus' last vision was of the casket dropping into the earth. Among rows and rows of white, uniformly arranged gravestones, on that bitter cold March afternoon.

CHAPTER 6

Cyrus lay cocooned in his sleeping bag, arms tightly locked to his side, zipper up to his chin, an insect waiting for springtime. Little did he shift or squirm.

A well-deserved rest which could have possibly continued for hours if not for the twangy beat of a pop song pulsating through the closet. The pitchy lyrics cried out of Cyrus' phone, a soft, bluish light dancing to their rhythms with opaque luminosity. His eyes sprung open. He wondered how long he'd been out.

Like a paranoid prairie dog, he swiveled his head. He was only slightly aware of where he was and why he was there. At first, he thought he was in his room at home, a deception which made a jersey hanging on a rack appear as the Chromiums jersey hanging on his bedroom wall.

Soon, the reality sunk in that he was in a supply closet in an arena, far from home. He drew down his sleeping bag's zipper, climbed out, cut his phone's musical ode to summertime revelry, and rooted around for his flashlight. He blasted a beam at the door. *Yes, still locked.* He whistled a phew.

His phone read 6:16 pm.

As he collected his belongings and was set to exit the supply closet, his phone rang. His mother's face winked at him from the home screen, puckering a kiss. He hit the speaker.

"Cyrus? Cy, baby? How did the fighting go? Did you win?" Her excited words raced out.

"Hi, mom. Uh, yes. I won. Three times. Then I lost in the semis."

"Fantastic, Cy. I'm so proud. You won," she yelped.

As with many mothers, Cyrus' mother is attentive to certain aspects of his life. The particulars of ComBot aren't one of them. Time after time, he had to explain the simple tournament format to her, highlighting three crucial, inner-related factors: winner takes all, no rubber matches, survive-or-go-home. So, when her excitement launched into a jump-scare at the word "won," he tried to hold back his frustration.

"Mom, the thing is, I lost one. If you lose a fight, you're done. I came close, really close, meaning the semis, but I didn't win the *whole* thing."

"Oh, honey. I'm so sorry. Sorry…what a shame. Well, there's always next year."

"Sounds familiar."

"Cy, have you made it to the bus yet?" she asked. "Shouldn't you be on the bus if you're not staying until the end?"

"In about an hour," said Cyrus, again checking the time.

"How about Spiral Cyclone?" she asked. "How did it hold up?"

"Uh, not so good. In fact, Cyclone was destroyed."

"Destroyed?"

"Completely. Like totally. Wrecked. Gone." He inflected each word with greater dejection.

"Oh, Cy. That's too bad, baby. I know how hard you and your father worked on that machine. So, so many hours…years. Maybe, you know, well maybe ComBot may have been a bit too much, given…." She fell quiet a beat, which was unusual for his mother. He realized she had either run her course on condolences or was delving far into a subject she didn't want to delve into. Something neither wanted to touch at the moment. But if he knew his mother well enough, she'd soon be moving swiftly onto something else. Like his grandmother and all the women of their clan, a dam could hold back the water only so long before it burst the walls. The Hampstead men, on the other hand, were sheets of ice on the tundra: frosty and mostly muted.

His assumption was correct. "By the way, how was your stay with the Mulvaney's? Did you give Lettie my best? I haven't seen her, or Popsicle, in years."

"Uh, they were good," said Cyrus.

"I just want to make sure you were comfortable. That was a big trip to take alone like that. I was really worried about you."

"Uh, I was comfortable, mom" he lied. "They had a nice room for me. Real quiet, too."

What Cyrus was reluctant to tell his mother (possibly because he was running on a tight schedule and was antsy to leave the "Staff Only" closet, although the notion that he would soon have to endure a battery of questions did cross his mind) was that sleep last night at the Mulvaney's was terrible. His parent's friends, with whom he was staying for the night, had recently adopted a puppy. That puppy had somehow found its way to the basement where Cyrus was lodging. The basement didn't have a door, so a curious, rambunctious puppy had no problem finding its new friend. Cyrus didn't want to disturb his hosts by tossing him back upstairs; they looked exhausted themselves from trying to train the little guy to pee outside and not eat their socks. So, he let the pooch stay.

It was fun at first. The pup licked and nipped and tugged and snuggled, which happened to keep his mind occupied from his crushing, pre-fight nerves. At least for a while, until Cyrus was worn by its boundless energy. As soon as Cyrus thought the puppy was about to crash out, it rebounded for more action. Five or six times that happened. Like clockwork.

When Cyrus heard Popsicle upstairs at four am rooting around in the kitchen, with the smell of coffee brewing, he lugged himself upstairs, puppy at his heels.

"Hi, Mr. Mulvaney," said Cyrus, startling the man.

"Oh, man. Hey, Cy," he jumped. "You got me good there. I think I've lost my edge. That's what happens when they keep you cooped up in a lab and not out in the field."

"Sorry."

"No, no. All good. And Cyrus, call me Popsicle, please. Everyone likes a Popsicle. I don't think your father even knew my real name. Hell, I think I've about forgotten it as well. Unless I happen to renew my license or something like that. Why ya up so earlier, boy?"

The night before, Cyrus overheard Popsicle telling Lettie he'd have to be at the airport early in the morning for a flight out. He knew the airport was near the arena.

"The arena's near the airport, right? Any chance you could drop me off?"

"Just off Route 118. Mile or so south. Lettie said she'd take you later, though. Don't you think four am is a little early? Contest begins, what, like seven, eight hours from now?"

"Yeah, but I've got some repairs to do. Stuff like that. Gotta prepare, you know," said Cyrus.

"Sure. No problem, boy," Popsicle said. "Always be prepared. No matter what, 'cause shit does happen. You heard that creed before, haven't you?"

"Yeah. From Dad. He also said shit is created."

"Boy, yes…it…is, you said a mouthful there. Especially with what we dealt with." He took a sip of coffee and gave a fond, blank look at the puppy, who sat innocently at his feet. "First time in a month I wasn't woken up by Muttly here. Man, I musta been out."

If Cyrus' eyes told the story, he didn't let them show. "Cute little fellow," he said, leaning down to scratch his ear. Muttly jumped cravenly at his hand, nipping his thumb.

Popsicle topped off his to-go mug. "Alright, then. Grab your gear and I'll get the ramp hooked to the truck's tailgate. Meet me outside the garage pull 'er up on in. I'll let Lettie know you're coming with."

Forty-five minutes later, Popsicle and Cyrus pulled up to the entrance of the arena. The sun, not yet risen, cast the great brick building in a gauzy shade. Cyrus watched the workers through the glass windows preparing for the day.

"Well, good luck, Cy. Should be an adventure from what I'm guessing," said Popsicle. He released the ratchet ties holding the wagon down to the pickup truck bed, attached the ramp, and together they wheeled the wagon off. "Wish I could see it myself, but you know, business calls."

"Understood. Thanks, Popsicle."

"I think your father would be pretty impressed. I know he loved this stuff, the fighting caught up in his blood after a while. It really did. I dabbled in the game myself, years ago back. Helped him out a bit, but he took it to a whole 'nother level."

"You made combat robots with him?" asked Cyrus.

"I did. We didn't spend all our talents and energies for the military, you know." Popsicle laughed. "He really loved the combatting part of it. That was his true passion. Looks to be yours too. Ain't that something." He shook his head. "Boy, I do miss him. Sure you do, too."

Cyrus looked away to the building. Inside, a man was mopping the floor in the dim yellow light. "I do. Yeah, he loved the sport. I just hope…"

"Boy, listen, no matter how it turns out, no matter how it goes down in there or whatever may happen, the fact that you got here, and doing it all be yourself at that, well, he'd be one hella proud. Hella proud."

"Thanks, Popsicle," said Cyrus, grabbing the wagon's side. "And thanks for the ride."

"Now, you know where to head for the bus stop, across the lot there. Your mother also said you might be staying with us another night."

"Hopefully. It's a long shot. If I make it to the finals, I'd be here too late to make the bus back home tonight. I can catch one tomorrow near your house."

"I see. Well, just give Lettie a shout if you'll need picking up to-night. Or not. She's got the details. And the other truck. And luckily," he patted the edge of the aluminum ramp, "a second ramp in the garage."

"Got it."

Popsicle squeezed his shoulder heartily, gave him a salute, and was off.

Once inside the arena, Cyrus' intention was spartan. Find a lonely hallway or corridor to lay his head awhile. A quiet space to cram all those nerves of his into a tight bundle and fall against a wall and sail away before the chaos began. With this purpose in mind, he wandered upon a "Staff Only" door, which was slightly ajar. He nudged it open with his foot. Providence came in the form of a dark, seldom-used closet. That was a little after five am.

Cyrus listened as his mother let out a sigh, the extended kind that longs for times past. "They're great people. Popsicle was so close to your father. They were like best friends in their unit. Seen everything together.

More than I ever wanted to know."

Cyrus thought back to the look in Popsicle's eyes when he mentioned his father. They glinted with forlorn affection, hinted at souls lost.

"Anyway, Cy, make sure you connect with Lettie to let her know you'll be coming back home tonight. Listen, are you sure you don't want me to come get you? I can be up there in little over, what, three and a half hours? You may be too exhausted to deal with the bus."

"No, mom," said Cyrus, "I'm good. I've made it this far. Bus's not so bad anyway."

"OK, then. I understand. I have to head out. I'm late picking up Cindy for..."

In his haste, Cyrus was purposing two hands for three tasks—holding his phone, turning the door handle, and pulling his wagon—so his mother's statement became a distorted muffle when his phone banged to the floor.

"A movie?" he questioned as he gathered the phone.

"Not a movie, an antique show," she wailed with exasperation. "Weren't you listening?"

"Oh. An antique show sounds so much more boring than a movie," he said.

"Who said anything about a movie?"

"You did," he said.

"I did not. Oh, forget it. Oh, oh, Cy, I almost forgot to tell you. Do you remember that reporter who interviewed you recently? From the

Beacon?"

"Yes."

"I emailed you the article he wrote. It just came out and it's really sweet, you'll love it. You can read it on your way home. You're catching the bus soon, right?"

"In exactly fifty-two minutes and twelve seconds, mom."

"OK, don't miss it. I can't wait to see you tonight. Love you, baby."

"See you tonight. Love you."

Cyrus shot Lettie a text before heading out in search of the repair room.

Hi LOST IN SEMIS. CATCHING RIDE HOME NOW THX FOR HAVING ME. GIVE MUTTLY A HUG

Muttly. Had he beat Ray Dokestout, he would've partied all night long with the pup. One step away from the ComBot27's trophy and the forty thousand dollars purse. Yes, he would've gladly been Muttly's besty.

Such was not the case. Cyrus was bus-bound in less than an hour.

CHAPTER 7

Cyrus weaved through the crowd like a poultry rancher through a chicken yard. His wagon crushed over dozens of empty cups. He two-stepped around food containers tossed flippantly to the ground. He pressed through people and their messes.

The music in the arena was vibing. Heads swinging, bodies swaying, fans rattling about with excitement. As Cyrus trekked through the throngs, he encountered a grappling, foul-mouthed ruckus. Little surprise that all that adrenaline from watching machines smash together spilled over into humans doing the same. One guy took a wild swing at another but missed. Flying backwards, that guy tried for a kick but also misconnected. In short time, the incident tempered and each guy was dragged the opposite direction.

Cyrus descended a short ramp. Eventually, he found the repair room. Inside, several long rows of workbenches stretched out with a scattering of hardware and tools: sanders, welding arcs, vises, soldering guns, pliers, wrenches, pinchers, hammers, bits and screws, cogs and rods, spools of rainbow-colored wire. Everything for the combat robotics trade.

He entered quietly and parked his wagon off to the side. His Chromiums blanket had slid off Spiral Cyclone's carcass, exposing a logo that looked like it was exhumed from a house fire. Not that the house looked much better.

A dozen or so people lingered inside, tinkering and talking. Cyrus paid no notice of them, or who they were, although he couldn't escape the fall of eyes upon him. A group huddled in the back seemed especially interested in his presence.

Cyrus looked around, trying to remember where he left his gas tank and repair kit.

As he walked the length of a workbench, he found it. The name "Hampstead" was emblazoned in a rough, scar-raised weld. His welding kit lay next to it. As he placed them in the wagon, a distinctive voice rose above the rest.

"I'd be careful with that thing," Ray Dokestout shouted across the room. "You might start a fire. And I think you've had enough of that for one day." Snickers rumbled from his camp.

From what Cyrus could tell, the man was forty-something years old. His onyx hair was parted to one side, matted and slightly greasy. His forearms were asymmetrical to his biceps, like Popeye's, though it was obvious the guy didn't thrive off spinach. His T-shirt was stretched across his gut to the point where the first and last letters of the rock band's name were indecipherable. His denim jeans were torn at the knees, allowing puffy white flesh to sneak out of the openings.

It could've been as simple as ordering an ice cream, but the voice had a blustering bravado. Anyone familiar with Ray Dokestout's internet tutorials knew it well, and Cyrus himself was no stranger to the brash cadences of the sport's legend. The series of tutorials called "How-to-Build-a-Battling-Bot" were Ray Dokestout's production. He was the guy who swung in tandem with every fighting season, the high imminence at every tournament. Ray Dokestout was the acclaimed king of ComBot. And if others didn't see it that way, Ray himself would find a way to set them straight.

If it had to do with the sport, his name would be the first to pop up on a search list. If there was an article written on the topic, his name would be featured. For a kid like Cyrus, the technical information on robotic engineering became invaluable once his father passed. Ever since that fateful day, and the weeks and empty months, Cyrus' only option for advice were internet tutorials, produced and copyrighted by the one and only, Ray Dokestout.

Of course, the tutorials were vehicles to promote his books and products. Even as a young boy, that notion wasn't lost on Cyrus. In fact, Ray Dokestout would tell the viewer, with a high dose of egotistic self-conflagration, the means of access: *Now listen, Folks, these elements I've discussed have been instrumental to my innumerable years of success. Now you too can benefit from my vast knowledge. You see, it's not enough to put your heart and soul into your robot, that's fine and good, but you must have the technical acumen. My longevity and championship runs have been developed by the highest standards in technical engineering. Right here in my own commercially successful, Doke-a-lab. Now you too can access these invaluable riches. Look closely, see this rack pin-ion feature on this arm station? It's one of the many innovations that can accessed through a simple purchase, investment really, in my series.*

Cyrus never bought the books or any of the products he pitched. He couldn't afford them. He did, however, watch his free videos, hoping to learn anything that would help him with the maintenance of Spiral Cyclone. As he continued to fight, and win, viewing those videos became ever more crucial.

If he had to build another fighting robot, he may very well have to buy into Ray Dokestout's bible of robotic knowledge. If the lone traveler wanted directions, he'd have to get a map. It was either that—or don't travel at all. As it now stood, Cyrus had no idea what direction to take. Let alone if he even needed a map.

Naturally, all Ray's content was to glorify his Doke-a-bots. His weapons were the most innovative and engineered to the highest standards. His fights, a showcase of supremacy. At the heart of it all was this notion: the viewer was witnessing a master at work.

And Ray Dokestout begged the world to dethrone him.

Cyrus ambled to his wagon and never looked over at Ray. He thought it best to keep quiet, ignore the goading. Let the king and his fiefdom have their glorious moment.

Then Ray's voice vaulted to a taunt. "Damn hot in that decagon, wasn't it? Damn, it was fucking hot. Hotter than the Sahara, huh, little buckaroo?"

Cyrus couldn't keep his mouth shut: "Like the Sahara in summertime. Yep, you got it."

"Hey, sport," one his teammates interjected, "you see that over there? The recycling clown in the corner."

Cyrus had seen it earlier in the day. A giant stylized clown robot with a punchy-red smile. One of the robot's hands pointed down to an open cylinder while the other held a sign: "Recycle Heap. Throw Scraps Here." The final resting stop of the defeated. Cyrus never imagined Spiral Cyclone would be eligible for the clown wasteland, but there it was, waiting to be fed.

"The clown doesn't pay for scrap metal, but it won't laugh at ya either," cracked another guy. "At least I haven't heard it yet."

Ray leaned against a workbench where two in his crew worked on Doke-a-lasher. "Nah, I wouldn't toss the thing in there. It's too darn cute. I mean, ya made a cute little thing there. Take it home and do something with it. You design that bot yourself, kid?" he asked.

"Had some help," said Cyrus tersely.

"Lieutenant Hampstead's kid?" Ray questioned after a beat.

Cyrus froze. He felt helpless and trapped, like an army of ants were attacking his legs as he sunk into quicksand.

"Yeah, my father built it. I helped," he said sturdily.

"I remember him," said Ray. A light rain of laughter filled the repair room. "He made some good bots. Not championship caliber, not second level either. Decent enough. Well, there's always next year, kid."

"Right, I know," replied Cyrus. The sarcasm caught the ire of Ray's right hand man, a wiry guy with bushy white hair that billowed from his cap. The man's eyes were pinched like a weasel. "I got it," he shot out. "I know what you can do with your little bot there, kid. Use it as a planter. Turn it upside, plant a little bush or something in it."

"A cactus," another guy shouted.

"The kind with those little arms sticking out," bleated the wiry guy.

"A saguaro."

"A what?"

"A saguaro. They grow in the Sonoran Desert."

"The Saharan?"

"No asshole. The Sonoran. Saguaros grow in the Sonoran," the wiry guy yelled jocularly. "Sonoran, Saguaro, get it?"

"Sonoran, Saguaro, Sonoran, Saguaro," Ray's crew chanted, as if this was the funniest thing ever conceived. Even the two guys fiddling with Doke-a-lasher got in on the action.

"Sonoran, Saguaro, Sonoran, Saguaro, Sonoran, Saguaro."

Cyrus opened the repair room door.

"Don't go into the desert looking for one," yelled Ray. "You might not like the heat. It's a real inferno in the Sonoran Desert."

Cyrus wedged his tank beneath Spiral Cyclone's disintegrated tires.

"Sonoran, Saguaro, Sonoran, Saguaro."

Heaves of chuckling followed him. Before he exited, someone called out: "Don't forget to water it every day."

It's a cactus, I wouldn't need to water it every day. You fucking asshole.

CHAPTER 8

The shortcut Cyrus thought he was taking turned out be one anxiety-inducing labyrinth. Far from a shortcut, not quite a long cut, more of a corkscrew cut. At least that's how Cyrus saw the journey, an ever-accelerating downward spiral that eventually led him to the underground parking garage. Once he had turned onto that first ramp, there was no turning back.

Pulling a wagon is hard enough, but going downhill with close to two hundred-and-fifty pounds behind you, then having to round corners and avoid crashing into walls, columns and railings, then finally decelerating all that free-wheeling momentum all the while accounting for the rattling, untethered weight of a hundred-and eighty-seven-pound robot, plus gas tank, is, to say the least, harder that it seems. Especially when one considers the wagon in question was controlled by a kid registering nowhere near the same mass.

After about a full minute of fighting gravity, Cyrus' muscle expenditure and fatigue became nearly unbearable. Along the way he passed a lone concessioner (who nearly lost a full tray of beers) and two surprised security guards. They were the only human impediments to a wild, unforeseeable ending.

At last, a pair of swinging double doors appeared out of nowhere, and before he knew it, he crashed unceremoniously through them. It was a miracle he came away without a broken bone, or even a scrape.

He found himself inside a dimly lit subterranean garage. It was as if he entered a morgue. The place was quiet, chilly. Nothing but cars, columns, cool air, and orange cones scattered about like lost chess pieces. Meanwhile, his head was a marbled sphere of sweat. His calves were strained, and his back felt like it had been yanked on a torture-rack.

Cyrus checked the time. The bus was scheduled to depart in eight minutes. He knew the kindly cool of the garage would be short-lived; outside a stark July sun was waiting. He rested a minute, swiping away the flow of sweat with the back of his hand. He then looked around for large the trash dumpsters, knowing they were always stationed near the exits. He walked around the garage until the smell of rubbish hit his nostrils. Next to the dumpster, an exit ramp curved up to level land. *Great, now uphill. And with a stench at my back.* No surprise, Ray Dokestout crossed his mind.

Steeling his stomach, Cyrus heaved a breath and made a running start for the ramp. He drove his legs with brave momentum...*screw that...* stalled...*shit*...cranked and gave out...*bag*...cranked...*ass*...stalled... *Dokestout*...cranked...*piece*...stalled...*of*...and cranked until he finally mounted the crest...*crap!*

He arrived in a stifling July humidity that attempted to wick every last drop of moisture from his already-drained body. In the parking lot, shimmering heat waves rose from the black asphalt, and thousands of cars radiated the sun from their roofs and hoods. The air was so thick the pores of Cyrus' skin had flooded his shirt, which clung to him like cellophane. He leaned over his wagon, suffering from salt-stung eyes. Everything appeared kaleidoscopic.

Cyrus raced across the lot, laying pods of sweat in his wake. The bus was nowhere in sight, but he huffed it nonetheless, anxiety over missing it fueling his feet. Timeliness was important to Cyrus. Timeliness was one thing that calmed his nerves, however much they could be calmed.

Cyrus landed in a weedy medium strip between the road that circled the arena. There, he waited. Twenty yards beyond, an electronic billboard intermittently flashed an advertisement for the weekend's offering. The synthesized colors turned his shirt the color of mud: *ComBot27. The Robots Have Arrived. Combat Robotics Finals, July 26. Limited Seating Available.*

While mesmerized in the billboard's trance, Cyrus suddenly recalled something. Something important. Something his mother said. *The*

LOCAL TEEN TO COMPETE IN COMBAT ROBOTIC FINALS

BY: KELVIN K. RUSSO
BEACON STAFF REPORTER

Like many competitors, sixteen-year-old local resident, Cyrus Hampstead, takes a determined approach to his sport. He reviews videos, strategizes for upcoming matches, and prepares to be in the utmost physical condition. This last avocation, however, is what separates him from the typical athlete, because it is not Cyrus who must buttress his body with strength training and fierce conditioning, rather his robot must.

Cyrus Hampstead is one of many devoted enthusiasts who compete in the specialized, winner-take-all world of combat robotics. On any given day, you can find the Stafford P. Ellicott High junior feverishly working in his basement workshop, upgrading, repairing, enhancing, and fortifying his own remote-controlled machine, a robot which fights under the moniker, Spiral Cyclone.

Built of steel, powered by a lithium battery, and endowed with a fearsome weapon—a pivoting, rotating arm equipped with an eight-and-a-half-inch circular saw—a device which would draw the envy of any horror movie villain. It is this combat robot which has conquered, and often completely ravaged, over a dozen opponents on its quest to compete in the nation's ultimate competition.

This weekend, Cyrus and Spiral Cyclone will take part in the sport's year-end finale, ComBot27. The event is considered the ultimate test in robotic warfare. Cyrus and his robot, or "bot," earned entry and a prime spot in ComBot27 by stringing together a series of victories in preliminary regional tournaments. According to Cyrus, there may have been "a few stars aligned" as well. The two teammates will compete in the event's MegaBot division.

According to Cyrus, the feat of making it into ComBot27 was not an easy one: "I had to do a lot of adjustments to my bot. A few upgrades to the battery unit, too, and of course every time Spiral Cyclone fights, there are tons of repairs. Fighting takes its toll, that's for sure."

Early last year, the Hampstead family lost one of their own, Cyrus' father, Lt. Colonel Francis Hampstead, who himself worked on robots for the U.S. Army. He designed and engineered them to disable improvised explosive devices, or IEDs. Now, it is Cyrus who carries on his late father's passion and competitive spirit for battling robots.

For Cyrus, winning the MegaBot title in ComBot27 would not only be the fulfillment of long family dream, it would also be a financial windfall. The winner would receive a check of forty-thousand dollars tabbed into the payment line.
"Yeah, winning would be real sweet. And the money's not so bad either," said Cyrus.

The televised episode of ComBot27 will air in November of this year. Look for Cyrus Hampstead and his well-oiled bot, Spiral Cyclone, to flip, slash, pummel and hack their way to a "riveting" victory in combat robotics ultimate test.

As it rolled in, Cyrus saw a blur of heads through the bus's windows. The driver stepped off, fiddling his fingers to his phone, seemingly unaware of Cyrus as he pushed his wagon out of the medium strip and crossed the road. As he thundered down from the curb, the driver's head shot up. A teenage boy wheeling a wagon with a massive hulk inside, barreling straight towards him, was probably not on his list of expected sights.

"What on God's divine earth have ya got there?" said the driver. His blue uniform's name tag said Earl. Earl's curly hair was silver-white, decades in the making. His pot belly told a similar story of years of good eating. His face was smooth and wrinkle-free and marked by a constellation of freckles.

Cyrus didn't quite know how to answer the question. Maybe the explanation he had in mind would become too long-winded. He thought of all the follow-up questions his mother might ask when given a simply answer. Maybe Earl was no different. So Cyrus said nothing.

Earl proffered a simple nod.

"Oh, I've got my ticket right here," said Cyrus, rummaging through his pockets and producing a crumpled paper. "Man, I'm glad I made it on time."

"Yeees, sir, you made it on time. Wouldn't wanna leave you stranded, not with all that contraption ya got in tow," said Earl with a wink. He flicked his thumb to the bus's lower luggage compartment. "Got 'nough room. Underneath, in the back. On the right."

Cyrus lifted the Chromiums blanket off his mangled machine.

"Boy 'o boy, looks like someone took a bat to it and set it ablaze."

"Sorta like that. Only it wasn't playing baseball. So, no bats."

Earl belted out a hearty laugh. "Hahaha, wasn't playin' baseball. I like that. No bats. I like that, too. Yes, sir, sumetin' got to that thang. That 'nough I can tell."

Just then, the lights from the electronic billboard caught Earl's attention. His bright hazel eyes squinted as he watched two animated robots clashing into one another, sparks flying like fireworks. The title "Com-Bot27" was superimposed against the bright screen display. Earl raised an eyebrow.

"Alright then," he said, "Let's get 'er off and put 'er in the back. Wagon can go after. What do ya call yurself, young man?"

"Cyrus."

"Nice meetin' ya, Cyrus. I'm Earl. C'ptain Earl."

They shook hands. Together they lifted out Spiral Cyclone' shell and pushed it to the rear of the luggage compartment, past a rusty, broken bird cage.

"Believe someone in this bus wanna keep that thang, Cyrus?" Earl asked. "Broken 'ol cage like that."

"Maybe they should recycle it," said Cyrus as he placed the gas tank in the lower wagon compartment. "But sometimes that's hard to do."

"Ya mean toss it?" asked Earl. "Heck, wife keeps 'bout every darn thing she gets hold of. No sooner it come in, I try to push it on out. All the same, it's me endin' on the short side of happy."

Cyrus unlatched a clasp and drew down a wagon's side, Earl the other. They then hoisted the wagon in the luggage compartment.

Earl stared at Cyrus a long moment before his eyes drifted away. "What's ya reckon you'll do what that thang? That 'ol robot? Don't quite function no more, do it?"

"No, it's gone. I don't know what I'll do with it, really. Yet."

"Looks so, looks so," said Earl, nodding slowly. A Cheshire grin crept across his face. "Guess we can't count on it to drive then." Earl laughed so hard that he slapped at the side of the bus. Inside, Cyrus saw heads turn. "Can't count on it to drive, I like that," he bellowed again.

Earl looked down to his phone, studying it. "Well, there's always…"

"…Next year," said Cyrus.

Earl looked up with confusion. "No. Next year ain't gonna get it. Talkin' bout a dif'rent route. Been some type o' accident on route three-two-nine. But I knows a way around. Skip 'cross Belleview, take McArthur most o' the way up. Then straight over onto the highway." He pointed to the bus steps. Cyrus walked ahead.

"I'll getcha home. Ol' Captain Earl knows how to outsmart 'em. You can't let 'em outsmart ya, kid," he said in a confidential, knowing way. Before going up the steps, Cyrus caught Earl's eyes, two electric pearls set within weathered oyster shells. "Takes just one time. Then they think it can go like that all the time. Slip, slide, super glide. No, oh, no, no, that's not how's it's gonna be, my friend. No, sir." He pointed to his head, then to Cyrus'. "You and I, we don't roll like that, know what I mean?"

"Yes, sir."

Earl reached into a cooler on the floor and handed Cyrus a bottle of cold water. He guzzled every last drop. Earl continued: "When they ain't expecting it, Cyrus, they think they got ya like made in the shade, an' believin' it all the while too, just watch how we go ahead an' flip that doggone script on 'em. Flip it right on over." Earl slapped his hands together as if he were clearing away some dust. "Flip that doggone script right on over on 'em, yes, sir, mister Cyrus."

Cyrus tried to decipher each of Earl's phrases. How they related to, or didn't relate to, navigating traffic jams.

"Thanks for the water, Mr. Earl," he said. With his head more focused from the hydration, Cyrus realized that what Earl was talking about wasn't traffic, or road accidents, or driving at all. It was something else altogether.

"Alright then, let's get this thang movin'," commanded Earl, sitting in the driver's seat. "People's all gettin' fussy and twitchy back thar."

Cyrus found a seat at the back of the bus and settled in. Before long, they were on the highway heading south. Cars sped by Cyrus' eyes like fence-jumping sheep, and the swiftly passing trees blurred into green daydreams.

Suddenly, waves of warm blood coursed through Cyrus. That was the difficult part of life, when things seem lost, and everything becomes one giant puzzle, and what seemingly was once there exists no longer. The gaps in life, the voids that have you wondering. Tricks of the brain. One moment, Spiral Cyclone was set to deliver a debilitating blow, its circular saw poised above Doke-a-lasher and its last remaining rotary blade, and the next moment everything went blank. *A complete blackout! Like it never happened.* It was as if a valve in his brain turned on and there he was, flushing down some strange, time-warping whirlpool.

Yes, his fingers were firmly placed on the knobs of the controller. They were still sliding up and down, sideways and backways. He remembered that. The light on his receiver was lit, so he was good there. And Spiral Cyclone's orange safety light was on, too. *Definitely. Everything functioned.* Yet still, no movement. *Yeah, the script sure got doggone flipped alright.*

He remembered Spiral Cyclone matching his nemesis, blow by blow, landing sweltering shots, a hurricane of sparks. He felt the tide turn. Spiral Cyclone was digging in its claws. Weakened, Doke-a-lasher spun to the other end of the decagon. It hobbled side to side as the floor's sawblade ripped at its wheels. *Yep. Yep.* Sputtering steam, hanging on with its last blade, beaten down, near dead. He prepared Spiral Cyclone for the final assault. *That was the script.*

Then it happened. Spiral Cyclone seized up. And so did Cyrus. His legs wobbled as if his bones were drained of marrow and filled with gelatin.

He could see it now, those last motionless seconds. Doke-a-lasher stood tauntingly over his bot. But not for long. Within seconds, Spiral Cyclone was methodically dragged to the decagon's blazing funeral pyre.

For its final salute goodbye.

CHAPTER 9

The bus was a half-filled, southern rolling vessel which bounced and shook only when Earl happened to hit a rough patch of asphalt, conditions which varied according to the wealth of the county they happened to be traveling through. Outside, the late afternoon sky blushed pale with streaks of crimson clouds. When Cyrus placed his hands on the window, he could feel both the heat of the day and the coolness of air conditioning venting up the glass, which left a specter of fog a quarter of the way up. Because it was dusk, more people were drawn outdoors than when the bus departed. In the small towns they passed, Cyrus watched citizens tending their gardens, walking their dogs, and watering their grass. At one home, kids were running through a spraying hose. All of this made the idea of home weigh heavy upon Cyrus' heart.

Cyrus figured anyone heading his direction was on the bus by now; no more detouring to pick people up, no more boarding and un-boarding and all that tossing of luggage and squeaky yawning of the door as it opened and shuttered, followed by footsteps and hollow murmurs of passengers as they made their way down the aisle. No more stops or wide, swaying turns which had Cyrus wishing for a double dose of anti-nausea medication.

It would be all momentum from here on out. Cyrus counted his blessings that each new passenger who had walked down the aisle reached only midway. At that point they would collapse into an open seat and complain that the July heat was too much for them. With the entire back of the bus to himself, he plopped his feet on the next seat over and kicked off his shoes. If anyone were offended by the waft two-day sweaty socks, they'd more than likely blame someone in the front than the kid in the back. Besides, he had enough attention for one day, included the desultory remarks made by one Ray Dokestout.

Cyrus grabbed his phone and looked through his call logs. His good friend, Blake, had called multiple times, sending a text message along with each one.

It was typical of Blake to fly headlong into whatever was consuming him, whether it be some fanciful idea or a random tidbit of encyclopedic knowledge that had him scouring the internet for days. For the last few weeks, it happened to be Cyrus' quest for ComBot glory which garnered his interest. Blake would call Cyrus all hours of the day asking if he was prepared, well rested, and deluge him with all the 'what ifs'—as in: "What would you do if you won? What would you do with all the G's? Do chicks even like robots?"

Cyrus usually ignored his calls and sent him to voicemail. Otherwise, he'd have gone insane with the incessant querying. He knew Blake meant well, but sometimes Cyrus felt he was wired on a closed-circuit loop without a breaker box. His friend, Tonmoy Chakraborty, on the other hand, was more mellow. Tonmoy mostly texted strings of Bengali-inspired emojis and phrases that were impossible to comprehend unless you were from Bangladesh.

Cyrus closed his eyes. He thought about taking a nap. The world outside, however, held more interest than the back of his eyelids. The woods along the highway zipped past his tired eyes, broken here and there by the speckled whiteness of a solitary house or the flashy billboard telling of treasures down the road. The trees in the woods were rowed like stacked dominoes, and as Cyrus followed with their recurrent patterns, he fell spellbound.

He tried to shake loose the spell. But for whatever reason he felt the compulsion to know if anything, or anyone, was wedged in those dirt-ochre recesses within the trees. As he looked down each narrow void, a cavity which showed darker and darker the deeper it went, he searched for some evidence of life. In one of the rows, he could have sworn he saw some kids running around, and in another he thought he saw a fox skulking about. Though no sooner than he'd establish what he spied, did a new row of trees flash by, followed by another dark, descending void of emptiness. It all whizzed by too fast to catch a good look, row after row after row.

Maybe it's better, he thought after some time, *to just stare mindlessly. Not keep wondering what's down those rows. Maybe it's better not to know.* Besides, by the time his mind registered what he thought he'd seen, maybe what he thought was there wasn't really there. Such was the case with illusions. And illusions he'd had enough of for the day.

But there was one image he couldn't shake. A vision, really, projected against the green rush. There he was in his basement sitting on a stool. His father was intently working on some circuitry inside of Spiral Cyclone. A slick lather of gray grease was lodged between his fingernails, and his wire-rimmed glasses were dangling precariously off his nose, a breath from falling off.

"See this, you lower it down like this. Make sure you've got one hand steadying it, otherwise…well, see?" He let the device drop for example.

Back then, Cyrus was always happy to reach over and grab a tool for his father. Or place his finger on a sliver of wire to hold it in place. Sometimes his father would mutter to himself if the connection wasn't right, but mostly he would describe to Cyrus what he was working on: how to ignite the welding torch, how to operate the grinders, rotary sharpeners, fasteners and drill press, explain the best method to solder a joint or secure wire connections.

When his father wasn't off somewhere ('deployed' was the word Cyrus eventually came to know) he would watch his father work with all those wonderful tools. The basement smelled perpetually of metal, oil, musk, and for whatever reason, wood shavings. Then Cyrus remembered the time when his father, without notice, threw a pair of goggles on his head and earmuffs that didn't have any fur. His father told him to go behind a tool chest, one no bigger than he was. He then showcased the fury. Sparks jumped; blue flames arced over the room. Cyrus could taste the char of steel and was enlivened by the eerie sounds. Seconds of excitement before things got too chaotic with a kid in the room.

Years later, Cyrus gained enough knowledge to piece together his own fighting robot. Forwards and backwards—a rudimentary bot. As with his father, combat robotics became an all-consuming passion.

An electrical substation darted across the bus window, a maze of wires and transformers, and Cyrus thought about the early incarnation of Spiral Cyclone, when the bot didn't have an arm with the circular saw. Serviceable, but not quite combat-ready. His father was having a difficult time integrating a main weapon.

One night, it came to Cyrus in a dream. He was twelve years old at the time. Restless of sleep, he decided to crawl next to his father in his parent's bed. His father stroked the perspiration off Cyrus' overworked head. He asked: "Why the busy mind?"

"Thinking about our robot, that's all," replied Cyrus.

"Ah, I see. OK, what's the most important part of a fighting robot?"

"A weapon. I think."

"Correct. So, think about that, but not too hard. Let your mind just wander towards it. Eventually you'll fall asleep. That weapon, maybe, I don't know, maybe it will just come to you. Like a light bulb over your head. You've heard about that happening, haven't you?"

"Yeah."

"Good. Because I'm having the darndest of time getting that light bulb to turn on myself."

He grabbed Cyrus' nose, twisting it like a knob. "A single offensive weapon. You understand? Something to be feared," he said, drawing out the "r" and crash landing the "d."

"I understand," laughed Cyrus. Cyrus was keen to the motives of adults. He wasn't quite sure if his father really wanted his input, or if he was just trying to settle his anxious mind. Either way was fine; the intent didn't matter, as long as his father was asking.

"Otherwise," continued his father, "the thing would just go careening around. Ram, ram, ram." He knuckled into the soft spot of Cyrus' belly. "Can't win like that."

Cyrus turned his body over, laughing, trying not to pee. "No way."

"Well, maybe. But your bot better have some good push and lift to prevent it," he said. He kissed on the back of Cyrus' head. "Better get some sleep now. But get yourself to the bathroom first."

A daylong bout of nervous energy could either keep Cyrus awake for bedsheet-twisting hours or collapse him in a single wink. That night, it was a wink.

He dreamt his playroom. One of those rooms in an old house that never had much of a purpose other than being a playroom. Toy construction trucks—haulers, loaders, big rigs—overran the place.

There was one toy Cyrus especially liked: the backhoe loader. The pivoting rear limb appeared odd and asymmetrical, like some giant tail on a terrestrial dinosaur. The loader did most of the chores in the playroom—twisting, pivoting, lifting, digging, spilling out all the colorful sand that somehow found its way in there.

In his dream, the backhoe loader's rear limb magically appeared on Spiral Cyclone. Right out of the dreamy blue.

Early the next morning, as his father lay in bed with his mother, he snuck in and whispered that very idea into his father's ear. His father eyes narrowed. He raised a single brow.

It happened a few months later. Spiral Cyclone's new endowment was a diamond-laced saw wheel attached to a pivoting, fully rotatable arm. The icing on a truly devilish cake.

And Cyrus was the mastermind.

How things have changed. How my life has changed.

As the bus eased into slower traffic, Cyrus thought back to his exchange with Ray Dokestout. A burning flush migrated up his face. His stomach tossed unsettlingly, as if coagulated by a pound of raw sugar. *That guy could have said nothing. Could have left it be, watched me pick up my gas tank and slide on out.* What really got to Cyrus wasn't so much Ray's moronic words, but the undertone of disparagement when he mentioned his father's name. In combat robotics circles, he knew victory sometimes is laced with a cocksure glint. That's all well and good. The point is to beat the other's machine to a pulp, after all. But the venom never enters the bloodstream. With Ray Dokestout, it did.

Maybe that's his MO. Acting like some mobster in a movie who spits on his enemy before stomping him. He had a suspicion Ray Dokestout's nature fell into the insidious realm—the black widow treachery realm.

He tried to recall if his father ever mentioned clashing with Ray in the decagon. He couldn't.

Cyrus cleared the fog off the window with his hand as the bus slowed for a railroad crossing. As he stared down the endless, barren tracks he was more certain than ever.

He'd return for ComBot28. Somehow, someway, he'd find a way to build another bot.

As for what happened back there in the decagon, that was the past.

ComBot28 was the future.

Flip the doggone script. Flip it right on over.

And if he came up against some Doke-a-bot in the process, well… *so the better.*

It's gonna be a busy year. A doggone script flippin' year.

CHAPTER 10

Cyrus stood at his living room's bay windows, mug of hot chocolate in hand. His favorite brand. Sweet and creamy, and though touched by subtle bitterness, it always brought back memories. What he was really after, however, were not memories but the warmth of the chocolatey liquid.

The chill in the air was more than a shock—it was a wakeup call that a new season was on its way. The days of high humidity and constant sweating were nearing their end, and the mosquitos would soon be calling their season of bloodsucking quits. Maybe it was the hot chocolate, or maybe it was the slow spectacle of the mist floating down his street, sweeping up and over the roof and around the chimney of the empty house across the street, which turned Cyrus' mind to deep thought. As he looked out, he ruminated on the creek behind that house, his old getaway place and his crayfish hunting grounds, his private childhood resort of all those years that were quickly passing him by.

Cyrus felt anxious for the future; the beginning of his junior year in high school (heralded by all as the most arduous one) was but two weeks away.

He returned to the kitchen and put his mug in the sink. As he headed back toward his basement confines, to the seclusion of robotic concepts and components, Cyrus again looked out the bay windows. Now propped up against the neighbor's real estate sign was a bicycle, with no sign of its owner. *Strange*. He hadn't seen anyone over at that property since early spring. No interested parties, no landscapers, nothing living except for the weeds which stood like scraggly sentinels watching over a forgotten land. The family had abruptly abandoned it, leaving a poorly manicured lawn and a stretch of driveway asphalt that had not a single bike-riding kid. In fact, he was starting to wonder if the agent, whose picture on the "For Sale" sign had become so weathered it was almost unrecognizable, had given up on the place altogether. And if the agent hadn't, Cyrus could foresee inquiries as problematic: the phone number had about peeled away to nothing.

The bicycle was about as rusty and worn as the sign it was leaning against. At last, Cyrus saw a figure moseying around the wooded lot. It didn't take long for Cyrus to notice the wintery-white on the kid's neck, which stood in stark contrast to his dark hair. And that hairstyle; it hadn't changed since second grade, as if someone had thrown a bowl over his head and cut around the bottom. For whatever reason, Blake Tinsley seemed proud of its uniqueness. But that didn't mean other kids didn't give him crap for it.

"Hey," Cyrus yelled from the front door, "the place's been sold already. You can't afford it anyway."

"What's up, Cy?" Blake threw up his arms and skipped back to the bike. "I'm baaaack," announced his good friend.

"Hold on. I'll be right out."

Blake trudged the bike through the yard, sending aerials of weed seeds across his face. He threw the bike down on Cyrus' grass.

"I thought you said you'd be back a few days before school started," said Cyrus.

"Came back early. Dad couldn't stand the sun any longer," said Blake.

"Yeah, that thing ruins more fun."

"I kinda get it though," continued Blake, "I mostly stayed inside the hotel and played video games. Now I'm sick of them. Vid crash. That's why I'm paying you a visit. You're never busy." He beamed a smarmy smile, all grin and teeth.

"Surprised to see anyone out this way anyway," said Cyrus. "It's not really the boonies, but it's not too far off from it either. And where'd you get that crap ass bike, anyway, Blake?"

"Next to old Vennari's old barn, laying in the back."

"Ya think for a second it might be old Vennari's bike," said Cyrus, spitting into the grass.

"Ya think for a second an old pizza maker who's been using a walker for the past five years even needs a bike, not to mention one that barely works," said Blake. "My legs are killing me.

"Point."

"So, Cy, give the low down on ComBot. You texted that you lost in the semis, but what the hell happened?"

"Can't say. I'm under a confidentiality agreement?"

"A what?"

"It's a written agreement that states you cannot publicly disclose the results, or post images of the results, before ComBot airs in November. Every contestant has to sign it."

"That's horseshit and you know it."

"Maybe, but true."

"How the hell can they keep the thousands of people in that arena from saying anything? So, I know it's horseshit. You got spanked, didn't you?"

"That's an understatement," said Cyrus. "I guess you'll have to watch it on TV to find out. But I can offer you a sneak preview, as they say. Spiral Cyclone met its match."

"No kidding? Busted, kaput?"

"In Spanish, they say, 'no mas'."

Blake contorted his mouth into some crazed laughter caught in freeze frame, a look he practiced hard to perfect. Cyrus shook his head dismissively.

"So I guess I can't count on a loan from all those G's you didn't win."

"Plan on buying a bike?" said Cyrus. "Anyway, the thing is, I don't know how it happened. How I lost that last fight."

"Cyrus, I've seen those contests. I can guess how it happened. I mean, what the hell? It's ComBot. Cyclone either got shredded to bits or it took a licking from all those things that pop out everywhere."

"Oh, it got hit by an obstacle all right. It's just that…"

"…what? Lemme guess, it ran into the corkscrew majiger-jobby thing…"

"…No. Ultimately, the fire pit. What I meant was that Cyclone just stopped working. Like the bot said, 'I've had enough and I'm not playing anymore.' And I never figured out why."

Cyrus was still groping for some explanation, so it was even more difficult to convey the reason of defeat to someone else. It wasn't like he could tell Blake that Spiral Cyclone took some mega-strike in the semifinal match, some debilitating hit that disabled its circuitry. No, that wasn't the case. He could possibly tell him that Ray Dokestout simply made the right moves at the right time, but even that seemed to confound reason; Spiral Cyclone was taking it to Doke-a-lasher every day to Sunday. Three weeks later and his recollection was still in the muck. But his brain's murkiness didn't quite explain the real sparks and deafening blows and violent slashes he and Spiral Cyclone had inflicted on Doke-a-lasher.

Yes, it still irked him. It haunted him, in fact. Was it his error at the remote controller? He concluded that it must have been something like that. Human error. For someone who prided himself on control and execution, that was a hard pill to swallow. As he tried to explain what may have happened to Blake, warm blood ran through his chest and pounded his heart. The same sensation he felt during those few seconds of inoperability, when his robot was dragged helplessly into the pit o' fire.

Seconds which remain a mystery.

"Huh," said Blake, "I guess all you can do is try again. Like the little ant and the rubber tree plant."

"Yeah, at least the ant has a friggen' plant. I'm left with zip. Nada, my old boy," drawled Cyrus.

"Think you'll make another?" Blake asked.

"Yeah. I have to. One way or another. I'm mulling some ideas. Been working in the basement."

"Just don't let it get in the way of your love life."

"What's that?" asked Cyrus.

"Oh, listen, speaking of. I got a message from a girl. It was like almost a month ago, and she…"

"That's great, Blake. After all these years, you're starting to make some headway," interrupted Cyrus.

"Wow, and I thought you'd outgrown your smartass phase," snapped Blake. "I was about to say, if you'd pause and let me finish, that it was about you, you spankin' idiot."

"Why would some girl message *you* about *me?*"

"Well, let's think about it. Since you never go on social because you're terrified of humanity and it conquest of planet earth…"

"Yeah OK, Blake. Just because I'm not addicted like you are to Flapjack…"

"It's FlapYap and you know it. But maybe you wouldn't because your never on *any* social."

"Not exactly true. Spiral Cyclone had its own page, which I recently took down. But as a machine it doesn't have to deal with the fucking anxiety that comes with social media. Anyway, go on."

"I guess she wanted to wish you luck at ComBot. For whatever reason Tonmoy gave her *my* number. Maybe by mistake, or maybe she digs these goods. Know what I mean?" Blake slid his fingers across his evenly cut bangs.

"Wait, you mean she's trying to get to you, by going through me, by going through you. Is that what I'm hearing?"

"Something like that," said Blake evenly. "I think. I don't know. Anyway, dumbass, Tonmoy knew her from working on a play over the summer. If that explains anything."

"What's her name?" asked Cyrus.

"Leslie something or other. You've seen her, or maybe not…I don't know…she's got reddish hair."

Cyrus, usually adept at recall when it came to the female gender, had little to go by. He pondered a moment as he watched the mist drift down the lane. "Wait, she plays field hockey?"

"That's right. Tonmoy told me she's on the field hockey team. So, you do know her."

"Uh-huh, I think. Wonder how she knew I was going to ComBot. Or when ComBot was. Or what ComBot is, for that matter. Who in school knows anything about ComBot?"

"Or even cares," said Blake.

"Bingo," said Cyrus, thrusting his index finger in the air.

Blake lifted the front of the bike and spun the rusty wheel. "I guess you'll have to find out when school starts," he said. "Otherwise, when we go on a double date, you'll have to bring your new robot along."

"Probably have better luck with a girl at this point," rued Cyrus. "Come on, Blake, let's go to the shed and get some oil on that crap ass thing."

"Hey, while you're at it, mix me up some of that hot chocolate I see stuck to your lip.

CHAPTER 11

"Hey, Cy, this way. Third period's down here." Cyrus, backpack flung over a shoulder, was two-stepping up the high school staircase and bounding for the third floor when Tonmoy reached out and yanked his strap. Cyrus caught the railing and righted himself before tumbling backwards.

"Nope," replied Cyrus, "I'm transferring out, Ton. I heard Mr. Evan's a full-on dictator."

"Who told you that?" asked Tonmoy in disbelief. "Anyway, you know the drill. First day you go to your class, sit there, listen to the deal about expectations and all that. Then later, if you want, you make a move out. Let's go."

"Not happening, Tonmoy. You can stick to that. New school year, I'm rolling the dice on another class." Cyrus bounded up the stairs. "And hey, good luck with Stalin."

If it hadn't been for Tonmoy all along, Cyrus would have dutifully made his way to Mr. Evans' class, sat there patiently with the rest of the students and listened to the math teacher issue his proclamations and protocols for the new school year. Space out, survey the collection of students, raise his hand "here" when his name was called. Yes, he knew the drill. But because of Tonmoy he was heading elsewhere. It was Tonmoy who had mentioned to Blake about a girl named Leslie.

The first day of high school is a frenzied buzz hive. It can be overwhelming for some students. Downstairs near the front office of

Stafford P. Ellicott High School is a bulletin board with a printout of all

the classes—who's enrolled in what and where they're supposed to go.

Hard proof of where to scour for that all-important first classroom of the

semester.

Cyrus knew which class to go to, where it was located, what sub-

ject Mr. Evans taught.

But after second period, he passed by that bulletin board. There

he noticed a girl fitting the description Blake gave him. She was peer-

ing closely at the printout, tracing her finger along the manifest. Cyrus

stopped in his tracks. Some vague memory of this girl popped into his

head. His pulse hit triple-digits. When she moved along, he went to the

bulletin.

PERIOD 3 – GEOMETRY II – SECTION 204 – MRS. WYTHE –

CLASSROOM 347

Near the top of the page: BOROWSKI, LESLIE

Sometimes life can reroute itself out of nowhere. Forks in the road

can often force a person to make a quick decision. And sometimes when

that person encounters a fork, bold impulsivity can be substituted for

sound judgment—and a new path is blazed. One which splits the fork

right down the middle. What lay ahead is anyone's guess. Despite his usual

temerity, right then and there, minutes before the third period bell rang,

Cyrus cut a new path. He was determined to include himself as one of

the students in Stafford P. Ellicott's Geometry II, Section 204, Classroom

347.

Cyrus stood outside of Classroom 347 and peered through the door's window. Dreary heads, burdened by not having a pillow under them at ten o'clock in the morning, waited for the teacher to arrive. Most of the seats were occupied, though in the rear were three vacant seats in a row. A girl with strawberry blond hair sat in the corner aside the three empty seats. *Now I remember her. We played dodgeball together last year in gym. We were the last two survivors before I got beaned in the leg.* Cyrus recalled her look of satisfaction.

As he stared at the glassy-eyed students, Cyrus calculated his odds of survival. He quietly debated those odds, which fluctuated like the bets at a racetrack. *So what if this Mrs. Wythe tells me I'm in the wrong class. I'm sure it happens all the time. A few chuckles and out I go. I get escorted right over to Mr. Evan's class. Big deal.* Then, on the flip side, there was the notion that sometimes things slide by. Government oversight stuff. Paperwork signed, names recorded. A clean getaway. *Cyrus Hampstead: official registrant of Geometry 204. Sounds good. Real good.* The lame, 100-1 colt rounds the homestretch and beats the odds.

Owing to a cumulative four-point-three grade average, Cyrus didn't have to worry about his mother questioning his academic deci-sion-making. *Besides, do I really need another AP math class? Especially this year?* He eyed the unoccupied seats and the radiance beyond them. His limbs shook. His pulse stammered. *No, this class is just fine.*

A jolting tap came on his shoulder. It was Mrs. Wythe.

"Too late to run for your life now," she said, "so let's move on in."

He followed behind Mrs. Wythe, casual of gait. As he prepared to split down the far aisle, the door opened. Two brutish football players wearing Ellicott Electron's jerseys lumbered in. Cyrus saw them spying the empty seats. He quick-heeled down the far aisle, trying his best to look inconspicuous. They took a more direct route.

Just before he could toss his backpack on the desk next to Leslie, one of the footballers curtly brushed him aside. The other crashed into the next seat over. Both plopped in the seats with grunts.

Cyrus was forced to settle in the last remaining seat, with five hundred-and-fifty-some-odd pounds packed in between he and Leslie Borowski.

The footballers were nearly identical. If the game of football had a gene pool, they could've been twins. Same height, same body type, near same weight, which was some combination of gridiron muscle and potato-turned-to-fat filler. Cyrus didn't know their true proportions, nor did he care. All he knew was that the massive presence of Number 71 and Number 79, respectively, obstructed his view. His beautiful view.

Mrs. Wythe got down to roll. Once finished, she never took stock of the kid in the back who never answered. The footballers, however, did notice. They glared over at Cyrus as he pretended to search through his backpack. When their smoldering stares abated, he looked up. And there was the girl with strawberry blond hair, craning her neck around the brutes, beaming at him. She had emerald eyes, high cheekbones that were slightly rouged, lips round and delicate. She reminded Cyrus of what might be found inside a Russian nesting doll.

Cyrus took a deep breath and tried to remain calm.

When class was over many of the students stayed behind to catch up on two months of separation. Leslie approached Cyrus. "Hey, how come you didn't get your name called? I'd go up there right now and talk to her about it. Straighten it all out."

Cyrus flustered. "Me? I, uh, um..." flowed the gibberish.

"Look, she seems kinda shaky about this attendance stuff," Leslie pointed out. "I mean, I know how these absences can add up. Then at the end of the term when you got like fifteen of them, you're screwed."

Cyrus' eyes focused on her strawberry blond hair, how it was tucked tight into a ponytail. She wore a white crop top and blue jeans with a shamrock patch over the thigh, pale-pink slip-on shoes. Her bottom lip shifted to the left. She bit at the right. Her floral perfume made overtures he couldn't quite handle. Her green eyes never left his.

"You're right. Maybe it's some mistake. I'll get it figured out," said Cyrus, zipping his backpack.

"Hey, if you can skim under the radar, more power to you. So... what's your name? The one that wasn't called on roll?"

"Cyrus," he said. "What's yours?"

"Cyrus? Hold on! You compete in combat robotics?"

He tried to temper his eagerness, keep his voice from cracking. He was caught in a whirling dizziness which made him think he was free-falling from an airplane. "Yeah," he blurted.

"Some of those robots are just crazy wild. I heard you went to…
to…" Suddenly Leslie looked in the direction of Numbers 71 and 79. She
tilted her head suspiciously, as if she viewed them as thieves in the dark,
or worse, unwelcome eavesdroppers.

"ComBot," inserted Cyrus.

"Uh-huh, I know. ComBot," her voice trailing off. She suddenly
twisted around.

The two footballers sat stationary, their eyes darting around the
room, their hands clenched to their desks. Number 79 was breathing
heavy. Number 71 produced a wheezing whistle from his nose. They were
zeroing in on something and ready to pounce.

Cyrus was as perplexed as Leslie.

Together, the footballers sprung into karate postures, their feet
planted wide apart as if they were about to go to town on some blocking
pads. Seconds later, a hand swiped across the top of Cyrus' head, centime-
ters from his scalp and whizzing a gale through his hair.

"You missed, dummy," spat Number 71 to Number 79. "My turn."

Cyrus followed Leslie's incredulous eyes as she too homed in on
the target: a rogue fly. It made a chaotic loop between the ceiling and
the footballers, goading them into a contest. Leslie shook her head as she
stood there watching the fly dive bomb the two.

"Gentlemen?" yelled Mrs. Wythe as she was leaving Classroom 347,
"what on earth are you doing? Class is over."

"We know, Mrs. Wythe," said Number 71. Their attention was half to the teacher, half to the fly. "Some kinda fly got in here," said Number 79, "it's been bothering us...and all the students in the back."

"It's a fly. So what? I'm sure it will leave by tomorrow. In fact, it probably has an appointment to keep with the other flies in the school cafeteria."

"We're trying to kill it," Number 71 responded.

"Then the other flies will be wondering where it went," Mrs. Wythe said sarcastically. "Please dismiss yourselves. Fourth period is waiting. Now!" Her tone was final.

The two simultaneously folded their textbooks and commenced a long stretch of their large frames, producing similar deep base sounds. They lurched towards the door. Before they exited, Number 71 threw a punch to Number 79's kidney, doubling him over. In retaliation, Number 79 connected a shot to Number 71's groin, which sent out a yelp.

Leslie rolled her eyes. Cyrus tried to hold back laughter.

"Well, at least we know who to turn to when the fly comes back," said Leslie. "My money's on the fly."

Cyrus and Leslie exited the geometry class and strolled down the school's third-floor hallway, mostly in silence. Silver and cyan, the school's colors, consumed the corridor; the greenish-blue and lively metallic were painted on doors, splashed on spirit banners, and adorned T-shirts and jackets. Even the large columns holding the school upright were painted silver and cyan. As a color scheme, it was a little overwhelming. But now, the only color holding Cyrus' attention was straw-berry blond.

They dodged oncoming students, yielded and rejoined. Leslie field-ed a few hellos, made a random comment or two to acquaintances. Cyrus gave a few head nods. He felt an unusual number of eyes on him, though it didn't take him long to realize they were directed towards Leslie. And mostly from guys. Swaggered bravely down the hall, he nonetheless felt a little unsure and out of his element.

Leslie broke the silence: "Can you believe those two guys chasing that fly around? What would they have done if they caught it, anyway?"

"I think they said they were trying to kill it."

"Oh, right. Problem solved."

"I have a theory on why," said Cyrus.

"A theory, huh?"

"You see, as football players they have a strong reaction to stimuli. Like moving limbs or an oncoming player carrying a ball or…"

"Or over-caffeinated flies," interrupted Leslie.

"Exactly. They're coached to react and attack. Kinda like a beast with prey," he explained as they moved through a clique of students. "They go on the offensive as soon as there's any movement. Whistle, snap, explode. It's all a direct consequence of their football training."

"Well, let me see," retorted Leslie. "Tennis players have to react quickly to a ball, then explode to it. Field hockey players, we do too. And, correct me if I'm wrong, combat robotic competitors do the same. But I see none of those people fighting flies in the back of a class," she said. "Too many helmet-to-helmet collisions is what I'm thinking."

"That's another theory, too, Leslie," said Cyrus.

Leslie stopped and side-eyed him. "Remember in class when you asked me my name. Before the whole fly thing."

"Right," said Cyrus, sensing a trap.

"I never told you my name. So how did you know it?"

Cyrus didn't miss a beat. "From roll call. I have a good memory. Comes in handy in classes, too."

"I see," she said, still staring him down, "then why did you...oh, never mind."

Cyrus pressed on. "You never told me how you knew about Com-Bot. Not many people here even know it's a thing."

She slapped him on the shoulder. "So, here's the deal. And what are the odds. My uncle used to compete awhile back. I watch ComBot every year, every season since I was like, ten, maybe eleven. It's compulsory."

"Compulsory?" asked Cyrus, hoping for another shoulder slap.

"Yeah, like I said, Uncle Carl used to compete a little. He was never any good, but he tried. I guess his robots weren't any good, which amounts to the same thing. But he's really into mechanics and, you know, engineering things." They walked on. "He never made it as far as Com-Bot. Which might account for an entire storage room of old parts at his garage."

Cyrus shifted his backpack to avoid oncoming students. He thought about his own graveyard of parts, the lurking of the disabled, the haunting of the dead. "But he still watches, huh?"

"Yep. That's what I mean by compulsory. He comes over to our house for every ComBot. Watches with the family. It's a big event for him."

Cyrus pictured her uncle as a lonely man without a family, or television. "Oh, I get it."

"Plus, my dad keeps a kegerator full of beer. That alone is incentive enough. Point is, I've learned to love it, too." She stopped at the top of the stairwell. "So, tell me, how did it go?"

Cyrus was ready to come clean, to spill his guts and every emotion boiling inside him. His heart wanted to pour everything out to this wonderful girl next to him in the high school hallway. He wanted to tell her about his defeat, his despair, his disgust for Ray Dokestout. He really thought himself capable of such an expansive emotional release. Uncork the bottle, a cry-out for the ages, a gush-out all over the silver and cyan carpet.

But his throat clenched, his mouth went feeble, his tongue pickled.

A girl in a field hockey sweatshirt approached them, phone outstretched. "Leslie," the girl gasped, "did you get the text about practice? Coach says we have to practice at the park. Our fields are like a soaking mess."

"That would have been nice to know, like yesterday," Leslie said.

"Can I get a ride?"

"Sure, Sydney," said Leslie. "Meet me in the parking lot after school. Cyrus, I'll see you tomorrow in class."

She flounced her ponytail to the opposite shoulder as she spun down the staircase. A few steps down she turned back to Cyrus. "Still betting on the fly."

As Cyrus watched her leave, a jubilant song wailed in his heart.

CHAPTER 12

Cyrus wasn't sure what the play was about, or the name of it really, only that it took place in some country with steep, snow-capped mountains where people apparently sang a lot. A musical, he was told, which he knew little about. What he did know about, however, was a certain Leslie Borowski was in charge of building sets for the drama department. Since that first day of school three weeks ago, they hadn't spoken much. She was always out of geometry in a flash, leaving he and his nerves in a trail of lonely stardust.

So, when Tonmoy mentioned an extra hand was needed for the set, Cyrus didn't hesitate to throw his hat into the ring. He even lauded himself as a highly skilled craftsman of set backgrounds, which was almost like saying he was a renowned composer of musicals.

What a trade-off, a no brainier. An opportunity to impress the crew chief with his work ethic and hands-on eagerness. He couldn't turn that down. In fact, the moment the question sprang from Tonmoy's mouth, an endless sputter of "yeses," and "no problems" spewed out of Cyrus'. All he had to do was put some final decorative touches on a two-tiered background facade which towered grandly over the school's library.

More than once, several times in fact, Tonmoy mentioned the height of the facade. Cyrus shrugged it off, listening absentmindedly to Tonmoy as he fretted over some tall ladder while thinking about Leslie.

Over and over, Tonmoy cried: "It's real high, so many friggen' rungs, man, that friggen' thing's so unsteady." *Ladder. Whatever, Ton.* Cyrus was consumed by other matters.

If there was one downside to the set endeavor, however, it would be spending less time in his basement developing a new bot. But he had to face the hard reality: he hadn't yet produced anything close to having a robotic pulse. Every attempt had stalled, and with each new failure he was met with the prospect of beginning anew. It was like his workshop was harboring a phantom, floating in spirit but without a corpse.

As Cyrus saw it, the robot reboot was just a temporary snag. Like a rainstorm that halts the repair of a highway. He knew he'd eventually get to it and get it done. Admittedly though, his enthusiasm for the master plan had waned once school began. The expectations were too daunting. Each attempt after the next produced nothing but incoherent designs, tons of shredded up mock-ups and increased frustration. Which beget more anxiety. Which beget more frustration, then more anxiety. It was a foreboding, stressful cycle.

His self-imposed deadline of entering ComBot28's preliminaries in the spring weighed on him like cinderblocks.

Cyrus needed a break, a submission to the restart button. Given all his fruitless frustrations, he probably would've accepted an invitation to clean the school's bathrooms had Tonmoy asked.

Fortunately, Cyrus was right where he wanted to be. Deep down, he'd told himself it's where he needed to be. In the library with an excused absence, climbing an eighteen-foot ladder and giving the background village a little spruce and flair. Tonmoy, who claimed to be dreadfully afraid of heights (hence the ladder fretting), was stationed several feet below, chewing a wad of gum and carelessly serving up the necessary supplies. Cyrus believed Tonmoy's "afraid of heights" but a ruse to have someone else go up the ladder, namely him. But Cyrus didn't care. He was beginning to take a mindless liking to adding straw to the village's thatched roofs and fluffing polyacrylate into clouds and snowbanks.

"You alright up there, Cy?" asked Tonmoy, chewing his gum languidly. "Need some more puffy white stuff?"

"I need for the ladder not to move," said Cyrus as he looked down, "which it has been. I've got to go up one step higher. Just keep it steady, Tonmoy, please."

"Hey, if you fall, you think you'd fall clockwise or counterclockwise?" Tonmoy had one hand on a ladder rung as the other waved to someone in the hallway above.

"I don't want to think about that right now, Tonmoy. What kinda of dumb question is that anyway?" scoffed Cyrus.

"Come on…which direction? Counter-clockwise or clockwise?" Tonmoy continued.

"Probably straight down on you if you really want to know."

"Why can't you answer a simple question," implored Tonmoy.

"Ah, I see where this is going…clockwise," said Cyrus, looking under his armpit.

"...Because it's shaped like a toilet bowl," they both said together, overlapping words they had repeated many times before.

It was a running joke among the students at Stafford P. Ellicott High School that the school's strange architecture—built in 1967, when utilitarianism dominated over aesthetic considerations—served as a punchline. A punchline which most likely began with the students of that era; a half century later, and the bathroom humor continued. Although there were different variations of the joke throughout its lineage, with setups going through infinite permutations, the kids always knocked it down the same: "Because it's shaped like a toilet bowl."

The fact that the building is concrete and brick, instead of porcelain, doesn't change the truth behind the wordplay. The building has an undeniable shape. Some students even claim the architect was in on the joke too. And that was the ultimate crack: that the joke's originator was in fact Stafford P. Ellicott's architect. Who that architect was nobody knew, but plenty of colorful suggestions have been tallied throughout the years.

The very idea of it resembling a toilet bowl was further cemented for Cyrus when he saw an aerial photograph of the school prominently displayed in the administration office. One day, when he was in the office sick and waiting to be picked up, he stared at the photo. A vision of his high school soon came into focus: a squatter plopped in the middle of the woods. Cylinder (main building) attached to a rectangle (gym/auditorium)—toilet bowl and water basin. What else could it be?

Back when the high school was built, Cyrus' hometown was a rural offshoot of a medium-sized city. Before the sprawl, the area had little in terms of a robust economy. It was a simple town. People farmed, some ranched, some were miners. Many hunted the swaths of woods for their dinner. Some, like his father, were soldiers stationed at the nearby Army base. Back then, the denizens built their public buildings with what they could afford, with whatever resources and architectural vision was at their disposal. Cement and brick made for simple constructions; if anyone had an eye toward modern architectural notions, they were in the minority. It wasn't quite Soviet bloc, though it wasn't Paris either. This was his hometown's origins.

It's a different era now. People migrated from the cities, escaped the urban blight and found themselves in a natural surrounding they could work with. And work in. Businesses seemingly sprang from out of nowhere. Roads turned from potholed patchwork to smooth asphalt. Eventually, the area became buttressed by tracts of newly developed homes, which grew in clusters and spread in every direction. The Hampstead home was but one of a dozen or so remaining farmhouses, although the land ceased its agrarian purpose many years ago.

With new homes came people. A lot of them. From everywhere. Cyrus was witness to the slow influx that changed the makeup of every school he attended—elementary, middle and high—into one big melting-pot. And he couldn't have been happier. That was the best part of it for Cyrus. When he heard others complain about how their town was so different ("ain't no space no more to do nothing" or "can't even go to the store without someone cutting me darn off" or "where'd all these people come from, anyway?"), Cyrus would smile, thankful for the injection of new blood. His hometown was different, but different had its upside, too.

The high school, however, never changed. It hadn't been torn down and reconfigured, as the lower schools were. Maybe that was coming someday. Then again, it might remain a toilet bowl for eternity, and the popular joke would continue its string of laughter.

Nonetheless, from a toilet bowl perspective, the drain was the library. Right where Cyrus currently stood atop an eighteen-foot ladder. The highest point of focus, smack in the center of the action.

Situated above this ecosystem of shelves and books and tables and computers rose three floors of classrooms, each with a hallway that cantilevered above the library. All of it resembled an ancient Greek theatre; spectators taking in the play from above, groundlings at library-level (which is exactly what it would be once the weekend rolled around and the Alpine musical sang its first note). Along the upper hallway railings, students would often hang out, lean over to see what was happening down below. It was like having a bird's eye view into a fishbowl (or a toilet bowl with fish in it.) If there was anything happening beyond studying going on down in the library, anything that involved kinetic motion, rest assured eyes would zero in on it—the spectacle of the moment.

As the last bell of the day rang out, students began to filter into the hallways. With them came noise, chaos, and Cyrus could feel his already precarious balance on the ladder becoming even more so. He felt them, and he knew Tonmoy was feeling them too. Indistinct catcalls echoed across the library. Someone popped off a whistle. It didn't take Cyrus long to conclude, that by virtue of him being high up on a ladder, most kids were keenly attuned to his tenuous mount. He felt eyes piercing his back. Above him, laughter from a group of girls. He stared uneasily at a bank of clouds.

"Bruh? Where were you in fourth?" Tonmoy shouted to someone above. The ladder trembled, which caused Cyrus' hand to yaw, which caused a squirt of glue to glob onto his shirt. "I'm not giving up my notes. Not this time you lazy sack of crap."

"Tonmoy!" screeched Cyrus.

"I gotcha covered, Cy. Don't worry," Tonmoy whispered up smoothly.

He felt like he was back at the decagon, clutching his remote controller with television cameras circling about. Only now, anything could happen. His backside was a bullseye, and not just of perceived mockery. A real target. A target for objects. Ones with airborne capabilities, like paper airplanes, gum, or half-eaten sandwiches. One direct hit coupled with an untimely shift of an eighteen-foot ladder, and Cyrus Hampstead would be the spectacle of the moment at Stafford P. Ellicott High.

As he clung to a rung with a sweaty grip, he began to second guess his decision to abide Tonmoy's "ladder phobia."

Subtle tremors shook the ladder. Cyrus didn't look down, not wanting to be met with disappointment…and fear. Easing down wasn't an option either: he wanted to appear brave in case the head honcho swung by.

"Cy, did you know that back in Bangladesh standing under a ladder is considered bad luck," said Tonmoy.

"News update, Tonmoy, it's the same here. Just steady it please. It's getting damn shaky up here. I have to finish this cloudbank," pleaded Cyrus.

When Cyrus realized he was out of polyacrylate, he leaned over and reached down to Tonmoy. His hand came up empty. He snapped his fingers hastily. Still, an empty hand.

"Well, you're in luck, my friend. The boss just arrived," whispered up Tonmoy.

Cyrus looked across his left shoulder, seeing only mountain peaks. To his right were village roofs. He had no idea which direction Tonmoy was looking, and since repositioning himself was out of the question, he had to go on Tonmoy's word. After all, a single-story pratfall is not a trait of human selectivity. Bravery and fearlessness, on the other hand, did have its evolutionary upside.

"Oh great, we're almost finished with the highland villages. About time, too. I've been asking for these to do be done for like a week now." Cyrus could hear Leslie's voice below. "We should add a few more hills in the distance, maybe three—no just two, there and there, one in the foreground and the other further back. That will give better depth perception, especially for those standing above." Cyrus had no idea who she was speaking to. It most certainly wasn't Tonmoy, whose idea of listening to orders is when a waiter repeats back his dinner request.

Cyrus peered under his armpit. One of the boys who had been tightening up the bolts on the set's backside stood woodenly next to her, listening attentively. Another boy craned his head around, but once he figured the commands didn't involve him, he fell back out of view. Leslie continued: "We also need to make sure the background panels are aligned correctly. They need to be framed in tight and secured by the time Mr. Asbaugh gives his approval on Wednesday. Which is in two days. The guy's such a stickler. Head of drama, what can I say?"

The boy next to her didn't answer. Neither did Tonmoy. Cyrus figured he was more focused on the happenings in the hallways.

"Sounds good," said Cyrus loudly over his shoulder. "Right Tonmoy?"

"Uh, yeah. Locked in on that."

"Cyrus? Is that you?" There was spryness to her voice. Soon, her whole body came into view. She was in her field hockey uniform. A loose teal sweater dipped just below her waist. Her lean, muscular legs were spotted with slate-gray bruising, decorations of her sport.

"Yes…up here…hi, Leslie, I didn't realize that was you," he sugar-coated the lie.

"Thank goodness," said Leslie. "We really needed more help." Her strawberry blond hair lustered despite the library's dull florescent lighting. She stood with her hands on her hips, looking up. "Because one might say that the help around here is, oh, I don't know…sub-par." She cocked her head towards Tonmoy, whose attention was on the upper rails.

"Yeah, some things never change," said Cyrus. *Shit, did that just sound like it came out of some cranky old man?* The thought caused his legs to shake.

"I heard everything you two said, by the way," Tonmoy said flatly. "But as my grandmother used to say: let negative words be like the rain-drops on a Bengal Monitor's back."

"Love to hear more lizard sayings, Tonmoy, but I've got to get to field hockey practice. Coach has been giving me slack because I've been dealing with this play. But someone's got to. Still, I'd rather *not* run wind sprints."

Cyrus didn't want her to be late, but he didn't want her to leave either. "I've never seen a field hockey game," he said as he lowered down a few rungs. "Is it like ice hockey?"

"Yes, and no. No puck, just a ball. And the stick is curved like a J, rounded on one side but with a flat face on the other." She used her hands to shape the description. "That's where you hit it. No side boards, either."

"Then no ice, I'm guessing?" asked Tonmoy.

Leslie froze him a stare. "Tonmoy, what's the national sport of Bangladesh?"

"Cricket, definitely," answered Tonmoy.

"Well, field hockey can't be far behind. So, why the dumb ques-tion?"

"It's sorta my thing."

She shook her head. "Anyway, let's just say that field hockey's more exciting than golf. That's like watching an ape knock a rock into a hole with a tree branch."

Cyrus had an image of a pre-ancestral human hunched over in the ancient grasslands, whacking a weathered stone with a knotty stick. "Yeah, that's about right," he said, smiling down at her. Her emerald eyes latched to his, beaming bright. Cyrus turned shyly back to the snowbank.

"Homo Erectus Country Club," said Tonmoy. "I can see the sign out front."

"Only members in *good standing*," said Cyrus over his shoulder.

"…Allowed on the *missing* links," said Tonmoy.

"*Cro-Mags* must carry own bags," added Cyrus.

Cyrus and Tonmoy both began to crack up, the type of laughter that comes from an inside joke.

"Two of you were on a roll there," Leslie said. Cyrus clutched onto a mountain peak as he continued to laugh.

"OK, what am I out on here?" Leslie asked quizzically.

"The ice hockey team," said Cyrus, peering down. "The Kettle-bridge Chromiums…"

"Oh, I love the Chromiums. My uncle, you know, the one I was telling you about, he's got season tickets."

"Yeah?" said Cyrus. "You go to the games?"

"Maybe three times a season," she said, "thereabouts."

"We call the Chromiums the Cro-Magnons. Or Cro-Mags, for short. Even if they were to have a winning season, which is pretty rare, we'd still call them that."

"Nickname of endearment," added Tonmoy.

"The Cro-Mags, I like that," nodded Leslie. "Yeah, I'm sorta used to them losing, too."

"Right," said Cyrus. "But I still watch anyway. Then complain about them afterwards. Complaining's part of the fun."

"I know. Losing's like almost a tradition in Kettlebridge," said Leslie. She lofted her finger. "But for the Electron Varsity field hockey team it's not. Coach is insistent on that. Gotta run. Gotta go Cro-Mag on some girls' shins."

"Sure thing," said Cyrus coolly.

Leslie looked into Cyrus' eyes with a sparkling smile. "Thanks for stepping in, Cyrus. The village is looking better now. And Tonmoy can thank you for relieving him of ladder duty. See you in geometry." Her voice was sugar and spice.

When Leslie was out of earshot, Tonmoy took the gum out of his mouth. "Geometry, huh? I guess you're happy with your new class."

"Just hold the ladder, Tonmoy. And steady. For once."

CHAPTER 13

Cyrus started bouncing his leg. The ball of his foot thumped and thumped like a turbine, powered by the piston of his calf. When one leg tired out, he switched to the other, alternating, he came to realize, to the staccato of Mrs. Wythe's geometry lesson.

"So, as we learned earlier, the (vocal rise) *major axis* is the longest chord of the ellipse which is (vocal fall) *bisected* by the minor axis. There-fore, as we attempt (vocal ascent) *to find the perimeter* we must follow this (vocal slide) *formula* in order to get our (vocal crescendo) *calculation*." She traced her cursor around the whiteboard. It looked to Cyrus as if she were conducting an orchestra.

Mrs. Wythe's vocal rhythms were her trademark, her way of staving off student's wavering attention. A fight against daydreams, boredom, sleep deprivation. Her vocal undulations were an attempt to make ge-ometry come alive, a way of shaping parabolas and cones and isosceles triangles into some distinct dimensional personality. Geometry wasn't a jump off the page and into your brain kind of subject. It needed claws and talons. It needed to fight for mental space. Geometry needed all the help it could get.

The footballers, too, needed all the help they could get. Which was the reason Cyrus had come to know them (well, but not too well) ever since hijacking his way into Mrs. Wythe's class. It wasn't that he developed any type of friendship with the lugs; it was more a mutually beneficial relationship.

Cyrus discovered early on that braving even the slightest glance towards Leslie Borowski was problematic, as his line of sight traversed straight through them. In moments when the footballers' heads weren't felled to their desks with mathematical overload, the two would stifle his gander and his longings would be curtailed by ugly sneers. Cyrus assumed they weren't keen on interlopers. Some side effect, he assumed, of football's quest for possession. And Numbers 71 and 79 guarded their domain savagely.

But Cyrus had a work-around, one that would give him brief visual access to Leslie Borowski. At times, it was a modest view, barely the profile of a head of a coin. Still, it was enough. Enough to get him through a month and a half of a class well below his level of mathematical ability, which, incidentally, was something else he discovered early on. (Not too much of a surprise, really.)

This work-around required tact. And a little foreknowledge. Such as: student athletes had to maintain a minimum grade point average to play at their sports. So, twice a week at the beginning of class, when the previous night's homework was due, Cyrus would surreptitiously expose his paper. He angled it invitingly to wandering eyes slumped atop broad shoulders. A full view access. Number 79 would accept the invitation, then duplicate the information to Number 71.

It became a ritual, an arrangement akin to an offering to the chief—or chiefs. Besides, Cyrus figured the team needed the brutes on the field—the Electrons were not historically known for their gridiron superiority. And in return, Cyrus was able to look right past them without interference, settling his eyes now and then on the most stimulating part of geometry class—period.

Nevertheless, there was another purpose served by Cyrus' vigorous leg thumping, beyond synchronizing to Mrs. Wythe's teachings. The thumping kept his blood circulating. The last thing he wanted was to follow the lead of the footballers or a few of the other kids in class, whose heads were often collapsed on pillow-substituting textbooks. Cyrus knew, if unchecked, he would go down that same path. Grogginess seemed to be the pervasive state of the class, and too often he found himself floating adrift.

No, Cyrus couldn't afford to divest his attention. He had to stay mentally engaged. His top priority was respectful attentiveness. Especially considering what Blake told him: that the school's administration was clamping down on class transfers, due to, they both reasoned, the mass influx of new students. So, for someone who wasn't supposed to be in the class in the first place, Cyrus knew what was at stake: third period purgatory without Leslie Borowski. Even if the material *was* below him, he didn't want to forsake his lot. By this day in October, he was still part of the roster. Which was a blessing.

"So, students, before the end of class I would like (vocal ascent) *each and every one of you* to review and study (vocal descent) *the problems* from pages (vocal ascent) *one-fourteen* to (vocal descent) *one-twenty-two*. This is the last section before our first test on Wednesday, so please don't (vocal rise) *be surprised* if you see this material (vocal descent) *then*. And students, I have your second quiz (vocal ascent) *graded*, so please grab it (vocal trail off) *on your way out*. The grades will also be posted on the portal, if you somehow you, and you know who you are, fail to remember."

When Mrs. Wythe mentioned the words "end of class," the students sprang alive. Numbers 71 and 79, however, remained slack-jawed and blank, eyes drooped as if nothing had changed. Cyrus ruffled some papers to get their attention. The hibernating bears finally awoke.

"Did she say test?" asked Number 79.

"Yes, Wednesday," said Cyrus, showing him the pages in the textbook.

Number 79 smacked Number 71 upside the head. "Big test, ya big Dummy. Next Wednesday." Number 79 then looked to Cyrus, who was watching Leslie mark her textbook for the pages to study. "Hey, Cy, you gonna be here?" he questioned. There was secret concern in his voice.

Oh, goodness. Here we go. "Sure, but..." he replied tentatively. Cyrus understood something else about the behemoths: despite obscuring his quizzes, Number 79 often took stock of the answers he marked down. Cyrus was beginning to worry the meathead might also copy *his* name down in the process. It wasn't like Cyrus' quizzes were flawless—he wanted an A, but he had to make some errors to hide his mastery—it was just that his answers couldn't be too close to the footballers' marks.

Therefore, he had to make a few changes before turning in his quiz. An exam, however, might be a whole different problem. Cyrus continued: "…I heard she gives different tests to different students." Cyrus had no idea if this was true, but it very well could be. The footballers took in this information. They looked to one another. "Different tests?" they repeated.

At the front of class, Leslie was waiting for Cyrus while she glossed over her quiz. Since talking at the stage set last week, Cyrus and Leslie made an informal pact to leave class together, walk to the top of the staircase, then sign off. She would leave for Political Science; he would attempt to simmer his bottle-rocketed nerves before Spanish. Naturally, Cyrus would have loved to have asked her out during those brief minutes between geometry and their salutes goodbye, but he never pushed the envelope. A response of "Sorry I can't, too busy" might translate to "Not a chance, not even close." He felt it best to bide his time. When that time was, he hadn't a clue.

As Cyrus approached Mrs. Wythe's desk, the teacher threw her hand on top of his quiz.

"Cyrus Hampstead," she said, "a quick word." *Great, the moment of truth.* He knew this time would come. The day of reckoning. The day of walking the plank, a resignation to the frozen waters. *Damn, administration finally sent word. Or did Mrs. Wythe herself finally sniff a rat? The brutes…they friggen' copied my name after all!*

Numbers 71 and 79 surreptitiously snuck up, snatched their quizzes, and trundled out the door. Cyrus and Leslie were the only students left in the classroom.

Certain phrases entered his mind: *"See ya later sucker"; "Check and checkmate"; "End of the line"; "Happy trails"; "Vayos con Dios."*

"And Ms. Borowski?" Mrs. Wythe said to Leslie waiting at the door, "I'd like to see you as well." Mrs. Wythe adjusted her thick, tortoise-shell glasses with measure and consulted a folder on her desk. Cyrus attempted to search it for something that read "Denial of Transfer" or "Wrong Class." All he saw was blank manilla.

"First, Cyrus. I guess it's fair to say that geometry isn't much of a challenge for you. You've done rather well on the first few quizzes."

Cyrus merely shrugged his shoulders and waited for the inevitable. His calling-out party. His return ticket to Mr. Evans' class.

"You probably should have been placed in a more advanced class in the beginning of the term," she said. "Though it may be too late at this point. It's really getting full around here. I don't know *what's* going on."

Cyrus saw an opening, a chink in the fortress of the administrative realities of Stafford P. Ellicott High.

"Oh, the school's been having some technical issues lately. Glitches in the new enrollment software. That's what I heard."

"I haven't heard anything like that," Mrs. Wythe replied, "and I work here." She combed her fingers through her short-cropped hair. "Boy, this place has changed."

"It's kinda low key," Cyrus remarked with an air of confidentiality. "You know, the number of students coming in is hard to keep up with.

Principal Worthers doesn't want to make a big deal about it. He doesn't want it to look like the new system he ordered can't keep up with the changes. Then he'd be, you know, on the whipping post."

"Whipping post! Sometimes I'd like to…" Mrs. Wythe stopped short. She sighed, eased her glasses off her head and deliberated. "Huh. Possibly. You know, Cyrus, it took a while to even figure out how to officially record your grades. I had to add you to the roster by hand, then Joyce in the office was able to import your name into the system."

"That's really weird. Really strange" shrugged Cyrus. "Huh. Anyway, I've learned a lot of interesting things in this class so far. I mean, I like the way you teach. It makes geometry less boring, you know. Like the material makes more sense how you teach it." Cyrus was thinking of stretching the praise out further, lavish it on like melted caramel over an apple. Anything to sidetrack her attention away from his hobo-hopping into her class. But truth be told, the material *was* below him. He knew it and she knew it. And all his fawning, like melted caramel, was verging on sticky sweet. And who likes that?

"I see," Mrs. Wythe said as she tapped her pencil. "Thank you for that, Cyrus. Ms. Borowski, on the other hand…" She shot Leslie a look. Cyrus looked down, pretending to page through his textbook.

"Mrs. Wythe, I just don't get all this geometry stuff," she exclaimed defensively, waving her quiz in the air. "I end up getting all confused with what formula to use with what problem. There's so many of them, and then there are all those shapes and angles. They get in the way of things."

Leslie's hands took on a life of their own. They groped at her quiz, her shirt buttons, the air. "I don't think I have that kind of logic in me."

"It's called practice, Leslie. Studying usually works just fine," said Mrs. Wythe. "OK, here's the deal. Here's what we can do. Cyrus, for extra credit towards next year's advanced placement calculus, which I will be teaching, and I *know* you will be taking, you can tutor some students."

Cyrus' head dizzied like he'd just stepped off the twirl-a-whirl. *Some students? Students, as in the plural? No! Please, please, no, no. Not the footballers!*

"Namely Ms. Borowski here," she said after a beat.

Blood rushed back to his head. The spell lifted, and better yet, it came with renewed life. He tried to hide his relief. He was stone-faced, as if he were one of the Mt. Rushmore presidents. He nodded in agreement.

"Are you good with this, Leslie?" asked Mrs. Wythe. "As a student athlete, I think you need to keep your grades up."

"Yes, I can agree to that," said Leslie.

"Good then," said Mrs. Wythe resolutely. "The two of you can arrange amongst yourselves the times. Then get back to me and I'll sign off on the hours. And I trust you'll put forth the effort, Mrs. Borowski?"

"Absolutely."

As they walked down the hallway, sliding in and out of oncoming students, there was an air of apprehension between them, like a reticent date proposal. "OK, how about Sunday? At your place?" Leslie offered at last.

The thought of Leslie coming over to his house wobbled Cyrus. He strode deliberately so that his feet didn't catch the carpet. "Sunday's good."

"Two o'clock, OK? The matinee showing of the play, the final one, thank God, ends at one o'clock. I have to stick around at least 'til then."

"Oh, I have to run errands with my mom in the afternoon. Maybe nighttime's better," said Cyrus. He knew his mother was less active, and therefore less intrusive, at the end of the day; a glass of wine usually settled her.

"Three?" said Leslie.

Cyrus rubbed his chin. "Five."

"What are you, like, in a poker game?" she asked.

"May be a bluff," said Cyrus. He knew nothing about gambling. He just thought it sounded clever.

"I don't do bluffs, Cyrus," she said. "But I do ro-sham-bo's." Leslie threw out her fist. Colorful rings were stacked on her fingers. "If I win, which I will, then it will be three o'clock. If you miraculously pull it off, then I guess five will be fine."

They stopped amidst the traffic. "Ro"… "sham"… "bo…"

At the very moment Cyrus was to extend a stalemating scissor a boy bumped his shoulder. His hand turned to paper. Leslie cut into it.

"But…"

"No buts." She lifted her hands in an "I told you so" manner.

They walked on. Two boys passed and made eye contact with

Cyrus. He waved uneasily at them. One timidly squawked, "What's up?"

"How do you know those guys?" Leslie asked when they passed.

"They want me to join their robotics club. They just started it."

"And? That seems right up your alley."

"I've just never..."

"You've just never what?" she asked.

"Never worked with anyone. Not with other kids, I mean. I dunno, I wouldn't mind the help, but I don't have time for the club stuff. Not with trying to build a bot specifically designed to destroy other bots. Besides, every time I run into them, they try to work me over. I'm kinda over it."

"They didn't seem too eager."

"That's because you're here. They're shy," he said with a shrug of his shoulders.

"Are you?"

"Joining their club?"

"No, shy?"

Of course I'm shy. Shyness is anxiety's second cousin. It's been a part of me since the first day I can remember. But I'm working on it. Hard. Especially now. "What makes you think that?"

"For the same reason that you made me ask the question," she said with a wink. "Anyway, what's this about some technical software glitch or whatever? Mrs. Wythe knows you've been in the class all along."

"Maybe she made some mistake. You know, like she's overwhelmed.

Actually, she might be losing things up here." He pointed to his head. "I made up the computer glitch part because I didn't want to hurt her feelings."

"Ahh, compassionate," she said, squeezing his cheek. He flushed. "I guess compassion is the same reason you wanted to help Tonmoy with the drama set. Because he's afraid of heights?"

Cyrus tried to remain calm despite of her soft touch, her silky voice, and the trap he was sensing. "Maybe. He told me when he lived in Bangladesh he had to cross over a tall, shaky foot bridge to get to school every day. It scared the 'you know what' out of him."

"Shaky foot bridge? I thought he lived in Dhaka. That's like a huge city?"

"I think the traffic shook it. Lots of cars there. I don't know, maybe that's just Tonmoy making things up."

"He wouldn't be the only one," she said as they reached the staircase.

Before parting ways, the two leaned over the railing and watched the usual bustle between periods. It was a blur of silver and cyan, currents of color. Noise lofted upwards and they listened quietly to the overlapping conversations from the valley floor. As he looked down, it occurred to Cyrus that the extent of his meagre relationship with Leslie—which up until now consisted mainly of a few minutes during geometry class, a handful of interrupted exchanges at the drama set, and a few minutes more walking away from geometry class—would soon enter a close relationship of personal hours. It made him nervous, but he also knew he had to adjust to the not-too-likely-to-go-away fluttering.

"Oh, by the way," said Leslie, touching his elbow, "did Tonmoy tell you that you could get shop credit for helping with the set."

"He never mentioned that," said Cyrus.

"Well, I'm mentioning it now. Go to Mr. Vincent, he's cool, he'll sign off on it. Last year, he gave Rozalyn and I full credit for just oiling the machines. Took us like ten minutes a week."

"Then you know what you're doing in a workshop. Because I could really use someone..."

"Good try, Cy," she chirped as she skipped down the steps. She spiraled at the landing, made a graceful ballerina twirl. "See you Sunday. Three o'clock. Not five."

CHAPTER 14

Cyrus had lived through many snow days. And occasionally a blizzard would plow through the region. On those days, it took one look outside to know what would be reported on the school district's website: No School.

But in all his years never once was there an announcement that school was closed due to a flood. Where Cyrus lived, the creeks were so numerous and the river channels so deep and wide that water rarely accumulated to overflow, no matter the extent of the deluge. But here it was, in bold glorious lettering: **No School Wednesday/Thursday: Flooding.**

The real shocker, however, was when he looked out his window. Not a drop in the sky, not a puddle in the grass. He consulted the website further. The flood, it turned out, was due to a pipe rupture inside Stafford P. Ellicott High School. School officials had a two-day slop-fest on their hands. Which meant two days of freedom.

After eating a bowl of fruity-puffed cereal, Cyrus headed to his basement workshop. Years of moisture, along with decades of dirt settled into crevices and caked into corners, made for a dank and musty subterranean dwelling. A century of farmhouse existence—that is not something easily remedied. One just had to deal with it. Or move elsewhere.

It was Cyrus' father who had tried to keep the place somewhat organized and in shape, though still that was a hard-fought battle. But that was his father's nature. Cyrus figured it came from all that Army conditioning, where everything was swabbed over and tucked tight and kept in its place. "Tidy up!" and "Easy retrieving, no thinking," were common phrases in his father's vernacular. In his world, systems of order allowed for efficient, optimal outputs. His father knew the location of every part and tool in their workspace—clamps, gears, lubes, tubes, rods, sprockets, circuits, and converters were all labeled, arranged, inventoried, catalogued, and stratified.

Now a collection of the purposeless sub-let the workspace environment. Discarded materials littered the floor—the slightly-off pieces, the rusted, the bent, the twisted and the misshaped. Whole carcasses of forged metallic appendages, designed by the original tradesman, were spread around, vying for tenant supremacy with the vast tools-of-the-trade clutter. Then, there were the instruction manuals and spec sheets. Many were crumpled and torn, tossed about like fallen leaves from a magnolia tree.

If his father had any allusion that his mentality for organization and orderliness would have somehow been engrained into his son, he would have been sorely disappointed. In fact, the only section of the basement still miraculously intact was the back corner where his father showcased his military memorabilia and photographs. There, a bookcase stood within a section of carpet and wood paneling; shelves replete with metals of valor and books on military history. Dozens of photos of Cyrus over the years bookended the collection.

Under bright fluorescent lights, Cyrus scanned the length of his workbench. Angst and disbelief welled up inside him. Screws, nuts, bolts, fuses, rivets, wires, sprockets—some obsolete, some not—managed to stake their claim to every square inch. To his far right, in an area devoted to machining parts, fine metal filings and nodules covered the floor. To his left, prototypes of half-finished flippers were piled on top of another like baby birds in a nest. In the far corner, an old welding torch stretched haphazardly along a table; it looked to be in a state of disrepair. In an area where all the electrical wiring was kept, Cyrus saw only unruly knots of hair. And though the case of multicolored fuses was bright and shiny, they brought him little joy.

The clutter made Cyrus' anxiety extremely palpable. It sored his head. All of it the consequence of his own actions. It wasn't like the proliferation was intentional. It had just progressively gotten out of hand. Considering his minimal experience in engineering a combat robot (and more than a few improvisational attempts), this was at minimum understandable, if not desirable.

Something had to be done about the mess and his mental state. Therefore, he made a decision. He was going to own that workshop, whip it into shape, get the sea-ravaged boat to the dockyard for repairs. Besides, what could be more appropriate than spending a flood day cleaning up?

He looked around, considered where to begin. He thought about what objects should go where, what objects needed temporary housing, what needed permanent homes. The toolchest would be a good start. It was a stellar disaster as it was. Once clean, it could serve as storage for most anything.

The toolchest was T-boned against a cement wall and lodged between a built-in cabinet and a drill press. Because of years of rust and dirt, the toolchest's casters barely rolled, so Cyrus grabbed one end, wedged a leg against the cabinet for support, and wormed it away from the drill press a few inches. A plume of dust exploded around him, leaving only cobwebs and floating particles and a choking spider on the run.

When Cyrus turned for the broom, something caught his eye. He leaned down to the base of the toolchest for a better look.

It was a large, sliced section of a tree. He inched the toolchest further out for better light. Without a doubt, a tree trunk—two feet tall and a foot-and-a-half in diameter, knotted and sectioned clean. *How long has this been here? Is that the elm tree we cut down years ago? What year was that anyway? And why the hell is it jammed back there in the first place?*

When Cyrus pushed the toolchest away from the wall as far as it would go, he realized something else: the section of elm blocked an alcove, a recessed cubby hidden within the built-in cabinet. A space Cyrus never knew existed.

He grabbed the broom and swiped away the cobwebs. Then there was movement. He waited tentatively. As he slid the tree trunk over, Mongrel suddenly sprang from the alcove. Cyrus jumped. He was expecting a scare as much as Mongrel was the disruption of his midday slumber? With Mongrel gone, Cyrus got to his knees and peered inside the dark, dusty alcove. He drew his hand inside. A fistful of gray hair came out. He reached above him, grabbed a lighter from the cabinet and flickered the light. Deep within was a tinseling glint, so he lowered his shoulder and reached back as far as he could, to where he could barely touch the object. It was smooth, metallic. He managed to grab hold of its bottom, and through dust and fur, he slid the shiny object out.

The remains of long forgotten bot. Stowed away since who knows when. He gave it a once over. He then decided to get it up on the workbench for a better look, so he pushed it over to the lift his father had installed at the end of the workbench, centered it on the platform, and slowly cranked the large wheel until the conveyance was even with the workbench. The bot yielded stubbornly on the table.

He viewed the thing from all sides. The stainless steel was dull, and there were rings of rust around the bolts and rivets. It was not as large as Spiral Cyclone and it seemed to weigh slightly less. It reminded Cyrus of a device from a 1950's science fiction movie. Cyrus could tell it was well balanced and had a well-proportioned center of gravity, fine qualities for a fighting robot.

From the top view, it was shaped like a spade, or an arrowhead. In the rear was a sharp pointed tail—a dagger. In the front (the arrowhead's tip) was a mechanical wedge, five inches wide and low to the ground, modulated so that the machine could upturn an opponent. End to end, the robot was longer than Spiral Cyclone. Its edges were jagged and sharp. It had quite a few gouges and chunks in its frame, reminiscent of a worn-out boxer who'd seen too many rounds. *Obviously, it's seen battle. But...I've never seen this thing before in my life.* It had no other markings—no logo, no name. Which usually meant no fighting history, at least any history *Cyrus* was aware of. Cyrus became very curious about its provenance.

He grabbed a flashlight from the toolbox, flipped the bot over, unscrewed the main panel with a drill, and looked inside. At first glance, the components seemed intact, although the wiring was flimsy and tangled. Its wheels were missing, and its battery compartment was a hollowed-out shell. The motor (if it had one at all) was in a separate housing, battened down by a bolted panel. Still, the chassis was solid and the axels were fairly straight, despite the strands of gray hair wound around them.

With leveraging muscle, he turned it back over with a thud. There was a conspicuous void in its top—a cutout. *Main weapon?* He shone his lighter into the opening, but the configuration was unfamiliar. *Definitely for a weapon.* The thing seemed solid enough. Still, he wondered: *How good is this old bot anyway?*

He had an idea. Since the thing was too heavy to haul upstairs by himself, he'd need some help. Tonmoy had a car, and because of the flooding, the time. Tonmoy could be over within an hour if he harassed him now, so long as he didn't fall back to sleep after hanging up. By Tonmoy's arrival, Cyrus could easily have four tires slapped on and given a fresh charge to a battery. *Now where did we keep those extra tires anyway?* Nothing came easy in the basement mess.

Tonmoy sounded like he was sleeping, or just waking up, or maybe some state in between.

"Ton, I need your strong beautiful body over here," he said teasingly.

"Am I dreaming?"

"Maybe. But I need your help. I have to move something."

"Do I look like I want to move something?" he slurred.

"I don't know how you look. I'm on the phone, not in your dreams. At least you're not at school. Get over here. Please."

"It's a flood day," yawned Tonmoy.

"Is it flooding at your house?" asked Cyrus.

"No."

"Great. Come on over."

"Don't you live in like…in the country?"

"Yeah. And don't you have like…a car? I'll owe you," Cyrus said, then disconnected.

Cyrus turned over the bot, unbolted the housing for the battery and remote receptor. As the machine sat patiently in repose, he coordinated the frequencies to his controller, then, with a needle-nose plier, screwdriver, and electrical tape, he re-wrapped the loose, intwined wires. He then searched through several large drawers in the toolchest and found four similarly sized wheels. He wrenched the lug nuts on after removing all the tangled fur. Next, he unearthed his battery charger, fit the clamps to the exposed terminals of a battery, and prayed the strange thing had a functional motor somewhere inside.

An hour later, Cyrus heard a hard knock. Tonmoy stood at the bottom of the basement steps.

"Your faithful servant has arrived," Tonmoy said with fish-dead eyes.

"Perfect timing."

"My specialty, sir."

Together, they hauled the bot up the steps as Mongrel trudged slowly behind.

"I can't see the steps," said Tonmoy from the rear. "And I feel your cat's tail on my feet."

"That's not his tail. Most likely he's trying to trip you with his paws. He likes to do that."

"Can't you get a dog."

"Did my mom answer the door, Tonmoy?" asked Cyrus as they reached the landing.

"I knocked but no one answered. I figured she wasn't home, so I came on down. Cy, this thing's really heavy. Especially for whatever time it is."

"Robo-time, Tonmoy. It's robo-time and I'm Robo-boy."

From the front bay windows, Cyrus looked out and saw that his mother's car was missing from the driveway. *Probably at the store.* "OK, let's bring it in the den. I'll show it to her when she gets back. She'll want to see this baby."

Straining from the weight, they set the machine down on the floor in the center of the den. Cyrus stared at it; in the natural light sweeping in from the French doors, it was a sign from the heavens. If machines like this existed in ancient times, Cyrus may have been convinced the object standing before him was a treasured relic. A talisman. A thousand-year-old genie lamp that needed awakening.

"Looks dead tired. Must be my soul mate," said Tonmoy.

"Time to wake it up."

Tonmoy peered at it closely. "The woman of your dreams."

"I already have one, Ton-Ton."

Meanwhile, Mongrel had timidly inched towards it. He stalked slowly around the bot and sniffed its tires, engaging in a tepid appraisal. Once he circled it, Mongrel became more comfortable with its presence. It was his long-term bunkmate, after all. His napping comrade.

Cyrus loved Mongrel, but the temptation was too great. He activated the remote just as Mongrel lowered to take a whiff of its underside. The once-dead motor came to life. A high-squealing whirr echoed across the den. Mongrel's back arched and the cat let out a roaring squelch, matching the volume of the machine. Cyrus eased his fingers on the remote and thrusted the thing slightly forward. Mongrel leapt two vertical feet straight in the air, landed, and made a hair-raising beeline through the den's double doors.

"Wow, that cat has hops," yelled Tonmoy over the motor.

Seconds later, Cyrus had his own surprise. The bot's impulse for motion was as controllable as a thoroughbred at the starting gate. It twisted. It spun in circles. The front flipper wedge shot out, retracting and extending in quick succession. Cyrus thumbed the remote's throttle to no avail. The bot then lurched forward and took off across the carpet, zigzagging from couch to ottoman to coffee table, all in a flash. After years of inactivity, the relic was on a rampage.

Cyrus feverishly tried to control it, but the bot was off to the races, spinning, bouncing, colliding, its tail dagger making mincemeat out of the coffee table legs and the front of the couch. It then came straight at Tonmoy. He jumped on the ottoman, saving his two-hundred-dollar kicks and both tibias. As the machine rammed into the ottoman, Tonmoy leapt to the coffee table, landed in a tight crouch and ready to spring.

The motor suddenly let out a woeful cry and died.

Between the thing's flipper and daggered tail, the den ended up looking like a lion cub had come for a visit to sharpen its claws.

The two boys stood frozen quiet. Cyrus looked at Tonmoy, whose mouth was agape. The dark puddles under his eyes had disappeared. "You know, I could be sleeping right now," Tonmoy bleated.

Cyrus stood over the fighting bot. He disengaged the remote and placed a foot on it in case it decided for an encore. "I had no idea it'd go all fucking maniac on me."

Through the double doors, Cyrus heard a banging in the kitchen.

"She knows I had nothing to do with this," whispered Tonmoy. "Robots aren't even my thing."

"Don't worry," moaned Cyrus. "I'll handle it."

Cyrus knew it wouldn't take long. His mother had a nose for such incidents. And right on cue, the double doors opened. She surveyed the room. Her demeanor was solemn, then sour.

"What on heaven's earth, Cy." She tossed her grocery bag on the end table. "What went on here? Look at this place. And what's that thing on the floor?" Cyrus figured she wasn't seeing a long-lost treasure, but an ancient curse.

"Mongrel found it, you could say." Cyrus looked around for the complicit cat.

"Mongrel? Doesn't look like Mongrel had any part of this. Mongrel didn't turn my furniture into shambles. I'm pretty sure that thing you're standing on did," she wailed, pointing with reproach at the silver object. "This is not ComBot, Cy. This is not some place to have fun with whatever robot that is."

Cyrus bit his lip. "I think it might have been dad's," said Cyrus, shifting gears. "It was in the basement. But I had no idea it had this kind of…power."

"I'm sure you didn't," she said. "Then why'd you turn it on in the first place? In here? In the den? For heaven's sake, Cy."

"You need help bringing in the groceries, Mrs. Hampstead?" asked Tonmoy sheepishly.

"Yes, thank you, Tonmoy." As Tonmoy made his escape, she stepped into the room to inspect her once-pristine furniture. Her look was of loathe and disappointment. "Look at the couch. And the ottoman. Ugghh. Where'd you say you found that thing, anyway?"

"Hidden in the basement. Down in a little spot where Mongrel was hanging out," he explained. "I came up to show you, but somehow the bot just started going crazy," he snapped his fingers, "just like that. On its own."

"Uh-huh, on its own? What's that remote for, Cy? I don't think there was any 'on its own' with that in your hands."

"Well, I turned it on just to test the motor, like a little a nudge, but then..."

"Yeah, I see the 'then.' 'Then' my couch gets ripped up, 'then' the coffee table legs get destroyed." His mother looked the bot over. "What the hell is it...this...this...I've never seen this thing before in my life. Hidden with Mongrel?"

"Yeah, where he sleeps in the basement."

"I have no idea where that cat sleeps. I hardly ever go down there." She bent down to inspect the slashes carved into the wooden legs of the coffee table. "My Goodness. You're gonna have to sand these down, Cyrus."

"I will. I swear."

"The couch, well...that's plain ruined. We'll have to get a whole new one. Which, by the way, I wasn't expecting to shell out for anytime soon. I really wasn't. Cyrus, and you know this is not something we have extra money for. Luckily, it's seen better days, so you may get off rather easy. Maybe." She sternly caught Cyrus' eyes. "I don't know about Mongrel, but you're in the doghouse, mister."

CHAPTER 15

A pleasant enough day, Sunday in early-October. Cyrus stood at his bay windows, hastily ingesting a peanut butter and banana sandwich and looking out towards the vacant house across the street. Still on the market and still in need of care. On the upside, however, the weeds had retreated for their fall slumber. The adjacent woods, greenish-yellow mere weeks ago, were now orange and yellow, and every so often a brisk wind shook their branches. Cyrus watched the leaves spin to the ground.

He suddenly felt a familiar tickle in his back pocket. A cartoon lizard holding a hockey stick appeared on his phone—Blake Tinsley. *Impeccable timing*. Cyrus shook his head.

"Blake, I can't talk right now," he said over the speaker.

"No problem, Cy. I gotcha. How did the tutoring go with Leslie?"

"Hasn't happened yet. I'm waiting. It's just that…"

"Oh, I see, a little nervous, huh. Yeah, that happens. One time I took out Franny Fournier, you know, from Haywood High, went to the movies I think, can't remember which one, oh, the one about the guy who takes advice from an old traveler on some deserted road and… anyway, it doesn't end well…but before the date I was in the bathroom, smelled like rotting flesh and my hair was all matted and scrappy…hey, I was doing some research on head lice, did you know those damn things…"

If the profusion of words were meant to calm Cyrus, they did the opposite.

"Love to hear about it, Blake. Just not now. Call me later," said Cyrus. As he disconnected, he alighted to something Blake said. The part (the only part he was listening to) about his hair being "matted and scrappy." He walked to the den to where he'd soon be studying with Leslie. He took a look at its scrappiness. "Oh crap," he muttered.

He went to the hall closet and pulled out an over-stuffed cardboard box containing every jacket, hat, coat, glove, and sweatshirt ever owned, loaned or inherited by the Hampstead family. He combed through it, assessing how much he would need: two chunked-out legs of a coffee table; the front upholstery of a couch; an ottoman, frayed and eviscerated.

Sometimes it takes creative ingenuity to cover up an *unnatural* disaster.

These'll do. He extracted the items and threw them on the floor: two large coats, his Kettlebridge Chromiums blanket, a pile of winter hats, and a scarf. He picked up the pile and headed to the next room, moving as fast as a stagehand between draws of the curtain. With one coat he covered the ottoman, the other the coffee table. The Chromiums blanket draped the couch. The assortment of hats he scattered for general disguise. The scarf he sent flying in for good measure.

It was quarter to three and Leslie Borowski was due over in fifteen minutes. He gave the den a once over. If only he had time to clean the crusted food from the chair cushions, the place might seem halfway presentable. But if he hadn't done that by this point, he probably never would. He figured there were times when things have to look lived in, appear in their natural state, although his mother would entirely disagree. At least the "going through my winter clothes" charade would be a respectable compromise.

His phone buzzed again. Again, Blake.

"Blake, I said call me later," he huffed.

"I am," replied Blake. "It is later. It's been five minutes. How much later did you mean?"

"Like tonight. Like after I finish tutoring."

"Gotcha, gotcha. She on her way, then? You know, because..."

Cyrus figured he had two options: hang up or come up with a believable lie. Blake could be very sensitive; it might take him days to get over being ghosted. Since Cyrus just then happened to be staring at two glasses of lemonade sitting on a silver tray in the den, it sprang out. "Blake, I just friggen' poured lemonade down my friggen' shorts. They're soaked. Look what you did."

"How the hell did I..."

"Somehow you did," he spouted before hanging up.

Cyrus stared at the lemonades sitting on the credenza. Proud as he was of his impromptu fib, he also began to wonder why lemonades were there in the first place. The glasses certainly weren't there to entertain the neighbors.

"Cy, what time is your friend coming over?" his mother yelled from the kitchen. He also wondered why his mother was referring to Leslie as "friend." She certainly knew the person coming over was not in the same category as Tonmoy or Blake. With those two, he wouldn't have combed his hair and splashed a dash of dollar store cologne on his chest. His mother and her disingenuous line of questioning certainly knew the difference.

"Not sure, Mom," he replied, feigning disinterest, "maybe soon. Why?"

"I made you lemonade. Maybe she'll like some. It's on the table in there."

"That's not really necessary, Mom. She's just coming to study for a test. Not to have high tea." He hoped to throw her off the scent, but that was never easy. Her nose was well seasoned, conditioned, up to any task. As he saw it, interfering is what most mothers do for sport, but in this arena his mother might be considered an all-star meddler.

"It's not tea, thank you very much," his mother yelled back.

Cyrus took a few moments to open the geometry textbook and review what they'd be going over. If his mother came in, it would at least present an air of scholarly commitment. Formulas and equations came easy for Cyrus, the answers seemingly materializing out of nowhere, like those images intentionally hidden within a painting. It wasn't like that for everybody. He knew it wasn't like that for Leslie. Or the footballers, which was a given.

As the minutes slid closer and closer, Cyrus became notches and notches more nervous. His stomach curdled and knotted. He debated in his head what he would say or even how he would open the door. Would he present himself as the debonair type, bowing with a gentle flourish? Or the laid back, no-problem guy with other things on his mind? In truth, he was altogether unfamiliar in these matters. He was as confused by such formalities of ritual as much as he was with the feelings uprising inside him. So, the moment his mother came into the living room with a plate full of cookies, he veered towards near skittishness.

"Uh, Mom? Thanks, I, uh, I really doubt she'll be hungry."

"Relax, Cy. I'm going to leave them here just in case. Then I'll get out of your way. You won't see me again. I'll grab a glass of wine and go upstairs, if that's alright."

"Upstairs of *this* house?"

"Good one. Let me know if you want me to bake any crumpets, because I'll gladly..."

"Got the point. Here, I'll take those," he said, intercepting the cookies.

Once his mother was upstairs, he ran the cookie plate into the kitchen. He was planning to do the same with the lemonade tray when a knock came to the door. Quickly, he slid the cookies along the counter and bounded out of the kitchen. Then, with a reckon to judgement, he slowed to a crawl a few strides before opening it.

Leslie stood on the porch, her backpack slung over her shoulder. Her eyes were fixed rigidly over his head.

"Don't move an inch," she whispered slowly. Cyrus froze. Leslie removed a small Electron's towel from her backpack and peppered the towel over his head. From the doorframe spiraled down several insects: beetles, black with red striping down their backsides, oblong creatures shaped like olive pits.

"They were about to attack you," said Leslie. "They were planning. I was watching them."

Cyrus smiled. "I thought I sensed something."

"What are they, anyway?" she asked as she slung off her backpack.

"Not sure. Some distant cousin of the cockroach. As soon as it gets cold, they invite themselves in," he said. "Here, come in before they attack."

Once inside, Leslie immediately seized upon the lemonades on the credenza. "Oh my God, I'm so thirsty. Thank you," she said, then downed half the glass.

"I always have some on hand. You know, when the neighbors swing by."

"Yeah?" asked Leslie with skepticism. "How often is that?"

"Not as often as the beetles."

Leslie laughed into her drink. She then followed him into the den.

"Find what you were looking for?" she asked.

"What?"

She pointing to the articles of clothing spilled around the room. "The clothes for winter. Find what you were looking for?"

"Oh, uh, not yet…I was looking for my Chromium's pullover. It's somewhere here. But I couldn't find it."

"Ah." Leslie rested her backpack on the table and scanned the open textbook. "So, this is the section we need to study. Goodness. Just looking at it jumbles my head. I'm really better suited for other disciplines. The kind that don't have numbers."

"Don't worry, I can make it seem easy," he reassured her. "Besides, if you think about it, the bottoms of the grade-curve are sitting right next to you."

"The football players?"

"Exactly."

Cyrus opened the textbook to the section on angle and hinge bisector theorems, trying his best to simplify the versions explained in the pages. He drew sketches of two-dimensional configurations, triangles, circles and angles, wrote out equations and simple formulas. Sometimes he would kneel on his chair and lean over to scratch with his pencil on Leslie's paper, other times he'd fall back in his chair, patiently respectful of her insistence to work out a problem on her own. But after nearly an hour and a half of teasing math out her brain (after which she reported positive gains but also an agonizing crush to her temples) Leslie's head began to nod languidly. Cyrus' explanations were now netting zero-point-zero returns.

"Ugghh, my circuits are shot," Leslie complained. "I was studying French all this morning. And not only did I have to study it, I had to translate an English version of some work into French. Like, exhausting."

"Really? You had to translate?" Cyrus closed the textbook. "We don't have to do that in Spanish. We mostly do conjugations, learn some new words. What kind of work did you have to translate, anyway?"

"Oh, it was a short thing by Mark Twain. Like "The Celebrated Frog of something or other county." I can't remember the name, but we had to come up with everything in French, which wasn't easy because there was a lot of old slang and old sayings and words that don't seem to even exist anymore."

"Oh, yeah, I remember reading that in Lit class. About this guy who was tricked out of his money in a frog jumping contest…You know, you could've just told your teacher there was nothing to translate because in the French version the frog doesn't have any legs. Get it?"

"No," replied Leslie, eyeing him suspiciously.

"Because the frog's legs would have been on someone's dinner plate."

Leslie rang out a quick laugh, which made Cyrus feel like a world-class comic. "Clever. Clever one. If the robot thing doesn't work out, you should go the comedy route."

The mention of *robot* made Cyrus think of the object sitting on the tree stump down in his basement. It was the perfect segue. At the very least, it would provide a distraction to the rigors of geometric calculations.

"Speaking of robots, how 'bout a tour of Frankenstein's laboratory? I'll show you what I found," said Cyrus.

"Sure. But just no creepy mad scientist stuff. Don't know if I can handle."

Cyrus and Leslie stepped down the stairwell and into a basement bathed only in a dim light that seeped through a small horizontal window. Brownish-red dirt lightly coated the outside of the glass, making it appear as though twilight had come early. Outside, the wind was playing games with tree branches, swirling soft shadows into the space.

"Let me snap the lights," Cyrus said. The room came to with a low hum and a saturating luminescence.

"I sorta see the Frankenstein part of it," said Leslie. "Rather, Frankenbot part of it."

Everywhere, on and around the long workbench, housed some aspect of robot building. Leslie stood for several seconds looking the place over. Cyrus had made a dent in his quest to clean the space. Still, the basement was a jungle of loose parts, power tools, devices, wires, springs, rods, nuts, bolts, schematics, and manuals. The dark sludge that followed everything like trails of a slug: fortunately, that had been dealt with.

Cyrus wasn't quite sure what was going on in Leslie's head. Was it incredulity at the mess, or impressiveness at the venture? He could see both sides; a madman's lab is often both.

At last, Leslie focused her eyes on the object sitting atop the elm stump. The spade-shaped object stood there stock-still and ominous, like an alligator ready to explode at the faintest twitch.

"Is that what you were talking about? Is that what you found?"

"That's it. I didn't even know it was down here until I pulled it from underneath that cubby," said Cyrus, nodding to the dark nook beneath the cabinet.

She took a stride towards it. "It looks like...well, cool but creepy." *And reckless.*

"I'm guessing your dad built it?"

"Yeah," he said. "Some time ago. I've never seen it before, nor had my mom. She had no idea about it. It's just one of those things."

Leslie looked at him earnestly. "It must be tough. I mean, not having your dad around," she said.

Time had filtered some of his despair. Though his sorrow never left, it had flatlined into something else. Something he had little words for. Yes, it was tough, especially if some event or passing statement happened to trigger the day he learned of his death. There was no escape from that wellspring of emotion.

"Yeah. But on the plus side he taught me how to build bots. I had Spiral Cyclone around, and I tinkered with him a lot," said Cyrus as he walked to the cabinet. With his forearm, he cleared a shotgun blast of debris from the top. "Here, help me lift it up." Together, they hoisted the bot from the stump and placed it atop the cabinet. "He and I always worked on things together. Now I'm the caretaker of all this. And this sucker, too, I guess."

"So, how's your mom doing?"

"She has her days, but they're getting better. She keeps busy."

Leslie leaned in close to inspect the sleek metallic hull on four wheels, giving it the once over as Mongrel did days before, although without the sniffing. She gathered her golden-strawberry hair into a bun and tied it with a scrunchy band. She craned her head to look underneath at the wedge mechanism that had caused so much damage to the furniture. She then inspected the sides. Lastly, she peered down into the square opening on top. "What do you think your dad had in mind with this?"

Cyrus peered inside. Across the center stretched a single steel rod. "I'm thinking it would've been for some type of weapon. Sorta like Spiral Cyclone had, but he had an arm with a circular saw. But this is different. I'm sure that's what my father had in mind. Haven't really figured it out yet."

"Good guess," she said. "Uncle Carl never was this advanced, he just designed some things that spun around all crazy. Some had a few spikes on them. At least that's how he described them. But this is on another level. I can see why Spiral Cyclone made it to the ComBot semis." She turned to Cyrus. "How did he learn to do all of this?"

"He was in the Army. There are some pictures of him in the corner," he said pointing to the section of memorabilia. "He worked with robots, designed and built them, fixed them, serviced them. That's what his unit did. The kind of robots that blow up bombs up before bombs blow up people."

"You mean like explosives that terrorists leave in the markets? In the streets? Those?"

"Yep, exactly. IED's. The robots would go in, snuff them out. Only thing is they weren't designed to move as fast as these. But they could move over almost any terrain," added Cyrus.

"Neat. Does it work? You try it?"

"Uh, not really…well, I mean, yes, just once. It's super reactive."

"OK, so let me know what you think. I'm thinking a hammer, a big hammer swinging over the top of it, like the kind you see in one of those carnival games. Where you strike down with a mallet to test your strength. You know, the ball thing goes up the pole, then says something like "weakling" or "mad muscles." And if you're really strong, the bell rings at the top. Same thing, same swinging motion, positioned on that rod in there," Leslie explained as she leaned over, her eyeball inches from the cavity.

Cyrus lost track of what she was saying. His mental connections had short-circuited. Anything to do with robotics receded to a distant realm. It became hard to focus on anything other than Leslie Borowski.

She tilted her head, waiting for a response. He stepped closer.

"A hammer…swinging thing…you think?" he stammered. A magnifying glass straddling a taught wire between two poles at each end of the cabinet hovered several feet away. He yanked the wire, sliding the glass down the line. He set it in front of her. "Thanks," Leslie said, surprised. She gazed, then crinkled a smile. "This thing must be prone to hair growth? Either that, or you really *are* a mad scientist." She reached in and pinched out some gray fur.

"Ha," chuckled Cyrus. "My cat, Mongrel. He naps in the same cubby. They're buddies."

"Oh…curiosity and the cat," she quipped. "Anyway, check it out." She slid him the magnifier.

"Maybe you're right," Cyrus said, looking in closely. "Why else would the rod be running between the cross beams that way." He angled his eye to the magnifier but saw nothing but shadowy mechanics. "Some type of swinging weapon, huh?"

"That's my guess. Either that or it's to raise a pole. You know, like a white flag for surrender."

"Now that doesn't sound *at all* like my father."

"Didn't you say Spiral Cyclone had a circular saw?" she asked.

"Yes." Cyrus slid the magnifying glass back down the wire. "The arm pivoted at a radial hinge, like an elbow." Cyrus moved her arm accordingly. "It could twist, chop down, go sideways." He eased down her arm, aware of his upswing of nerves. "It was awesome. But this one, this one seems to have all its fight right down there. In the space missing on the rod. I'll have to open it up soon and find out."

Leslie cradled her chin. She stared intently at the stainless-steel object in front of her. "Did it stop working?" she asked after a moment.

"Uh, I haven't really activated it. I mean, like I said, just once briefly…"

"No. I meant the saw on Spiral Cyclone," she said. "You made it to the ComBot semis, and it seems like a circular saw would be pretty tough beat. But it could get damaged too, especially if it took a lot of blows. I've seen that happen more than twice. That's what I meant."

Cyrus rubbed his thumb against his bottom lip. A series of flimsy flashbacks crossed his mind. Whenever he thought about that semifinal fight his memories tended to unspool. Even though he understood her question, he really didn't know how to answer it. It's been the same for months: Was it a damaging blow? A snapped circuit? A connective piece that severed and caused the eventual meltdown? Or was he at fault for his robot's undoing? Then the thought would always cross his mind that Ray Dokestout was simply unbeatable. Whatever the truth, he didn't have a single explanation.

"Not sure, really," he confessed.

Leslie regarded him earnestly. "Sometimes the opponent just has a better day, no matter how good you think you're doing. Happens in field hockey. You're out there on your game, your teammates, they're doing their part, everyone's dialed in and making passes and defensive stops. Then, for whatever reason, it all breaks down. Ball goes in. Then from there everything washes downhill. No one's on the same wavelength anymore. It's hard to get that mojo back, you know."

"I guess Dokestout just had a better day then. Better mojo."

"You lost to Ray Dokestout?"

"Yeah. One of many who have. Wait, you know Ray Dokestout?"

"Like I said, I've been watching ComBot for years. What's he like anyway? I only know him from those splashy, 'get-to-know the champion' intros."

"Like nausea in a bottle."

"Figured. Seems like he is. So, you and Spiral Cyclone give him a fight?"

"Guess you could put it that way. For a while at least. I was in control for a while, until the end."

"Like I said," said Leslie coolly, "right when you least expect it, there goes the mojo." She swiped her hands together with a flourish. "Forget about giving me a spoiler alert. Does Dokestout win the title again?"

"Yep. Once again."

Upstairs, Cyrus heard pots and pans clanging over the faint sounds of an old-time song playing on the radio. A pungent scent wafted down the basement stairwell. Cyrus had lost track of time, not noticing (or maybe not really caring to notice) that beyond the small basement window the pale light of the evening had turned slate gray.

"Better wrap up the geometry stuff," said Leslie. She nodded to the stainless-steel creature on the cabinet. "Thanks for the Frankenbot tour." As they walked up the staircase, she asked: "What was the Doke-a-name this year?"

Cyrus was impressed she knew Ray Dokestout named his bots some iteration of his own name: Doke-a-devil, Doke-a-crusher, Doke-a-bull. The list goes on.

"Doke-a-lasher."

"Wasn't last year something like Doke-n-round. I remember some bat-out-of-hell tornado thingy that ripped everything to shreds?"

"Yeah," replied Cyrus, "that was last year. The one I most remember was Rope-a-Doke. That bot bounced like a pinball off the sidewalls and came hurling back at like a hundred miles per hour. With a flying machete."

"Geez. Hey, does the guy have any kids?" she asked as they reached the top of the stairs.

"Not sure. Why?"

"He thinks pretty highly of himself. Wouldn't be surprised if he gave his kid a name like, Doke-a-boy."

"Doke-a-bloke," snapped Cyrus.

"If it was a girl, Raymonda."

"Raylene!" they shouted simultaneously, laughing.

In the kitchen, Cyrus' mother stood over a pot on the stove, humming and stirring to the music of yesteryear. To Cyrus, the kitchen resembled a greenhouse during a summer storm circa 1955. Like floating spurs, the spices scrabbled his eyes and the weepy tunes gave an aura of mid-century depression.

Cooking to music was his mother's serenity, but in terms of tastes of music and food, they couldn't have been further from Cyrus' own. She listened to vaudeville; he, industrial pop. She favored rich spices; he, blandness.

"Mom, this is Leslie," he said over the music.

"Nice to meet you, Leslie," replied his mother, turning around with a cheery smile.

"Nice to meet you, too, Mrs. Hampstead." A polished reply.

"Mom, you want me to open the window? Or turn on the vent?" Cyrus choked.

"No, not really. Here, give this a taste, Cy. It needs something."

"Not a chance," he recoiled.

"Want me to give it a try?" asked Leslie.

"Thank you, Leslie." His mother scooped a dollop of the sauce with a wooden spoon and handed it to her.

"Humm. Right amount of salt. Maybe a touch more cumin."

"At least someone's developed a culinary palate," his mother said, glaring at Cyrus. "You're welcome to stay for dinner, Leslie," she added.

"She has to be home soon," Cyrus said hurriedly.

"Thank you for the offer," said Leslie. "It tasted great, but I really do have to get going."

Once they left the kitchen, Leslie said: "You're lucky to have dinners like that. She's a better cook than both my parents."

"Cook? She could win a worst cook-off contest."

She slapped him on the shoulder. "Cooking's not easy." She gathered her backpack and Cyrus walked her to the door. On the porch, she released her bun and let a waterfall of strawberry-blond cascade down her back, then whipped it around. "Hey, you never told me what happened to Spiral Cyclone after you lost. You have it still?"

"What's left of it, which isn't much. Its insides were left in the decagon. Like roadkill. I dragged the shell back here." He paused, looking in the distance. "Someone suggested I use it as a planter."

"A planter? For what?"

"Who knows. A cactus, I think. It's in the back shed."

"Maybe you can show me some time," she said with an easy smile. She then leaned into his ear. His knees staggered. She whispered. "As long as Mongrel doesn't mind."

Cyrus hiccupped but managed to clip a laugh. As she walked to her car, he knew the last image he'd have that night as his head hit the pillow would be of her lips, whispering softly in his ear.

CHAPTER 16

Cyrus, Tonmoy and three other boys stood atop the bleachers overlooking the Stafford P. Ellicott football stadium. Clear, early November day, with a top view of the undulating hills and the trees in their Autumnal hues. The sweet, musky scent of burning leaves filled the air.

The boys watched as the gym coach labored his way up the bleacher steps. With his commands calling them down to the track going unheeded, the coach seemed frustrated at having to huff up the steep bleachers.

"Couldn't you boys hear what I was saying? I was saying get back on down to the track," he yelled.

"It's windy up here, we couldn't quite hear and we thought you were telling us to stay put," Tonmoy explained. Cyrus was glad his friend came up with the somewhat believable fabrication.

"Stay put? What'd ya'll think my arms were flailing around like this for?" The coach flapped his arms erratically, his face pinched in wry sarcasm. "Anyway, I don't mind you boys being up here. Not one bit. In fact, once you're nice and settled in, you can go down there"—he pointed to the bottom of the steps—"and then back up here"—pointing now to where they stood—"then there, and then back. Twenty times sounds 'bout right to me. Got the drift? Sweat, pain and tears, sons." He hiked up his shorts and pivoted each leg deliberately down the steps.

The boys began the circuit with half-hearted enthusiasm.

"He's used to having the football players obey his orders," said one of the boys. "They got him coaching special teams."

"Well, we're a special team," said Tonmoy. "Can't he see that. He should be glad the Electrons are doing so well and just leave us alone."

"For now they are," said another boy.

"For now, what?" asked Cyrus as he jumped the last three steps and thudded to the bottom of the bleachers. "Aren't they kicking ass?"

"Yeah, but I overheard Coach Belnitch in the weight room telling... well, you know those two dudes, the star players?"

"Let me guess, Numbers Seventy-one and Seventy-nine," said Cyrus.

"Yeah, them. He told them yesterday he'd have to yank their asses from the field if they didn't get their grades up."

"Interesting," said Tonmoy, leaping next to Cyrus. "Aren't they in your geometry class, Cy?"

"They're there. Physically at least. Who could miss them."

The boy began to imitate Coach Belnitch's gruff voice, in how he explained the situation to the football lugs. "'Left with no other option, boys. Ya here me? Rules are rules and you're not above them. Hell, sons, I'm not above them. That's just life, flat out, plain ol' life.'"

Tonmoy threw his arm around Cyrus' shoulders. "Lemme see. The Electrons' bid for a state title is rising, those boy's grades are falling. Looks like you may have your work cut out for you, my friend."

Cyrus looked to the green turf where smash mouth football was the talk of the town. "Huh, Friday night lights...out. That's what I'm sensing."

The information, incidentally, rang true. Spot on. The next day, Numbers 71 and 79 came into geometry class in a deep funk. They looked comatose when Cyrus spoon fed them the previous night's homework. The following day, a quiz came around and they seemed to rather walk on coals than have a crack at it. The day after, they came in dressed like normal students, not jocks. They were emotionally sunk. Sunk as low as their grades. Their depression even depressed Cyrus.

After class, Cyrus asked them how things were going.

"OK," they moped.

"How's the football season going?"

"Nine and O," mumbled Number 79.

"Best record in nineteen years," brooded Number 71.

"That's great," said Cyrus. "You guys play offense or defense?"

"Both."

"What...wait...Wow."

"I'm leading in tackles," said Number 79.

"I've got the most sacks in the league," said Number 71.

"Because I flush the quarterback your way, dummy," said Number 79.

"Bullshit."

"Hey, is my homework helping you guys? You know, and the quizzes? You guys getting by?"

They became sullen. Their eyes glassed over.

Yikes!

The two confided to Cyrus that their gridiron season was on the brink, that suiting up in their Friday night's finest was in peril. "Screwed, dude, like, really, totally screwed."

They were wounded warriors in desperate need of salvation. No way Cyrus could turn his back on the brutes. That might upset the football gods. The two were the linchpins to the Electron's offense, and so it seemed, the defense as well. He had to do something. Something that didn't involve the time-consuming act of tutoring (he was certain that wouldn't have worked anyway.)

Nonetheless, Cyrus managed to get one tidbit of information: one good test result in geometry would keep them hanging on until the end of the semester. That would at least allow them to "beat some ass in the playoffs."

After class, Cyrus and Leslie walked to their usual spot before heading to the next class. They leaned against the railing and looked down on the open toilet-basin. Students intersected in all directions. At a bank of computers, a dozen or so students were gathered around a teacher like ducklings, stiffly trying to pay attention as a stampede of teenagers roamed by and floated above them.

"Coach Belnitch told them that?" asked Leslie. "Yeah, they're in deep. Coaches won't threaten that for nothing."

"I know their grades in other classes aren't that great," said Cyrus. "But I also know a good result on next Wednesday's geom test will keep them on the field. That's what they said coach told them, and I'm guessing that came from Mrs. Wythe herself."

"Can't they just study?" It was less of a question than a statement.

"Uh, maybe. But…you really think cramming material into those two guy's heads for several days is gonna tip the scales?"

Below in the library, the teacher had dismissed all his students except two boys. His arms swung animatedly, pointing now and again the computer screen, and Cyrus could hear his vague, inspiring words that conveyed some importance. The commotion around the two boys, however, was far from conducive. "Look," continued Leslie, "I was clueless with this stuff before you started helping me. I mean, studying works. I'm living proof. Now I can at least get by without getting a call from the friggen' school board police."

"School board police?"

"Mrs. Wythe. She called my mom once to say I was 'borderline failing.' Or 'in need of intervention,' or whatever the lame term was. That was before you helped me. It's not like I enjoy racking my brain over this stuff. I don't know…what's that part of the brain that math uses?"

"Left. More analytical."

"Left, right, center, whatever, I don't have it. I mean, I really appreciate you getting me to understand it all, Cy, but it's no stroll in the park. As I'm sure it's not for those two."

"Which is exactly why I think I…well, *we* should help them," said Cyrus.

A shifty look came across her face. She deliberated while smoothing out the wrinkles of her blouse. "What're you thinking, anyway?"

"Maybe a little test assist. Not sure how, but you've seen what all goes on in there. Like at nap time. Nothing major, just enough to keep them in the playoffs. Which, by the way, starts next week."

"I get it," said Leslie. "I *do* get it."

"I know what it's like to be in a tough spot. I've been there. I mean, I feel bad for them. Those dudes need *serious* help. Maybe if this all works out, they'll get to sit on the mountaintop. I have a similar dream myself."

"And I hope you *do* get to that mountaintop. Sit up there and take it all in. As for them, if they get there, hopefully they'll just like stay there. Ugghh." She laid her backpack down and casually knotted her ponytail into a bun. It looked to Cyrus that she was turning over some ideas, but then again, she always seemed to be in a state of operational planning. "I got it. In the fourth grade we had a little system. If it can work for a fourth grader, it should work with them." Leslie went on to explain how the pencil tapping scheme worked; erasures on two pencils, the other two pencils without. "As long as the two numbskulls can count."

"They count the ticks of the clock every day," said Cyrus. "It's only that…we'll have to shuffle the seats around. You know, with the alternating tests and all."

Leslie eased her backpack over her shoulder. "Now that sounds like a plan," she said. "Kinda getting tired of being sandwiched between cement wall and muscle."

Oh, how he craved to ask her to the Homecoming dance right then, if not for his shackling nerves. *How come I can tutor her, confide in her, laugh with her, but when it comes to asking her to that dance, I'm like some medical school dummy?*

"So, you ready for a new neighbor?" he asked tentatively.

"Yeah. But you never know, I may turn out to be the neighbor from hell." Her cheekbones blushed rose, her eyes sparkled green.

"I'll bring lemonade," he teased, holding out his hand.

"Fresh squeezed for me?" she cooed, laying a hand to his.

His heart measured a hundred count. "Who said anything about fresh squeezed?"

"Then who'd say I'd drink it." She slid her hand along his, a slow draw until their fingers parted.

Blake strode up as the fourth period bell made its warning. Together, they watched the slow exodus of students from the library. "Now there's something of interest," said Blake.

Below, a quiet tussle between the two boys broke out behind the teacher's back. Soon it turned into a ground-grinding wrestling match. Finally, the teacher shot around, his face flushed with anger. He tried his best to disengage them, but the two kept scraping mightily on the ground.

After a flustering minute, the teacher escorted the boys from the library. As they exited beneath, Blake clapped his hands: "Bravo, boys, bravo. Standing ovation from the gallery." One of the boys shot Blake the middle finger.

"Guess you had that coming, Blake," said Leslie.

"I would've been disappointed if he hadn't."

CHAPTER 17

By Cyrus' account, taking an exam in Mrs. Wythe's geometry class is like a prisoner being watched by a vigilant, yet narcoleptic, guard. Immediately after passing out her test, she paces the room as if surveilling from the guard tower. Although the temperature in the room is cool, the atmosphere is oppressive. Her prisoners perspire. They're on edge.

From the back row, Cyrus watched Mrs. Wythe set her timer. She then canvased the rows, eyes alert and ears perked to any misdeed. She leaned over desks, terrorizing one's personal space. Hands and arms were systematically inspected for cheat sheets. No ink tattoos or scraps of paper hidden between thighs. Phones wedged under butts? She'd find them. Electronic watches had to be removed.

The quiet of the room was broken only by her footfalls, or a pencil scrape which rose over another, or the solitary squeak of a chair which had the effect of a thunderclap. Cyrus knew she was listening for conspiracy, and the slightest shuffling of one's foot could be construed as an exchange of prisoner contraband.

In his opinion, all that hovering and roaming about had a detrimental effect on the concentration in the room. A severely debilitating effect. Cyrus could tell some students were so rankled by this intense supervision that they simply decided to wait it out, bide their time, pretend to work out some formula before she headed back to her desk.

Because they knew it wouldn't be long. Within minutes, Mrs. Wythe would transform from vigilant guard to narcoleptic guard.

With an Italian Renaissance-patterned scarf wrapped around her head, she leafed through her papers. Then the scarf slowly recedes. A nod of the head and the scarf slides lower, and lower. Soon her eyeglasses are enshrouded. Any astute observer (as most students are) would see her eyelids turn to blinders. Off to La-La Land. Fifteen minutes, max. That was Mrs. Wythe's routine during test time.

Not a bad idea, Cyrus concluded, to keep pace with her steadfast napping schedule during these monthly exams. To bide one's time before siesta-time was simply good strategy. Some of the students needed to relax. Some needed to concentrate. Others needed the advantage.

The prison guard affect never really bothered Cyrus. Yes, at first it sweated him like the rest. But at this point in the semester, it was no problem. He figured Mrs. Wythe's routine of surveillance was but a tactical maneuver to combat cheating. Any yard guard would do the same. Cyrus, however, ignored it, pressed on, scanned the questions quickly, efficiently whipping through the test.

Per usual, the questions this day dutifully synthesized into correct answers. No problem at all.

After the last question, he looked up. Mrs. Wythe's scarf obscured her face from the bridge of the nose on up.

On test days, Cyrus had his own routine (aside from breezing through the exam.) His routine was to completely zone out during the final minutes, and focus, as he always did, on that poster of the Eiffel Tower hanging on the wall. He would stare at its enumerated degrees of triangulation and think things over. Different test, same routine—watch Mrs. Wythe zonk out, finish before everyone else, zone out to the Parisian monument, wonder in awe over its geometric perfection, let his mind wander.

But with twenty minutes left in the exam, things were different. His routine was broken. Cyrus had to stay focused. Uber-sharp. Listen for pencil tapping, respond in kind.

Before he was bothered again (and he was certain it wouldn't be the last of the tapping) his mind thought to that troublesome robot of his. With its shell removed, Cyrus had set about overhauling its guts. Metal shavings and rusted wire were the easy parts. What was really flummoxing him was the CO_2 chamber. *Why wasn't it producing enough power? Was there a crack? A broken seal?* Without the gas-charged cylinder, the bot couldn't generate any power to the weapon. *A weapon I still don't have!*

The weapon. Now that is a problem. He needed to find something, a good…

A swift kick to his shin jolted the thought. He counted his blessings the kick came from Leslie and not from the mighty leg of football player Number 79, who until recently had sat in the seat over. Leslie had a perturbed look. She thumbed secretively to her right. Cyrus, it seemed, had daydreamed through some important pencil tapping.

He counted six metal-to-paper taps. He responded with two taps of his own.

Cyrus had explained the seat switch to the footballers like this: "You see, the deal is, Mrs. Wythe hands out two different versions of the test. They alternate according to the seats in the rows. One test, then the other, and so on down the line. So, if the person who is seated against the wall, the seat where Leslie now sits, needs an answer, they can pencil tap over to her because she's only two seats away. The person one seat over from the wall can tap a pencil to me, also two seats over. That way we'd be able to hear the number in question and tap out the corresponding letter and not rouse any suspicion from Mrs. Wythe. Make sense?" The two lugs stared blankly at one another. They nodded their heads. Cyrus wasn't sure if they fully understood how the whole pencil tapping thing worked. He wasn't quite sure himself.

Despite his ethical reservations about Morse-coding the test answers to the footballers, Cyrus felt it was the obvious solution. (Truth be told, he wanted Leslie seated next to him all along. It was sort of the reason he ambushed his way into the classroom in the first place.)

With one eye on the Parisian tower and the other on his dozing teacher, his mind again travelled back to his bot.

There was little doubt the thing had a metaphorical "screw loose." It was entirely unpredictable. Like last Saturday when Blake announced himself at his front door. Cyrus led him to the basement to check out "that bot."

"What makes that hammer-that-isn't-yet-there even swing?" Blake asked while looking it over. Cyrus pointed to the CO_2 cylinder, explaining the potential transfer of compressed air into raw force.

"How fast does it move?" Blake asked. Cyrus was stumped. He had no idea. He only knew of its bloodthirsty, honey badger tendencies on furniture.

"Don't know. Let's find out."

They hauled the bot to the driveway.

"I think it needs to stretch his legs a bit, get the rust out," said Blake as they set the bot down in front of the carport, feet from where his father's boxy, gas-loving pickup from the seventies, nicknamed Brown Toro, was toad stooled. The carport was once a robot training ground where Spiral Cyclone worked its muscle. Now it was truly a carport.

Cyrus coordinated the radio frequencies and activated the "on" switch. He and Blake retreated to the end of the driveway. Blake had his phone out to capture the action, while Cyrus gripped the controller. He let it rip.

The machine blasted a straight line toward them like a low-flying arrowhead, tail-winding dust as the sun's rays reflected from its top.

Halfway down the drive Cyrus throttled it down, decelerating it into a sliding stop along the cement. He turned it around and pulled hard on the throttle again. They watched as the bot sailed past them and crossed the street onto the driveway of the house still for sale. Cyrus slammed it to a stop. Fine particles clouded the driveway. He turned it around again and aimed it back. It was behaving like a good little robot.

And it was fast.

Blake, head down to his phone, cued the replay. They had a laugh. Cyrus' attention had then drifted to the new "For Sale" sign across the street, a picture of a woman flanked by two younger women, all arms crossed—a "Team" it read. The lawn had been recently mowed.

When he glanced back to the bot it was gone. It had moved unexpectedly midway up his driveway. They watched it make a one hundred-and-eighty degree turn in one direction and then the other. Before long, it was racing towards the carport. Cyrus' desperate commands of the controller were ignored.

They watched as it caught a wheel on a plastic container, spun sideways in the air, and hurled itself at Brown Toro's tailgate. "Oh shiiiiit," cackled Blake (heard this many times over as Blake had recorded the feat.)

Cyrus approached his overturned bot as Blake held out his phone behind him. When Cyrus reached down to deactivate the bot's underbelly switch, the stubborn machine decided to flog him with its flipper. It then spun its wheels, taunting him. At last, Cyrus hit the orange deactivation switch.

The bot's dagger had gouged a deep slash into the tailgate of the old truck. He figured the tailgate damage was something his mother might not notice, or care about. He was wrong.

Cyrus cursed his luck. He cursed "that bot's" insolence. He cursed its strange predilections. His concerns, it seemed, were justified. "That bot" wasn't such a good little robot, after all.

More pencil tapping from two seats over. One short tap, three closer together—question thirteen. He slapped a three-beat to his paper—letter C.

He dazed on. Alone with the Eiffel Tower and his wandering thoughts. As he thought about his bot he was reminded of the time when he was little and his mother took him to the petting zoo. She bought a cup of oats and poured some of it into his cupped hands…and that stupid goat bit his fingers. It nipped his flesh without the slightest concern for what it was doing. Oats, fingers, shirt sleeves, it didn't matter. The craven creature knew more hands would soon be around with more offerings. "Pull your hand away," it might have said, "I don't care. I'll get more." It was the same with that intransigent machine of his: no consequences, no regrets. He likened his robot to a pigheaded performer who only sings what they want to sing, dismissive of anyone who suggests they sing in a new style. In this case, the "anyone" was Cyrus.

If only all this robot building was as easy as when he was a kid. Back when robotic engineering was but a budding obsession, sitting in the basement watching his father build Spiral Cyclone. He wasn't quite at the age where he could help his father, but that didn't stop him from fantasizing about his own mechanical creations. Watching television, half listening to the teacher at school, sitting at the dinner table, riding in the car as he watched mailboxes and trash cans morph into objects for battle. In the workshop he would imagine all those deliriously detailed and complex schematics miraculously breeding into existence: Poof!—Insta-bot.

Designs took shape, fuses and wires fired up motors, everything magically humming and purring to life. And the weapons. Their bizarreness and weirdness were only that of a child's imagination. Simpler times for Cyrus Hampstead. Simpler, for sure.

Now bot-engineering was like approaching Deadman's curve with a boulder in the center of the road. How to proceed, where to turn, how not to crash. How to purchase materials of unknown type and quantity. Painstaking hours trying to get wires properly aligned so the thing could follow basic commands. Reassemble, reinstall, reattach, reconfigure—it left him frustrated, bewildered, near-mad, a true Dr. Frankenbot in the making. And his laboratory nightmare awaiting his attention, every day. There, without fail.

The geometry classroom now had a pulse, like woods at sundown as birds eased into their nests. A shuffling of feet, an odd scratching sound in the front. Two boys in the third row communicated with each other in primitive hand signals, approaching it as an artform. Cyrus waited for the next series of taps. They came seconds later—question fifteen was D.

In the next seat over, Leslie gnawed on her pencil, full of mean concentration. She fielded one short tap and eight corresponding quick ones, then beat out a single tap without hesitation. It seemed to Cyrus as if she was taking the process in stride. But he could be wrong.

As he waited for more taps, Cyrus leaned his head on his hands and stared at Leslie as if he were a toddler enamored by a kid's show, without a care in the world. A sudden swell hammered his heart. It was a common symptom. More than a crushing love, her proximity turned into something real: his anxieties went on hiatus. He knew they'd inevitably return and correct to their typical state (maybe even come back with a vengeance) but when she was around, all was good. For Cyrus, Leslie was an elixir. She was the ease to the worry, the one who rounded out life's edges. And he certainly wouldn't have had the gumption to help the footballers without her.

Leslie's foot twitched. Cyrus drew back his leg instinctively. He double-checked Mrs. Wythe's status. Her head was fixed to a post. As the footballers got closer to the finish line, Cyrus could sense their spirits pep, their burdens sink. They were nearing the end zone, the stadium's clock counting down, a touchdown in the lead. Smiles crept on their faces.

The clock indicated one minute left—wake-up time. Cyrus held up three fingers and silently mouthed to Number 79: "Last three." The lug nodded his head as if he was getting crunch-time instructions in the huddle. Cyrus beat out three taps, waited, two taps, waited, and ended with four taps. Number 79 nodded with each one.

Leslie, meanwhile, had finished her rap score with Number 71. She lay her head on her desk. She appeared exhausted.

Cyrus saw Mrs. Wythe's head pop up. She groggily fought through the invisible cobwebs, lifted the scarf above her glasses and shuffled around some papers. Right where she left off. Her old-school timer made its usual buzz and rattle. Cyrus counted it as a sixteen-and-a-half-minute snooze. Better than average.

Leslie let out a huge sigh, folded her test, and shrugged her shoulders. Cyrus looked over to Numbers 71 and 79. Although mentally spent, they seemed to be euphoric, as if they just got whiff of an opponent's reeking fear. *They might not be all that bright, but at least they're focused. Like good football players should be. Maybe they'll take that to the gridiron and get the silver and cyan a state title. For once.*

When Mrs. Wythe collected their exams, they fist bumped each other with canyon-wide grins.

Walking down the hallway with Leslie after class, Cyrus never felt their massive presence come from behind. They approached as stealthily as polar bears in the snow. Suddenly, each brute placed a hand atop Cyrus' shoulders. Their meaty paws had no sense of restraint. A shockwave was sent down his spine.

"We owe you, Cy. Like huge," said Number 71.

"Big, baby, big. You know we gotchur back," said Number 79.

"Like literally," said Number 71, slapping him hard on the butt. The two fell out with laughter, tromping in the opposite direction down the hallway.

"Not that I get any props," complained Leslie. "What the hell! Not even a thanks."

Cyrus was still wincing from the vise grips that had been attached to his shoulders. "I think they're afraid of you. You know, like, with how you kick and all."

"Oh, that, right. Sorry. I was getting frustrated. Hey, least it wasn't higher up," she said with a smirk.

"For that I'm grateful."

"Those two were pretty busy with all their tappings," she fretted. "Tap, tap, tap, that's all I heard for like a solid straight minute. Tap, tap, tap. How could I pay attention to my own problems? I was in the middle of that one about alternate and converse angle theorems, then, all of a sudden, tap, tap, tap. Remind me, why didn't we do hand signals like the two guys near the front?"

"Because I'm not sure what's going on behind Mrs. Wythe's glasses."

"That's really good to know." She mocked the footballer's baritone voices: "Like, literally."

CHAPTER 18

One plastic container filled. Onto the next.

In his basement workshop, Cyrus separated the clusters of odds and ends, placing them into separate containers. He arranged them according to three criteria: the absolutely necessary, the maybe's, and the possibly's. In short order, the workbench was close to respectable, enough to work a rag around. The rag went from white to black in seconds. The workbench began to look less and less like a toy train scrapyard.

With a clean slate, Cyrus reached for a bucket of stainless-steel rods. He spilled them onto the workbench. At the other end of the workshop, atop the built-in cabinet, was an old canvas tool bag. Inside, more steel rods. There were steel rods in buckets along the wall, too. Steel rods everywhere, too many of them. Cyrus collected every one he could find and rattled them into a pile on the table. Once again, the table resembled a toy train scrapyard, albeit without the oil spill.

Cyrus set out to systematically sort the rods by diameter, then catalogue and store them away. He slid the wire-straddling magnifying glass to his right eye. He watched the slow dance of dust particles float across the lens in the stagnant air, then grabbed his micrometer caliper, twisted the adjustable ratchet knob with his free hand until both spindle and anvil clamped a metal rod. He recorded the cylinder's diameter at four-point-nine millimeters and tossed it into a small wooden box he labeled "4 to

5 mil." The next one measured three-point-three millimeters; he threw it into a different box. The steel rods clanged loudly into their respective boxes. He was moving right along.

Cyrus heard a noise. Some weird shriek. He thought perhaps all that rummaging around and the clanging of rods was creating a false buzz in his ears. He stopped and listened attentively. Nothing. No buzz. Nothing but a quiet basement and the sound of a reclusive cricket chirping faintly in the dusty recesses.

Cyrus reached for another rod; the screech again pierced his ears. He was sure of it this time. A sound without distinction, as if either the wind or a wolf was howling across a remote lake. Cyrus waited a few seconds. White noise. Even the cricket was muted. He shook it off it, grabbed, measured, and tossed another rod in the bucket.

That noise again! What the hell. It was unmistakable. The sound now belted out in quick succession, each one higher than the next. Cyrus remained perfectly still in the interludes, ear to the ready.

"Cyrus? Cyrus, can't you hear me?" his mother screamed down the basement stairwell. Startled, Cyrus knocked his forehead against the magnifying glass.

"I'm down here," he yelled up the stairs. "You alright?"

"I know you're down there. I've been screaming my head off for you."

Cyrus ran to the bottom of the stairwell. "What is it? You OK?"

"Come on up here please," she demanded. "I really need your help."

He switched off the lights and headed upstairs.

His mother was seated in the kitchen, staring at the ceiling like she was a lonely stargazer on an exotic cruise. But she didn't look content, or dreamy, or stargazery. She looked glazed, distant. And that worried Cyrus. It was that very same look which confined her for weeks, months, after she received that knock on the door that day. The day when the two soldiers stood solemnly side by side. During that stretch, he would find her rocking idly in her chair, stricken with sallow, vacant eyes, stroking her cross and rosary. As time passed, Cyrus discovered less of her in that forlorn condition. Now, he was alarmed.

"You all right, mom?" he asked warily.

She lifted her finger to the ceiling, pointing to a water-stained area. One of those residual areas of neglect in an old farmhouse. Cyrus remembered the initial cause being an upstairs toilet overflow caused by a toy soldier drowning during battle.

"Those things. They're outta control, Cy. They're getting in through that small hole. Right there near the water stain. See it there in the corner? See?"

There was a tiny breech near the strain where the ceiling met wall. Cyrus saw a bug scurry out and head down the wall. Moments later, a small invasion followed its lead.

"They've ruined my chocolate cake," she cried. "Crawling all over it. Some were even digging inside. Can you believe it? I made that cake specially for Aunt Margie's birthday party."

"Aunt Margie might like them. She's really into lean protein diets. And if they're covered in chocolate..."

"Not funny, Cy!"

"You throw the cake out?"

"Of course I did. And don't get wise, either. Not now. I spent a lot of time on that cake and I don't have it in me to start another. When we're done here, we're heading straight to the bakery." She rose from her chair, eyes still stewing at the ceiling.

Going to the bakery had not been on the top of his "to do" list. "What do you mean, 'Done here'?" he asked.

"What I mean is you need to take care of them. And I don't mean take care of them like you did when you were little and collected them in that container so they could work at your construction set. You *do* know what I mean?" She walked out of the kitchen.

Cyrus watched the bugs. He considered the insects, they're laid-back, causal manner, roaming the earth as if their existence was foreordained. Never scampering and burrowing for cover. Massive numbers: that was their selective advantage. They simply played the odds. The things reminded him of that time he attended that second-rate summer camp, where the kids whittled the time away by visiting each other's cabins all day. *They'd probably been hanging out here since the first day the house got framed. Must've loved finally getting a roof.*

Cyrus searched below the kitchen sink. Fate now stood before them with a towering can of insecticide. Their farmhouse numbers were in peril.

It wasn't like Cyrus took any pleasure in what he was about to do, but he nonetheless flipped the nozzle, aimed steadily, and gave a decisive pull of the trigger. A bitter, toxic taste befell his mouth. He spat and spewed and hacked and heaved. He lunged for the sink's faucet handle, gulping fistfuls of water into his mouth, shaking his head violently. A seven-cycle gurgle and rinse, which had little effect. The poison was a palate-sticker; it took all the effort in the world not to retch it up.

He peered closely at the reversed spray tip and groaned. *Stupid!*

With resolve, he took aim again and landed a direct hit. The foamy poison sent the insects spiraling down the wall. Some fell motionless, others squirmed. Moral pangs knocked around in his heart. Aside for the robot variety, killing wasn't his thing. Still, if his mother were to ever solicit him again as executioner, he knew he'd have to oblige. She made that clear enough.

"OK, Mom. I think I got most of them," he called from the kitchen.

"Great," she yelled back. "You're driving to the bakery. You need the practice. You haven't been behind the wheel since…"

"OK, Mom."

"And please try to remember what you learned. Like looking for bicycle lanes, yielding, looking both ways when you come to a…"

"Stop…"

"…that's right, a stop.

"No. I mean, stop," he said, walking out of the kitchen. "I know how to drive. Remember? Driving's second nature for me."

The moment Cyrus jumped into the driver's seat of the SUV, he began tinkering with the knobs on the radio and adjusting the temperature controls. Instinctual reactions cultivated from years of listening to the oldies piped into an insufferably hot car. Now that he was the one behind the wheel, he determined the physical environment and musical offerings would be to *his* liking. He'd at least get those out of the way before steering towards some bakery, insecticide lingering on his tongue like a bad infection, and his mother seated next to him issuing cautionary commands and well-intentioned vehicular strategies.

It was the first time his mother occupied shotgun seat, though it wasn't his first time behind the wheel. Not by far. He watched her examine her face in the visor's sun mirror, working her finger under her eyes as if Braille reading the creases and deepening wrinkles. Patches of silver-gray had begun to expose themselves against the edges of her brown hair, untimely signs, as she called them, of a lady rounding her forties. She pursed her lips and casually wiped away a smudge of lipstick. She flipped up the visor, tossed her handbag to the floor, and turned to Cyrus.

"Now remember, Cy. When you first get in a car, you have to set the seat and adjust the steering wheel. Correctly." She indicated each task with brisk hand directions. "That's so everything's in reach. You really have to be in a comfortable position before driving."

"I did all my adjustments," replied Cyrus, "you just didn't see me do them."

"And you didn't see me watching you *not* do them. I've got eyes, Cy. And fooling with the radio was the first thing I saw you do when you got in. At least you put your seat belt on," she said. She paused, then emphatically cut off his music. "Really, you shouldn't even have music on, not until you've become acquainted with driving a little better. You know how distracting music is. And don't even get me started on texting or looking at your phone. Zero-tolerance. Does the driving instructor have music playing?"

"Playing?! The guy blares it. It's like a rolling rock concert in there. The guy wears a green fedora. That's how he rolls."

"Sure, Cy," she said sardonically, lifting her eyebrows.

Cyrus considered himself a good driver. Better than average, in fact. He had a firm grasp of the rules of the road, having paid close attention since he was little, when he would intuitively shout out, "wandering dog, one o'clock," or "man on phone." By nature, he was vigilant, cautious. As he saw it, those dispatches usually proved fortuitous, although as the thought back on them maybe some were a bit too much. Like the time when he loudly announced the appearance of an indecisive squirrel zagging across the road, causing his mother to slam on the brakes. The only outcome then was a backtracking squirrel and a long harangue.

Cyrus certainly had the technical skills mastered: pedal manipulation, steering, blinkering, shifting gears, all of it learned in that old pickup truck. With a solemn promise not to mention anything to his mother, Cyrus' father often took him out to race the rolling, one-lane backcountry roads. The forays were under the guise of errands—picking up fresh vegetables or spare robot parts. Sometimes that was the case. Mainly, the two would veer off and frequent their favorite country barbecue stand. Afterwards, Cyrus would jump behind the wheel of Brown Toro.

As Cyrus backed out of the driveway, he recalled the first occasion when his father directed him to splinter off-road. It was a groomed trail and a spur of the moment decision, one that shined like a beacon. There Cyrus was, rollicking over uneven tire tracks, banging through foot-deep ruts, spinning tires in an open dirt field. He was seized by a wondrous sense of freedom, and it was in those free-wheeling moments when he really learned the art of driving. *Somewhat masterfully, too.*

Nevertheless, Cyrus figured his mother was preparing for a rough ride, bracing herself for those sudden nose-to-the-dashboard stops and head-to-the-seat starts which are the hallmarks of new drivers. Cyrus didn't want to expose *too* much mastery. Flaws were expected. Flaws needed to be executed. Besides, being an overconfident driver did give him pause. Unknown variables in life existed, and more than anything else, Cyrus valued certainty. Unknowns produced anxiety, worry. And although there were "unknowns" in those backwoods turn-outs ("unforeseen variables," in his father's military parlance), his father was there with a watchful eye, righting the wheel when need be.

Cyrus eased out of their quiet woodsy lane and yielded onto the main road. His hands were at the perfect ten o'clock/two o'clock position on the wheel, a driving instructor directive. He passed the defunct gas station that had been turned into an upscale bar, and the new office building where Dr. Rivers had recently filled some cavities.

The day was slightly breezy, a cloudless blue sky. Leaves coasted in the wind, occasionally crashing at his windshield. The type of day he could keep vigil on other cars, pedestrians, the occasional biker. A day of reduced unforeseen variables, which eased his concern.

"Wow, Cyrus," said his mother after a few deft turns and smooth accelerations, "you seem to have the hang of it. How many times did you go out with that instructor?"

"Oh, just a couple. But I've been prepping for this for a long time. You see, it's not much different than operating robots. It's all about attentiveness, coordination, you know, eye-to-brain-to-hand reaction time. Those kinds of things. Maybe it's a little of a gift, too," he added with aplomb.

"Is that right?" A glimmer of suspicion rose on her face.

As Cyrus came to an intersection, he pumped the brake using his left foot instead of his right, giving the SUV the right amount of hitch and lurch. "Shoot," he feigned. His mother remained indifferent to the jerk. As he glanced over, he thought he saw the corner of her mouth smug up.

"So, how long have you known Leslie?" she asked. "Pleasant girl. You two seem to get along real nice when she's over."

Cyrus hesitated. A round-a-bout was approaching. He pretended to intensely concentrate as he navigated through the confluence of cars entering and exiting at varying speeds into the confusing circle. Once he straightened onto the boulevard, he let out an exaggerated sigh of relief. He was hoping the tension would diffuse her line of questioning, send it drifting like the leaves passing the windshield.

It didn't work. "Cy, you didn't answer me."

"Oh, right. I've known her since the first day of school. We're in the same class."

"That I know. But is that all? I mean, do you see her outside of class. Outside of studying with her at the house?"

"Where did you say this bakery is?" asked Cyrus. The insecticide was still on his tongue, which hovered to the side of his mouth, making it seem like he was hiding a smile.

"Post High Road. It's going to be on the left. Anyway, I think she's lovely, and sweet. That's all I'm saying. But you don't have to comment," she said with a slight huff, "if you don't want to."

They stopped at a red light. He could feel his mother's eyes keenly on him. He knew she wasn't going to let up. She might well keep on about Leslie until the stars twinkled. "Your dad would be so proud of you, you know that, Cy. Who've you become and what you've done." *Good, she's onto something else.* "You're just like him, in many ways. Strong willed. Confident and determined in what you want. I know he was with you when you travelled to the robot contest. He was there all the way."

Cyrus thought about his father, how he would often leave on deployment and then return. Even though it was a regularity, the man always seemed present. Like he was there without actually being there.

Which was why it was hard for Cyrus to reconcile the truth of his death; his heart would often fool him into believing that he would return some day. As he always had.

"Yeah, I miss him. Just having him around," said Cyrus, "Building robots with him especially. I miss that a lot."

"I know you do. That was very special to him, having you there to share his passion and then taking it as your own. We both miss him. A lot." His mother caught his eyes. "It hasn't been easy. Let me tell you that."

"I know."

"At least he left you that robot in the basement. For better or worse. Worse being my furniture." She let out a whimsical yet melancholy laugh. A tear beaded on her eye and she dabbed it with a tissue. "What are your plans for that machine, anyhow? I know you said you want to go back to ComBot. But how far have you gotten with it? I went down there the other day to flip the electric breaker and it looked about the same as when it tore up the den."

"I'm still working on it," he said as he accelerated at a green light. "And yes. I do want to make another run at ComBot."

His mother drew up in her seat slightly and crossed her hands over her purse. She fiddled with the clasp. "Cy, do you remember when I drove you to those fights before you entered ComBot, those qualifiers that were in the middle of nowhere? Where I sat in the car, usually reading…well, actually I was thinking about your father most of the time. I don't know if I have it in me to do that again. Not only that, I have to get a job soon. For me, and for us. I don't want to live on just your father's pension alone, and I need to work for my own sake. You'll be heading to college before I know it and I'll be by myself, alone...I've been applying, you know?"

"I know...wait...you mean applying to colleges? For me?"

"No, I was talking about jobs. For me. Remember? And yes, we'll be doing the college search soon enough."

He came to another red light. Cars whizzed through the intersection. Cyrus considered the chaos of traffic, the mystery of how, despite their proximity to each other and all that was going on inside of them, they rarely collided. At least statistically. The implausibly of metal avoiding metal seemed illogical, considering combat robotics. "So, have you gotten anywhere? With the job search?" He rapped an awkward foot to the gas pedal, jerking the vehicle off the red signal.

"I have an interview set up next week. A financial company. They're needing someone in sales, which I did before you came along. Did you know that?"

"No."

"Well, I did. And I was good at it. I know the industry very well."

"Then I'll have no problem getting a loan. For competitive purposes."

"Huh, not likely, mister. Which brings me to the point of next year, and this run for ComBot." She paused for emphasis. "You'll have your license by then, but you'll have to find a way to do this by yourself. That includes paying for it."

"I'll find a way," said Cyrus as he weaved around a car with a bumper sticker that read, "New Driver." The *ways* have been beating through his head for months. A conveyor belt of various *ways*. But as the sole quality control officer on the conveyor line, not a single *way* got through inspection. "You sure you don't have any gum on you?" he asked, "I'm suffering here."

"I don't," she replied without looking through her purse. "I can help out as much as I can financially," she continued, "but I do know the kind of expenses your father paid out to build those machines. I really do. I just don't know if we have that kind of extra money floating about."

"I can get a job on the side. It won't get in the way of school, either. I can hustle a lot of parts and equipment, I mean, there's a bunch already down there. So that's not an issue. I can figure it out. I know what I'm doing." If he was convincing his mother, he was still having a hard time convincing the quality control officer in his head.

"I see," she said, smoothing out her blouse.

"See what?" he said defensively. "I've learned enough."

"I didn't say that. However, you and your dad had Spiral Cyclone up and running well before it ever saw a single fight. This new one's in nowhere near that kind of shape."

I've noticed. "Mom, do you realize how much you get for winning ComBot?"

"I do know the prize amount, yes," she replied.

"Dad always referred to it as a calculated gamble. That's how he phrased it. Like in any other sport, it takes money up front. But you can also pay yourself back tenfold on the back end. By winning." Cyrus made the turn on Post High Road and continued down the heavily trafficked commercial boulevard. Cars zoomed by even though he too was exceeding the speed limit. In his head, he saw the glorious moment of winning ComBot. The rapture, the excitement, the relief of the long quest. Then, a mirage unexpectedly floated across the windshield: Ray Dokestout thrusting his arms in the air. The mirage disappeared in an instant.

"Watch your speed, Cy. You're not an Indy car driver. Where'd you learn to drive like that anyway?"

"Like I said, driving's my second nature."

"Uh-huh…Look, I do understand this competition your passion. And I realize it's something you need to do. Something you had with your father. I know you two had plans, what events to go to and things of that nature. And I never wanted to get in the way of that. But here's where I stand, because I have to look at it realistically. It's what mothers do. If competing helps you get into college, or say an engineering scholarship, then I can agree it's a good bet. A 'calculated gamble', as your father called it. At the very least it looks good on a college application. But what I don't want is for you to waste too much time and too much money, which neither of us really have. This is your junior year, mind you."

"It does look good on a college application," said Cyrus in agreement.

"Cyrus!" shouted his mother. Cyrus was close, very close, to pumping the brakes, but somehow reason trumped panic. He figured her frenzy could be about anything, and understanding this about his mother usually served him well. He scanned the roadway, detecting no imminent danger. "Bakery's up ahead. Quick, get in that turn lane," she said, pointing across his chest. He aimed the SUV two lanes over.

"I could have sworn it was up three blocks further," she said.

"Don't worry. I needed the adrenaline rush." *And to wash this damn poison from my mouth!*

Inside, the smell of baked goods sent Cyrus' stomach grumbling. The rich sweetness teased his toxic-laced tastebuds, which were crying out for help. Pink and blue frosted confections, sprinkled chocolate donuts, strawberries and blueberries glistening in a pool of a semi-transparent glaze—he wanted to shove them all in his mouth and eradicate that poisonous spell.

As he passed a counter, the baker reached over and offered Cyrus an oatmeal raisin cookie. He immediately swooped it up and chewed it, thanking the man through a full mouth.

Soon, Cyrus realized his mouth needed a lubricant. He cased the bakery aisles, searching for a refrigerator; in the back was an open cooler with rows of milk. As he approached it, nearly choking a swallow, his mother suddenly hitched him by the waist. "Cy, is that Faye Smith over there across the bakery?"

Cyrus gulped. "Dunno." He didn't know who Faye was, nor did he care. All he cared about were the luscious containers of milk beckoning his parched, contaminated mouth.

His mother dragged him by the arm. Across the bakery was a heavy-set woman was waiting at a counter to be served. She wore a bold floral dress in matching tribute to the bright colors of bakery—orange and red and lime and azure. The colors were everywhere: on the signs, the walls, the laminate countertops, and this woman's loud dress.

Cyrus recognized her. She was a friend of his mother's, the one with the hearty laugh and predilection for whimsy. He often imagined her house full of trinkets and glass figurines, and a perennial smell of cinnamon and cardamom. Cyrus also remembered her husband, whom he once met when he was dragged to a musical recital. The husband was the exact the opposite of Faye; the man affected an uncanny stiffness and blandness.

"Hello, Faye," his mother cried out cheerfully.

"Bridget? My goodness," the woman fluted loudly. "Oh my, oh my. Isn't this a treat. It's been too long. And I think I remember this handsome young man as …as…?"

"My very own chauffeur. Though he refuses to wear the cap," his mother said. "You remember, Cyrus?"

Faye merrily gathered both Cyrus and his mother into her cavernous, floral dress. "Oh, I love it. A legitimate driver now. Little Cyrus out there on the roads."

"He's still learning," said his mother. "He only has his permit."

"Haha, wonderful. Won-der-ful! Just do me a favor, Cyrus. Let me know when you'll be driving so I can stay off the road, huh?" Her guffaw filled every corner of the bakery, and turned heads.

"I'll include you on the group chat," he replied through a half-ingested cookie.

"Ah, you got yourself a real wise acre here, Bridge. A real charmer, I can tell. I could use someone to chauffeur me around town too, you know."

"That can be arranged," Cyrus' mother said, "but he *has to* wear the cap."

"Gladly!" Faye belted out.

As Faye and his mother talked about the cake overrun by sinful insects, Cyrus watched the woman behind the counter pile dozens of pastries into large boxes. Her speed was transfixing; no sooner did she shutter one box, than another was half-filled. Cyrus again tried to peel away to the refrigerator, but his mother's arm was locked onto his.

At last, Faye held up her finger in an exclamation point. "Bridget, Horace and I have been meaning to have you over to the house. And of course, Cyrus, too."

"We'd love to come. That would be wonderful. Anytime."

"How does next Saturday night sound?" asked Faye.

"Mom," choked Cyrus, pointing to his mouth. "Sorry, need milk."

"Oh, dear boy. You've gone prim polly pink," said Faye. "Here, drink this." She reached in her cart and handed Cyrus a pint of chocolate milk. He guzzled it down, mindless of the brown river cascading down his chin. The insecticide, for now, had abated.

"Better now, Cy?" asked his mother, brows crossed. She turned to Faye. "Saturday night is perfect," she told her.

Did she say Saturday night? The night of ComBot? He couldn't imagine watching it any other place than his own den. Alone, by himself, maybe with his mother and Mongrel. "Uh, Mom. I might not be able to. You know, ComBot," he pointed out.

"Oh, right. Sorry, Faye. Saturday may not work after all. The robot competition Cyrus competed in last summer airs on television that very night."

"Robots!" Faye squealed, her voice reverberating off the walls, shocking customers out of their pre-sugar doldrums. "What's this about robots? Like the kind they use in factories? My goodness, they're everywhere now. My vacuum's a robot, my car's almost one, too. Goodness gracious, Cyrus, what's all this about robots?"

"It's a combat robotics event," he said, waiting for a glimmer of understanding. It required further explanation. "You see, I have a robot, which I'm operating with a remote control, you know, the kind with knobs and switches, and the other person operates their robot. They both have weapons and things like that. Whichever one gets destroyed loses. The competition's in its twenty-seventh year," he added.

"Mercy! Twenty-seven doggone years of robot fighting," said Faye. "Bridget, where have I been?"

"Trust me, Faye, I know. Hey, it's more exciting than, say golf."

"You kidding? I'd rather watch my toes freeze off in a blizzard than watch that snoozer of a sport. Chasing around a ball with a club, trying to drain it down a hole. Ha."

Once again, Cyrus envisioned a hunched over pre-human aimlessly wandering the grasslands with a stick and a stone, and their progression from the tall savannah to the groomed golf club landscape. He thought of Leslie and smiled.

"Next Saturday, you say. Horace and I will surely be watching that. In fact, I'll force him to. I really do need to get him weaned from watching golf. It's on endlessly on our TV. And, as you might have guessed, I need something a bit livelier. Especially if this handsome boy's at the helm."

"Number seventy-three," called the woman from across the counter.

"Seventy-three right here," Faye yelped, waving her ticket. "Well, I can't wait to see Cyrus compete in Com…Com…"

"…Bot…" said Cyrus.

"…Bot. ComBot." She rumpled his hair into a bowl of spaghetti, then enveloped Cyrus and his mother into a smothering sea of orange and red and lime and azure. "I've got an idea. Friday night after Thanksgiving. You'll be in town, I hope?"

"We'll be here," said his mother. "No away plans."

"Great. We'll have you over then. And don't expect any turkey leftovers. The day after Thanksgiving we take a culinary trip to the Szechuan Province," she cackled before turning to place her order.

CHAPTER 19

The tint of gunmetal gray slid up the walls of Cyrus' room. His Chromiums' jersey slowly darkened, his posters washed of their color, and the ceiling took on a murky shade. Cyrus never noticed the waning light. He never noticed the heavily soaked mid-November clouds encroaching from the west. His mind was focused on ComBot27.

Soon, Cyrus heard the pelting of rain on his window and roof. The steadily thumping presence gave him clarity, lifted his spirits, put him at ease; odd, considering rain had the ability to slog others down into a gutter. The rain even lessened his nervous anticipation over the evening's telecast. That morning he had awakened with a jolt, and since then he'd been as restless as a raven.

He knew the rain would win eventually. It always did. It'd caress him back to sleep at some point on this ComBot27 Saturday. But for now, Cyrus was good.

To keep his mind occupied, he'd been at his desktop computer researching bots in battle since dawn. He watched them slam and hack with fervor, taking notes of the different modes and styles of attack, and the ingenuities employed by the developers. But one type of robotic weapon had him lasered focused: the hammer swinging variety. The idea had been consuming him for weeks.

Each day after school he downloaded videos from the internet, watched for hours, typed his notes, sketched designs on a notepad. The single-minded pursuit for "that bot" to be ready for the upcoming fighting circuit. That was his new routine. He thought about his father and how he might approach the venture. It'd take strict discipline.

After reviewing video footages, Cyrus made notations on vulner-abilities and capabilities, successes and failures. He detailed the modes of attack, the condensed stocked force, the power systems, and how often an arm would swing in comparison to the number of times it got clobbered. He was grading those hammer wielding machines, assessing their potency and potential, determining how best to implement his own iteration of a "whack-a-bot." Nothing was left to chance. The season would be kicking off in few months and all he was looking at was a basement full of tools, semi-worthy parts, and a slumbering, armless hell-spirit, along with a wallet full of nothing.

With his friends busy with after-school extracurriculars, and Leslie's field hockey season in its final weeks, it would be all robot all the time for Cyrus Hampstead. Still, if given the option he'd spend every available minute with Leslie. If that could even be a reality. Those two minutes after geometry before they skittered their own directions pained his heart. It left him asking: *Why can't I get up the nerve to ask her out? Just ask her to Homecoming? Just do it!* Then the excuses: *What would I do, go looking behind old Vennari's barn for a bike to take her out on?* With his driver's license months away, the thought of asking her out and then saying, "Can you pick me up at eight?" seemed kind of lame.

Cyrus was tugged by extremes of emotions. So much second-guessing. Insecurities rattled about his sixteen-year-old frame like antibodies waging a war against a foreign virus. By default, robotic focus was the cure-all.

Despite his resolve, Cyrus knew that robot conceptualization that morning had perhaps a few more hours left. He promised his mother he'd sand down the legs of the ottoman and coffee table before ComBot27. As a result, his brain was on hyper-focus as the earthbound drops crashed onto his roof and window.

"Cy, I think the delivery people are here," interrupted his mother from the other end of the upstairs hallway. "Go get them before it gets too wet?"

"It's already too wet. They probably have raincoats," Cyrus yelled absently at his door. He was intently watching a bot named The Mustard Hyperion, a yellow bot with a horizontal spinner and an overhead striking claw, take on a vertical chainsaw contraption named Snag-L-Toof. It escaped Cyrus why delivery people were there in the first place, or what they might be delivering.

"I'm pretty sure they have rain gear. It's pouring," she squelched. "But I'm talking about the couch. I don't want it sitting out in the rain too long. They just pulled up and are getting it out of the van now, so please go and help them get it through the door."

"One sec." He plucked a Chromiums hat from his rack and headed downstairs.

In the front yard, a large puddle in the grass made like an agitated sea. Two men stood next to it on the sidewalk carrying a couch covered in plastic. Cyrus waved them in.

The men exchanged the new couch for the one ripped apart by his steel devil-bot. Before the crew carried it off, Cyrus made sure to double-check the couch—something was always lodged in the slots and folds. Sure enough, he filled a jar of coins and good batteries. He left the pencils and candy wrappers in the recesses with the years-old grime.

He lay on his new couch, enjoying the freshness and firmness of the new cushions. He closed his eyes. The rain, it was taking hold. He was succumbing to its power. ComBot27 began to circle in his head like one of those roadway round-a-bouts.

But the rain was fighting. To offset its effect, he forced himself to think about where he left off at the computer: The Mustard Hyperion versus Snag-L-Toof. The tiny yellow sucker's hammer-claw was set to rapid speed, ferocious and windmilling. But it lacked endurance. The Mustard Hyperion's final, inglorious moment came at the corkscrew. Cyrus' eyes drooped.

Finally, he held one last image—Leslie. She was rushing off down the staircase, harried over some place she needed to be. Her beautiful face lingered at the edge of dreaminess. Rain, it's a formidable force. Like a branch caught on the precipice of a waterfall—stable, teetering, gone—her face disappeared. Cyrus was asleep.

"Oh, it's wonderful!" His mother was standing over him, coffee mug in hand. "I thought it would be a darker tan, but I love the contemporary style. Don't you, Cy? Cy, do me a favor? No robots *anywhere* near this couch, *anywhere*! Don't even dream about them. Were you dreaming about them? And while I'm thinking about it, no eating on the couch either. Let me enjoy it for some time. OK?"

"K, Mom," he replied groggily, rubbing his eyes. He had no idea how long he'd been out. "I'll treat it like it belongs in a palace."

"Oh, and by the way," she said in a more chipper note. "I bought sandpaper yesterday."

"Great. Almost as exciting as buying a new couch."

"Don't get smart. Not today."

"I'll save it for tomorrow."

"Maybe you should. Because today you're going to do some serious sanding. Make sure you have all your tools together before you begin, that way you'll finish in plenty of time for your big night. Remember what your father always used to say. The key to success is…"

"…preparation," he slurred as he rolled off his royal throne with a thud.

Cyrus looked over his handiwork. The splintery notches and jagged gorges had been transformed to a rounded polish, and despite being attacked by a feral, oversized appliance, the only sign that the legs had been roughed up were a few spots where the graining was mismatched. His mother would be impressed. He considered the possibility of one day staining it, then dismissed the idea.

A lizard holding a hockey stick popped up on his phone.

"You jacked? You jacked for ComBot? I'm jacked, baby. Straight up jacked, racked and cracked, like a poolhall hillbilly. It's like, what, a couple hours away?"

Cyrus lost track of time. Thankfully. He checked his phone. "Uh-huh, comes on in two hours. Oh, man…I'm trying not to think about it."

"Not trying to think about it? You're gonna shine like a star, Cy. How many other idiots in school get the spotlight like you're gonna have?"

"Wow, since you put it that way."

"Hey, all I'm telling you is there will be no more walking around in obscurity. No more high-nose sniffing from girls when they walk right on past you like you don't exist. Ha, barely a glance your way. That's not gonna be you, and that's not gonna be me. You know why, baby? Because I'm your fucking wingman. The shadows *will not* be our legacy. No, it's gonna be all eyes on Cy, and to kick it into a higher gear you're gonna need a power broker by your side, booking appointments and sinking deals. That's me. Hell no, no more 'who's that kid's, what's his name?' while they look through the yearbook. None of that shit. We're *done* with that crap. It's show time and it's fucking go-time. ComBot, baby!"

"Ya done?"

"Yeah. For now."

"Well, you said one thing that's true. It's gonna be show time alright. Show time for all those who enjoy seeing a kid going down in flames. And his robot going *up* in flames. With not a lick of any friggen' dinero to show for it. What kinda of power brokering is that gonna get me, Blake? Look, I'm just keeping my eyes on the prize for next year."

"Next year is next year, tiger sport," said Blake in his best agent lingo.

"Hold on. Yes, you're right. Just checked my calendar. It *is* next year." Cyrus' phone buzzed. "Leslie" appeared on the screen. His pulse rate increased twenty beats. "Gotta go, Blake."

"Hey, hey, wait, wait," pleaded Blake with hint of dejection which turned quickly to resignation. "Ah, shit, it's probably another agent cutting me outta the deal. Don't worry, Cy, I'll be watching tonight, rooting for my old friend anyway. Oh, and by the way, I'll have my fire extinguisher on standby." Cyrus switched the call over, cutting off Blake's hysterical laugh.

"Hey," he said excitedly.

"Hey, you getting ready for tonight?

"As much as I can be. I guess you could say I know the outcome anyway. Was never much for surprises."

"Guess not," she laughed. "Hey, my parents are having a barbeque. You probably hear all the commotion. Many are staying around to watch ComBot, including Uncle Carl, as usual. Hopefully he won't dry out the kegerator before it starts. I'm already playing barmaid over here."

"Any tips?"

"Tips? Yeah, like don't put too much foam on top of the beer. You know, you're welcome to come over tonight and watch. I was gonna ask you earlier."

"Thanks for the offer. But I don't know..."

"I get it. And don't worry, there's too much going on over here anyway." Her voice softened. "It can be a little nerve-racking watching yourself on TV. I know you sometimes get a little anxious. It seems that way anyway."

The subject of his anxiety was a never a topic between them, though it didn't surprise him that Leslie had figured it out from the get-go. She was more than astute; she was uber-aware. It seemed nothing much escaped her.

"Trying not to be," he admitted. "I've been keeping busy. My mom has me working on some home projects. Breaking me like some donkey mule," said Cyrus.

"Which one, a donkey or a mule?" she laughed.

"Aren't they the same?" he asked.

"Kinda, not really. Different breeds. One is smarter than the other, that's the mule. And the mule can't breed, so it loses out there, too. I guess that accounts for it being smarter."

"Huh."

"Anyway, I'll explain their genetical composition later. But it's good that you're taking your mind off tonight. I do that a lot, you know, keep busy with other stuff so I don't have to deal with what's really on my mind."

"You don't seem like you get too stressed," said Cyrus. "Not like I really know, but…it seems that way. Like nothing much gets to you."

"I guess you don't know," she said quietly, cryptically. The phone line became stagnant. After a pause, she spoke: "It's the small stuff, or the big stuff, depending on how you look at it. The stuff that really matters."

"Field hockey?"

"Like relationships," she said.

"Relationships?"

"Yes, Cyrus, relationships."

Cyrus wasn't sure how to handle that. He wasn't even sure if it involved him, but he had more than a fortuneteller's guess that it did. Otherwise, she wouldn't have mentioned the word *relationship*.

"Hey, how'd your field hockey game go? That was a playoff game, right?" he asked offhandedly.

"Like garbage. I scored twice, but our defense stunk *soooo* bad. I swear! And yes, that was a playoff game, as in, 'was' the playoffs."

"You're out?"

"In French, the term is 'au revoir'." There was a long sigh on the end of the phone in which Cyrus imagined her flouncing her strawberry hair like they do in shampoo commercials. "Just as well, maybe the bruises on my legs will begin to heal."

Cyrus thought of her lean, coltish legs specked with blueish circles, and how different they would look without the discoloration. And how it didn't matter either way.

"Oh, speaking of playoffs," she continued, "I got word from Rozalyn that the football team won their second playoff game today. Slaughtered them. She said those two knuckleheads dominated. Had a ton of sacks."

"See, Les? I told you. They're natural born football players."

"Cy, I'm not even sure they're natural born. Anyway," Leslie continued wearily, "it's been a long day of ankle-smashing. I'm about toast. Soggy toast, if there's such a thing. And I still have to keep up with this bunch over here."

"Well, I'm sorry you lost, Leslie."

"Like I said, no biggie. I guess now there's some certainty in my life. Unlike with other things."

"Other things?"

"Yes, other things. Things in the personal realm."

Cyrus kept mute.

"Uh, OK. Oh hey, I forgot to tell you, Cyrus. The fam's heading out early for Thanksgiving break to my grandmother's house, so I won't be at school next week."

That seat next to me is going to be one lonely piece of plastic. The Eiffel Tower, Mrs. Wythe, the footballers' vacant stares. It's gonna be a long week. "Really," he replied.

"Really," she answered. There was a short pause. "Was that a 'really' as in, 'I'm going to miss her' or another kinda 'really'?"

How would he answer such an obvious question? The 'really' was an over the moon 'really.' But it was only obvious to him, not her. Unfortunately, his feelings were always tucked inside a deep pocket where anxiety kept them from sneaking out. *But I'm trying. I'm 'really' trying.*

"A really 'really'," he said tentatively. "Like really."

"I like hearing that. I *really* do. You know, it's going to be kinda boring up at grandmas. If you're not too busy, call me."

"I'll squeeze you in. Blake's my agent now. You'll have to go through him."

"Just don't let it go to your head, big shot. But hey, I'm rooting for you tonight anyway. Even if I do know what's going to happen. Still... don't disappoint." She disconnected. Cyrus looked at the dead phone, and laughed.

CHAPTER 20

7:15. The two-hour telecast of ComBot27 was fifteen minutes from airing. Aside for the quick nap on the new couch, Cyrus had been up since five-thirty in the morning. He was drained, just as he had been after Com-Bot, *especially* after that confrontation he had with Ray Dokestout. Not that he wanted to relive that guy right now; he'd have plenty of a reminder of him soon enough.

His phone buzzed rhythmically. An emoji assault from Tonmoy—a robot followed by an explosion, a pitchfork, a hay pile, three different smiley faces, and a bunch of Bengali words. Cyrus returned his own emoji string, a purely random assortment.

7:30. His mother came into the den with a root beer and a bucket of popcorn. She scratched his head with her long nails, then sat silently on her new couch behind him.

His heart began to palpitate, his throat constricted, his hands moistened with perspiration. The French doors to the outside were slightly ajar and a gentle waft worked its way in. The white noise of the splattering rain was a welcome relief. Cyrus propped his feet supine on the recliner and waited for the commercials to end. They seemed to drag on forever.

Nearly four months since he competed at ComBot27. He was as eager to see Spiral Cyclone in its original condition. A final visual fare-well. And maybe, just maybe, resolve the mystery of his prized bot's fateful undoing. All the scenarios of what could've happened—from a motor cogging to his controller not syncing to a lapse of his own accord—vexed and perplexed him to no end. Maybe now—finally—he could reconcile the truth and get a clearer picture of what went wrong before Spiral Cyclone crisped to death.

On the television, an overhead shot of the ComBot arena crystallized into view. Seconds later, the spider camera swooped and dove over the crowd like a soaring hawk, its images filling the screen. The spider cam landed inside the decagonal polycarbonate enclosure and panned the maddening arena.

"ComBot27" floated across the screen, accompanied by a wailing electric guitar riff. Superimposed over the title was a montage of robot battles over the years. Cyrus quietly remarked how stylized the broadcast production was in comparison to how procedural the event was in reality.

He laid his head back on the headrest. It had been a pit-in-the-stomach kind of day. His loose-knot queasiness and bristling nerves were beginning to give way to a tranquil ease—an amble down a horizoned road.

At last, the mayhem began. Cyrus yanked back his chair's lever. *Can't change the outcome. Let's just hope I don't look the fool.*

Cyrus and his mother watched ten fights before his semifinal battle against Doke-a-lasher aired. (Of those, only one showcased Cyrus and Spiral Cyclone, a forty-five second hack job he won in less than a minute.) After an insurance ad, the music faded in and a woman with shiny, flowing black hair and a sleek purple outfit and a toney voice came on. As she paced the decagon's exterior walls, the camera followed her astride. With an indulgent smile, she cast out her arms. "I'm Shon'dae Marquette, and metallic madness is back as warfare of the hardware returns for the semifinal action. We welcome the robots in the MegaBot division, their final chance to prove their mettle by proving their metal before the ComBot27 championship." Cyrus couldn't recall ever seeing Shon'dae Marquette. It was like she appeared out of nowhere, sent by the ComBot gods. He did, however, remember the two guys now fronting the frame. "Without further ado," said Shon'dae Marquette, "we'll send it up to the booth to the maestros of the mechanical, Jack and Skip."

"Great to have you back," said the man under the white cowboy hat. "Skip, before the heavyweights of the illustrious MegaBot division enter the decagon, I'd like to reacquaint our viewers with the reigning champ. This man is the most decorated contestant *ever* in the arena of combat robotics. If you follow the sport, you know his name, and last week our own Shon'dae Marquette caught up with Ray Dokestout in his workshop as he prepped for ComBot27. Let's have a look."

The screen filled edge to edge with the last image Cyrus wanted to see: a close-up of Ray Dokestout's meaty head, grinning ear to ear. Cyrus' glands excreted a double dose of sweat. He wiped his temples and took in a deep breath.

"So that's what that guy looks like," his mother said.

"Uh-huh. That's Dokestout," replied Cyrus.

"I was expecting someone more…I don't know, polished."

"No. You got that."

Shon'dae Marquette stood outside on the main steps of an industrial building. Tall black windows extended on either side of a gold door. A sign overhead read: "The Gold Standard of Robotic Engineering." Shon'dae Marquette spoke into the camera: "Over the years, Ray Dokestout has earned a few titles, and with them, legions of fans. This is a man who knows a thing or two about engineering robots. Dokestout Industries provides businesses around the globe with robotic machinery designed for everything from the manufacturing sector to the service industry. Then of course there's the combat part of the enterprise, which, it turns out, ignites the passion of the hard-working individuals who are right behind me within these doors. We were honored to have Ray Dokestout himself invite us in to take a peek at his laboratories, and to give a preview for what's in store for the evening. Let's head inside," she said with a graceful sweep of her hand.

Inside, Ray Dokestout addressed the viewer. "Welcome to the world of champions," he beamed, signaling the camera to follow him as he walked the floor of his lab. Ray spread his arms to show the extent of his cavernous, industrial space. The place was high-ceilinged and high-tech, stocked with industrial-grade tools and machines for building robotic machinery. A gleaming display of prototypes lined the walls. In the rear was a long table with computers and monitors. Two men leaned over a motherboard.

Ray Dokestout continued to a separate room devoted to combat robotics. "In this space we have every weight category represented. Every type of bot, every conceivable weapon system, designed and engineered, right here. Shon'dae, you are witnessing the echelon of the sport, the birthplace of every top victory in combat robotics. They all came out of this laboratory. We've had a few rare defeats, that sometimes happens, and that's when we acknowledge the opponent's good fortune. But the whole point of the Doke-a-lab..." he said, giving a quick wink to the camera, "is the ultimate prize. Winning ComBot. That's what we do, what we've always done, and what we will continue to do. Win."

Ray continued the tour of his domain. "Over on this wall is where I hold the hardware. And I don't mean the tools. I'm talking trophies." The camera spun to a large case with ribbons, medals, and polished ComBot chalices emblazoned with the names of various Doke-a-bots. "Of course, I'll need to expand," he laughed.

"Now, last but not least, the moment you've all been waiting for..." Ray gestured to a table covered with a golden drape. "In action tonight, I present..." with a flourish he removed the drape, revealing the machine of Cyrus' nightmares, "...Doke-a-lasher. Enjoy the action, folks," he cackled menacingly into the camera.

Cyrus thought of the invectives which might be spewing from Leslie right now, like fire from a dragon.

Shon'dae Marquette was back in the ComBot arena. Crazed fans pumped their energy behind her. "What a remarkable, gracious champion we have in Ray Dokestout. And what a treat to have toured the gold standard in robotics. It's a visit I'll never forget. Skip, Jack, back up to you." The occupants underneath the two large cowboy hats appeared in the frame, heads shaking as if they just witnessed the messiah. "What a champion," said Skip. "Thank you for that, Shon'dae. Now introducing the contestants into the decagon."

The screen cut to Cyrus and his sandy mop of hair. He glared into the decagon, concentrating intently on the battle to come. "Now that's a face I'd rather see," his mother said cheerfully.

"Let the mayhem begin," the ring PA announcer bayed.

CHAPTER 21

ComBot27: a bitter-sweet affair. "Bitter" because Cyrus relived a traumatic ordeal of four months prior, which brought back the painful memory of watching his bot's near-victory, then its flaccid last stand and blackened incineration. "Bitter" because Ray Dokestout's ComBot reign lived on, topped off by the revolting dance party and raise of the challis. And "bitter upon all bitter" because the answers he was hoping to have discovered remained unrequited. Nothing indicated anything other than a Spiral Cyclone system breakdown. He could only come to one conclusion: connection failure between receptor and controller.

Maybe it was, as Leslie put it, a mojo breakdown. He'd have to leave it at that.

But there was also the "sweet" to the bitter-sweet. The telecast didn't air an image of a teenage kid with sandy mopped hair seized by panic as his bot went inactive. No closeups of the kid's body going limp or almost losing his stomach or tucking his tail between his legs as he exited the decagon. Most of the shots, for better or worse, were focused on Ray Dokestout and Doke-a-lasher. Only a brief cut-to of Cyrus and the officials lifting his bot into the wagon, which showed him in stable spirits. Any undignified images had been left in the editing room. His fear of a lifetime of embarrassment was as baseless as his fear of asking Leslie Borowski on a date. Such is the chaotic loop of insecurity. And that, naturally, fell into "bitter" category.

When the final note of the rock score faded and the telecast concluded, Cyrus lowered his feet, tipping over the bucket popcorn kernels. A commercial came on. It was a trailer for an upcoming war movie. Soldiers were conducting operations, moving through hostile urban environments on a mission to save someone, or some people, or an ideal. He thought about all the times his father might have been in similar situations. Events his father never discussed though alluded to in rare moments of self-disclosure. Tragedies muted even if the realities were impossible to ignore.

As Cyrus watched, a primal feeling came over him. An instinct which told him things weren't quite right. He himself felt like an outpost of resistance, just like the soldier's compound in the movie trailer. His churning stomach, he figured, was a telling sign. It was as if a bugle call commanded: "March on, keep fighting, the enemy's closing in, don't surrender." *But for what? To avenge some injustice? Revenge? Honor? A test of character?* He would have given anything to have someone tell him the true meaning. The soldiers in the movie were at least provided that, or so that was his understanding.

He went to the kitchen for his phone. He took stock of his messages: one from Tonmoy (again Bangladeshi emojis) and eight from Blake, a combination of preliminary advice (like that would do any good) and post-battle commentary that left him a daze. There were two from Leslie. One wishing him luck at 7:25. The other coming in minutes ago: CALL

ME!!!

He quickly typed replies to Blake and Tonmoy, then scrolled to Leslie's recent and hit send.

She answered in half a ring.

"First of all, let me just say I thought you did great. They were cheering like crazy for you and Cyclone over here. It was a nuthouse. And TBH, if you would have made it past the great wizard, the one and very only Ray Dokestout, which, yeah, you were bringing the heat, well, then of course you got dragged into, but that's not the point right now, the point is how you would've destroyed that other bot in the finals. Like Dokestout did. And now that I'm the subject of the great and wonderful…what an ass. You think he's part of the sport for any other reason than serving his own huge ego? The guy's full of himself. Hero? Ha, he's about as gracious a champion as my aunt Nellie in the bingo hall. And she's a sneaky devil, the other players hate her. So, what I'm telling you is this: the guy's a ratchety sewer snake that sucks on dirty sewer water." He pinched his eyes and imagined Ray's head on a snake, slithering around a wet drainage pipe.

Leslie's tirade was music to his ears.

She kept on. Cyrus put her on speaker, walked to the den, threw back the footer of the recliner, and listened to her sweet hymn.

A wonderful ending to a long, fretful day.

CHAPTER 22

"There's the handsome devil." Faye's vibrant dress melded into his vision, nearly blinding him. Next was his mother's turn to be smothered.

"Come in, come in," Faye exclaimed. She pulled Cyrus and his mother down short wooden steps into her sunken living room. The room was decorated to the hilt: long pale curtains, leather chairs, a modern chenille davenport, paintings and eclectic statuaries. It was much less cluttered than he imagined, and he didn't pick up a lingering scent of cinnamon or cardamon or nutmeg. Only Chinese food wafting in from the kitchen. He was starving.

"Cyrus, this is Horace," said Faye. "I believe you two have met once before." Horace offered him a slack hand which Cyrus held like a dead fish.

"Nice to see you, Sir."

On the living room's television was a recap of a golf tournament. The usual hush of the broadcaster was replaced by a spirited host and a fast, dynamic score. As Faye showed his mother the outside patio, which fronted the eleventh fairway of the town's illustrious country club, Cyrus stood uneasily next to Horace. Horace seemed both perplexed and enraptured that his genteel sport had gone stylishly upbeat.

"Golf is about tradition and character," Horace explained tonelessly. "It's about self-reporting and integrity." Before Cyrus could regurgitate something regarding the virtues of golf, something he'd overheard once in passing, Faye and his mother briskly walked back inside. Both of their coifed tresses were tossed from the high winds.

"My oh my, what a blustery day," said Faye, fixing her hair back in place. "Cyrus, do I have a surprise for you. Strawberry rhubarb pie. Your mother said that is your absolute fave. After dinner, we'll have a slice."

At the dining room table, Cyrus slurped down wide noodles and spooned in his favorite soup, Miso, like a human sump pump.

Afterwards, everyone headed for the kitchen. Horace sat glumly on a counter stool; Cyrus next to him. The woman stood on the opposite side of the counter, preparing the pie.

Soon, Faye barraged Cyrus with questions about ComBot. He explained the governing rules, the mechanical constraints, the quarter-century history, how a hazard could break apart a bot just as easy as a rival's vertical spinning sawblade. Cyrus didn't mind explaining combat robotics, but in a sense the sport was self-explanatory—white-hot sparks and shrapnel-inducing collisions meant destruction. "If you roll away after all that, you're the winner. Spiral Cyclone didn't roll away," he concluded.

"Horace and I watched from start to finish," said Faye heartily.

"Er, yes, quite the show," coughed Horace. Cyrus figured old Horace had probably skipped out once the first robot rolled in.

"That semifinal fight of yours was pure high drama," said Faye, "I understand you and your father built that machine. What a feat, what a feat indeed. But sorry for my ignorance, Cyrus, but how'd you make it there anyway?"

"By bus," replied Cyrus.

"By bus!?" shrieked Faye, looking to his mother in awe.

His mother whipped the cream with a utensil. "It's true Faye. He went by bus. He was determined to compete by himself, no matter what. That's what he told me he would do and that's what he did."

"I had no idea." Faye shook her head in disbelief. "But what I meant when I asked the question was how did you qualify for ComBot?"

"Oh, right. I entered some preliminary fights," said Cyrus, "Mom took me to all the regional contests. They were nearby. Dad had them mapped out already."

As he stared intently at the strawberry rhubarb pie, Horace asked: "Your father? Did he ever compete with that robot of yours?"

"We were meaning to, but each time the fights came around, he'd get called. And then…you know…well, then, I went by myself. I was old enough by then."

"That took some real courage," said Faye. "What an incredibly brave thing for someone your age to do."

"Spiral Cyclone had been with us so long it was almost family," reminisced his mother. "My heart just about broke seeing how it ended."

"That's the name of the game," conceded Cyrus.

Faye placed her palms on the countertop. She looked to the ceiling; a rare moment of quiet contemplation. Her face lit serious. She turned to Cyrus. "Do you have another robot, Cyrus? Will you be competing again?"

"Yes. I found one of dad's old bots down in the basement. He built it some time ago, but I don't know exactly when. It's kinda stripped down. I'm working on it, when I have time. It's sorta a one-man operation."

"Then it needs to be a two-man operation," said Faye.

Cyrus had no idea what she meant, what she was getting at, but Faye had a look of conviction that was hell-bent on something. "It does?"

"Yes, it does. Just watching you fighting that robot was enough for me. I knew right then and there that this kid's in for a penny, in for a pound. That's not your last stand, certainly not the final act. You've got more to prove. Isn't that right, Horace?"

"Yes," he replied automatically, still fixated on the pie.

"Here's what I noticed," Faye continued. "Something I picked up on in those fights…"

"ComBot, Dear," chimed Horace. Cyrus was dumbfounded Horace remembered the name.

"ComBot. Thank you, Horace. In ComBot, there were robots with company names on them. Not just the names of the robot, those were on there too, but I mean on their sides. Corporate logos."

"That's right," said his mother, "I noticed that, too. You see it on sport's jerseys all the time, too. Tennis, soccer, even race cars. They all have corporate sponsorships."

"Right, Bridge. So, here's what I was thinking: Cyrus Hampstead needs a sponsor!" yowled Faye.

Cyrus had never considered the idea. He never had to. His father always took care of things, equipped Spiral Cyclone, procured the parts, did the installs. But in the wake of ComBot27, and with the prospect ComBot28 looming, he had to consider the stark realities involved with combat robotics competition. It took money and resources. Motors, batteries, pneumatics, machined parts—they weren't going to materialize out of nowhere. Not to mention the expense of travel and entry fees.

He knew that stainless-steel hellion wasn't going to become the bot he wanted it to become by dreamy will power alone. That wasn't sensible. That wasn't realistic. His father wasn't around anymore and that was the stone-cold truth. The protege needed serious help.

As he thought about it, he did remember seeing a robot with a "Spittle Spattle Vodka" logo on it, and another that read "CorwinMining-Services.com" All along he thought they were fancy embellishments.

"I like that idea," said Cyrus.

"It's a great idea. And I know just the company to sponsor you. Don't we, Horace?"

"Er, uh…" choked Horace.

"Smitty's Lighting, Lamps and Shades," announced Faye, spreading her arms wide as she held two plates of pie. "One of Horace's companies. But really it's my baby."

"Faye?" interrupted Cyrus' mother. "You don't have to do that."

"Are you kidding, Bridget. I'm looking at it as publicity. We're looking to expand into franchising."

"I didn't even know you owned a lamp shop. Car washes and restaurants, yes, but not a lighting business," his mother said incredulously.

"Just got into it recently. One day I went in to purchase a lamp, bought the thing, then I said to the lady, 'how 'bout a lamp shade for this?' She told me I'd have to go down the street to get those, that they didn't sell them. Well, I thought, isn't that stupid. Who's ever heard of lamps without the shades? So, I bought the store and we're now selling shades too. Smitty's Lighting, Lamps and Shades. Isn't that so, Horace?"

Horace looked up. "Round shades, oval shades, rectangular…"

"…Cyrus, I'm going to send our design to our printer and get you set up. We can discuss the terms later after some research, but we need to get going on this soon. That way you can secure what you need. How's that sound?"

The idea shocked Cyrus. A well-oiled operation, a properly funded one, always seemed like a fantasy. Now that ComBot28 was firmly planted in the field, he'd have to till the soil, fertilize it, water it, and reap the sweet nectar. He needed to nurture "that bot" to a championship-level pedigree.

"That works. Sounds great. Thank you," rang Cyrus. He tried to temper his excitement.

"Perfect," said Faye, "because if I have to see that arrogant jerk win ComBot next year, I'll break a vital neck vein. Doesn't that sound about right, Horace?"

"Yes, we don't want that, Dear," Horace said drily. "Let's celebrate with pie."

Cyrus' mother doled out the slices of strawberry rhubarb pie and dolloped on the whipped cream. By the time Horace was handed his, he was mid-bite.

CHAPTER 23

The next day, Saturday, Cyrus called Leslie. She was still at her grandmother's house.

"Hey, Les, I found a sponsor," he said.

"A what?"

"You know, someone to finance me. A sponsor. So I can finish getting that bot built. To help pay for travel and fees and things like that. So I can make a solid run at ComBot."

"That's great, Cy. How does that work?"

"You ever notice that some of the bots had logos on them, names and such?"

"Yeah."

"They're sponsors, like companies who advertise," explained Cyrus. "There was a pretty decent one that had Corwin Mining Service on it. Wedgebot, I think. I'll be sporting Smitty's Lights and…Shades… uh, something along those lines."

Leslie went quiet. Cyrus looked to his phone to see if it was still connected. "You there?"

"Oh, sorry, I'm here. Just thinking. Brain fry from all that turkey talk. Leftover this, leftover that, baked, fried, cornbread or potatoes, goodness I'm glad it's all over with. Hold on, I'll call ya back."

Ten minutes later, his phone buzzed.

"Cyrus? I called Uncle Carl. He was vacationing down in Costa Rica, but I got hold of him. He was at a beachside bar. Sorta outta character for him, go figure. Anyway, he wants to see if you want to go to a Chromiums' game. He's got season tickets on the boards, says I'm invited too. Can you believe it? And here I thought he wasn't a gentleman."

"Oookaaay!" Cyrus protracted the syllables. "I mean, don't get me wrong, I'd love to go to a Chromes game, but…"

"…oh, and he told me to tell you 'Tatwak Fitness'."

Perplexed, Cyrus asked: "Tatwak Fitness? That a gym or something?"

"I think it translates to 'To talk business.' Uncle Carl was pretty buzzed. It means I'm trying to convince him to be one of your sponsors, too. He wants to take you to the Chromiums to discuss. To talk business—Tatwak Fitness. Get it?"

Cyrus thought how fortune seems to have a momentum all its own, how the gods bestow their divinities all in one fell swoop. "Sounds awesome," he exclaimed. Then he had flash of concern: her uncle's business dealings could be anything. "What's his business? Not that it makes a difference."

"Mechanic. Mostly big diesel stuff. Owns three shops. You'd never know it by like how he dresses. Or acts. But he does pretty well."

"I'm in. When's the game?"

"Lemme pull up the Chromiums' app." She put him on speaker. "In like two weeks they're back in town. Friday night, December third, seven o'clock. They're playing the Turbines."

"Perfect," said Cyrus eagerly.

"I'll swing by and get you, then we'll pick up Uncle Carl. Since it's a Friday night, you never know what condition he'll be in," she groused under her breath.

"Uh, OK."

"JK. He'll be fine. I'll make sure of it. Oh, by the way, you have any idea how much to charge for robot sponsorship? You don't want Uncle Carl, or Smitty's, getting off too easy."

"No," he said. "I barely know the cost of building one of those things, let alone their advertising rates."

"Alright, me find out. What's the name of that mining service you mentioned?"

"Corwin's."

"Corwin's. Got it." She swung into a sultry Southern drawl, "Call ya right on back now, hear."

Later that evening, as he tinkered in his workshop, Cyrus received a text from Leslie.

Leslie: FOUND SOME INFO 4 U

Cyrus: GREAT WHAT

Leslie: GOT W MINING CO IN AZ

Cyrus: WTF...? THEY TALKED TO U? ITS A HOLIDAY...PLUS CORPS R TIGHT W INFO

Leslie: WHAT R U TALKIN ABOUT!!??

Cyrus: U ASKED HOW MUCH?

Leslie: COURSE HOW ELSE??? 7000 EACH…MR CORWIN SPONS 2 BOTS

Cyrus: WOW!!!

Leslie: HE LOVES HOCKEY TOO…WHOS THE GREATEST???

Cyrus: MR CORWIN?

Leslie: NOOOOOO

Cyrus: LESLIE?

Leslie: YEP

Cyrus: UR UNCLE GOOD FOR HALF?

Leslie: PROB…CALL ME

"I wouldn't put it past him. He's known for some carefree spending," said Leslie as soon as she answered.

"Yeah?"

"Yeah, one time he invited an entire youth baseball team over for a fish dinner."

"That's cool. Like a fish fry or something?"

"No, not exactly. They were a team from Japan travelling around the U.S. for the summer. He read an article in the paper about how homesick the kids were, and that they were coming into town. He held this big shindig at his shop, you know, invited the newspaper over for publicity even. He purchased a whole yellowfin tuna from the North Atlantic. Sushi grade, a bunch of eel and squid too. Had it all shipped overnight and like hired sushi chefs from in town and everything."

"Wow," said Cyrus, laughing. "What do you think that cost him."

"Not sure the exact figure, but I called some wholesale market and they told me yellowfin ran twenty-nine dollars per pound. I did the math, and he was in over two grand for just the fish alone. And I'm thinking, just thinking, that there were several bottles of rice saki consumed. For the responsible adults, of course. Excluding Uncle Carl."

"What? He doesn't drink saki?"

"No, I meant the responsible part," said Leslie. An exaggerated sigh came over the line, then an extended silence. It was like waiting for a train to pass. Cyrus could feel the shift in conversation.

"I'm bored," she said.

Cyrus watched Mongrel emerge from under the cabinet and make a slow, lazy pad up the basement stairs. He considered the boredom of the domestic cat, or maybe the "non-boredom" in which they lived their lives. "You want to come over and watch, uh, a movie?"

"You're sweet, Cy, but if you remember correctly, I'm still at my grandmother's house"—she swooped into a high note—"for Thanksgiving."

"Oh, right. I forgot. Can't you stream movies there."

"Barely, the WiFi here is garbage. Did I mention grandma lives in the boonies? There's absolutely nothing out here," she fussed.

"Is there a creek?"

"Cyrus, what am I going to do with a creek? And a near frozen one at that. We're coming back tomorrow, anyway. Are you looking forward to the Chromes game?"

"Of course. I can't wait to hear what your uncle has to say. I'm starting to put together a spreadsheet of expenses and…"

Leslie let out a long, high wheeze of exasperation.

"What's the matter?" asked Cyrus.

"Nothing…"

"What?"

"It's just that you think it's a date with Uncle Carl. I feel like the third wheel. That it's like you two who'll be going to the hockey game, and I'll be just, like, trailing along."

"You're not a third wheel, Leslie. I wouldn't even be going without you," said Cyrus.

"I guess it's how I feel."

"Do you want to go with me instead. Then your uncle can be the third wheel?"

"Are you asking me on a date?"

After a nervous beat, he replied, "Yes."

"Good, because I was tired of dropping hints. So, did you miss me last week? Did you even notice I was gone?"

Cyrus did notice. He noticed just about every step she took, every smile or toss of her hair or pensive bite of her pencil, so of course he noticed she wasn't in school. Beside him was one sad, empty seat. And two seats over, two near-comatose brutes. *Why didn't I say something earlier? Stupid.* Having other things on his mind wasn't an excuse. It wouldn't get him off the hook, either. Still, for better or worse, his solution was to wash over his shortcomings with a crack at lame humor. "I couldn't see past the footballers. They've bulked up for the playoffs."

"Cute. But doesn't quite work. If you remember correctly, they sit on the other side of me now. Oh, and speaking of those guys, I heard the team beat Belfry Christian last Friday. They're heading to the finals."

"After all these years, Stafford P in the championships," said Cyrus. "You know, Tonmoy traveled to every game and he told me those two guys had like twenty sacks in the first three games. And on offense, they haven't given up a single QB sack."

"And who's to thank for that?"

"You're talking to him."

"Uh-huh. Right. So, you didn't answer me, Cyrus. And be serious for once. Did you miss me?"

"Did you ask me that?" he questioned coyly.

"Yes, I asked you that. Say it," she teased melodiously.

"I," creaked Cyrus.

"Here, I'll help you…miss…"

"Miss."

"Leslie Borowski."

"Leslie Borowski."

"See, you did it all by yourself. Sort of."

"I could claim I was under duress," said Cyrus.

"You could. But then where'd that get you?"

CHAPTER 24

Cyrus looked at his Chromiums jersey hanging on the wall. The shiny chrome exhaust pipe severing the cobalt C twinkled in the light. He remembered when his father bought it for him at a game; since it was too big, way too big, they decided instead to mount it on the wall above his chest of drawers. Even though he had pushed past the taller stature of most human beings (three inches plus) in the past year, the jersey was still too big. In fact, when he took it down recently to try on, it hung like a drape.

His upward expansion, however, did result in him outgrowing every Chromiums T-shirt he owned, which unlike the jersey, snugged him too tight to the frame. He vowed to take a trip to the team's store, Chromiums Corner, that evening. Only issue: every item in the store was a bank-breaker. Given that his pursuit of ComBot28 may take every loose dime, frugality was essential. But there was a fine line between being money-tight and miserly, and Cyrus didn't want to come across as the latter. *It is a date, after all.*

He donned his old Chromiums' hat (which never seemed to get any tighter) and headed for the den to wait for Leslie. He had the place to himself—his own castle. He settled nervously on his royal couch and waited for his princess to ring.

When the doorbell sounded, he sprang from the couch and tripped over the ottoman and cracked his shin against the coffee table leg. *This thing in cahoots with my mother?* "Not going down that easy," he muttered as he hobbled to the door.

Leslie held a burlap sack. Inside it, sprigs of leaves flounced from a small tree like curious baby fingers. Her blush-pink sweater, which bore a small blotch of soil, breezed in the wind and exposed her navel. "I got something for your robot planter," she said.

"Thank you. But what, no cactus?"

"I don't do cactus. Too prickly. We clash."

The two headed for the tool shed in the back yard, crunching through a smattering of leaves which had fallen since Cyrus had last raked. Cyrus spun the shed's lock and unlatched the door, releasing the scent of wet leaves and wood musk and gasoline. Sitting beside his wagon, below a row of hanging tools, was the derelict shell of Spiral Cyclone. It looked more worn out than the day of its last fight. Rust was beginning to find a home, and by the looks of it, so was a spider. Thin webs stretched across the upturned hull, and somewhere inside its arachnid denizen was waiting to pounce on an unsuspecting insect. Cyrus grabbed it, wiped away the webs, and looked it over. "A fighter past its prime," he said ruefully.

"Maybe it's time it took up gardening," said Leslie.

Cyrus wanted to kiss her at that moment, right then and there in the confines of his secret aristocratic garden, but as soon as the notion set his heart hammering, Leslie reached for a shovel in the corner and headed outside. Cyrus followed carrying his old fighting robot.

She found a patch of loose dirt next to the shed and dug. "You know, sometimes things need to be repurposed. Once they've outlived their use," she said as she dropped small loads of dirt into the metal carcass. "When I was little, I had a quilt I loved so much, never left my sight. Then, after many years of being dragged around, and maybe washed too, who knows, it just started crumbling apart. Holes began to appear and the patchwork became all tattered. I was in tears. But my mom would have none of it. That summer she signed me up for a sewing course and I turned it into a stuffed animal."

"That's cool. Good idea." Cyrus knelt down, unfurling the sapling's burlap casing and pulling apart the hair-thin roots. He laid the sapling in. "So, what is it?"

"It's an alligator now," said Leslie.

"Oh. A gator. I love gators." Cyrus looked up, hands covered in dirt. "But I meant the tree. What kind of tree is it?" he asked.

"An elm," she smiled.

The arena's marquee read: **Stallsborough Turbines v. Kettlebridge Chromiums. December 3. 7:00 pm. Tickets available at box office window.**

"Now whatever you do, Cyrus," said Uncle Carl as they walked across the arena parking lot, "don't go banging on the glass right from the get-go. You gotta let the game evolve, gotta let the players find their rhythm. Then in the third period, when the Turbines are run down and skating on shaky legs and blowing go-cart fumes, we start hammering the rink glass." He laughed like a handful of marbles were stuck in his throat. "Shocks 'em every time. They hate that."

"We'll make a note of that, Uncle Carl," said Leslie, rolling her eyes.

"Do you ever yell at the players?" asked Cyrus. He didn't know what else to say, but he figured he was in the right neighborhood.

"Of course. Never hold back on that," said Carl, pulling up the tickets on his phone. "Anything goes in that department."

The arena was just as Cyrus remembered it from three years ago when his father took him to a game. One of those old brick and cinder block structures from a time when fans didn't expect or require anything more than a solid-standing venue to watch sports or see a concert. Cavernous, grayish-brown, bare-boned accommodations for the masses and all their primitive needs. One could even smell the years seeping from its concrete pores. It was nothing like the venue for ComBot27, which was as polished as one of those newly sprung foodie bars in the upscale section of town. Somewhere along the line, thought Cyrus, spectators became more like honored guests than herded animals. The Chromiums' home arena definitely fell into the latter camp.

After their tickets were scanned, they entered a large foyer bathed in black, cobalt and chrome. Leslie tapped Cyrus' shoulder, pointing to a giant wall banner. "That's kinda funny," she said. Before them, spilled in light, was a Chromiums' season ticket advertisement—four players in tuxedoes holding sticks, flanked by a goaltender with a bruised-up face.

Underneath, it read: POLISHED CHROME. SEASON TICKETS ON SALE NOW.

Cyrus continued staring at it until Leslie grabbed him by the hand and whisked him along with the fleet-footed Uncle Carl, who was on the move to their seats, declaring he never missed a pre-game warmup. It was during this ritualistic skate around and puck handling session, he assured the two, that the tensions between players raged to a boil. All subsequent fights were predicated on these initial interactions.

As they entered the front row, Carl proudly attested he had an eye for which players would be dropping gloves with whom that evening. Cyrus was curious about this phenomenon. When they finally found their seats, with the teams skating ovals on their own ends of the ice, Cyrus became transfixed by the prospect of a good hockey fight. *If it's in an arena, why shouldn't there be fighting.*

Leslie didn't seem so enthralled. "I'm heading to the concession stand." Cyrus stood up to go with her, but she leaned in and whispered in his ear. "Stay here, get the Tatwak Fitness out of the way before the game starts." Cyrus nodded, then reached into his pocket and handed her two twenty-dollar bills. "Here, I'd like to buy something for Uncle Carl. And for my date. Oh, and I'll have a root beer, please."

"Get me a beer, Les," Carl shouted as she crossed the seats.

"They do card, you know," she yelled back.

"Ah, hell. I'll get one after the first period. Now, Cyrus, let's get down to brass tacks here. That was one hellava fight you had at ComBot.

You knocked that sonabitch Dokestout around, you sure as hell did. For a while at least. And for what's it worth, you should've beat that corncob asshole. I've been watching ComBot for years, and he's no stranger to me. No sparklin' gem either, I can tell you that. Not that I'm being partial or anything…well, I can't stand the guy. Not in the least. Favor him as much as a weasel in a windbreaker. But that's neither here nor there, because everything's already been laid out in that department. You gotta look forward."

"Yep," agreed Cyrus. They watched as the opposing coaches slid on shoes across the ice to shake hands with the refs. Some fans booed, several cheered. "I've been working on that. That is, I have a decent bot right now. I just need to get it into fighting shape. You know, up to speed."

"And that's where I can come in. Leslie, I'm sure, told you about my own attempts at combat robotics." Carl then raised his arms high, hysterically yelling, "I coulda been a contender!" People at the end of their row stared at him, perplexed.

On the ice, the teams surrounded the circle for the first period faceoff. When the referee dropped the puck, Carl shot out, "Let's go, Chromes!" It nearly severed Cyrus' eardrums. "Anyway," continued Carl as the players chased the puck, "my venture into combat robotics was a generation ago. A long time passed. But look here, I've gotta lot of extra unused parts laying around the shop, and you're welcome to them anytime. But you'll also need some capital. Buy yourself some quality, top-of-the-line items. Having gone through the process and dealing with

222 | JOE G. BECKER

equipment every day, I know that's the truth. Because one can't run the rails stuffin' horseshit into a steam engine."

"Right," said Cyrus. He imagined a man in a conductor's cap tossing a shovel full of manure into a train's boiler. "I've got one sponsor," said Cyrus, "but Leslie said you might want to advertise, too."

"Correct-o. It's great publicity, especially if you can make it to ComBot again. Better than a friggen' billboard on the interstate that tears apart faster than a wet flag in a hurricane. Thinking three grand, one half of the bot could be mine, the other half the rights of your other sponsor." Cyrus' jaw almost dropped at the spoken amount. Then again, he'd never had to incur the expense of a fighting robot before.

Carl suddenly shot up out of his seat and ripped the cap from his head, smacking it at the glass. "Right there, see right there, Cyrus, number forty-five on the Turbs just cheap-shotted number sixteen on the Chromes. Those two are throwing down, guaranteed."

Cyrus decided to follow the movements of the two players Carl called out. They weaved the ice and slapped the puck like a couple of haggard hockey pros going through the motions. "I guess so," remarked Cyrus. "But I got my eye on number eight of the Cro-Mags, Seidler, and number thirty-nine on the Turbs, Clark. There's some bad blood there."

"Nice call, my friend, nice call. So how does that sound? Three thousand dollars can get you plenty up and running by time of the pre-lims."

"Sounds good," Cyrus hemmed. "But, uh, I have to mention that to

Faye, she's my other investor. She owns Smitty's Lighting and Shades. Or maybe it's Smitty's Shades and Lights. Something like that. I'm charging her thirty-five hundred a side," he confided. He was working solely off the figure Leslie reported from Corwin Mining Service's investment.

"Well, sometimes they have multiple signage. That's part of the business. At any rate, if she's in for thirty-five, it's a done deal. Thirty-five hundred it is." Carl offered his hand.

"OK," said Cyrus, shaking the deal.

Leslie squeezed through the row, juggling food and drinks. "Hey, Les, the Monkey Wrench is back in the fighting game," Carl yelled over some people's heads.

"Great, the Monkey Wrench can now grab the pretzels and sodas."

For whatever reason—luck or intuition—the second period of the hockey match found Cyrus' designated players in a glove-dropping scrum. Both players had their opponent's jerseys clutched while their opposing arms swung furiously at each other's ducking face. The referees circled cautiously as the fight proceeded along. It was a scoreless contest, and since goal scoring wasn't in the cards, the players gave the fans what they wanted. They had to earn their keep; Chromium 8 and Turbine 39 honored that tradition with a no-holds-barred slugfest.

"Can't they just get back to the game," said Leslie to Cyrus. She nuzzled in close to him, pawing at his arm. "I get queasy, especially when the blood pours." Her emerald-green eyes locked into his.

"Doesn't this happen in field hockey?" questioned Cyrus. He rattled his root beer as he nervously tried to land the straw to his mouth.

"We beat sticks to shins, not fists to skulls."

As the fisticuffs migrated to their end of the ice, and as blood began to seep from the eye of Turbine 39, who rallied in a last-ditch effort with some free-swinging haymakers, Leslie grabbed Cyrus. "I don't have the stomach for this," she said, kneading his biceps.

"Maybe next time we can go to a movie," he said, leaning into her. The crowd, Uncle Carl, the fighting players, the game itself receded into some distant parallel universe. Cyrus saw only a pair of bright emeralds.

"No, they're too violent," Leslie whispered as she came close to his face. "Besides, I just wanted to go somewhere. As long as it was with you."

"Me too." Cyrus met her lips. It was soft heaven, all sweetness, a touch of salt caressing his mouth. A blissful universe. All their own.

As the players fell to the ice, jerseys clutched and tugged, the referees began prying them apart. Exhausted and bloodied, the players skated wearily back to their benches, carrying their gloves and sticks and pride. Whether they were injured or not was a problem in a far-off universe.

"Hey, there's a hockey game going on here," interrupted Carl. They fell out of their embrace like dripping honey.

Leslie blushed, her eyes sparkling. She leaned across Cyrus. "Then tell us when it's hockey, and not MMA."

When the period buzzer sounded, Carl said: "You're lucky the two guys fighting were on the Jumbo screen, and not the two of you." Cyrus smiled and Carl patted him on the back. "I'm getting a beer. Leaving you two by yourselves."

"I'm sure the fans wouldn't have minded," Leslie said to him as he passed. She squeezed Cyrus' arm. "Hey, let's go to the store?"

At that, they took off to Chromiums Corner.

After the game, the three of them swept along with the departing crowd, many of whom were distraught over another Chromiums loss (sometimes it's the 1-0 defeat in the last minute of a game that hurts the most.) Outside, the night was crowned by a harvest moon, its light suffusing with the yellow umber of the parking lot lights, creating a margarine and champagne glow. Taffy-like clouds stretched over the adjacent woods. The air was cold and crisp. Vapors from their breaths expelled as they walked to the car.

Cyrus and Leslie walked, swinging hands together like a pendulum. Leslie wore a long-sleeve V-neck Cyrus bought her, solid cobalt in color with a puffing chrome exhaust pipe on the front. He decided to wait until next year to buy a new jersey. By then, he hoped to be flush with prize money.

Still, that didn't stop him from trying on the entire selection of jackets in Chromiums Corner. He and Leslie were there most of the third period, and with each new style he tried on she played the role of wardrobe consultant, assessing the fit with gentle caresses, sweetening it with a kiss. No surprise Cyrus couldn't make up his mind, even if he was priced out of the market. Something he never mentioned to Leslie.

Not like he was ever going to mention it either. Because the night was his no matter what. And he was going to savor it. This night made his month, made his year. It was the best night of his life. A night like this was not to be forgotten, and he cherished every second of it as he walked with a dancing heart, his head swooning under the cold-stretched clouds and the lingering salty-sweetness of Leslie's lips.

Despite the absence of one person in his life, all seemed perfect in the world.

Soon, Uncle Carl broke his reflective spell. "Cyrus, I didn't hear yet about this new bot of yours. I mean, the technical details."

"Well, it's set up in a modulated pod structure, for serviceability. Runs on lithium polymer batteries, brushless DC motor—dual, has a decent speed controller, with reversibility, runs on a FM 75 megahertz…"

"OK, enough of the tech talk," said Leslie.

"It's not much right now." said Cyrus. "I found the body in my basement…" Cyrus stopped short by the strangeness of the words. "Uh, not what I meant to say."

"Let's hope so," said Leslie, looking at him sideways.

"What I meant was that the bot was tucked way back in a nook," explained Cyrus. "Behind an old tool chest. It was probably abandoned by my dad years ago, maybe before we even started working on Spiral Cyclone."

"Or maybe your dad had it there as a backup, you know, in case one system crashed he'd have another on standby. If he was serious about competing, that'd probably've been the case."

"It's pretty impressive, Uncle Carl," interjected Leslie, "there's an opening at the top for a swinging hammer. Something menacing."

Menacing?...more than you know. "Most everything's intact except the main weapon," explained Cyrus. "The drive train functions well, although it could still use some tweaking. The center of gravity is solid. The flipper seems reliable, pretty accurate. It's got a compartmentalized CO_2 cylinder, for the top swinger, which I'm still trying to figure out."

"Is that right?" said Carl, scratching his gray chin stubble. He looked to the moon. "It could've also been some concept bot, maybe an idea your dad was tinkerin' with, playin' with some. I do that with engines, experiment to see which parts work most efficiently. Then again, you never know, your ol' man could've fought with the thing. But you said he never mentioned it, so, you don't know."

"I'd like to know," said Cyrus.

"Only one way to find out," said Carl definitively. "I have a friend, Lester Hofstied. He's got footage of just about any fight that's ever been filmed. Has a huge archive, from the small events all up to ComBot, from Seattle to Shipassaokie…"

"Shipassaokie?" said Leslie dismissively, "there's no such place."

"Whatever, Les. It should be a place, but that's not the point. The point is, I think if your father had ever fought with that bot, Lester'd be able to round up the footage. You have any idea its name, anything along those lines?"

"Like I said, it just looks like a silver arrowhead. Nothing else on it.

Aside for some scratches and scrapes," noted Cyrus.

Leslie unlocked the car and Carl climbed in the back. "I'll see what I can find," he said once inside. "See if Lester can cross-reference your last name. Begin there for starters. Or with its general description."

When Leslie started the car, producing a puff of steam which matched her shirt, she turned to Cyrus: "Any word on the Stafford P. championship game?"

"Tonmoy stopped texting after the first quarter. They were down a field goal, so it musta been a close game," said Cyrus.

"The better question is this: How did the Cro-Mags blow that one with a damn minute left in the game?" asked Carl.

"I don't think you were banging on the glass hard enough," said Leslie.

"Me? Didn't see you two around in the third period for any glass work," replied Carl. "And I'll leave that, at that."

CHAPTER 25

That night, Cyrus had a dream. He was at a creek surrounded by an ambient purple sky. Across the creek, lounging on a rock, was a hyena which occasionally morphed into Mongrel. It didn't matter which animal appeared (both were fine with dreamland Cyrus) because beside him was Leslie. She was in a pale green dress with coffee-colored stripes—like a candy cane. The rings she normally wore had turned into soda bottle caps. And she was going on and on about how wonderful the creek was, how she wished that she'd come here earlier, and how...

It was at this exact moment when Cyrus was awoken by the sound of a vacuum cleaner. It was so loud it sounded as if it was outside his bedroom door. He listened more intently. No, his mother was vacuuming downstairs. Definitely. And it was super loud.

The disquiet interrupted his Saturday morning ritual, a ritual which consisted of freeing his mind from whatever dream it was attached to (in this case, Leslie at the creek), tapping on his phone's music library, crawling from out of his covers, forcing his muscles into service with a protracted stretch, then hanging from the edge of his bed like a bat, or if his muscles weren't quite up to it, like a sloth.

Today, he was neither bat nor sloth. He was simply annoyed. His ritual was broken by a vacuum sounding like a motorboat struggling to get out of the flats at low tide.

As he lay there, wondering when the vacuum would finally suck in its last speck of dust, he reached for his phone. He came up empty. It wasn't on his nightstand. He winced, because nothing would have been better than donning a pair of headphones and drowning out the whirr of an appliance on the verge of death, then falling back into his Saturday morning dream.

Suddenly, the vacuum came to a halt. Cyrus moaned. He curled himself into a ball and let out a groan. He knew what was coming down the pike: his mother, into his room, announcing that they'd have to go shopping for another vacuum cleaner. Salesmen, vacuum models, register lines. What could be worse on a chilly Saturday? Especially after the night he just had.

He heard his mother walking up the stairs. His stretch of agony was complete by the time she reached the landing.

"Cy, you left your phone downstairs and it's blowing up. Leslie's been texting. I think she's looking for her knight in shining armor."

"How'd you even hear it over that vacuum?" he questioned, not caring if he sounded put off.

"Because your phone lights up, too. Haven't you noticed."

"Oh, right. So, when do you wanna go?" There was little enthusiasm in his voice; it was the tone of capitulation.

She looked at him like he was crazy. "Go? Go where?"

"To get a new vacuum cleaner," he said, "didn't the thing just die?"

"There's nothing wrong with the vacuum. I just turned it off because your phone was going crazy." His mother tossed his phone onto the bed, then started to close the door. She stopped halfway. "Oh, and I meant to tell you. You have an appointment next week to test for your driver's license. So please be prepared."

"Uh-huh." He was preoccupied with his messages.

"Are you paying attention, Cy. I want you passing the first time, OK?"

"Got it. Like I said, driving's second nature for me."

His mother spawned an evil stare. She pointed to the ground next to his bed. "I didn't know there was a hook down there."

"Hook?" he muttered absentmindedly.

"On the floor. Where your towel is." She walked over, snatched it and whipped at his dangling feet.

"Hey! What's with all this cleaning stuff, anyway? It's Saturday morning."

His mother's face turned to a glow. "Because Cy, it's called turning over a new leaf. I was offered a position at Linseed Financial, as a financial sales rep. I'm excited, and as I'm sure you can relate, a little anxious. This is my way of getting my jitters out. I'm very excited...did I mention that already?"

"You did. Sounds like a good job. Nice work, Mom."

"Better still, my office is right in town. So, I'd be able to drop you off at school and then head in to work."

"Sweet, in town. Wow. That's perfect. So, how would I get *back* from school?" he asked.

"You're familiar with that bus stop down the lane." His mother threw the towel on his bed and headed down the creaky farmhouse stairs.

Leslie: HAVE SURPRISE 4 U

FORGOT TO TELL U LAST NIGHT

OR MAYBE I DIDNT

BECAUSE ITS A SURPRISE

HELLLLOOOOOO?

U THERE?????

Cyrus: I LOVE SURPRISES

Leslie: THERE U R…DRESSED YET?

Cyrus: BARELY WHAT SURPRISE?

Leslie: EARLY CHRISTMAS PRESENT. BE OVER IN 30. GET DRESSED

They drove seven miles outside of town on a road that winds through the hills and eventually leads to a remote field, where once there was a daylong battle that turned to night and all that was left by sunup were human remains and scattered munitions. Cyrus went there once on a field trip. The road mostly bisects through industrial graveyards, decimated structures of humanity's industrious nature. In front of those worn-out structures of busted brick, worn mortar, and splintered iron re-bar, stood many "Danger, No Trespassing" signs. As Cyrus looked at them, he assumed only rats and mice would ignore those warnings. *Probably not even them.* The road looked even bleaker in leaf-less December.

The two talked about the Ellicott Electrons winning the state championship the night before, and who of their friends travelled across the state to watch the team's close overtime victory against the powerhouse St. Michael Marauders. They avoided conversation about their kiss, even about the Chromiums loss and Uncle Carl's investment. Cyrus still felt a tingle of nerves that never settled from the evening, nerves that had seeped into his dream. It was safer to talk historical battles, industrial graveyards, and football, than their nascent relationship.

Leslie pulled up to an antique shop. She told Cyrus she happened upon it with her mother last week; she always dragged she and her brother to such places. To Cyrus, the place looked more like a warehouse of the tired and forgotten, a sign of the times in that area. If there were treasures in that antique shop, as the sign advertised, Cyrus figured they might take some effort to find.

"OK, so, don't mind all the junk…" started Leslie once inside.

"…I'll try not to…"

"…but there's a section in the back you'll want to see. I found it while hiding."

"Hiding?" asked Cyrus.

"Yes, from my brother."

"Like three-year-old's playing hide-and-seek?" he laughed.

"Yes…like three-year-old's, Cy. Just listen. I wanted to surprise you. Check it out." She yanked him by the arm, gave him a quick kiss on the cheek, and led him to the back.

Cyrus poked around some in a section devoted to kitchenware—glassware, silverware, serving ware, all types of "ware." After a few minutes, he turned to Leslie in confusion. He didn't see any "ware" of value. He offered a half-smile.

"Seriously, you don't notice anything? Something you've been looking for? Anything unusual?"

"There's a lot of unusual, but…" Leslie grabbed him by the chin. Cyrus wholly expected a repeat performance of last night, but instead she spun his face around and pointed to a dusty table. Laying on top of it were old mixers and meat grinders and other culinary instruments facing the prospect of their eternal rest.

When he stepped closer, he saw it: an industrial-sized meat mallet. He lit up.

He picked it up and heaved it up and down. Swung it around like a Nordic hammer. It weighed about twenty-five pounds, flat on one side with tenderizing spikes on the other, which were still sharp after what most likely was years of pulverizing metric tons of meat. It had a dull finish that wiped to a shine by rubbing it on his sleeve.

Cyrus figured it was wielded by either a Paul Bunyanesque butcher or a heavy-duty machine, but regardless, technological upgrades in the industry had made the thing obsolete. It had no price tag (or maybe it had fallen off the handle) but Cyrus couldn't imagine it being on many people's buying list—only someone who wanted to turn it into a giant wrecking hammer atop a combat robot.

"And look. On the handle," said Leslie.

Imprinted onto the tenderizer was a single word: Titanium.

Cyrus and Leslie approached the counter. An old man in a flannel shirt and a blanched complexion stood behind it. Leslie placed the meat tenderizer on the counter. The man looked at it as one would a dormant anthill.

"Didn't have a price tag," Leslie said to the man, "but I'm thinking it's worth no more than twenty." Cyrus knew it was a low-ball offer.

"Looks to be," said the man, nodding his head.

"Great. We'll take it," Leslie said.

The man kept nodding. "Looks to be runnin' a value 'rond sixty. That, plus some."

"I really can't see paying no more than thirty," chimed Leslie.

"Well, I can't very well see takin' no less than fifty."

"Forty it is," she said, reaching into her purse.

"Receipt?" mumbled the man dully.

"Naturally," said Leslie. She turned to Cyrus, winked. "Especially since I plan to expense it to your number one favorite investor, Carl's Monkey Wrench." Cyrus was glad Leslie had the money; his wallet had been drained the night before.

Outside the store, Cyrus gripped his new tenderizer in one hand and his new girlfriend (hopefully) in the other.

"I think it's perfect, Cy. I think it's exactly what your dad had in mind. What it was built for. Don't you think?"

"Yep, that bot seems designed just for this thing," he replied. He mimicked his machine's swinging motion, leaving an imprint of dots on the palm of his hand when he stopped its swing.

They walked along the street. On the corner was a newspaper stand. Inside the scuffed plastic door was a stack of Beacon Newspapers. Cyrus saw a photo of the entire Electrons football team surrounding a trophy. He reached in and pulled one out.

The headline: Finally! The subheading: Ellicott High Claims State Championship.

"I still can't believe it," said Leslie. "In field hockey, we've had like seven or eight titles, and with baseball we like win it about every other year. But in football, we've just plain sucked. Until now."

"Sometimes it's more brain than brawn, if you know what I mean," said Cyrus, turning the front page for the rest of the story.

"Yes, I do," she said. There was an icy chill in her voice. Cyrus looked up from the paper. "I don't know," Leslie continued, "you really think we should have helped those two like we did. It was kinda like cheating. It, you know, still bothers me a little."

"Think of it more like an assist. Like an assist in a field hockey game. We assisted the team. Those two are the pieces, the mega-sized pieces, the team had been missing," said Cyrus.

"And say, hypothetically, that they were on the school's baking team. Would you have helped them with their tests then?"

"We have a baking team?"

"I said, hypothetically."

"Oh. Of course I would've helped them. I'd been right there with them when they hoisted the silver spoon or the golden mixer or whatever you'd get for winning that event," he rambled. He could tell Leslie was close to rolling her eyes, but he pressed on. "But that's not their thing. They don't bake. Or, I don't think they do. They play football. Born football players."

"Trying to learn geometry could've been their thing. I tried. I did it."

"They try hard on the football field. It's what they live for," explained Cyrus. "They're naturally gifted with superior gridiron prowess. That's what makes them who they are. We all have gifts and strengths, and theirs isn't the study of mathematics."

"I don't know." She looked down at the paper in Cyrus' hand, reading over the stats the two footballers compiled in the game. She turned to him. "I don't know if you thought about it, maybe you have, I don't know, but what do you think your dad would have done? Would he have helped them in the same way?"

Cyrus had thought that over, several times in fact. Every time it crossed his mind he always came to the same conclusion: his father would have done what was best for those around him, for those with whom he went to battle, for those he loved. Given the circumstances—circumstances that were not so much for the Electrons football team, but for Numbers 71 and 79 themselves—he felt helping them cheat (or assisting them with a test) *was* the right thing to do. His father was a man bathed in principle and honor, but sometimes, Cyrus determined, one has to look beyond the rules, bend them slightly, for the greater benefit. If football made the man, if football was *life*, then that should supplant the nominal comprehension of geometric measurements by two gridiron-loving lugs any day. *Shouldn't it?*

"He probably would have done the same. He would have seen the position they were in and helped out. It was pretty dire at that point, with the coach about to bench them."

"I'm not saying it was the crime of the century or anything. It's just that…well, we could have helped them another way. Like tutoring." She slipped the paper back inside the newsstand.

"We do have more tests before the end of the school year. So, maybe," said Cyrus.

They walked across the vacant lot, kicking up granite dust that whisked away in the breeze. "Hey, if you're so into helping people out, how 'bout helping me practice for my driving test. I'm scheduled this week," he said, reaching for her keys.

She slapped his hand away. "Not a chance. My mom would kill me. And so would yours. Besides you need to study the manual, not the roads. You've already told me about your driving history, remember?"

"Oh, right."

"But I will make you a deal," she said.

Cyrus flushed thinking about what the deal might be. "A deal? OK."

She opened the driver side door, speaking to him over the hood. "Since I'm not busy anymore with field hockey, I'd be able to drive you home after school."

"Really, you would? It's not too far?" Cyrus asked, opening the door.

"It's far all right, but I agreed to look after my dad's friend's daughter until the holidays, to give the grandmother a break. They live out past your way, in Everett Springs. Anyway, that'd give your mom a break from driving, wouldn't it?"

"She's starting a new job, but at least she wouldn't have to worry about me getting home. Not that she would. I guess the only thing bothering her is me complaining about the bus. Plus, I'd love it. I always have to answer so many questions in the car with her."

"That won't change."

Once inside the car, Cyrus asked, "So, what's the deal anyway?"

"The babysitting? She's a four-year-old. Sweet little thing."

"Oh, that sounds cush. Feed her, play with her…wait, you have to clean her?"

"Of course, Cyrus," she laughed, throwing over the seatbelt, "it *is* a full-service gig."

"Oh, right. Uh, but the deal? You mentioned something about a deal," said Cyrus.

"Oh, that deal. The deal is you take that meat tenderizer there and smash it on every Doke-a-bot that gets in your way, and don't stop until the spikes go dull."

"On it."

"And…wait for it…I'll need your help on set construction," she grinned wide. "The play this spring is Man of La Mancha."

Unrestrained joy wended through Cyrus. Simply knowing he'd be able to spend more time with Leslie made his heart jump and goose-bumps rise from his skin. Lifting him home from school *and* working with her on the set, now that was a treasured bargain.

"Perfect," said Cyrus. "I can do it. I've become a pro at the set thing. Not that I really like musicals very much."

"Nor do I."

"Really? I thought you loved them. That's why you're in the drama department."

"No, I work on them because I like bossing people around." She gave him a knowing smirk. "And think, the best part is you'll get ladder duty again. You and I both know Tonmoy's not getting up on that thing. With his fear of heights and all."

"Tonmoy's got a phobia all right," said Cyrus. "It's a fear of work."

Leslie leaned in and pinched her fingers gently on his chin. "How about you? Do you have any phobias?"

"A few, uh, I guess," he stammered.

"Fear of girls?" she whispered, inches from his mouth.

Cyrus leaned in, his lips pressing gently to hers. "Just one," he said before their long, uninterrupted kiss.

CHAPTER 26

The following evening, Sunday, Cyrus sat in his room reviewing for a test in AP American Government. A "micro-test" is what his AG teacher, Mr. Oppenheim, called it. A pre-test before the semester's final. Micro-test, pre-test, mini-test, quiz, whatever you want to call it, it was still a test. And for whatever reason it was going down first thing on a Monday morning.

Cyrus never understood it, how some teachers yearned to wield that "I can do whatever the hell I want" tyranny, all to satisfy some deficiency in their souls. And if that truly was the case, which he was sure it was, how and why this Oppenheim guy took that tyranny to a whole new level, to the deepest pit-of-the-earth realm, haunted rational reason. *A Monday morning exam? The guy's a true friggen' sadist!*

So, there he was, Sunday evening slogging through legislative procedures and judicial responsibilities hour upon hour as another round of rain worked itself through town. Chilled air, a strong northernly zephyr, soaked terrain. Legislative bill wrangling, Congressional motions, Supreme Court voting schedules. Even if he wanted to tinker with his bot and new weapon, or perhaps take a step outdoors to feel the temperature, he wouldn't have had the time. And on top of it all, his driving exam was scheduled for Wednesday; he had yet to crack the practice book.

A picture of a cartoon lizard holding a hockey stick startled Cyrus.

He put Blake on speaker.

"What the hell does bicameral mean anyway?" boomed Blake.

"The splitting of the House into two parts," answered Cyrus.

"I mean, what jackass named it that? Dude musta been riding a desert animal and looked down and saw two fuckin' humps and decided to call it bi-cameral. Shit, it just doesn't make any fucking sense."

"Yeah, agreed. Guess he was inspired. Like Oppenheim's inspired to give Monday morning tests."

"Why not bicuspid or bilateral or bi something else," Blake raged on. "I mean, what the crap in a shit bucket is that! My god! Anyhow, how did your date go on Friday? Was there any hooking up? Huh, Cy?" he asked excitedly.

"Yeah, once. The guy got a two-minute minor penalty for it. But the Chromes failed to convert on the power play."

There was a long silence. "Real. Clever. You're so fucking clever. You really know how to avoid answering a direct question. So, I'm guessing that double date we've been talking about for the last seven years just may be in the works."

"Eh, it may be in the cards," said Cyrus nonchalantly.

"Well, what's in the cards is me wringing Mr. Oppenheim's neck. Why a test on a Monday morning? Why?" yelled Blake at the top of his lungs. His voice echoed throughout the room.

Cyrus didn't notice his mother standing at his door. "Tell Blake he won't be wringing any teacher's neck."

"Alright, Blake, I gotta go. Call me back later."

"He deserves it, Mrs. Hampstead!" Blake shouted before Cyrus hung up.

His mother shook her head. "Cy, Faye Smith didn't have your email, so she sent me something to forward to you. There's an attachment but I didn't open it. I'm sending it to you now." She tapped her phone and left the room.

Cyrus needed a break from the torture of AP American Government, so he launched his emails.

From: Smitty's Lighting, Lamps & Shades
To: Cyrus Hampstead
Subject: Robot Sponsorship/Investment

Hello Cyrus,

Hope this email finds you doing well, both in school and with your robot. I enjoyed our conversation at dinner, as did Horace. And we had a blast, absolutely looooved watching combot.

I received your recent email re: investment in the Cyrus for president campaign...ooops, wrong one, the Cyrus wins combot campaign. Sounds fantastic. I'm all in for $3,500. Send me your bank accnt. info for deposit of funds. I understand you'll have another sponsor as well, which is great...more the merrier.

Find attached to this email a very uncomplicated agreement between Smitty's and you, as owner/operator robot competitor. Since it spells out the expectations and deliverables, you may want to reword and use it for Monkey wrench as well, if you choose to do so. Electronic sig is fine, just send it back, dated. And bank info, as mentioned.

If all good, I'll have graphics designed and will send to printer. I'll request an order of a dozen or so in case they peel or get shredded. Judging from what I saw in combot, that might be a smart idea. You may also want to have MW submit graphic to same printer for convenience and better rate.

Take care Cyrus, and please keep me up to date as to how you're progressing. And let me know the name of your new "bot" if there is one. Can't wait until next year's big event. You'll get there, I know.

(Give your mom a big hug, please.)

Love and kisses,

Faye Smith

Cyrus downloaded Faye's attachment and looked it over. As Faye stated, it was an uncomplicated agreement (he feared having to sign anything that looked as if it belonged on a prescription drug advertisement), although it was rife with legal terminology—naturally, that would be his mother's department.

RELEASE AND AUTHORIZATION AGREEMENT

EFFECTIVE BETWEEN SMITTY'S LIGHTING, LAMPS AND SHADES, LLC AND CYRUS HAMPSTEAD.

Smitty's Lighting, Lamps and Shades, LLC (herein "Smitty's") agrees to pay the sum of $3,500.00 to robot owner/operator Cyrus Hampstead (herein "Cyrus") for consideration of <u>corporate mark placement on robotic entity</u>, name to be determined, (herein "Entity") for the duration of said Entity's existence presently and through the time of combat robotics event, ComBot28.

Payment of sum will guarantee placement of Smitty's name/logo/likeness on one (1) side of Entity. Size, style and color will be determined by Smitty's, however shall not exceed ten (10) inches in length and four (4) inches high, the approximate proportional dimension determined and stated in conversation with Cyrus.

Should Entity fail or become destroyed during events leading up to ComBot28, due to handling, transportation, engineering malpractice or engagement in respective pursuit, namely combat robotics, then Cyrus may retain ownership of agreed upon sum, which is, and shall be, disbursed according to Cyrus' discretion, i.e., how Cyrus sees fit. This sum does not entitle placement of Smitty's name/logo/likeness on any robotic entity controlled or operated by Cyrus subsequent to ComBot28. Any future agreements and sums, if any, will theretofore be determined by Smitty's and Cyrus at a date TBD and within a separate document.

If it was good enough for a businessperson like Faye, it should work for a businessperson like Carl. Cyrus sent the document to his desktop and made a copy for the "more the merrier" Carl, in which he changed Smitty's Lighting, Lamps and Shades to Carl's Monkey Wrench. He composed an email to Carl with the amended attachment.

From: Cyrus Hampstead
To: Carl Borowski
Subject: Robot Sponsorship/Investment

Hi Carl,

Thank you for taking me and Leslie to the Cro-mag game. I had a great time, even if the outcome was a loss. I wasn't expecting much more than that anyway. Can you blame me?

In our conversation you said you were willing to advertise on my robot for $3,500. Thank you. You will be able to get one side of the bot to place your company name, see attached agreement.

It will be a great experience and a lot of fun. It will be hard work but I love building and competing. I'm glad you do too. I'm excited about the upcoming season.

Speaking of seasons, I hear the Chromiums may be getting a forward from Saskatchewan, he's got like 30 goals and 18 assists there. And he knows how to drop gloves. Maybe we can keep him long term and watch him play...or fight...this season and next.

Thanks again. See you soon.

Cyrus

Before hitting send, Cyrus called his mother into his room.

"Mom, can you look this over. You can act as my lawyer."

"My life's dream." She stood behind him, quickly scanning Faye's agreement.

"Yada, yada…yes, looks good. Very professional. The only concerning part for me is the "Cyrus' discretion" line. I want to see that you're spending this money wisely, not frivolously. Understand? These are your funds. Your only funds. Because extra funds around here don't exist."

"Got it. But since I've never before *had* any money to spend frivolously, I really don't think I'd know *how* to spend money frivolously."

She lowered her brow. "Trust me, it's not that hard."

"What about a bank account, mom?"

"We'll go to the bank to set up an individual account this week. You'll get your own, that way you can track the money that comes and goes. Like an adult."

"My life's dream."

CHAPTER 27

For the umpteenth time over winter break, Cyrus checked the website. Nothing. No dates, no schedules, no locations. He figured with less than a week left before the new year, there'd be some word about when and where the ComBot regionals would take place. The only message on the website told prospective entrants to stay tuned. Cyrus didn't really like being told "stay tuned"; it made his nerves pop.

Periodically over winter break, he combed his emails for updates. He weeded through enticements from stores he never cared to shop or apps he'd never think of downloading, and still nothing. In fact, no one in the chatty cyber-world of combat robotics knew a thing. *Nada.*

The reasons why the tournament announcements were delayed began to run across his overactive mind: entangled lease negotiations; a prickly fire Marshall; financial constraints that might cancel the events indefinitely. He dreamt up every scenario possible. Whatever the situation, he was left with no other choice: wait.

And live life.

He earned his driver's license, having passed the written (just three wrong) and driving (minor curb scrape he blamed on the vehicle) portions of his test. His grades were no cause for concern either—straight A's across the board. And because it was winter siesta, he was sleeping in every day, a much-needed respite for mind and body.

Of course, his romantic life was flourishing, too. More than he could have ever imagined. Since being driven home every day after school until the holidays began, his relationship with Leslie had grown closer, more intimate. (She even had him doing most of the driving once his license was in hand.) His teenage years were truly beginning to feel like teenage years, with a romantic relationship validating all his expectations.

If anything, his life wasn't the same routine of waking up, going to school, saying goodbye to friends at school, being driven home by his mother, having dinner, doing homework, whittling time in the basement, going to bed—the typical cycle of wash, rinse, repeat. No, Cyrus' life had up ticked for the better. Several notches better. It had variety, spontaneity.

It had love.

Holiday nights at the movies and the coffee shop, drives to the country to watch the stars shine and comets shoot into blackness, finding areas of remote seclusion as chilled backwoods scents entered through cracked car windows. Moon blushes and drifting conversations, testing themselves and the curfew clock. He loved every minute of it.

Life was riding smoothly.

He even had opened a bank account. With Faye and Carl's investment, minus $1873.45 for an order of assorted robot parts (a new battery, a backup motor, a dozen wheels as spares, plus tax), $98.88 for dinner and movie expenses (Leslie told him she deserved to be treated for a finder's fee), various runs to the store for treats, and a ten dollar roll of quarters for the greedy parking meters in town, the total in his Iron Mill

Bank account currently amounted to $4,077.67.

Which was the exact total at the top of his spread sheet now on his desktop computer. In the columns: robotics events he planned to attend. In the rows: a tally of charges incurred, yet to be incurred, and which may someday be incurred—if only he'd receive notice from those molasses-moving event officials.

Again, he checked the status on the website. Again, the same disappointing wording.

For Cyrus, there was great deal of practicality in knowing when and where the robot contests would take place. Real factors of place, distance, and timing, which equated to real considerations of transportation, gas expenses, and whether or not he'd have to worm his way out of school for a day or two. He obsessed over these "unknown variables." *Was there some venue change I was unaware of? Is one coming?* If so, would the events be close enough that his mother, who drove him to every contest last year except ComBot, be willing to relinquish her car to her teenage son? *Where would I stay overnight? Would Mom even let me drive the distance? What about school? What about Leslie!?* Then, of course, there was his bot. *Is that damn maniac even fight worthy? Would it cooperate like a good little bot that it mostly wasn't?* The questions beat around his head. If he was looking for a sagely monk on a distant mountaintop to answer them, he was sorely out of luck.

Cyrus soon became tired of rows and columns and combat robotic events not yet slated. He was tired of worrying.

He noticed an envelope on the edge of his desk with his name on it. He figured his mother had probably placed it there. He opened it. Inside were the decals from a printing company. Two different sleeves, a ten count of each: Smitty's Lighting, Lamps and Shades and Carl's Monkey Wrench. Both decals were the exact size: ten by four inches. *Sweet!*

Smitty's logo was sharp and colorful, with lighting objects artistically rendered in the name Smitty's: a lamp for the "i"; a shade over the two "t's"; a lightbulb in place of the apostrophe. Carl's was black and white, a monkey's butt sticking out of an engine hood with the garage's name on it. The monkey held aloft what looked like a wrench, though on second glance Cyrus noticed it wasn't a wrench after all, as one might expect, but a crucifix.

Instructions for application (and removal) were included in the envelope. They called for an alcohol prep and a hot air gun to seal them. He grabbed the sleeves, went to the bathroom for the isopropyl alcohol, and headed to the basement.

Cyrus flicked on the basement's overhead lights and walked over to the workbench. His bot shone a low luster from the fluorescent lights. Atop the stump of elm was the massive titanium cube, and the iron pipe with its broken footer. He poured some rubbing alcohol on a rag and shimmied it over the weapon. The alcohol evaporated immediately, exposing the persistent glow of the immense tenderizer.

Weeks of studying for finals, nights with Leslie, sleeping in until eleven o'clock. The little time he devoted to that bot, no wonder the giant titanium tenderizer wasn't yet installed. Besides, mounting it was causing him nothing but fits.

Cyrus knew that in any given battle the weapon's handle might bend, or completely snap off. So, the week prior he decided to sleeve it with an iron pipe, making the tenderizer's handle longer, stronger, more formidable. With his caliper, he had measured the handle's diameter. In a tool drawer, he had found a fifteen-inch iron pipe with almost the exact same diameter. He beat the handle through the iron pipe's interior, leaving no wiggle room. He welded the ends shut. If the arm handle were to ever become damaged, he could cut off the ends and beat out the handle and slide in another pipe in its place. (He was certain this might happen at some point.) After that, he had machined a footer for the hammer's handle and welded them together. He then slotted the footer though the bot's interior rod, tightening it with heavy-duty lock nuts. When he tested it manually, it chopped down smooth and seamlessly in a seventy-five-degree arc. He was on his way.

But the final test—when he activated his controller and switched on the weapon—proved to be a different story. For starters, the rate of acceleration was a mixed bag. On any one attempt, the downward smash was flawless—a crushing blow. Other times, it bore down haphazardly—with sporadic hesitations and glitchy midway vibrations. Overall, it was more a clunky mess than a reliable, faultless force. After tinkering with it some more, Cyrus launched a final attempt: the weapon slammed against the edge of the worktable and the footer cracked apart. His welding skills, it turned out, weren't as masterful as his father's.

Cyrus looked at the project with despair. Instead of messing with it more, he found the hot air gun in the tool chest and doused the rag with alcohol and stroked it across the bot's frame. Using a wax pencil and a ruler, Cyrus marked the spots for the decals and then set them inside the parameters. He hit the decals with the gun.

He stood back and looked at the bot approvingly. The graphics made the difference. *Maybe they will give it an attitude adjustment. Like I wanted to with that damn finger-munching goat.*

He walked over to the small rectangular window coated with seasonal smudge. His view outside was just a foot above ground level. He looked out, silent, thoughtful. Sometimes a mood would come over Cyrus. From out of nowhere. An unexpected funk which ate at his mind and niggled his soul. He tried his best to temper it, but eventually he knew he'd be forced to listen to it. Address the cause head on.

As he looked out, he knew the emotional tug had nothing to do with when or where the ComBot prelims would take place, or if his robot was in proper fighting condition, or anything to do with school or Leslie or friends. The tug was emptiness. Reason told him that "emptiness," in some form or another, would linger with him his whole life. But this emptiness was different; this was more a pestering of the conscience. Not so much foreboding (he wouldn't term it that), more like the feeling one gets when something ominous is around the corner they're unable to see. Something they know will haunt them until it comes out into the light.

Cyrus needed to see it for what it was. He needed to see it in the full light.

In the corner of his eye something caught his attention. A drifting shadow. He soon saw a wheelbarrow's wheel. It was followed by his mother's garden boots.

He headed upstairs and went outside.

His mother was in the side yard garden on her knees, tilling the hard soil with a three-pronged cultivator. Mongrel sat on the edge of the garden, hoping to catch a critter weaseling out to freedom. "Hi, mom. Must be some hard ground?"

"It is, Cy," she said as she clawed a deep trough through dead roots. "Should've got to this last month but I didn't. At least it's not frozen yet."

"Dad used to do that. Turn it over in the Fall," he said, grabbing an auger from the wheelbarrow. "He told me the weeds could survive anything, any temperature, and then come back stronger. Like those insects in the house," he quipped.

"Probably just like those insects. Yeah, your father liked to keep busy." She looked up with a soft smile. "Here, work that area over there by the statue," she said, pointing to an ornament in the garden that looked a rainbowed dragonfly. "Anything you pull from the ground, roots, weeds, throw in the barrow. Unless it's a bulb, keep those planted."

"Mom, do you know if dad ever did anything dishonest? You know, like cheat a little. He didn't seem the type, I mean, you know how he was."

"Yeah, I know how he was. Why do you ask?"

"Just curious."

"Good Lord Jesus, no. Not that man." She stopped clawing the soil and looked to be consumed in thought. "Well, there was this one time, and I only know about it because I was told about it, because they all laughed about it afterwards…for years even…but he and some guys had a deer hunting trip planned, planned it for some time, then at the last minute Popsicle decided he wanted to go too, said he just got some time off work and needed to get away. So, there they all were, out in the woods, with Popsicle hunting in a separate group from your father. Popsicle kills a buck. But the only thing was, since he came late to the party, he was the only one in the group without a hunting permit. So, late in the day, Popsicle's driving up to meet up with your father's group, but right before they joined together your father sees a ranger in a vehicle hightailing it towards Popsicle, who was all alone with that big buck, antlers dangling over the side of the truck bed. Your dad steps on it and splits off on a side trail, parks, gets out and runs through the woods, then jumps into the passenger side of Popsicle's truck. Seconds before the ranger gets out of his own truck. Popsicle almost had a heart attack from the scare. Well, when the ranger approaches your father whips out his hunting permit with a big grin and tells this big lie about nailing it from hundred meters out or so while the animal was in full sprint. 'Best shot of my life,' he tells the ranger. I remember the details because they told it so many times. They loved telling that one. Saved Popsicle's you know what."

"Huh. I guess that doesn't seem too out of character. For him."

"No, it doesn't. Aside from that, there may have been other instances, but he...well, took those with him," his mother said, wiping away a tear that came with the memory.

Cyrus looked across the dormant lawn. He was staring for some time at the tailgate of Brown Toro in the carport, lost in thought as the scene with the ranger and Popsicle's pickup truck played out in his head. *Brown Toro!*

"Hey, mom," he said suddenly, "does Brown Toro work? Is it even drivable?"

"Could be, I guess. I never liked to drive that thing, so I don't know much about it. But I do remember, now that I think about it, how your father talked about it being yours one day." After tossing a collection of weed roots into the wheelbarrow, she paused and winked at Cyrus. "You have a driver's license now. Guess it's all yours."

It had been at least two years since Brown Toro felt real pavement. His father, Cyrus recalled, didn't drive it very often, only those few times to teach him how to "drive stick." Maybe because it had a few issues. More than a few. For whatever reason, it had no front bumper, which may have been lost to the roadways. Its cloth upholstery was a patchwork of tears and tape. Its brown paint was mostly given over to rust, making the truck look splotchy and sickly. In fact, the rust was so pervasive it left several holes in its undercarriage, allowing driver and passenger to see asphalt as it passed under their feet.

Cyrus didn't have much issue with those holes underneath. His father claimed they were like portholes on a ship, a glancing view of a world one would normally never get to see. A unique feature. Cyrus agreed. What was disconcerting, however, was Brown Toro's steering—a full quarter turn one direction set the tires in motion. Anyone driving the thing looked like a captain on an ancient ship, crazily spinning a large wheel. Cyrus figured that was the reason why it had so many scrapes along its sides (not including the one in the rear courtesy of his mercurial robot.) Narrow lanes and tight corners were a major challenge. He knew that from the times he drove it himself, events never disclosed to his mother. *The steering would definitely need adjustment.*

His mother continued: "I'll call tomorrow for the shop to come and get it and take a look at it. It'll definitely need a tune up before you take it out on the road."

"Wonder how it is in the snow."

"Like I said," responded his mother, "I wouldn't know. But I do know there's a plow attachment back there." She pointed behind the carport.

"That thing under the gray tarp is a plow?"

"Yes. You remember how your father would connect it to Brown Toro to plow our driveway. Sometimes he'd keep rolling down the road if the city hadn't come by. You can do the same for us this winter. I paid a fortune last year to have that guy Collier down the lane to come by. Thank goodness I have a job now. Extra income helps."

"Huh, extra income. Maybe I can be the guy who does the neighbors' snow plowing. Make some extra money."

"Not a bad idea. Work hard, have more. That was your grandfather's motto," she said, lifting from her knees.

Cyrus' "tug" abated. Then he got to thinking. Once Brown Toro was running properly and was out of the carport, he could park it off to the side and revert the space back to the robotic training facility it once was. There were two-foot-high plastic barricades filled with sand in the rear used to keep reckless bots at bay. Some were damaged, some leaked sand, but most of them were functional. And in the rear were training dummies that could take an unrelenting abuse. Of course, he'd have to sweep the place and scrub away a few oil slicks. In his head, he had the carport reimagined to its glory days.

Two days before New Year's Eve, Cyrus was awoken by his mother and a mechanic talking outside. When he looked out past the willow tree, he noticed Brown Toro was back in the carport.

He watched the mechanic get into another truck with a woman and drive away in a cloud of steam. Cyrus laced up his shoes and headed for the carport. He found his mother stuffing papers inside the vehicle's glovebox.

"Let me guess," said Cyrus, "the hunk of junk isn't road worthy."

"On the contrary. The mechanic gave it a quick tune up, replaced some belts and a hose and did some work on the transmission. It's all set. Just putting in the repair receipts in case there's ever a question. Like the one you just asked."

"Really? How about the steering? Did that get fixed?" he asked.

"No. Steering's fine."

"Steering's fine?"

"Fine."

Vacuum cleaners, steering wheels, fighting robots. If these machines weren't so damn important, they'd almost be useless.

CHAPTER 28

"Yeah, I'm pretty sure I won't run it into a river," replied Cyrus. He had his feet propped up on his desk, phone in one hand as he scratched behind Mongrel's ear with the other. He was listening to Leslie's worry and concern.

"Because I really don't feel like going for a swim," said Leslie, "especially in the dead of winter. And see, I really shouldn't even have said that word."

"Winter?"

"Dead! It's a bad luck word. In fact, it's the worst luck word. Are you sure that thing's safe?" she asked for the third time. "Because I *seriously* have my reservations."

"Leslie, we got it checked out by a legit mechanic. It's got all its papers and everything," he explained.

"It's not like having a proof of rabies shot. It's a machine. And your machine sorta looks like a rusted tomato can. *And* I do also remember you telling me how the steering works, or should I say, doesn't work. Goodness, Cy, I mean, thank God the bridges around here have strong railings." She let out a long sigh.

"You can drive it yourself to see. It's really not that bad," Cyrus said, downplaying the tension in the steering.

"No thanks."

"Have you ever driven a manual?" he asked.

"All the time."

"Manual means stick shift."

"What's that?"

Cyrus cracked up so hard Mongrel sprang from his lap. "Well, as long as I can see the road, I'll be fine. It's just a matter of making the adjustments, finding the catch patterns in the wheel. I've done it before. Besides, it's no different than operating robots," he told her as he plopped his feet to the floor. "You just have to understand the machine, and then once you do, it becomes second nature."

"Yeah? Second nature? What happens to your second nature when it's dark out? Like country road dark, like dead of night dark? Ugghh, there I go again with that word. Listen, do me a favor..." she trailed into silence.

"Hello?"

"Call ya right back," she said and hung up.

As Cyrus waited for her return call, he browsed the internet looking for a good electric winch so he could hoist his bot up and down the basement stairs. Given his resources, he was seeking a used one, something not too beat up. Last night, he dreamt up a way to install a pully system at the top of the stairs, using easily accessible items: a chin-up bar, a clamp, a toboggan, and a winch. Cyrus was tired of asking his mother for a lift assist every time he wanted to take the bot out for a spin; the last few times, she complained about the strain on her back, upgrading its severity (and her level of grievance) each time. So, if she happened to gripe about the bulky intrusion at the top of her stairwell, then at least he could claim it was there to save her back. Besides, a winch might also help with getting his wagon into Brown Toro's bed.

His phone rang several minutes later.

"Hey, is your mom home?" Leslie asked.

Cyrus' blood heated up, took a quick trip through his pumping heart, pounded it silly. "Uh, no, no, come on over."

"Not for that," she said flatly. "I just wanted to know if someone was there. To lift your bot into your truck. Both are going for a little ride to Uncle Carl's shop."

"They are?"

"I just got off the phone with him. He wants to look them over. Especially your truck. That's what he told me."

"I'm guessing the emphasis on the truck is more you, than him," said Cyrus.

"Possibly."

"Well, Carl's one of my top investors. Let's go."

"He's heading on vacay tomorrow, so I better get over to your place soon. From the sound of things, the tropical party's started early."

"OK, sure." Cyrus thought about how much the girl with strawberry hair and emerald eyes meant to him. How he'd be lost without her. "I'll be ready. Just knock. No use ringing the doorbell."

"Why?"

"It's *dead*."

"Ugghh," she screamed before hanging up.

It was near twilight by the time they arrived, the sky radiating silvery-pearl above the rolling hills of the countryside. The flagship facility of Carl's Monkey Wrench, one of three statewide, was one of those freestanding industrial buildings on the outskirt of town which welcomed guests as they came or saluted their departure as the left. Either way, it did so without much fuss to how it looked or what condition it was in. Or what objects were strewn around it. From the exterior it was as non-descript as they come, unless the description included a dozen or so long-haul trucks in various states of repair parked behind a razor-wired chain fence, beige corrugated siding with peeling paint, a neon sign of indeterminate age, and a gravel entryway with two old dogs collapsed in sleep along its side.

Across the highway from Carl's was a small diner called Lucy's. The place sat alone in front of acres of meadow which gradually sloped to the hills. Lucy's looked to be as old as the hills, and given its supposed longevity, Cyrus was certain the food was decent enough. As they passed, Cyrus noticed an elderly couple sitting inside. There was also a lone trucker whose brim of the hat rose just above a complacent stare. Maybe he was waiting for his truck to be repaired, or maybe he just liked Lucy's. Whatever the case, the sight of him eating made Cyrus' stomach growl.

They drove through an open gate and curved around to the rear of the building, into a vast yard where semi-trucks, some shelled of their engines, were haphazardly parked. Tires, rims, side panels, front grills, back bumpers, the odds and ends of the trucking world, took up the spaces between. Two of the four large bay doors in the back were open. Cyrus pulled into a spot next to the first one.

Leslie hopped out from the passenger side. Cyrus noticed how she dropped down with attitude, as if she was proud to be associated with Brown Toro's retro legacy. Still, he knew if anyone were to ask her, she'd scoff at the truck's decrepit condition. She didn't care for the wonky seating, despised watching the road pass below the floorboard, and absolutely hated the steering. She expressed as much the entire ride over.

One of the dogs slowly ambled around the corner.

"Look at my sweet Ginger-loo, my baby girl," Leslie swooned, petting the dog's head and rubbing its neck. "This is Cy, Ginger-loo."

The dog languidly walked in front of Cyrus, casually sniffing his leg. He patted the dog's head. "I think she smells Mongrel."

"My Ginger-loo has no use for such a lowly creature. Cats are below her. She has royal blood."

"I can tell by her ears," said Cyrus.

Leslie looked at him askance, then escorted him through the open bay door.

Inside, Carl's Monkey Wrench didn't look anything like its outer appearances. It was an immaculate, highly organized shop. The floors were glossed yellow. The truck lifts were bright red. A taut network of pipes ran along the ceiling and down the support beams, from which hoses and electrical cords sprang. Alongside each lift was a toolchest, the tools properly stowed. It didn't take long for Cyrus to become envious of the condition of the workspace. He imagined how his father might have stood there nodding in confirmation of its stratified layout.

Inside, a pair of semi-trucks rested on lifts. Their engine hoods were propped open as if abandoned in mid-repair. At the far end of the shop were some windowed offices for both customers and employees. Cyrus didn't see anyone around.

Leslie snatched a socket wrench from a toolchest and cracked some chimes on a stanchion. "Carl? Uncle Carl?" she trilled after each ding.

Carl emerged from an office with another guy, a bearded man in coveralls who looked bathed in soot. "There y'all are, I've been waiting," Carl yelled from across the shop. "Where'ya been, over at ol' Lucy's?"

"Lucy?" she turned to Cyrus, "Who's Lucy?"

"That's the diner across the street," explained Cyrus.

"Eek, looked awful," she whispered back. Her voice boomed again: "Carl, where should Cyrus...?"

"Cy, ol' buddy, how's it going?"

Cyrus waved. "Hey, Carl."

Leslie yelled once more, "...so, where do you wa..."

"...Been fine, just fine, Cy!" Carl waved one arm wildly, the other clutching a bottle of beer.

"Uncle Carl!..." Leslie hollered.

"This here's Gerald. My main mechanic."

Cyrus gave a perfunctory wave as Carl loped over to the last bay door and rolled it up by a switch. "Swing 'er back in over here, Les, would ya. Whatcha waiting for?"

She turned to Cyrus in disbelief. "Gee, I can't imagine."

Over the next half hour, Carl and Gerald were hunkered under Brown Toro's hood and chassis. They dove under the steering column in the cab, swinging tools into hard-to-reach places, calibrating this and that, hooking up devices to all kinds of mechanical systems Cyrus knew were there but knew nothing about. Meanwhile, Leslie had retreated outside to play with Ginger-loo.

Gerald cackled heartily at just about everything Carl said, jokes and non-jokes alike. It seemed humor was an integral part of their communication. Cyrus lingered around the truck, pretending to be interested the language of the grease arts.

"Cy, I'm figurin' what's under that tarp in your back bed is your bot," said Carl, on a wheeled sled and hidden under the truck's front end. "Hey, by the way, ya get my graphics on 'er yet?"

"Yeah, I just got them on," replied Cyrus. "They look great. Like a real contender."

"I coulda been a contender!" Carl yelled from underneath. Gerald cracked up inside the cab; Cyrus reckoned he'd heard that one once or twice before. "Anyway," continued Carl, "I hope this one is a real contender. Ya hear from ol' Lester yet? Any word on him findin' a video of your bot?"

"No, nothing yet."

Carl slid out from under the truck, upward facing, his shirt smudged in oil and his neck lathered in grease. "Huh. Well, I know Lester's been outta the country a lot for work. But hang tight on that. He's generally slow to getting' to things, but he's a follow-through type-a guy." He wheeled the sled back underneath Brown Toro.

"She's in purty good shape," Gerald said once he was finished. He wiped his hands on the only area of his coveralls not smudged with grease. "Seein' 'bout 'er age and all," he laughed.

Carl slammed the hood and walked over. "Made some adjustments to the steering, Cy. Might not be as tight as a beaver's dam, but it won't spill the lake either." An image came to Cyrus of Brown Toro steering wildly into a beaver's dam, one big cascading tower of water—wood, debris, and truck. "And by that I mean it's better than it was."

Gerald rumbled with laughter as he stowed away his tools.

"I appreciate it, guys," replied Cyrus, "Leslie was really, you know, she was worried about driving in it. Steering probably, though the canyons in the floorboard don't help much."

Gerald guffawed loudly. "No 'preciation for the finer vintage things."

Carl slapped Cyrus' shoulder. "Yep, you got yourself a fine vehicle here. Now let's take a good look at that monster under the tarp there. That thing's really got me piqued."

They released the ratchet ties and carried it over to a metal table.

Cyrus unscrewed the outer panel with a drill.

Gerald sent out a long whistle. "Lobos alive, ain't that something. A real beaut."

"That she is. Your ol' man really had a mind for these," said Carl. "Smart that he modulated it in pods, that way everything can be fixed just like that." He snapped his fingers. "Even if it does get damaged. But judging by the thickness of the sheathing, might take a missile to shred through this armor."

"The motor and the speed controller work OK. My main problem is figuring out the mechanics of the hammer. It's been kinda glitchy." Cyrus reached in the truck and extracted the meat tenderizer.

"I saw that big 'ol thing in there and figured t'was for protection purposes," quipped Gerald.

Cyrus placed the tenderizer's handle in the slot to show the intended swinging motion. Gerald issued another long whistle.

Carl said: "That tail dagger might slap an opponent around, keep 'em at distance, and that front flipper's a hot item too, but let me state the obvious. You'll wanna strut that hammer around like a moose does his antlers."

"Yeah," said Cyrus, "if I can perfect its timing and position, a wedgebot will feel a load of titanium." Cyrus held up the damaged footer. "If only the weld would hold. Snapped off after a few tries."

"Yeah, it did," exclaimed Carl. He examined the tenderizer, the iron sleeve and the footer separately, twisting them in his hand, giving a "hmm" as he laid each one down. He thumbed his stubbly chin. "Tell ya what, Cy. Give Gerald here a good 'ol crack at soldering these together. He's a master at the wire-and-weld, then we'll slip it right on through once he's done. Ya say the glitching's in the weapon, not the motor? Or the transmitter and receiver?"

"I mean, I've had some issues, incidences where it didn't respond. You know, like tweaking…misbehaving."

"Misbehaving, huh?" asked Carl.

"That's kinda an understatement."

"Well, we'll see how that goes once were done," said Carl.

As Carl and Cyrus worked on the CO_2 cylinder, Gerald took to the welding. Leslie briefly popped in, then seeing everyone was working popped back outside.

A half hour later, the pieces were reinstalled. "Let's test 'er right in between the lifts," Carl said. He raised two of his platform lifts by their hydraulic posts, creating space.

Cyrus flipped up the orange kill switch. He and Carl stood back while Gerald hid behind a toolchest. "Let 'er rip," yelled Carl after the motor revved a minute.

The hammer was a free-swinging maestro, a smooth swatter that pounded the floor in coordination with each of Cyrus' punches to the remote. He couldn't have dreamt of a better result. "That's what I'm talking about," he shouted.

"Hey, where's Leslie?" Carl called to Gerald. "She outta see this.

And Seevie, too. Round up the ladies."

Gerald found Leslie outside, then entered one of the offices. A woman sauntered out. She was older, gray-haired, a diminutive build, and labored under a slight limp. Cyrus could tell by the way she carried herself that she handled the business around the shop.

Leslie sidled up next to Cyrus. Heart thumping, he slid one of his arms around her waist as the other thumbed the controller.

Gerald combed his beard and chuckled. "Seevie, ever seen such a thing?"

Seevie pursed her lips. "Yeah, back when Carl was messin' with 'em all the time. Back when he should've been doing other things around here."

"Hey, ya can't tame the boilin' blood of a warrior," said Carl with a wink. "And look there, Seevie. Got my name on it."

"Never too late for glory," she rasped.

Cyrus wheeled the bot around some to show its movement. He caught the shine of Leslie's green twinkling orbs. A moment of delight.

Which soon turned to shock.

With unrestrained momentum, the bot wedged its arrowhead beneath the toolchest Gerald was using as a rampart. Its flipper then caught a caster and the whole assembly began an erratic spin. Gerald quickly side-stepped to one side, back to the other, trying to keep himself between the toolchest and Cyrus' rebellious robot.

"Whoa now, Nellie," yelled Carl.

"Do something, Cy," implored Leslie.

Frantically, Cyrus worked the knobs and switches of his controller, but nothing worked. His bot had moved the chest in the shape of an ampersand. It then dislodged itself and meted out a thunderous blow against its side, leaving a deep indentation of punctured dots.

Gerald slowly crept away from the toolchest, both eyes leerily fixed on the robot. Cyrus disabled his remote. He eased over to his bot, ready to skip at the faintest flinch, knowing full well its spurious tendencies.

The hammer's head was inches from the chest, ostensibly content with its exhibition of power and defiance. Cyrus carefully reached his arm underneath his bot and killed the orange switch.

"Sakes alive, that sucker has one hella thumper," said Carl.

"Yes it does," added Seevie insipidly, arms folded.

Gerald bayed with delight. "Whatcha call that thing, Cyrus? Cujo?"

"It just somehow went berserk," apologized Cyrus, though not surprised. "Sorry. I think I can bang out that dent?"

"Hey," said Carl, "don't worry about the dent, Cy. That's nothing but a day in the life around the shop. Ain't that right, Seevie?"

"Seen worse."

"Look, every bag of peanuts has a few cracked shells," said Carl.

Leslie leaned into Cyrus and whispered, "What the hell does that even mean?"

"Look, we just need to find the root of the problem," continued

Carl, "before you put 'er in the decagon."

"That won't be happening today," said Seevie emphatically. "You got a plane to catch in a few hours and we've got to close this place down. Plus, we gotta check to see if Gerald's pacemaker's still tickin'." Her cackle was long and gravelly.

"Nothin' a few at the tavern can't fix. Nice meetin' ya, Cyrus."

"You too, Gerald," replied Cyrus, "sorry about the scare."

"Was a rodeo man once. That ain't nothin' compared." He gave a chuckle on his way out.

"On the subject of these robots," continued Seevie to Carl, "I was going through the last of the day's emails and saw an announcement come in. Robot combatics, something on those lines, dates and such. Might want to check it on the plane, which is where you need to be heading. Right now."

"Yeah, Uncle Carl," said Leslie, "you don't want to miss your flight. Like last time. And the time before."

"Alright, OK," yielded Carl. "I'm going."

"So, where's the tropical vacation this year?" Leslie asked, as they walked back to the office.

"El Salvador. But vacation nothing. Goin' down there to build a water storage facility with my mission group. Sweatin' and gettin' my hands dirty. Like usual. But I gotta say, the locals do make a fine horchata de morro."

CHAPTER 29

"Not half bad," said Leslie. The two were sitting across from each other at Lucy's, sipping milk shakes and waiting for the rest of their order. Cyrus got the banana pancakes; Leslie went with a Rueben sandwich and fries. They were the only customers at the nine o'clock hour. A mainly dark, empty highway stretched in both directions beyond their windowed booth. Occasionally, headlights would approach, then pass, and the two would watch the fleeting lights tail away in the distance—Leslie one way, Cyrus the other.

Their conversation eased in and out of subjects, like the merits and drawbacks of social media and whether or not Cyrus would ever get a FlapYap account (he swore never), the eventual obsolescence of clowns at circuses (they both agreed clowns elicited fear, not joy), and if peanut butter was better than hazelnut spread (very far apart on this one.) They discussed people they knew, who was right for whom, who needed to chill and stop all the drama. Cyrus was enjoying his time with Leslie. After the terror caused by "that bot," a little time to chill was a good thing.

"Cy, I hope you're not too worried about what happened in Uncle Carl's shop."

"Well, I didn't mean to rough up his toolchest, but I'm glad it was there for protection. For Gerald. But if something like that chest had a two-thousand RPM spinning-sawblade, and I'm not able to control this thing of mine, then what? It'll be toast. And so will I. Extra crispy."

"I have confidence you'll figure it out," said Leslie.

Cyrus slouched into his booth and plopped his feet on the opposite bench next to her. Along the cold highway he watched a car zoom by with one headlight out. Its obsolescence triggered something. *Missing! What am I missing?*

Cyrus suddenly came to an upright jerk, whip cream splashing from his glass. He snatched his phone from the table. *That email Seevie mentioned! Maybe it's the one I've been waiting for.*

Leslie stared at him with perplexity. Her straw dangled from her mouth. Cyrus launched his emails.

From: The Robot Relay

To: Cyrus Hampstead

Subject: ComBot Dates Slated—and a Major Announcement.

Dear Faithful ComBotants:

Welcome to the qualifying rounds for the twenty-eighth annual ComBot tournament. After some delay, ComBot28 is pleased to announce its host locations by region. This email offers robot-ready contestants the opportunity to secure their spots in the preliminary rounds. For entry information, click on your region. See below for dates, locations, fees, and registration requirements.

Cyrus clicked on the link to his region. A bulletin popped

up.

Round 1: Crags Claw Business Park. March 21, Saturday. One-day event. Free Parking. Contest fee: $300.

Round 2: Sterling Woods Industrial Complex. April 18, Saturday. One-day event. $10 Parking. Contest fee: $325.

Round 3 (Final qualifying round): May 24. Exact Location TBA. Stay Tuned!

Come prepared and be prepared—for destruction!

"Here we go. Sweet," cried Cyrus. "Hey, what's a Crags Claw?"

"Not sure, why?"

"That's where the first round of the prelims take place. Some business park called Crags Claw."

"Cool, so they've given you a time and place," said Leslie holding out her hand. "Let me see. Crags Claw...what a dumb name. I'll find out where it is." Cyrus slid over his phone.

"Looks like it's no more than eighty miles away. Southeast. And Sterling Woods, that seems to be just a little further away, opposite direction."

"Definitely Brown Toro territory. I guess I'll find out where the third round is, at some point. If I make it to the third round, that is."

"Trust me, you'll make it. I'd love to go with you, Cy, but the school play will still be going on that time in March. I'm committed to sticking through to the last curtain. Then that weekend in April the fam's heading to Charleston for spring break. Oh, and we fly to Denver for a wedding in May, not sure exactly when." She slurped the last of her milkshake. "I need to stop living such a busy life, go full hermit."

"Maybe go full monk first, ease into it a bit," said Cyrus.

"Nah. Too quiet."

"And being a hermit isn't?"

"At least hermits get to talk to the birds and squirrels."

Cyrus spun his straw into his milkshake and thought about it. "Guess you're right. Anyway, thanks for considering it. You've done a lot for me already, Leslie. I mean, you found me the meat pulverizer, found out about sponsorship rates, you even got me that deal with your uncle. Oh, and you brought me the cute little elm tree. Thanks for being there, you know, helping me out with everything. I wouldn't have been able to do those things by myself, like, I don't think I would've even known where to begin."

Leslie continued reading his phone. She looked up, squeezing his hand. "I loved doing it. And I've really enjoyed being with you these last few months, you know that, right? It's not just because you *needed* those things done."

"I know. It's just that...well..."

"Cyrus, you don't always have to say what's on your mind, you know. Sometimes it's nice to hear, but I get it. I get you."

"It's just that everything you've done for me has meant a lot. Regardless of the outcome. And when ComBot comes around, if I make it that far, which sometimes I have serious reservations about, then maybe you can come to that, too."

"Don't worry, you'll make it back to ComBot. I'm certain about that. And as far as it goes, when it does happen, I'll do everything in my power to be there." Her eyes sparkled bright. "I've always wanted to go. I'm a lifer, remember?" Her attention returned to his phone.

Cyrus watched as she read. "Those smaller contests I've done before. They're really no big deal. Competition…eh, some of them just average, just depends. But ComBot, that's a whole different story."

"I understand," she said tersely, her eyes intently scanning his phone. Cyrus was amazed at how her brain could simultaneously retrieve and process two discrete modes of information—listening to him and reading the phone—without missing a beat. For him, multitasking was a fallacy.

"Besides, I'd most likely have to drive Brown Toro to the local events, and I know how much you like the road passing below your feet," he said as he followed the taillights of a truck as it faded into the night.

"Good point."

"And the bridges, with all that water below."

"Uh-huh, bridges."

"And don't forget the tunnels. Long, narrow tunnels," Cyrus said teasingly.

"Tunnels, uh-huh." Her response was short and sober.

His eyes flipped from the road to Leslie. She looked as if she'd just seen a tractor trailer overturn on the highway. She slid back his phone.

"What is it?" he questioned apprehensively.

"You may find this interesting. This major announcement."

After more than twenty years of chasing and fulfilling his dream, current ComBot champion (MegaBot), Ray Dokestout, will be putting his fighting robots and his competitive spirit to rest after this summer's ComBot28. Mr. Dokestout has been exemplary champion and a pillar of the combat robotics' community, introducing the sport to countless individuals who have aspired to join the fighting robot ranks by viewing his Web tutorials, instruction bibles, and winning ways. With hundreds of battles under his belt (and operating countless name-sake robots) Mr. Dokestout's pedigree is second to none. Four championships in the MicroBot weight division; five in the MacroBot category; and almost twice as many (9) in his favorite, the MegaBot division, where he is a three-time consecutive title holder.

Mr. Dokestout comes to this juncture in his life with a heavy heart, but with little regret. "It's been a great ride," says Mr. Dokestout, "one I wouldn't trade for anything. I'm living proof that with a positive attitude and strong work ethic, even some-one not as talented can be nearly successful. Knowing how important my involvement in the sport has been to so many people is the reason I'll be setting my sights on one last ComBot championship. Once victorious, my total wins for all my Doke-a-bots will number two-hundred and fifty. Therefore, I've crowned my latest and final bot, Doke-a-250. I've saved the best for last. Can't wait for the honor to battle one last time. See you at Com-Bot28."

That's right, ComBot enthusiasts: Ray Dokestout will look to record an unparalleled 250 wins if he notches another ComBot title. It will by far be the most ever recorded in the annals of the sport. If ComBot had a Hall of Fame, Mr. Dokestout would certainly have his own wing in the complex.

Fans, stay tuned for the exact date for this summer's ComBot28, and don't forget to put it on your calendar. Happy battling!

"Who's got the Rueben?" asked the server.

CHAPTER 30

As Cyrus waited for his bot's battery to charge, he went over to the small rectangular window and looked out. The basement was cold, very cold, which made him wonder about the outside temperature. *Twelve, thirteen degrees?* It felt at least that cold as he left school that afternoon. Add the wind-chill factor and the thought of venturing outside made him shudder.

But he had no choice. Cyrus had to go out into the elements. Once his battery was charged, he'd get right back after it. Time was precious.

Cyrus both loved and loathed winter. In his region, December was always a craps shoot; either an uninvited blizzard blew in or Autumn kept lingering, one being just as likely as the other. But by this date in mid-February, it was almost a certainty—the frosty heavens would unleash their offerings many times over. By Cyrus' count, there had been five major snowfalls. Oh, how he loved the mesmerizing blanket of the quiet snow. But after so much of the white stuff his assessment of it began to change.

Yes, he made over two thousand dollars plowing snow for neighbors up and down the country roads. It was time-consuming work, but relatively mindless. Slip the chains on the tires, line up Brown Toro's mount with the guides of the plow, bolt and lock it in place, connect the wires, and fifteen minutes later he was captaining the snowplow express, looping the steering wheel around like a cowboy's lasso, grinding treads through slush and ice as he kept mindful attention on the physics of a one-

ton machine as it scraped and pushed around mother nature's dumping.
Pulling into prearranged accounts, driveways owned by the Primeaux's,
Giuffre's, and Myers'. Collecting payments, working hard, watching the
digits rise ever higher on his Iron Mill Bank ledger.

Still, he couldn't wait for it to be over. He dreamt of springtime.
Spring meant warmth. In spring, he could train with "that bot" without
his limbs succumbing to frost bite. In spring, he wouldn't have to devote
so much of the available daylight hours to working Brown Toro like a
mule in the tundra. Cyrus loved spring. In spring, the earth shows what
it's capable of overcoming, tree buds awaken, bulbs emerge as yellow and
pink flowers, the creatures of the creek realize their rock caves are useless
and come out of their hovels. Spring yielded more daylight, more time
to prep for the prelims. The battles would be knocking. Spring was robot
fighting season.

Winter: school in the day, two hours to twilight once he returned
home, frost and snow and freezing hands, always freezing. Winter equaled
dreariness, darkness. For Cyrus, winter was the enemy of time, as much
an adversary as Ray Dokestout. Winter meant an hour and a half a day
training in a cold carport, and maybe a few more hours (possibly) on the
weekends. Since much of his weekend was spent with Leslie, time literally
flew by.

In winter, he had to take what he could get out of those small
chunks of the clock. Man of La Mancha was coming in spring, and the
play butted up against the first prelim at Crags Claw Business Park. His

first true test.

Time was indeed precious to Cyrus Hampstead.

The snow hadn't quite reached the top of the small rectangular window, having stopped just short of the upper frame. Looking out, Cyrus had but a sliver of a sightline which paralleled the accumulated snow in his backyard. He wiped a small bit of frost off the glass. Because of the dirt on the other side, and the plumes of snowflakes being pushed by a gusting wind, the bare-limbed trees in the distance appeared in a gauzy haze. The world looked cold. Very cold.

He was dreading the thought of it. The sun was lowering, the wind was picking up. *I can't stay inside. Nothing doing. Gotta get right out there in it. Just deal. Man up, Cyrus!*

He looked over at that silver, arrowhead-shaped bot, thinking of the last few days of smashing things in his converted carport, obliterating toys bought at yard sales, pummeling old equipment he found discarded at school, crushing the curbside leftovers of people's trash, taking it to just about anything and everything that could bear the brunt of the mighty tenderizer. He knew "that bot" was his last shot, his only shot, the one and only robotic entity to his name. No backups, nothing on standby, just "that bot" and a quest for fifty grand and a lifelong family dream. *It's got to hold up. That's it. Wedge, spinner, flipper, ax, cutter bot…any of those coming its direction. Beat them all down. Including that Doke-a-250 thing. Ray Fucking Dokestout!*

As far as "that bot" behaving like a good little robot and not going wildcat rogue, the addition of new components and adjustments Cyrus made on the fly seemed to have done the trick. *Thankfully. Maybe the thing actually likes being in the cold.* He stared out into the snowline, contemplating. *Crazy as it is.*

A robin landed a few yards from the window. It trotted in the snow, pecked around, found something of interest, burrowed down, then emerged to shake off the powder. Watching the bird, Cyrus thought about a name for his fighting bot. He'd been hoping one might appear organically—swoosh, from the heavens, then permanently heat-sealed on—but every time a name surfaced he reconsidered it. *How about I paint it red and call it "Robin's Revolt?" Nah. Too cheesy.* He was always left with "that bot."

Cyrus wondered what the robin thought of the cold, the snow. *Do birds just deal with it, like the guys working in Carl's shop?* Having retuned there several times over the winter, he noticed how the large bay doors were always open, the elements encroaching on their workspace. He was certain hands were numb and raw by day's end. *Do they just get used to it?* He wondered about ice fishers in Minnesota. *How do their hands even bait a line, much less grapple with a fish? Do they too just deal?* He looked closely at his own hands, light-purple, dry, and slightly more functional than ice sickles, and reflected on the number of times he had to run warm water over them upstairs or hover them over the basement's small space heater until they could at least wiggle. Cyrus considered adaptation, the ability to adjust to any environment. *That's all it is? Adaptation. Otherwise, how would people living in the cold be able to hook a fish—or fix a transmission.*

As he contemplated auto mechanics and Minnesotans, he realized he was deliberately trying to avoid the outside. The battery charger had turned green; he was wasting time. Trivial matters—they had no place. He had to get to work and train "that bot." If he stood there looking out the window too long, thinking of this and that, watching the robin hunt for food, avoiding the inevitable, his anxiety would prick up. He could hear his father's measured voice, "sedation may be seductive, but it never yields." The man always kept busy. And he never seemed anxious.

He unclipped the battery from the charger, inserted it into "that bot" on the workbench, and cranked the hoist to lower it. Mid-suspension, his phone rang. A cartoon lizard holding a hockey stick. He hit the speaker.

"Blake."

"You working?"

"Working, yeah, but not plowing. Hopefully that's the last of the snow for the season. I'm getting ready to train with what daylight's left. An hour, maybe."

"You're in luck. I'm coming over. Scored a bonanza at a thrift shop in town. Practically giving away old remote-controlled cars and trucks. They're all beat to shit, so they won't mind what's gonna happen to them. At least they work. I tested them. Hey, what the hell's a bonanza and why the hell did I say it? The shit I come up with."

"I think it was an old TV show, about a ranch, so I guess the bonanza referred to the number of cows they had stinking up the place. But come on over. You can run 'em and I'll smash 'em."

"Alright. Make sure your driveway's plowed. I'm coming in hot with toys for bots," he shouted before disconnecting.

Cyrus loaded the bot on the toboggan (another yard sale find) at the base of the stairs, chocked the wheels, strapped it down, headed up the stairs, set the chin-up bar (again, yard sale) between the two brackets on the door frames, clamped the winch down in the center, plugged the cord into the socket, flipped the switch, and waited at the top of the stairs. No more than two minutes, which was an efficient use of time.

Blake arrived in his parent's station wagon, skidding and plowing into a snowbank at the end of his driveway. He squeezed through a narrow opening between door and snowbank, wearing only a sweater.

"I see your driving's improved," teased Cyrus. "And aren't you freezing?" Cyrus was layered three flannels deep, plus a thermal coat.

"Eh, I'll adapt," said Blake. He went around to his wagon's hatch and opened it. Several remote-controlled toy vehicles spilled out into the snow.

"Whoa, look at all of those. What the hell, you've got dozens. So, what do I owe you?" asked Cyrus.

"Receipts right here," said Blake, pulling out a slip from his pocket. "Oh, add a tenner for the batteries." Blake tossed him a package of D batteries. "No delivery charge. This time."

"Thanks, I'll instant transfer it. Look, had you driven all these over on old Vennari's bike, then *maybe* I could see a delivery charge coming into play."

"Yeah, right. My legs never recovered from that day."

They loaded up the toys in a box. As they carried them into the carport, Cyrus could see an eagerness on Blake's face. A pleasure to come. A pleasure from destruction. Cyrus knew the look.

"Tell the truth, Blake. You know you love seeing this go down," said Cyrus, pointing to his primed robot.

"That I do. Yes indeedy-reedy, I do."

Three weeks. That's how long it took for Cyrus to obliterate the entire thrift store collection, not to mention all the other stuff laying around. Three weeks of filling up his recycling bin and hauling it to the end of the driveway, then bringing it back empty for another week's worth of shattered cars and trucks. Cyrus would have Blake drive hard at his bot (on several occasions, it was Tonmoy operating the toys), or stop tight, or verge quickly to the side, anything to simulate a robot on a kill mission. Sometimes he'd tell his friends to freewheel them around until dusk, bombing the pint-sized vehicles in as if on a frozen rope, or skidding them to the side, or maneuvering them in frenetic counter/clockwise circles. Any blazing movements so that Cyrus could perfect his turnouts, timing, slants, angles, reverses, positioning. Then, when all the chaotic steering was over, or when darkness prevailed, or when Cyrus' fingers had stiffened to uselessness, or when the itch for atomization became too overwhelming, Cyrus would give the signal, a lowering of a thumb: it was time. That virile titanium extension would rain down and send up a plastic explosion.

The next day, Cyrus would sweep up the debris. Then they would do it again. Different toy, same outcome.

Three weeks. Three weeks to perfect his operational skill. To enhance his maneuverable defenses. To master the attacking execution of that once industrial meat tenderizer.

Three weeks.

And Cyrus was ready.

March 21, Round One, was just around the corner.

CHAPTER 31

The earth's orbit finally forced a real rise in the mercury. When Cyrus checked his weather app, the report said it was going to be the hottest day of the year so far. Well above average. High temperatures he could stand; those in the single digits that turned his basement into an ice chest, he had problems with.

The basement was his place of seclusion, his insularity from the world. In the basement, worries abate, things got done. A place for quiet mental focus, a space devoted to robotic fine-tuning and improvements. Repairs and fixing issues. The basement is a world unto itself, and he could see why his father loved the place—no one was there to make demands on you; only those you made on yourself. The tools, they have their own pull, their own demand to be held, but generally they were reposed, sedentary. That is, unless they were being used, in which case the basement could be a very noisy place. Still, it was his space. Their space.

In the basement there is a small rectangular window, and unless one looks outside the window, only then would they know about the outside world. Cyrus went to the window. He wanted to see for himself what the weather report stated. The heat outside had fogged the glass, so he grabbed a cloth and wiped it off. He dreamily watched a calm breeze push spores of pollen through the air. Near the woods, stubborn pockets of snow long that had been sheltered by shade had finally withdrawn into the underground aquifer. Merely a month ago, there was an icy pile.

What a harsh winter. Brutal. Gone now. Hasta la vista. At least it covered two of my tournament expenses. A straight up even deal, plowing for fighting. Maybe I should name that bot Snowplow…Nah. Can't jinx it now when everything's working. Because we're still in the fight. One more tourney win and ComBot28. Damn, I got lucky. Seriously lucky. I thought I'd be licking my wounds by now but here we are. Lute in the bank, mojo on my side, heading to the third round.

Cyrus walked back to the workbench and to "that bot." He wondered where he should begin. After two tournaments, the bot showed a good deal of battle scaring. He would need to solder some stitches, smooth out some rough spots, fortify the damage to the flipper. But those projects would have to wait; he had only a half hour before he was off to school.

In the meantime, Cyrus went to work stripping both his sponsors' decals, which had taken major lickings. Little remained of Carl's monkey, and "Smitty's" had been reduced to one "t" and a lampshade. As he heat-blasted the logos, the scent of roasted coffee made its way downstairs, competing with the smell of burning plastic rising from his bot. He could hear his mother's banging and clanging, and he knew she'd soon be calling him up for breakfast. Her new obsession. She'd been harping about him losing weight, not getting enough sleep, and other problematic deficiencies she'd noticed. *Maybe all this fighting has been wearing me down. Eh, I'll relax when it's all over. Gotta keep pushing, keeping the mojo going.*

"Cy? Come on, breakfast." The decals could wait. His third-round tournament was a few weeks away, anyway.

In the kitchen, his mother studied him as he sat down to pan-cakes—blueberry jam and a tall glass of milk. Cyrus didn't look up. He waited for the words which were certain to come.

"Cyrus, do you recall what I told you about the sun in winter? How you should get some of it while it's out."

"Uh-huh. I remember."

"Well, the sun is certainly out now."

"Uh-huh. Point?"

"Point is you've had too much of it. Just look at what it's done to your face and neck. Look how red you are!"

"My mirror wasn't working this morning for some reason."

"Watch it."

"Mom, a couple of weeks ago you told me to get some sun. So, that's what I did. That's why I went to the park with Leslie."

"Yeah, well, guess what? Now I'm telling you to apply sunblock. Which is what you should've been doing all along."   It seemed to Cyrus that his mother's promotion of vitamin D from the sun had made an abrupt about-face to the caustic nature of its over-exposure. Deriding his sickly-white skin one day, upbraiding his red face the next. He just couldn't keep up. Listening to the virtues of applying a moisture-rich sun-block sent his pancakes and blueberry jam into his stomach at a faster than normal clip. He gulped down his milk and aimed for the kitchen door.

"Running late," he said as he grabbed his backpack off the counter.

She stopped in front of him. "Cy, I know I've been on you lately, and I'm sorry. That's what mothers do." She wiped a smudge of jam from his cheek. "I thought you were going to get yourself a haircut? It's a mess."

"I will, Mom."

His mother squared him with a stony, worrisome gaze.

"You know I worry about you, that's all. I hope you understand that. I've been through enough worry to last both of our lifetimes. And with you driving all that distance in Brown Toro, and not getting enough sleep, it makes me more than a little concerned."

"I understand. I get it," said Cyrus.

She shoved a sandwich in his backpack and plastered him with a kiss. "I love you. I'm proud of you. And put on sunblock. Please."

At lunchtime, Cyrus, Tonmoy and Blake sat outside eating their sandwiches. Cyrus had his typical concoction of peanut butter and banana, Blake ate tuna on rye, and Tonmoy nibbled on roust chicken on ruti. All were dressed in jeans and long shirts. All had failed to adjust to the change of weather.

With the high-noon sun beaming directly down on them, it didn't take long for the boys to notice that the newly installed picnic table made of recycled plastic composite generated a lot more heat than the old wooden table that was there a month ago. But at least with the new bench they wouldn't end up with splinters or be compelled to read odes of love carved by students from generation's past.

"Cy, where's your third rounder?" asked Tonmoy.

"Voerrs Ravine. That's north and to the east a little. In the mountains."

"Day trip?" asked Blake.

"Nah, too far. I'm staying the night at a cabin Faye Smith and her husband own up there, you know, my investors. She's giving me the keys. It's Green Fly country."

"Nasty little buggers," said Blake.

"That's why they lead the conference."

"What are *you* talking about?" asked Blake.

"The Voerrs Ravine Green Flies. The hockey team plays in the same civic center I'll be fighting in. What are *you* talking about?"

"I'm talking about Tabanus Nigrovittatus, the flying insect commonly known as the Greenhead Fly," said Blake with an air of haut. "They can suck the blood right outta you. Nasty feeders, especially the females before they lay their eggs. I did my research. They love the heat, too."

"Yeah, well I don't," said Tonmoy. "Whose idea was it to eat outside, anyway?" He eyed his sandwich as if the spices inside might be partially to blame. "I'm burning up here."

"My idea," replied Cyrus. "Mom's been getting on me about being in the sun."

"Looks like you've followed her advice so far," said Blake. "You look like Hellboy."

"That's what she's getting on me about, too much of it." Cyrus reached into his pocket for sunscreen and applied some to his face, without bothering to rub it in. His face was a mottle of red and white.

"Now all you need is the stubbed horns," said Tonmoy.

"Fantastic. A few weeks ago she told me I looked like Casper. I don't even know this Casper dude."

"That's a cartoon ghost, Cy, many moons removed" said Tonmoy. "We even had that in Bangladesh."

"Everyone knows Casper, man. The friendly ghost," said Blake, tossing the crust of his sandwich to some pigeons stalking behind a nearby tree. "Where *you* been?"

"Clearly not watching old cartoons," replied Cyrus.

"It would be so hot in Dhaka, that's all we would do sometimes. Sit inside and watch old cartoons. Either that or help my father cook, which would be worse than being outside with the spices he favors."

"Well, I watched cartoons because I liked them. And I was lazy. OK, just plain lazy, and I'm friggen' good with that," said Blake, throwing his arms up. Cyrus noticed that the loose fat below Blake's triceps was about as pasty as his own face before it turned into a beet.

"No argument here," said Tonmoy. He went to hurl the remainder of his sandwich to the rabidly cooing pigeons, but Blake intercepted with a stiff arm.

"You crazy?" Blake interjected, "you wanna kill those pigeons?

"Maybe. Vultures gotta eat, too" said Tonmoy, heaving the heat-bomb over Blake's shoulder. "Now they're spiced just right."

"Whatever. Let's talk dance here," said Blake, changing the subject.

"Who's in?"

"In what?" asked Cyrus and Tonmoy simultaneously. They both rose from the bench and pulled their clothes from their sweaty legs and butts. "Aren't you hot, Blake? That table's like sixty centigrade," said Tonmoy.

"I'll adapt," said Blake, remaining seated. "But let's not skirt the issue, because skirts are the issue. Well, really dresses are, but you get my point here."

"No, we don't," said Cyrus. He took a careful sip of root beer and spit it out.

"Prom, gentlemen. Prom," Blake said.

"Oh right, prom," said Cyrus plaintively. He sat down. He turned the base of his root beer on its axis, lost in thought.

"What is it, like a few weeks away," asked Tonmoy, "because in Bangladeshi time, that's an eternity."

"It's not a few weeks away, its two weeks away, Tonmoy, which is not an eternity," said Blake stiffly, "in fact, it's an oncoming locomotive. One that we must jump on, that is, if we want to go. You have to find a date, and that said date has to find a dress, arrange for a stylist…by the way, this comes from an overbearing mother…and then there's all the coordinating, the ride sharing and stuff."

Prom, an upperclassmen's entree into the social realm, a rite of passage, a couple's journey. Cyrus knew it was upcoming. It shrouded over him like a harbor's fog. As Cyrus prepared and competed in his robotic events, the dance formal hovered on the radar screen, unable to be seen through the harbor's fog. For a girl knocking on the door of womanhood (or in Leslie's case, kicking it in) he figured it to be a meaningful, memorable night. Now that Blake brought it up, he had to confront this very fact: prom was the same day as ComBot's final preliminary round.

"Remind me," inquired Tonmoy, "is this the dance where we have to get dressed in that black and white outfit?"

"Yeah, Tonmoy, a tuxedo. And getting that takes time too. Going to some shop to have all the fittings and adjustments, all of that," said Blake. "Again, overbearing mother."

"Well, what's your deal, Blake?" asked Tonmoy. "Who are you asking to prom?"

"Depends on you two," said Blake.

"I'm not taking you," laughed Tonmoy. "Not a chance, ask Cyrus. He's more your suit."

"Dumbass, I'm talking about who you'll be going with, if at all," shot Blake. "If Cy takes Leslie, which I assume he will, I'll start knocking on Roz's door. If that fails to work out, then whoever goes with you, miracles aside, I'll aim my sights that direction. Get it? Because I'm not doing this alone. I'm weak. I'd collapse under the pressure."

Cyrus stopped twirling his can. His sullen face caught their attention.

"What's wrong, Cy?" asked Tonmoy, "you look like you've seen a Casper."

"Prom's the same time as the last ComBot prelim. The very day, in fact" he said morosely.

"Crepes and crap-ola," said Blake. He lifted himself from the picnic bench and fanned his chest, pumping his shirt in and out. "Now it's really getting hot."

"Well…what's the verdict, Cy?" prodded Tonmoy, placing one foot on the picnic bench.

"Not sure," he replied. "It's just…uh…" Cyrus dumped the rest of his root beer on the ground. The pigeons feinted in clumsily, uncertain whether the brown liquid was worth the effort. When the lunch bell blared, the commotion sent the birds in flight. "…I just know I have to keep going. I can't stop fighting now."

In the halls of Stafford P. Ellicott High, Cyrus was garnering more attention than usual. Word was getting out—much more than the year before—that he was on the cusp of another key victory. A berth in a prestigious event which might earn him a good deal of "Benjamins," a term he overheard once or twice in hallway whisper.

Typically, Cyrus flew under the radar. But given the conversational brush-fire high school students are prone to, and the fact that he made it to last year's semifinal, kids began mentioning his name, pointing him out. He could feel their eyes on him when he walked the halls; it wasn't just the beautiful girl beside him they were staring at. Even the boys who wanted him to join their robotics club approached several times, inquiring what it was like in the big arena (Cyrus figured they had dreams of competing as well.) Cyrus lied: "No biggie." He didn't care for all the fuss.

"Hey, Cy, listen," said Tonmoy before they parted ways, "don't sweat it. Leslie will understand."

"I don't know…she's been talking a lot lately about dresses. Like what color she looks good in. And shoe styles, too. Like I know anything about that."

"Really? Well, there's always…"

"Next year."

"Correct, my friend. You still got time to think it over some. Maybe not an eternity, but still."

I'll need an eternity to get the courage to tell Leslie prom's a no-go.

CHAPTER 32

Later that night, despite his exhaustion, Cyrus lay restless in bed. He tossed the covers and shifted from side to side and shuffled around his pillows, stacking and restacking them against the headboard as if they were Jenga pieces. When that didn't solve the problem, he piled them like a litter of kittens. The result was a strained neck.

There he was, convulsed by nettlesome sheet-tangled anxiety. Leslie had texted stating she was out to dinner with her family and wouldn't be back until late. That she would call before she went to bed. He waited for her call lathered in a thin sweat.

When he finally heard his phone ring, Cyrus skyrocketed out of bed. He fumbled to get his sweatpants on, one leg struggling to find a slot as the other bounced for balance. The moment he hit the speaker and heard Leslie's "Hey," Mongrel came cantering out from under the bed and knocked his foot. His attempt to brace himself against his desk failed and he thudded helplessly to the floor.

"Mongrel!" he cursed. The cat jumped on the chair to lick his paws, oblivious.

"No, it's Leslie. Good guess though," he heard over the speaker.

Cyrus reached for his phone. "Hi. I know. It's just that…never mind." He gathered himself and sat on his bed. "Listen, Leslie, I wanted to talk to you about something," he stuttered awkwardly, "well, you know how…well, there's this thing coming up…"

"Yes, Cy, it's called prom."

"Yeah, prom."

"Look, I've already had an offer, which I accepted."

Cyrus' heart dropped. He felt the torture of hundreds of bullets, the aching of sharp, steel knives, the amalgamation of thousands of lovers who have felt such pains in their crushed hearts. His stomach churned to cement as he gasped for air that wasn't there.

"My little brother's taking me," she laughed.

Cyrus was caught for a second, a constriction of his vessels. Then he smiled. Wide. His stomach settled as his blood flowed back to normal. "Good one, Les. I guess you know?"

"Tonmoy happened to mention something."

"Tonmoy's a friggen' bonehead."

"Well, he didn't really. You know, not really, it's like he mentioned something subtle, like vaguely. He had this, you know, look in his eyes like he didn't want me to know something. I could tell he was trying to hide his cards."

"Sounds more like he was blabbing his mouth."

"Look, I'm really good at prying information out of people when I know they're trying to avoid telling me something. It's a gift. That's why we get along so well. You're an open book. I don't have to fish around for what you're thinking."

I'm an open book? "Yeah, what am I thinking now?" he asked teasingly.

"That you love and appreciate me."

He had but one word. "Yes."

"See, open book. Because I love and appreciate you, too. More than you know. Which is why it's no big deal."

Cyrus lay back on his bed and gazed out the window with a full heart. A firefly flittered through the willow tree's branches, passing aimlessly through. He watched the firefly as he did those trailing headlights that night at Lucy's diner. "It's just that I thought you really wanted to go. You know, you were asking a lot about dress colors, and shoe styles."

"Cyrus, do you remember when I told you I'd be going to Denver for a wedding next month. Well, that's what that's about. That wedding is the same day as prom. So, I wouldn't be able to go, anyway. We can do prom and homecoming and all those other dances next year, but this year you need to focus on one thing. Getting back to ComBot. That's your goal. That's the one thing, and I know this from the bottom of my heart just as much as you know it, you need to do. It's what you *have* to do. For many reasons. This whole thing has been called on you, Cyrus, and you've accepted that calling. And nothing, I mean nothing, no dance or anything else, is going to get in the way of that. Nothing."

CHAPTER 33

AREA TEEN SEEKS COMBOT REDEMPTION

BY: KELVIN K. RUSSO
BEACON STAFF REPORTER

Some say lighting never strikes twice. This may be true, but local teen Cyrus Hampstead is hoping to prove that saying wrong. In fact, he's looking to capture a double dose of that energy and harness it within his very own metallic fighting fortress as he heads to ComBot28.

For the second straight year, Cyrus Hampstead has been granted entry into the nation's premiere combat robotic competition, the illustrious contest with a grand prize purse now of $50,000. The Twenty-eighth annual event takes place in late July and telecasts in November.

Last year, the Stafford P. Ellicott High School junior and his fighting robot, Spiral Cyclone, made it to ComBot27's semifinal match before losing to the most decorated competitor in the sport, Ray Dokestout. The contest was neck and neck until Cyrus and his prized robot fell by way of knockout, a defeat which saw the total obliteration of Cyrus' machine.

Although Spiral Cyclone, a bot designed and built by Cyrus and his father, the late U.S. Army Lt. Major Francis Hampstead, had met its ultimate demise, this fighting season has seen its replacement. Cyrus' newest incarnation is one he refers to as "that bot" (for competition purposes, it fights under the moniker "Smitty/Carl," the names of his two sponsors.)

Unlike Cyrus' previous machine, whose primary weapon was a pivoting arm endowed with a tornadic circular saw, "Smitty/Carl" utilizes a destructive titanium cube positioned atop a steel armature—a creative use for what once was, states Cyrus, "an industrial meat mallet." Another notable distinction between the two is appearance: whereas the previous robot was shaped like a shell-backed amphibian, the new robot best resembles a sleek arrowhead.

According to Cyrus, the fighting machine was built some years ago by his father; all it needed was the final menacing touch. "One day I discovered the bot tucked into a cubby behind a toolchest," recalls Cyrus. "It seemed to be in good shape and only needed a few repairs and parts. My girlfriend found the main weapon for it. After that, I just practiced with its movement, delivery of attack and fighting execution. I guess you could say most of the hard stuff was already done. Now I get to do the fun stuff, fighting."

This year, the fighting hasn't been quite as easy as it was the previous season, where Cyrus ran the field leading up to ComBot27, conceding not a single fight. In all three tournaments he entered this year, "Smitty/Carl" suffered defeats. However, due to the round-robin formats, the pair was still able to advance through in the lead-up tournaments, prevailing in the MegaBot division.

Cyrus attributes the losses not so much to "Smitty/Carl's" mode of attack or his opponent's superior hardware, but to the unpredictable nature of his machine.

According to Cyrus, it has an ornery streak, like a "bad goat or something." He expands further: "I guess the thing has a mind of its own. That's the only way I can describe it. In the first tournament in March, I went to launch its flipper and instead it suddenly spun around and my opponent was right on it. Then in the April tournament, I went to fire down the hammer but the bot launched its flipper instead. Same thing in the May tournament last week. But I still made it to the finals, and there it actually worked out because I won the contest by an overturn. Like the bot knew better what to do than I did. I don't know, maybe it does. At least it came through in the clutch."

Cyrus was certain the hiccups he experienced were due to mechanical malfunctions, and not human errors at the remote controller. Cyrus claims he had practiced these maneuvers "hundreds of times" flawlessly; in battle, however, it was a different story. Nevertheless, he says, "he's happy to still be standing" and hopes to learn from the experience. "I'm still working on getting the kinks out."

Since March, Cyrus Hampstead and his meat-pulverizing bot have been traveling to nearby contests in his pickup truck, which he describes as an "ocean liner rust-bucket."

The teen's next stop is two months and two states away. It will be the final leg of a year-long journey that places him back in the thick of it as he battles the best-of-the-best in combat robotics at ComBot28. If you see his ocean liner rust-bucket on the local roads, give a few honks of support.

CHAPTER 34

From: Smitty's Lighting, Lamps & Shades
To: Cyrus Hampstead
Subject: Hooray!!!

My Dearest Cyrus,

Thank you so much for your nice letter. I am soooo happy you were able to stay at our mountain retreat (Horace calls it his castle in the pines) and spend time on the lake with your pole—yes, those squirmy things you men call fish really can be difficult to hook. It's why I stick to eating them and not touching them. I'm truly glad you had a wonderful time up there in Voerrs Ravine.

But what I'm really excited about, and what I'm jumping over my socks about (if I could jump) is how you pulled off another win. When your mother called me to say you'd be making another trip to combot, well I grabbed Horace by the shoulders and yelled, 'we're going to the big dance, H.' I don't have to tell you that Horace nearly collapsed from the excitement. I was worried I may have startled him too much. But at the moment I didn't care because the reality is that you are one step closer to your dream. A dream a long time coming, one older than your short years, one which began with your father. You should be so proud for what you've accomplished.

I've been hesitant to tell friends, family, neighbors about

the potential of Smitty's LLS being on a fighting robot, simply put, I didn't want to jinx it before you made it to combot (curses work like that, you know). Now I can't wait for July to come around and see what happens with this robot—Have you come up with a real name for it yet?!!!

I've already reached out the event organizers to run a combot promotion at our locations this summer, as a tie in. They're sending the paperwork over soon (We'll pay a small licensing fee) and they suggested you send a good pic of your robot to me (side facing with Smitty's logo of course) so I can make some banners and floor signs. Are you in, because guess what?—for each robo sale, you get 10% of profits. How's that for a business relationship?

Take good care of yourself Cyrus. Make sure you get plenty of rest and eat well, but not too well because everyone needs a treat now and then. If you need anything please let me know. We can't wait for summer.

Love and kisses,

Faye and Horace Smith

From: Carl Borowski
To: Cyrus Hampstead
Subject: ComBot28, here we come

Hey Cy,

You did it!! Again!!! ComBot28! When Les texted to say you took the last qualifier I almost cracked my nogg. I couldn't believe it. Congratulations. Big time. More to come.

Les said that last fight was brutal. A two wheeled spinner bar, holy jeepers. All I can say is you must have laid some serious hammer on that bot because those kind are nasty, especially when they come in like a pissed wild boar. Les also said you prob need me to look it over before ComBot. Some damage to the undercarriage? As long as G can weld it back, we'll be good. So bring it on in and we'll double check that swinger too. Friday is best.

I had a look at the website for ComBot28. I see your name is listed-still fighting under Smitty/Carl? How about Herculean Hammer? Thor's Thumper? And I see Doke-a-shit came thru too. No surprise there. Doka250? Straight demon it looks like. No joke, you seen the pic of it? If not let me explain...Two wheels, wide axel, two large titanium disks and both are toothed and spinning horizontally at an ungodly speed. But here's the kicker. Ray's got one of those disks rotating on the top, jutting outward, and the other one is spinning inches from the ground on the bottom, jutting out the other direction, so if the thing ever gets turned (from what I can tell it happened a lot in the prelims) the disks flip directions without missing a beat–the upper disk goes low, and the one that was skimming the ground goes top. A reversed polarity. And a damn good idea. And a damn asshole that guy is. But I didn't say that did I? But hey, if force meets force, like a giant hammer, you don't need me to tell you what could happen. In combat robotics you never know. That's why we fight.

Looking forward to hearing about ComBot and getting the Monkey Wrench some good pub. But it's not about that...I want Dokestout to snag his foot on a glacier crack and get dragged out to sea.

And hey, last thing. Can you believe the Chromes? Not ending up in last place in the conference. Talk about a miracle. Next year-contenders.

I could've been a contender!!!

See you in the shop.

Carl

CHAPTER 35

With a mid-July air stagnating around him, Cyrus took aim and delivered a blow. Direct hit. He watched as it twirled to the ground, leaving a splatter of blood on his palms.

Cyrus wasn't in the habit of taking his hand away from his controller. Certainly not in the week before ComBot28. Pulling his hand from the device was just begging for trouble, like a mountain climber who kicks out both feet to dangle by their fingertips. *Not good conditioning. Not smart.* The act made him uncomfortable, wary, especially considering "that bot" of his was already prone to misfires, mistakes, and misdeeds.

But what choice did he have. The mosquitos were simply not letting up.

One week before the biggest contest of his life, Cyrus was in his carport practicing a few maneuvers with his bot. Although they weren't specifically designed for Doke-a-250, he certainly envisioned them on Ray Dokestout's machine. In the "split-step beat-down," Cyrus races his bot forward, stops, rotates one direction with a slight slip, quickly reverses back the other way, then utilizes the backspin of momentum to deliver down a lethal hammer blow. Draw the opponent one way with a fake, counter against the grain, unleash the mallet. A simple yet effective combat maneuver designed to catch a horizontal spinner right at the edge of its blade.

Cyrus employed the "split-step beat-down" so often in the preliminary fights he was beginning to think he should patent it, an extravagantly boastful idea he immediately reconsidered. It was a repetitive tactic, one which might spell trouble. There were too many variables in robotic warfare, thousands in fact. Being turned upside down was a common occurrence, so Cyrus had begun practicing the counter to that dilemma: the "hammer handspring." A simultaneous activation of the arm swing for leverage and a reversing sidespin, and his bot was fully righted on four wheels. An absolutely necessary skill. Nevertheless, he had to acknowledge one crucial aspect of the sport: metal, even fortified metal, was metal nonetheless, and that could mean destruction for either side.

When he considered Doke-a-250, with its two reversable titanium frisbees, the prospect of a fireball did cross his mind. The thing would be coming in headstrong, regardless of its opponent's maneuvering or position.

As Cyrus orchestrated the maneuvers again, he envisioned the splat the hammer would make on the little flying vampires now attacking him. Their incessant hums and light tickles before penetration, it was driving him crazy. It seemed they instinctually knew when his hand was back on the remote, too. *Smart little bloodsuckers*. He smacked at another.

His carport was their destination of choice. And he was their fresh meat. *But why here? Weren't they more active at the creek, where they breed?* That thought alone made him wonder: *What's the creek like now? Is the water pushing hard? Had it crested above that dogleg section of knee-deep silt like it usually did in July?*

He would've enjoyed a visit to the creek. An hour-long excursion to take in the scent of the rich mud and dank fauna. And yes, knock a few mosquitos off and toss their languid bodies into the drink for the aquatic creatures to consume.

It wasn't like Cyrus was so busy training and preparing for what was probably his last run at ComBot that he couldn't allow himself *some* creek time. It was more an issue of access, at least for now. A new family was currently moving into the house across the lane, and he didn't want to seem the entitled, trespassing neighbor who traipses through *their* backyard and walks down *their* path, along *their* gateway to the creek. Not since the family was still hauling in their furniture from that mammoth truck parked in *their* driveway. Which made him wonder: *Are they getting their fair share of these damn mosquitos?*

A visit to the creek, at any rate, would have been a lonely venture. Gone were both Blake and Tonmoy on extended family vacations. Blake took west while Tonmoy departed east, to Dhaka. But really, it wasn't those two he was missing. It was Leslie.

While practicing the "split-step beat-down" and the "hammer handspring" and swatting all those mosquitos, all Cyrus could think about was Leslie. She'd been gone only two days—forty-eight hours of pining, agonizing loneliness which grew worse each hour and each minute.

Earlier in the week, Leslie had swung by to say goodbye before heading two states away to the south. There, she would have two weeks of intensive field hockey training courtesy of one of the school's well-heeled boosters, an anonymous figure who serendipitously paid the sizable expense for the entire Electron's varsity squad—room, board and coaches. Cyrus had little doubt Leslie was already exhausted by wind sprints and excessive strikes to her shins. But he hoped she was happy. And missing him as much as he was missing her.

He had a feeling it might turn out this way: her not being able to attend ComBot28. Again, he'd be alone at the winner-take-all, high-stakes event. He so badly wanted for her to be there with him, for physical and moral support. But what did he expect? Her mother, who nonetheless liked Cyrus, would never have granted her daughter's release. The writing was on the wall when Leslie mentioned the week before that it would be "an extremely doubtful scenario." First, it would be a five-hour drive in his decrepit pickup truck; second, Cyrus was planning to stay in a motel, by himself.

Which was another thing he was very nervous about. The lodgings were his mother's idea, a plan she hatched out of the blue when Cyrus mentioned how far south he'd have to travel for ComBot28 ("I can't get off work. The weekends are the busiest and I'm scheduled.") The plan, accordingly, was for the underage Cyrus to use her credit card to check in to the motel, explain to the hopefully non-officious, hopefully preoccupied desk clerk that his mother was in the car, was sick and couldn't make it inside, or was planning to show up later. "Cy, it's really no big deal," she explained to him, "people do it all the time. If need be, just call me and I'll explain the situation. Don't worry." A statement which led him to worry, naturally.

Again, alone at ComBot. The differences being this year he was a year older and operating a different bot—and he was planning to be behind the wheel of his own vehicle, and not in the back of Earl's. *Earl, good ol' Earl. Gonna flip that darn script, that's what I'm gonna do.*

After a lunch break and a splash of water (to relieve both the heat and the itch of mosquito bites), Cyrus was back in the carport taking hammer strikes on an improvised "medi-swivel" contraption, which was a rope anchored to a ceiling joist with a ten-pound rubber medicine ball attached to it, similar to tetherball. Cyrus would launch the ball outward, let it find its rhythm, then practice the timing of the hammer swing. It was the type of training he could do alone. He was getting quite good at it. The alone part he was having difficulty with.

As he propelled the "medi-swivel" and waited for its comeback, something in the corner of his eye caught his attention. He turned around with his bot stalled in a half-pirouette. *What the hell is that?* The closer it came down the driveway the more it crystallized into view. *But is it? Can it be? A walking roof?* There were definitely four legs underneath it, but what exactly it was had him scratching his head.

At first, his natural assumption was that there was a mix-up. Stuff was being delivered to his new neighbors' house at a breakneck pace over the last several days. Whatever *it* was, was not his, so *it* had to be theirs. But as *it* came within thirty yards, a portrait of *who* was carrying *it* began to emerge. Those two behemoth-sized frames were unmistakable: Numbers 71 and 79.

When the two footballers reached the edge of the carport, straining under the ostensibly heavy weight, they lowered the object to solid asphalt. The brutes then doubled over, hands to their knees. Their cut-off Electron Football T-shirts were drenched, their muscles glowing with taught definition. Cyrus walked over.

"What's up guys?" It was about all he could think to say. He knew an answer, however crazy or inane, would be forthcoming.

Dripping and fatigued, Number 79 leaned his shoulder against the object. "Remember when we said we gotchur back?" he panted.

"Now we gotchur truck's back," followed Number 71.

"Wait? A camper shell? For real?" said Cyrus, canvassing the fourteen-foot portable camper top. It was dingy white with a faded blue stripe down the side, and slidable windows on either side. "You mean, like, to use for travelling?"

"Yep," said Number 79. "Look, got yourself a little fold-down cot in there, too."

"We read in the paper how you'd be going to that robot thing in your truck," said Number 71, "like real far away."

"We borrowed this from our uncle. Never uses it," continued Number 79.

"Man, thanks guys. You sure?"

"Use it all summer," said Number 71, smacking a mosquito with his bear-paw.

"Hold on…your uncle? You two related?" asked Cyrus.

"Cousins," they said at once, gurgling their laughter. They simultaneously stopped laughing as they beat mosquitos from their faces.

"Um, cool. Wow, this is awesome. But I have to ask. Why didn't you
drive it over?"

"We did," said Number 71.

"We didn't know your house, only the road," said Number 79, "so
we parked near that bus stop down there. Carried it 'til we found you."

"You carried this thing all the way from the bus stop? That's like a
hundred yards down the lane."

"Needed the workout," said Number 71. "Good workout, too." The
footballers high-fived each other before laying waste to another flying
bloodsucker. They then looked at one another, their brows lifting the meat
of their foreheads high to their scalps. Without a word, they split around
the sides of the carport, one heading the opposite direction of the other.
Curious, Cyrus followed behind Number 71.

When they reached the back, they looked at one another. They
then hurled the tarp off the snowplow, which Cyrus had put to rest in late
February. The plow lay upright like a trough, cupping a pool of stagnant
brown water. "Mosquito grounds," said Number 79.

The two footballers grabbed either end of the plow, and with a
yank they upturned the water to the ground. "They like old tires, too,"
said Number 71. Cyrus knew they weren't good at math, or many other

subjects, but they had a savvy country wisdom which was enviable, indispensable.

Number 79 stopped, arched his eyes, looked to the sky. He pivoted to his right, stared above the tree line of the woods. "You feel that?"

"Yep," answered Number 71.

"No," said Cyrus.

"Storm's brewing. From the northwest," said Number 71.

"Get your truck, Cy," said Number 79, "let's get 'er up before it pounds."

Cyrus reversed Brown Toro into position. The three of them heaved up the camper, a little overhang to spare. They then twisted the leg poles until they locked into the bed and clamped down the sides. A decent fit.

Feeling the weight of the camper himself, it seemed impossible to Cyrus that the two could have carried it such a distance. *I knew they were powerful, but what the hell.*

The footballers squeezed their hearty hands on Cyrus' shoulders.

He winced. "Hey, Cy, thanks a lot for helping us this year," said Number 71.

"Yeah," said Number 79, "and tutoring us before the final. Oh, thank that girl, too."

"Oh, Leslie," said Cyrus, his heart leaping from her mention, "I'll let her know. So, how'd you do on the final?"

"C's," trumpeted the footballers, crushing their forearms together. "Mrs. Wythe even gave us C's for the whole term."

A crack of lightning announced itself deep beyond the woods. Cyrus lurched and looked that direction. The footballers remained unaffected.

"Guess you guys were right," Cyrus said, watching the dark gray clouds tumble above the woods. He could feel the pressure of the approaching storm. Even the mosquitos took cover.

"Yeah," drawled Number 71, "summer's like that."

Two more lightning strikes echoed the sky and a hard gust blew into the carport, twisting debris in a vortex. Number 79 gave an intense stare-down to Number 71, locked on him like a guard dog. "Race you to the stop, dummy." He sent a fist into his crotch.

"Shit bag ass-face," yelled Number 71, chasing after him.

Cyrus watched them race down the driveway until they were out of sight. An idea sprang to mind. A wonderful, beautiful idea. He hustled past the first pelts of water and raced upstairs.

In his room, he texted his mother at work: CHANGE OF PLANS ON MOTEL ROOM

At his computer, Cyrus launched the ComBot website and browsed it until he found the page for parking. He recalled that cavernous space he exited below ComBot's arena last year; most certainly the host arena for ComBot28 would have the same. Sure enough, there was the heading: **Premium Parking – Underground & Secure.** Cyrus grabbed his Iron Mill Bank card and paid for two days. Bunking overnight in the underground lair seemed a lot better than a lonely, uncertain motel room.

Cyrus sat back and allowed himself an unrestrained smiled. *Footballers came through in the clutch. Just like they did in the playoffs.* He was riding high, feeling confident about next week's contest. Fortune was hitching on his back, and he was letting it ride along.

CHAPTER 36

Even before reading the email, Cyrus was hit by the notion: "that robot" *did* fight. *Why else would I receive this email from this guy Lester?* As it was, he never could quite explain the notches and deep lesions imbedded across its steel frame the day he first found it. Then there was the phenomenon of the bot itself, like mayhem was bred within it. How it flashed to life with a roguish, channeled fury like fighting was metabolized within its genes. *Friggen' thing always was somewhat off. Still is.* He imagined it as a reptile that seeks refuge the moment it first breaks out of its shell—all genetic instinct. *Like it has a mind of its own. And heedless of most commands.*

Now, the proof, it seemed, was right there in his inbox.

Lester's email had a series of five thumbnail videos: two seemingly shot in a different location than the last three.

Cyrus dragged his cursor over the first video, then the next. Peering close, he could make out the same headline in both: "Dragonoya."

A lightning strike startled him from his concentration. He waited a second. After the thunder, he clicked play. The first video was rolling.

It wasn't quite grainy, nor was it high-res, and despite a pervasive umber tonality to it, the production quality wasn't the worst he'd ever seen. The fighting obviously took place in a large warehouse, similar to the venue of his first-round preliminary. A camera mounted atop one of the polycarbonate walls above the safety netting showed a top view of the action. Another was held by someone at floor level. The two angles were edited together, giving the footage a more professional vibe than would normally be associated with its industrial outskirt location.

Cyrus figured Lester was the cinematographer, maybe also the editor. Then again, maybe old Lester was simply steward for all things combat robotic.

Before the first buzzer sounded, the title of the combatants floated across the screen: Shelby Gamble/Give My Respects v. Francis Hampstead/Dragonoya. As Cyrus watched, he knew immediately that Dragonoya was not the same bot from his basement. It was shaped like a geodesic dome, not an arrowhead. In its front was a giant pneumatic claw, enabling it to grab hold of its adversary. Meanwhile, a horizontal lawn-mower blade attempted to finish the deal.

The man fighting it, however, was definitely his father. He wore an U.S. Army insignia cap and a plain navy-blue T-shirt. Francis Hampstead appeared strained with intense concentration. The raised scar on his neck, which Cyrus used to touch as a kid, appeared redder, more distinctive.

Cyrus' chest welled as the camera narrowed in on him. A strong wind gusted. It pierced and howled through the century-old farmhouse glass, vibrating the panes. Cyrus smiled.

He watched Dragonoya's two fights: one win, one defeat.

He clicked the play arrow for the third fight.

The object was almost exactly as he imagined, or more precisely, as Leslie had envisioned it. *Almost exactly. Except for the industrial meat mallet.*

A low-profile wedge, quick, agile, flipper in the fore, dagger in the rear, a black hammer clobbering from the top. *Like an arrowhead on steroids.* When he saw the name suddenly appear on the screen, he knew then and there the moniker pertained to his testy, strong-willed robot—"that bot."

Cranial Concusser.

Stainless steel, polished to a sheen, expertly welded and constructed, poly weaponized. That front wedge flipper mechanism could lift and drive an opponent with seamless momentum, and when it spun, its tailing dagger could lacerate deep into hardware. *Furniture, too.* Above it, cocked at a hundred-and twenty-five-degree angle, ready for downward explosion, was a black Roman-God hammer, a star on one side and crossing arrows on the other—Army insignias. Cyrus watched as all three devices worked in concert—the flipper, the dagger, and the overhead sledge; together, they made for a glorious display of fireworks.

At least that was the case in the first two Cranial Concusser videos. In those fights, Francis Hampstead, now dressed in a beige camouflage cap and a starched Hawaiian shirt, came out victorious. In those, Cranial Concusser created tons of intentional damage.

In the background of the second fight, Cyrus could hear a man's baritone voice over the loudspeaker, which blanketed the shrill of the couple of hundred people in attendance. The voice proclaimed Cranial Concusser the event's second finalist. The voice then went on to announce that with one more win, Cranial Concusser and Francis Hampstead would earn a berth to ComBot20.

Cyrus watched Lieutenant Colonel Hampstead's demeanor—impassive, stoic, restrained. *Typical father.*

Several sidewinding branches of the willow tree slapped against Cyrus' window. The snap-cracks created a strange rhythm with the shrieks of wind. Cyrus stood up from his computer and looked out. The woods swayed. Lightning struck. The willow tree whipped and whipped at the glass. He waited until the storm pushed through, listening as the final drops fell on the roof and the wind gave a final groan. Cyrus returned to the computer.

He queued up Cranial Concusser's final fight, clicking the thumbnail image.

A title card floated into view: **Francis Hampstead/Cranial Concusser v. Ray Dokestout/Doke-a-stroyer.**

There on Cyrus' computer, smiling smugly and surrounded by his typical cast of characters, was Ray Dokestout. He was testing the mechanics of Doke-a-stroyer while discussing some detail with his crew. Ray's mouth moved rapidly though what he was saying was inaudible. All Cyrus could hear was the announcer's disembodied introductions:

"On this side, we have the undefeated Doke-a-stroyer, over a hundred-and-sixty pounds of craven metal on two tracked wheels, ends spiked and skewered like a barbaric shish kabob. When emergency personnel use the jaws of life, Doke-a-stroyer deploys the opposite—the jaws of death." A crescendo rose from the crowd, nearly drowning out his last words. "The only animal on the face of the earth with greater crushing torque bestowed in their jaws was the extinct Megalodon. And one last tidbit. This robotic monster is flanked with two horizontal rototillers, spinning with such deliriously insane RPM's that it would make a psychotic farmer swoon with envy."

Goosebumps rose on Cyrus' arm, his skin sprouting with disbelief and repugnance. *My father did go up against Dokestout.* The distillation of humanity's banes. The antithesis of humility. The same person who, when the time came, he'd never want his own kids to become. *That fucking Ray Dokestout!*

The announcer introduced his father. Cyrus watched as LTC Hampstead tipped his cap to the crowd; other than that, his father was staid, focused on the battle to come. "On the other side of the decagon is a once defeated bot, Cranial Concusser, a rabid, sinister machine which sports a terrifying tail and wielding true terror in its nefarious nightstick. Folks, get set for the final fight of the evening, with a one-way ticket to ComBot20 to be punched."

Cyrus leaned into his computer, hands cradling his chin. He noticed that Cranial Concusser, after two hard-fought victories, showed noticeable scars of war.

The buzzer sounded. The two machines looped around the decagon, testing the temperature, both drawing into the center but reluctant to offer a first strike. For more than half a minute, they circled, danced, retreated. Doke-a-stroyer moved ploddingly, steadily, as if Ray knew his bot couldn't be hurt, that it alone would be the one to inflict the pain. As

Cranial Concusser padded around the edges, Cyrus could hear the crowd expressing their displeasure. The contest was an exercise of repetitive nothingness. They wanted collisions.

At the thirty-three second mark of the contest, the two machines finally clashed. Cranial Concusser launched into a contorting somersault several feet in the air, where it ended upside down. His father deployed the "hammer handspring" and came upon its wheels. Doke-a-stroyer fired in again, its dual rototillers carving a chain of canyons into Cranial Concusser, igniting a fireball plume and shrapnel-filled sparks. The collision pushed Cranial Concusser back to the other side of the decagon, where it bounced off a decagon wall, rebounded like a pinball, and returned with a jousting flipper strike. The jab hit just below Doke-a-stroyer's wheels; LTC Hampstead's attempt at an upend failed. Doke-a-stroyer's center of gravity was too strong. It had too solid a grip on the floor.

In the center of the decagon, Cranial Concusser struck a blow with its hammer. The attempt was a complete miss. It tried several more, but each subsequent attempt found only floor.

The only measure now was retreat. Cranial Concusser fled to a near sidewall with Doke-a-stroyer coming on strong from behind, nipping with its high-velocity rototillers. Sparks filled the screen. Cyrus figured his father was trying to afford himself time during the barrage, but no sooner did the bot find sanctuary than did the corkscrew crank up. Cranial Concusser lurched, spun, and darted away from the scrabbling hazard's tenacious clutch.

Again, Cranial Concusser was on the run.

And into a minefield of spikes, which blasted out from the laminate floor. Cranial Concusser's tires took hit after hit. The machine yawed right, then left, tottering like an unpiloted canoe going over rapids. Weaving and dodging, it finally emerged through the spiked gauntlet unscathed.

Like a rabbit running with death-panicked legs, Francis Hampstead's machine sought refuge, any place to hide within that polycarbonate cage which might provide it precious seconds of life. It sought reprieve beside the saw blade, circled around the floor spikes, straddled the corkscrew, bounding to any place where LTC Hampstead could evaluate the situation, regroup, strategize, neutralize, survive. Meanwhile, Doke-a-stroyer steadfastly stalked its prey, flushing it from each location.

With its rototillers in top gear, Ray made a calculated move. Doke-a-stroyer maneuvered Cranial Concusser back along the corkscrew, thereby trapping the bot against the wall and the churning obstacle. Francis Hampstead's bot was stuck with escape valve. And making things worse, a sidewinding wiggle had resulted in the tail dagger lodged into the corkscrew. A screech shot out of Cyrus' speakers. The corkscrew's churn was insatiable, unrelenting, unsparing.

As the dagger fell deeper and deeper into the abyss, Cyrus noticed the Cranial Concusser's hammer twitch awkwardly. Cyrus looked closer at the screen. The hammer was pinned against the wall. *Not good. Not good at all.*

Doke-a-stroyer angled a quarter turn and prepared to dig in. It extended its pneumatic razor-edged teeth.

Suddenly, Cranial Concusser's flipper shot out, zapping one of Doke-a-stroyer's tillers. White sparks filled Cyrus' eyes. It was a last ditch, perfectly timed maneuver. Cranial Concusser kept jabbing, letting its foe know the game wasn't over, like a burrowed animal fighting off a hole hunting predator.

The flipper repeatedly caught Doke-a-stroyer—two, three, four, five times—but still Doke-a-stroyer didn't back off. It stood its ground, searched for answers, zipped in and out like a maddened dog. With each encroachment, however, came a stiff punch. Cranial Concusser was trapped, but the game continued.

From what Cyrus could tell, Ray Dokestout had second-guessed his decision to remain in that spot. Cyrus could see it in his body language; the frustration from the pesty, annoying jabs was exasperating him. At bay, Doke-a-stroyer was impotent, and worse yet, the rototillers were taking a beating from all those flipper strikes. Cyrus figured the hokey-pokey dance wouldn't continue much longer, even with the grinder working hard on Cranial Concusser.

At last, Doke-a-stroyer shifted tactics. It was an all-in gamble with the jaws of death. The machine lunged forward and tried to snatch Cranial Concusser away from the churning obstacle. Ray wanted to snuff out the bot right then and there.

It was an ill-conceived gambit, or more precisely, ill-timed.

Because the moment Doke-a-stroyer lurched in, it had also hesitated. A split-second stutter. Cyrus had no idea if it was luck, or some stratagem on his father's part—or a combination of both—but at that very instant between Doke-a-stroyer's indecisiveness and its forward commitment, Cranial Concusser dislodged itself from the corkscrew and outstretched its flipper like a battering ram. It caught the oncoming Doke-a-stroyer above a tire, lifting it and banking the bot sideways. Doke-a-stroyer gyrated, attempted one last snap of its jaws, but missed by mere inches; the teeth grasped only air.

Cranial Concusser bull rushed Doke-a-stroyer, pushing it backwards. Unbalanced, Doke-a-stroyer flailed and struggled, and the more it tried to reposition its posture and hold true, the worse it faired. Now, the field of spikes. It hit one row, teetered; another row, tottered; the third row and fell to its side. Tiller side down, it spun around like a beetle suffering sunstroke.

Cranial Concusser stood over Doke-a-stroyer. It beat its hammer down, beat it down with such force that the scurvy-like tillers facing upward were soon flattened into the machine's frame. Cranial Concusser then twisted a degree, stopped, leered over the jaws of death. To Cyrus, the mouth, agape and frozen, appeared in a state of shock. The mighty hammer rained a single blow. The upper half of the jaws severed from the lower half. The mouth was a disfigured mess.

Cranial Concusser kept on hammering, inducing a hail of sparks and a roll of thunder as noisy and violent as the storm that had passed outside Cyrus' window. Doke-a-stroyer squirmed. Squirming was all it had left.

The mercy-rule buzzer, as far as Cyrus could tell, was but a touch of the finger away. Ticks of the clock. Academic. An easy 1-2-3. Entry into ComBot20 was his father's.

Then, suddenly, Cranial Concusser died. The hammer reached its apex, halted. Not even its flipper, which had been pestering non-stop, made the slightest twitch.

Cyrus checked the video for buffering. He then noticed Doke-a-stroyer moving slightly. It wasn't the video.

His father's bot was frozen. Stiff as if it had been zapped by an alien spaceship.

Cyrus watched in shock. It was all too unbelievable. All too familiar.

Blood ran to Cyrus' head. He felt his body seize and become woozy. *Déjà vu. That's what it is? Simple déjà vu. Right?*

Seconds later, Doke-a-stroyer writhed to its side. Spinning and spinning, it gained an upright leverage and came upon its wheels. It revved up its other still-operable rototiller.

Sparks flew over the decagon. A ten second flurry which filled Cyrus' screen. He looked on in disbelief. Seconds later, the mercy buzzer horned.

Cyrus stopped the video. He couldn't watch any longer. He couldn't watch the dancing and celebration he knew was coming, even though this all happened more than eight years ago.

Two bots, two Hampstead's, two freeze ups, two Doke-a-bot victories. Too many "twos."

Déjà vu? Can't be.

Right?

CHAPTER 37

Cyrus grabbed his phone and hammered out a text.

HI LES. I KNOW UR BUSY BUT WHEN HAVE CHANCE PLS WATCH VID I JUST EMAILED. LMK WHAT U THINK. HOPE UR HAVING GOOD TIME. MINE...EVENTFUL.

He copied the link to the last fight, pulled up Leslie's email address, hit send, and collapsed onto his bed.

He lay there, staring blankly at the ceiling.

Thinking. Contemplating.

But really, there was nothing to think about. Contemplation wouldn't change anything.

He jumped out of bed and headed for the basement.

Cyrus opened a cabinet drawer where his father kept old cans of paint. He pried open a quart of bright red. He then grabbed a brush with thin bristles from the drawer below.

On the stump of elm sat "that bot." He traced out the name on the top, one word above the other. Cyrus painted, diligently, as always staying within the lines.

He stood back and took in his handiwork.

Cranial Concusser was born.

Cranial Concusser, reborn.

CHAPTER 38

With its tailgate down and camper door ajar, Brown Toro looked as if it was poised to swallow feed. And Cyrus was ready to provide it: his wagon with the newly minted Cranial Concusser inside.

Cyrus hooked a ramp to the tailgate and placed the wagon's front wheels to its edge. He then secured the winch cable to its handle by way of carabiner and crawled through the camper's wide door and squeezed inside the pickup bed, where he anchored the winch to a hook on the back wall and plugged the cord into the power adapter that dangled through the cabin' back window. He then reversed himself back out. His mother, there to bid him farewell, watched his orchestrated movements with keen focus.

The July morning was muggy but bright, a cloudless start to the day. Brown Toro seemed eager for the road trip south, as was Cyrus. His mother, however, appeared to harbor all the nerves.

"And remember how that truck eats up gas. You've got to keep your eye on the gauge. Don't let it fall below a quarter tank, because before you know it, you'll be out of fuel with not a station in sight. Might be miles down the highway before you see one. So stay vigilant because that gauge gets finicky." His mother had on that serious look. Maybe it was because she was dressed in her professional work clothes and ready to head to work on a Friday. Maybe something else was eating at her.

"I'll keep checking it. I've got the gas gauge timed pretty good."

"And that reminds me. Keep your speed under sixty miles per hour. You'll use less gas that way. Besides, it's safer." She leaned over and gave Brown Toro's tires a circumspect look. "Just be careful, Cy. That's all I'm saying. Please."

"I'll be careful," promised Cyrus.

Cyrus jumped down from the truck with the confidence of a spry gymnast. His mother steeled him with a look. "I know you don't want to think about it, but…Cy, it's not outside the realm of possibility that your bot might not come back in the same condition it's leaving in. Like what happened last year. I just want you to be aware of the consequences. You've worked so hard…I just don't want you coming back…crushed. Like you did last year."

"I understand the consequences, Mom."

"This sport you and your father got into is…is unpredictable. Anything could happen, and not winning ComBot, really it's not the end of the world, Cy. You have plenty of life ahead of you. I mean it."

"Destruction's unpredictable. That's the nature of it," he replied. Cyrus didn't want to sound blithe, but he also wanted his mother to know that he wholeheartedly understood that in certain environments return is not a given. That the expectation of survival, no matter where you are or whatever the conditions you face, is a fool hearty and naïve notion. That life can be as fickle as the weather outside a small basement window. "That's combat robotics. Every time I fight losing crosses my mind. How could it not?"

His mother's eyes blurred. When Cyrus looked up, he saw a pained history on her face. He understood then and there that all her sentiments manifested beyond robotic machines; they became the embodiment of flesh and blood. As she wiped away a tear, he gave her a hug. When he looked again to her face, her eyes beamed not with despair, but with resiliency and hope.

"I know, Cy. Loss is always a possibility," she said, giving him a kiss.

He climbed up into the camper and flipped the winch's switch, which began the wagon's slow ascent up the tailgate ramp. From inside he said: "I can't go into this with the idea of losing. I can't think that way. Not being this close again. I've spent too much time, and well, it's something I've got to do. Something that I need to finish." Cyrus never told his mother about the video he received from Lester. He just couldn't. Doing so would have opened up too many cans of worms, and he was in no mood for her to go fishing. Besides, it seemed a matter he had to handle on his own—or with one other person. A vested partner.

He climbed back down and dusted himself off, ready for the trip.

"Cyrus, just because you lost last year doesn't mean you have to make things right. I don't think all the other competitors think that way."

"It's more than that, mom," said Cyrus, heaving the ramp into the truck bed sidelong. "The reality is…well, it goes beyond winning and losing." He looked to the cloudless sky. "I'll explain later, OK?"

"I know. I understand. You want to finish what your father started," his mother said. "To see what he could have accomplished, if he had had the chance." Cyrus was content to leave it at that. In part, it was the truth. A whole lot of truth.

"Kinda like that. But don't forget about the fifty grand tangling out there for the winner. Solid college money if I ever heard it. Bet you didn't even know they increased the purse this year."

"There's a lot that I don't know. I only know things if you tell me." His mother paused for reflection, brushing her fingers through her strands of hair. "Well, that's not exactly true. I may not have known all that you and your father were involved in, but that doesn't mean I didn't know *some* things. I'm your mother." She squeezed him tight and planted a kiss. "You wanna try me?" she asked with a saturating smile.

"No. Not really." He gave her a dubious look.

"That's OK, Cyrus, we'll have time for that later," she said, releasing him from her hug. She plucked some debris from the front of his T-shirt. "Besides, you've got other things to get to. Like driving. Which, by the way, you are very good at. It's almost like you instinctually knew how to drive Brown Toro from the get-go." She winked. "Like you were born into the machine, you know, that second nature thing you keep going on about. But I know *I* didn't teach you how to work a manual transmission."

Cyrus threw his backpack into Brown Toro and climbed in the driver's seat. He was itching to release a wide smile, but he kept his expression detached, guarded. Some things, like the video and his driving history, were better kept close to the vest. Someday, it would all be exposed anyway.

With a turn of the key, the old truck coughed to life. "A mother knows best," said Cyrus plaintively. "I'll call you when I arrive. Love you, Mom."

As Brown Toro carried Cyrus and his fight down the driveway, he peered into his rearview mirror. His mother blew him a kiss, Mongrel standing faithfully at her feet. He blasted a couple of honks, turned left down the lane, rolled past the bus stop, and headed south for to that "something" in his heart he knew he had to finish.

CHAPTER 39

The next morning Cyrus awoke to the sounds of rustling equipment and the murmurs of whispered conversations. He reached down from the bunk bed for his phone. It seemed impossible that he had crashed out so long. Then again, staring continuously at white lines on a highway doe stake a mental toll. The only thing that got him through his boredom was the blasting music and Leslie—those few breaks she called from field hockey camp helped to fill the void. The thought of her laugh lasted him for miles.

Outside his camper window, several vans and trucks with tow pulls were parked, many with insignias of university engineering departments. Like Cyrus, the road-wearied teams had filtered into the underground garage throughout the night. He wondered last night why the on-duty guard didn't think anything of his late-night appearance. Now he knew.

He scrolled his messages. He tapped the most important one.

LESLIE: WISHING U BEST THIS WKEND. FIGHT LIKE CRAZY THEN FIGHT HARDER. AND RIDE THAT MOJO. ALL GOOD W ME CEPT 4 BLACK & BLUE SHINS. XOXO

Cyrus released a smile, gathered his gear, threw it all into the wagon, and covered it with his Chromiums blanket. He followed the signs to registration.

He was early. A woman in a red-and-white striped shirt sat at a desk looking bored. When she noticed him, she pepped up a smile and opened her laptop. "Hello there. Your name?"

"Hampstead."

She traced her finger along her laptop.

"You must be Cyrus?" she stated by way of question. "And Smitty/ Carl?" She pointed to his covered wagon.

"Yes. Nice meeting you."

"Welcome to ComBot," she said. "And congratulations." She beat her fingers to the keypad. "Oh, I see you were a semifinalist last year in the MegaBots. Quite impressive. Hope you can repeat that kind of success at ComBot28."

"That's the plan. If anyone can have a plan at ComBot."

"Many come with plans, then sometimes that first collision them. Out the window, as they say." She laughed and continued to peck on the keyboard. "On the topic of plans, Cyrus, here's what you can expect. Similar to last year, only different. Over there on the wall, you'll see the official contest bracket posted." She pointed to a printout. "Now let me explain the arena layout and schedule. Once you've registered, which is now, you can head to any one of the auxiliary rooms to rest and prepare for your fights. Those are holding rooms numbered 277 to 280, and two smaller rooms on the opposite side of the arena, 209 and 213. There will be monitors inside each room so you can watch the other fights throughout the course of the event. And some refreshments, too. If you need to make modifications to your robot, legal and within the guidelines of course, or if you simply need to service it, the repair room is on the lower level, room 139, which you'll see by all the signs around pointing that out. There will also be an official in the repair room to designate your radio frequency, which you'll coordinate and test. As with any sanctioned contest, this will strictly be yours. Plenty of tools are provided in the RM as well. You'll have access to everything unless you want to use you own. Your choice. Within every holding room will be monitor remote," she held up an example, "and you can push this button to see the tournament bracket in real-time for all divisions. Many officials, as you'll see, will be moving all around, between rooms, the decagon, the corridors, and even around here, some too often, unfortunately. These officials will notify you of your upcoming contest. They'll give you fifteen minutes heads up, generally. Once you're notified, they'll escort you to your mark prior to the contest introduction. Then you'll hear the PA announcer call the rodeo and from that point on you'll be blinded by lights and insane yelling and all the rest, and try to make it to your fighting pod within a reasonable time, without much fanfare. As I'm sure you're aware, winner moves on, loser heads home, and much of this is old hat, all except for the increase in the purse, which you must already know, is fifty thousand to the victor of each division." She let out her breath. "Any questions?"

"Uh, I have just one," said Cyrus. "What if I have a name change? Can you, like, change a name before everything is officially set?"

"You mean change your name?" she inquired.

"Yes. I mean, no. Not my name. My bot's."

"Huh. Yes, that's been done before. Some teams will enter another robot other than what they previously competed with, because of a malfunction or inoperability. A backup. It's a technicality, in a sense. But I have to get the change in before everything becomes official."

Cyrus wrote down the name Cranial Concusser on a sheet of paper. The women searched her laptop for a document, imported the name, printed a sheet, and handed it to him. The heading read: ComBot28/Contestant Name Designation. Under the one-page declaration was a space for a signature, which Cyrus signed and dated. Cranial Concusser was officially recorded.

Cyrus grabbed his gear and aimed for the upper concourse, hoping to avoid one particular person and his entourage. A few maintenance workers and operations people lingered around. He became keenly aware of a door that read: "Staff Only." He shook his head. *Not this year.* He strolled down an aisle towards the open arena.

The cavernous space was bathed in yellow and light blue, the colors of the sports teams which normally took up residence there. The banners hanging from the ceiling attested to their history and greatness. He looked down on the decagon: fourteen-foot-high clear polycarbonate walls of ten panels, see-through ceiling, two separate fighting pods, two thwackers bunked against opposite walls, a six-foot corkscrew and the pit o' fire on two other opposing walls, and hidden somewhere beneath the floor, a sawblade able to inflict so much pain. On separate ladders, members of the production crew attended to a bank of lights and tweaked with the wire-high camera. Others in the crew moved about, blocking their shots.

The stage was being set.

He imagined what it would be like down there in a few hours.

Madness.

CHAPTER 40

The camera slid majestically across the taut wires, taking it all in. Spotlights crisscrossed the stands in whip-like fashion. Bass pumping heavy metal. A carnival of green, yellow, red and orange lights flooded the space. Everything and anything being yelled, hollered and screamed. The crowd: a single swaying, amorphously deafening, near-boiling tempest.

Cyrus stood at the threshold waiting to be announced, a darkened specter in a turbulent sea. He nervously rocked his wagon back and forth. Amidst the arena's clamor, he could hear the light squeaking of its wheels. Standing alongside him was the same cantankerous official who presided over his semifinal fight a year ago. He held a sober expression, nose ruddy and upturned. Cyrus figured he was annoyed by his continuously swaying wagon, and its creaking. *Too bad, deal with it.* With two fights down and number three moments away—the quarterfinals—Cyrus had to get the shakes out somehow. And he didn't care who he bothered in the process. It wasn't like all these people were waiting for the snubbed-nosed official to come rolling down the aisle. *So deal, dude.*

As Cyrus peered through the decagon walls, he noticed a bright orange dress shining in a camera's light. After half a ComBot dozen fights, this was first time he'd ever seen Shon'dae Marquette in person. Maybe he'd been too anxious and hyper-focused to notice her before. Moments later, the camera's light clicked off and Shon'dae Marquette and her cameraman walked up an aisle. He watched the theatrical antics that followed her.

The Jumbotron then came to life. Taking up the frame: two cowboy-hats, one black, the other white. The crowd simmered to a buzz as the two announcers launched into their dialogue.

"Skip, this quarterfinal square up is a much anticipated one. The fans are ready, we're ready, and we hope everyone out there's ready. So get your popcorn ready. I've got mine. Hopefully this will be a continuation of the rip-shredding demolishment we've seen so far in the MegaBot division."

"Darn right, Jack. No question there's been a bunch of hungry mongooses out there on the decagon floor. Crazy good stuff. Just how we like it. Take for instance one of our next competitors, Cranial Concusser, which is operated by seventeen-year-old Cyrus Hampstead,"—a flurry of whoops and whistles filled the arena—"Whoa, Jack, you can hear what a fan favorite this young man's become."

"Fan favorite?" questioned Jack spiritedly. "This kid's entering into boy-band fanatic status."

"Spot on, Jack. Only seventeen and a semifinalist from a year ago. Now that's an accomplished, early career resume. Much like last year, Cyrus Hampstead's solo quest has made quite the impression."

"But don't forget what twenty-five pounds of hardened-titanium destruction will buy you in this place, Skip. o be able to use that hammer of his in the first two contests with such precision and accuracy and ferocity, well, it's been simply mind-blowing."

As they continued to banter, Cyrus thought back to his first two rounds. How he was in lockstep with his machine, like an avatar. In his fingertips, in his bloodstream, in his heart, he sensed Cranial Concusser's willingness, its desire to unleash a sinister assault. Thirty-one seconds into Round One and the tenderizer left a pile of mincemeat on the floor. He could hardly describe the sensation (maybe because of all the turmoil the machine had put him through over the last year) but the way the bot responded was uncanny. Cyrus knew it sounded stupid, but it seemed as if Cranial Concusser was operating on its own accord, like there was some cerebral motivation (*nah, robots don't that!*) for its rampaging. Yes, he gave his machine the first taste of blood; in return it salivated for more, turned rabid. As if thirty-one seconds wasn't enough. A paltry carnal teasing. As he repaired Cranial Concusser's first-round wounds, he could feel this strange emanation coming from within it—an unquelled, insatiable appetite. *God, that was strange.* And sure enough, Round Two it went on an unbridled march of destruction. He knew his fingers were in control, but it all…*it all seemed…surreal? Otherworldly?*

Whatever, I'm just happy the thing's behaving. Like a good little robot.

"Let's see what Cyrus Hampstead's hammer-wielding, arrow-head-with-a-scorpion's-tail can do against the snaggled-toothed harvesting sickle in Foraging Banshee from the team of Northwest Crest School of Engineering."

The roaming spotlights settled into a single beam on the PA

announcer outside the decagon. Once he finished with the call, Cyrus strutted Cranial Concusser down the aisle to a riotous reception.

Before the opening buzzer, Cyrus flicked out his thumb and waddled it over the knob, sending Cranial Concusser on a loping war-mup around the perimeter walls. He wanted to give his opponents, and the fans, a glimpse of what was in store, so he parked his bot in front of Northwest Crest School of Engineering's pod and uncorked the mallet, sending out a shockwave when it hit the floor. The fans loved it. His adversaries not so much.

Cyrus looked across the walled pod at the operator of Foraging Banshee. The guy was dressed up in an arm sleeve of colorful tattoos, and his spiked blonde hair suggested limestone stalagmites had sprouted from his head. He looked to have all the confidence in the world. He returned Cyrus' stare with a smug-superior sneer. He bobbed his head to the heavy metal music as he pointed around to the crazed fans. In turn, Cyrus sprang Cranial Concusser's hammer back into the cocked position. The guy's eyes suddenly drained of their eagerness.

Cyrus took a good look at Foraging Banshee. The machine was streamlined, low to the ground. Its front weapon was a laterally sweeping sickle that rotated on hyper-sped. A spike protruded from the end of the sickle—a gorging instrument if there ever was one. Exactly how long the spike was Cyrus had no clue; it wasn't like he wanted to break out the measuring tape. He knew the damage it could inflict. To go along with it, flat radial metallic discs were imbedded on either side of the bot—counter measures to the sickle, though maybe more lethal in their own right. Running at full RPM's, Cyrus knew even a slight lick from one of those spinning discs would be problematic for Cranial Concusser. A solid lick into an obstacle, that might spell disaster. Proximity and timing were the key. He had to pick his spots.

At the sound of the buzzer, Cranial Concusser and Foraging Banshee raced in, compressing their distances. Instinctively, Cyrus went for the "split-step beat-down," but the oncoming speed caught him by surprise. The split-step stage was a success; the beat-down stage, however, was a moment too late. The result was a spectacular head-on collision that propelled both into an aerial show.

Cranial Concusser landed topside down, but righted itself with the "hammer handspring." Only superficial injuries were the result. Cranial Concusser then turned sharp and sped towards the edge, skimming under a resting wall thwacker and waited. (Cyrus knew obstacles never came to life before the half minute mark of any fight.) Cyrus had little time, however, because the fellow in control of Foraging Banshee wasn't here to hesitate or second guess himself. His sole aim, Cyrus gathered, was to inflict as much damage on the teenager's machine as quick as possible. Cyrus sped Cranial Concusser into a wall slot, Foraging Banshee racing in from behind. Its spiked extremity was revving high. It was looking to split Cranial Concusser like a log.

It missed full puncture, but still the spike carved out a screeching trench on top of Cranial Concusser, above the tail dagger. Cyrus reversed his bot from the assault, but behind it the corkscrew had cranked up and was steadily churning. Cyrus zagged his machine out of reach. He found open space, pivoted sharply, accelerated forward, and closed the gap on Foraging Banshee. He laid down the hammer—three good thumps, each one a missed message. Over the fog of war, Cyrus could hear the crowd's collective gasp. Foraging Banshee reversed out and aligned itself in the center of the decagon; there, the sawblade came from the floor like a bad omen. Foraging Banshee tempted fate as the blades nipped its side and spat out sparks. It shot away and escaped oblivion. Cyrus' foe was soon free and on the loose.

Once Cyrus thwarted the initial offensive and had space in front of him, he decided on a new tactic. One he even didn't expect to deploy. No more feints, no more pullbacks, no more reverses and jockeying around for position. Cyrus figured his opponent would be switching gears anyway, come sidewinding in with those radial discs. In an instant, Cyrus thumbed his knob and spun Cranial Concusser around. He accelerated his bot in reverse with all its God-given speed. A bullish, unsophisticated strategy. *So what...Let's do some spearfishing.*

Seconds later, Cranial Concusser's dagger jousted into one of its spinning discs. White hot sparks and a grinding screech. Cyrus kept pushing, ramming, jamming, until his dagger ground the disc to a halt. Foraging Banshee sputtered; its organs compromised. Its spiked arm flailed with fatalistic patty-taps. Cyrus pulled out, pirouetted Cranial Concusser one-hundred-and-eighty degrees. He extended the flipper and drove back

Foraging Banshee into the floor's sawblade. A flurry of yellow-and-white flashes exploded over the floor. Foraging Banshee shredded into discrete shards.

Cyrus sensed the crowd wanting one last thump. A baseless hammering. He parked Cranial Concusser adjacent and meted out a splattering blow. Foraging Banshee exploded into its last pieces.

The buzzer signaled the call of death.

Whistles pierced the arena, a chorus of ear-squelching cries and yells. Cyrus caught the eye of Foraging Banshee's operator. His once smarmy grin had turned into a grimace.

CHAPTER 41

With the number of contestants in ComBot28 dwindled to only the survivors of each division, Cyrus found himself alone in the repair room. In its pre-robotic capacity, the room was a training room for athletes; a cold bath sat in the corner, stretching tables were pushed against one wall, stationary bikes shoved against another. In their place, workbenches were aligned in five rows.

Cyrus looked around. The recyclable-loving clown receptable was at full capacity. Which got him thinking about last year and the two officials who cleaned up Spiral Cyclone's remnants. How their omission from this year's event was almost foreordained. *What is that word I recall from English Lit? Recalcitrant?* At any rate, he counted his blessings that he had not seen hide or hair of the one person he didn't want to see, not until the moment he had to. Ray Dokestout.

At the furthest workbench, Cyrus did his best to erase the effects of the quarterfinals. He sutured the gorge above the dagger with his welder, wrenched down some interior bolts, and heated up the air gun for the replacement of the Monkey Wrench decal, the original being all but a shredded blur. On the other side, Smitty's logo was unblemished, but he gave it a gentle buff nonetheless. With cameras hovering all around, it was important that his investors were well represented. Cyrus knew without them he wouldn't be here.

The emptiness and quiet of the room, which an hour ago was a scattering of tools and parts and people and their messes, reminded Cyrus of how far he had advanced—the semifinals. Once again. He felt a sense of relief, but as expected, it came with an uptick in nerves.

Twenty minutes later, his machine was primed and ready. And so too was Cyrus. Rallying to unknot that thing in his gut that had been hog-tying him since he first entered the repair room. Whatever it was, was now unraveled, stretched out mean and taut. And it became vicious, to where in his head he saw only sparks and shrapnel, heard only the whining shrill of metal-on-metal contact. Cranial Concusser, it seemed, wasn't the only one under the spell of bloodlust. In the repair, an echoing scream was let out.

Destruction, obliteration, annihilation. If that resulted in his own demise, he decided, so be it. At least he'd go down swinging in the semis. The journey, for better or worse, would be out of his system. He could accept that, move on. Nothing to show for it except for what was in his bank account and a return to normal life—Leslie, friends, his mother, college in a year. This was his thinking; he couldn't help it. But some voice told him not to think that way, that that was a reckoning to contrition. The easy way out. As he waited for the call to the semis, he listened to the voice—or rather, voices.

After an hour and a half of keeping one eye on the monitor and the other on his repairs, the official popped her head in. "Time," she announced. He loaded Cranial Concusser in his wagon and headed for his semifinal introduction. *Ride the mojo!*

Jack: "As we wait for the PA introductions, let me remind every-one about the skirmish we have in store inside the decagon. Once again, it's Cyrus Hampstead and Cranial Concusser taking center stage. Overall this season, the tandem has compiled ten victories and two defeats, and oh, I'd be remiss to add, they enter the decagon with one hellava maniacal mallet."

At this, the arena shook the marrow in Cyrus' bones. Over the darkened arena he could see the shadows of hand-held signs and the blur-ry aspect of bodies.

Skip: "But let's not get too far ahead of ourselves, Jack, Cranial Concusser has to get through a three wheeled wedgebot that's on a major roll. Tumultuous and its crew have taken out a total of eleven bots to advance to this semifinal outcome. Their machine is revved like a Formula One car and just keeps coming and coming. Out there in the decagon, that means only one thing: prepare...for...liftoff."

"Skip, let's not forget who's waiting on the other side of the brack-et. A phantom in the wings, and he's not here to play a part in any opera. Ray Dokestout and his Doke-a-250 are only two wins away from earning that two-fifty distinction. But they too have to get through a semifinal contest, with the winner to meet this winner for the lucrative ComBot championship title."

"Wow, what a MegaBot lineup we have in front of us," interjected Skip.

"Sure is," announced Jack. "Let's go down to the decagon for the call of the first semifinal showdown."

The moment Cyrus carted his warring bot into the decagon, hollers for carnage rang from the stands. Cranial Concusser was anointed with a nasty reputation, and it showed. Cyrus soaked up the screams, the whistles, the baying, the calls for chaos. It mimicked his own feelings.

Stepping into the pod, Leslie's message kept ringing through his head. *Fight like crazy. Then fight harder.* One more win and he'd be fighting for the title. *The trophy. The Benjamin's. The dineros. The glory. The redemption.* But deep down, more than anything else, it was the matchup with Dokestout that he really wanted. *Just have to get through this one. First things first.* His adrenaline started pumping. *Fight like crazy. Then fight harder. Ride the mojo.*

Cyrus took Cranial Concusser on a pre-fight spin around the decagon, and as he did, he sent a glance to his opponents. The team—two men and one woman—seemed twitchy. They bounced like jumping beans. They all wore the same caps with a picture of Tumultuous on them. The two men argued over something which Cyrus was unable to comprehend, and during the ruckus the woman grabbed Tumultuous' controller. Cyrus was figuring—hoping—the stage might be too big for them. Although only seventeen, it was he who had the advantage of experience.

The woman guided Tumultuous around the decagon. The bot moved clumsily, like a bull running between rodeo clowns. Cyrus hadn't yet seen Tumultuous in battle, had no idea about its zero-to-whatever torque. But despite its awkward movements he could sense a condensed raw power. Wedgebots can be unpredictably dangerous—simple yet effective, straightforward but lethal. *Rushing and overturning little devils.* He figured his flipper would be a good defense, or offense.

After all the introductions and the hell-spilling from the crowd, the cockcrowing between the two machines and the blinding arcade of spotlights, the semifinal horn finally sounded.

The obstacles—the opossum-playing thwacker, the stagnant corkscrew, the hibernating sawblade, the un-ignited pit o' fire—all lay quiet but would soon be coming to life. Each bot maneuvered the floor at a hesitant distance. Cranial Concusser cased the perimeter along the walls, testing the tepid waters. Tumultuous roamed like a shark, tentative but with a resolute hunger. For his part, Cyrus was determined to remain patient, keep the distance, wait it out. Despite the crowd's hiss of displeasure, neither ventured an attack.

Twenty seconds in, Cyrus called the stalemate quits and weaved Cranial Concusser into Tumultuous' zone, deploying the "zip and release" maneuver. The feinting gambit sent Tumultuous scurrying in reverse. On the chase, Cranial Concusser launched its flipper and clipped Tumultuous. The machine wobbled on two wheels, rebalanced and then regained speed. It raced along a sidewall with Cranial Concusser on its heels, twisted right, found open floor, accelerated and then straightened a path directly towards Cranial Concusser. Cyrus blasted the hammer. Tumultuous abruptly curved out and avoided the bashing. Still in stride, Tumultuous found itself on the wrong side of a downward thump: the sidewall thwacker. It was a direct, pummeling hit.

Cyrus heard a faint volley of curses from the opposing pod. He briefly glanced over. One of the guys was frantically adjusting his glasses as he jostled the remote, which he had wrested away from the woman. The resulting moves were hasty, fitful, unsure. Tumultuous threshed like a minnow out of water. *How about a double dose of the hammer to get you back on track?* Cyrus laid one down—a fractional, glancing shot. On his second attempt, Tumultuous spit out and careened wildly around the floor like a dog with an itch.

Cranial Concusser advanced on its opponent with Cyrus delivering longshot flipper slaps. One, two, three fruitless strikes, all missing the target. Still focused on the chase, Cyrus never saw the floor open up: the sawblade, whizzing at full throttle. He yanked his knob with quick-twitch panic, but Cranial Concusser's dagger was clutched by the upsurging metallic teeth and the bot rode a violent wave of white-hot sparks. Cranial Concusser catapulted several feet in the air and screeched to a landing, topside down. *Oh, shit!*

Cyrus handsprung the hammer and his bot came onto its wheels. Realizing an opportunity, Tumultuous about-faced and barreled in with full juice. Cyrus had but two options: hunt or be hunted. *Not going down like that.* He grounded Cranial Concusser, fronted up, readied his thumb, and as Tumultuous came within range he launched the flipper. The flipper appendage hitched into Tumultuous' undercarriage. With all its possessed power, Cyrus throttled and turned Cranial Concusser, whipping it back and forth, whipping his opponent as a dog does a toy rope. With a drive of savage momentum, Cyrus strong-armed Tumultuous into the grind of the churning corkscrew.

The gnashing teeth found metallic skin. A high-pitched bawl echoed across the arena. One of Tumultuous' wheels found a home in the twisting wave, and despite its best attempts at freedom, the wheel was gnawed to eviscerated rubber.

For good measure, Cyrus rained the meat mallet down several times on the moving target. Some hit the mark, others missed, but it didn't take long for Tumultuous' top to cave. Its wires spilled like guts. Its skeletal frame compressed into a jumbled mess. The wedgebot resembled pizza roadkill.

Against the roar of the stands, the buzzer at last shrilled its mercy.

The camera on wires swooped down and landed several feet in front of Cyrus. He offered it a hearty, pearly smile. He then realized the full extent of what had transpired. What he had accomplished. He dropped his remote and pumped his arm as if pulling down a train whistle. A quick jump in the air landed him clean. He sprung again. It was a victorious release, one built over a long, trying year.

The crowd surrounding him was maddening. He turned to them and pumped his fist, and they saluted back with the same, and more. Cyrus felt their power, consumed their energy; they were like a B-12 injection into a tired soul.

But it was not all about him and he knew it. Cyrus then turned towards the decagon and pointed in acknowledgment of the single-minded tenacity of his fighting robot, Cranial Concusser. A bot that had proven itself by earning a spot in the ComBot finale—despite being dormant for the better part of a decade.

Damn! What a good little robot!

CHAPTER 42

Exhaustion snuck up on Cyrus Hampstead. It took its toll the moment he entered the repair room. But he knew he still had work to do. ComBot28 was not over. In a sense, it was just beginning.

Cyrus hustled up his repairs. He smoothed Cranial Concusser's wounds the best he could, then heat ironed on a brand new Smitty logo. He unscrewed the bot's top panel and wrenched down the lock nuts of the hammer, which had held firm in its iron sleeve but had been jimmied at the footer. He replaced the CO_2. He adjusted some mechanics of the drive train. Put the rotary grinder on the tail dagger to smooth out the damage. Changed out two tires following their appointment with the saw-blade. All minor fixes and calibrations.

A half hour later he was back in his favorite auxiliary room, 213. He liked Room 213. He could rest in Room 213. In room 213 no one ever bothered him. It was a small room, detached and removed, a space maybe to tell a basketball or hockey player that he or she was traded or let go. The last of auxiliary rooms along a mostly quiet corridor. A quiet haven away from the buzz and hustle of ComBot28. A space to gather his thoughts, watch the other divisional fights, and tap out the messages he had been constructing in his head as he repaired Cranial Concusser. Despite what his body was telling him, he had to stay mentally alert and at the ready. No napping this year.

Through group chat, he apprised everyone in his world of his victory—everyone except Leslie. She got her own message. In a long-winded text, he told her about his semifinal win, gave her a snapshot of his rollercoaster of anxiety, related the damages to his machine, and compiled an abridged version of all his repairs. After sending it he was still pensive, fidgety, so with fingers moving at rapid speed he sent her a follow up text detailing his nervousness as he awaited the other semifinal outcome. His last sentence: GIVE ME ONE LAST CRACK BEFORE THE GUY RETIRES. Writing everything down eased his worries. Eventually though, he decided all these long, drawn-out texts were probably all she could handle, or were appropriate. She was probably exhausted, too, from all the field hockey.

Cyrus took a snap of his feet up on the table, tapped a sweet note of endearment and hit send for the last time. He was hopeful a reciprocating message would come sometime before the final, which was less than two hours away.

He looked over messages. Fourteen came from Blake, two from his mother, two from Carl, and strangely enough, one from Horace Smith. As he threw his phone atop the wagon a knock came to the door. The force jarred it open a crack. A head of dark hair pushed in. He instinctually threw his feet off the table. A familiar voice said: "Do have a moment for a quick interview, Cyrus?"

Shon'dae Marquette's television personality was flamboyant and lively. But that was television. After being introduced, Cyrus was soon enraptured by her earnestness and genuineness, and her calm demeanor. She took a seat in front of him as her cameraman stood in the corner.

With a cuing whisk of her hand, the cameraman snapped on a light which temporarily blinded Cyrus. "Now Cyrus, just try to be comfortable," said Shon'dae. "You can sit on the table if you wish, if that's easier. No need for formalities with us."

Over the next ten minutes, she asked Cyrus about his junior year of high school, the circumstances of finding Cranial Concusser, and his journey to ComBot28; Cyrus filled in all the blanks. He even rehashed some of the stories he told The Beacon for filler.

Shon'dae Marquette made a slash with her hand and the cameraman snapped off the light. "So, any idea what you'll do with fifty thousand dollars, if you win?" she asked.

"Hopefully it will last four years of college. Hopefully, that is. You never know. Oh, and I plan to do something nice for my girlfriend."

"That would be a great idea. Women always appreciate that." She stood up and smoothed out her dress. "Fantastic, Cyrus. You were great."

"That was easier than I thought it would be."

"It always is. By the way, Cyrus, I did a quick search of our database and cross-referenced the name Cranial Concusser. To get some background info. It's interesting, the only thing I came up with was an event roster seven, maybe eight years ago."

"That's right, my father did fight with it back then. Had a good run, almost made to ComBot20," he explained. He conveniently omitted the more controversial aspect of its demise.

"Now there's an interesting story lurking there, huh, Chuck?" The cameraman nodded. "Great follow up piece if you happen to win, for sure. Cyrus, it was a pleasure, but we've got to get back to the arena." Cyrus hopped off the table and shook Shon'dae and her cameraman's hands. "Oh, one last thing. Now that I've mentioned it," she continued. "Along with Francis Hampstead listed as the builder, there was another name associated with it. A name of Mulvaney."

"Popsicle," bleated Cyrus, "I mean, Mr. Mulvaney. He helped build Cranial Concusser?"

"Seems to be the case," she said as she walked towards the door. "We're rooting for you," she said with a turning wink. She then stopped, raised an eyebrow and gave a deceitful smile. "Especially if you end up meeting you know who. Then I'm really rooting for you."

Once they exited, Cyrus stared numbly at Cranial Concusser. *Why didn't I think to ask Popsicle about you? That was stupid. Would've saved me a hell of a lot of trouble.*

Cyrus grabbed his phone from the wagon. He found Popsicle's contact and punched out a message.

HI POPSICLE. HOPE ALL IS WELL. MADE IT TO COMBOT FINALS. TOUGH ROAD BUT I'M ON THE DOORSTEP. QUESTION…U REMEMBER A SILVER ARROW ROBOT NAMED CRANIAL CONCUSSER? THAT'S MY BOT. HEARD MAYBE U HELPED BUILD IT. LOVE TO LETTIE AND MUTTLY.

An hour later, Cyrus watched Ray Dokestout and his crew on the monitor parading up the aisle in victory. Dokestout held up his index finger as he passed the hysterical crowd. "One more" he seemed to be mouthing. As he fronted a camera along the way, he stopped and looked into it with a wide grin, held up two fingers, then all five, then made a circle with his hand. Cyrus got the message—250. Adrenaline pumped through Cyrus' veins. His temples crushed. His appointment in the decagon with Ray and Doke-a-250 was on the horizon.

A message buzzed his phone and his heart leapt from his chest. *Leslie!*

It was Popsicle.

HEY CY, FANTASTIC. CONGRATS. HOPE YOU CAN FINISH WHAT ME AND FRANCIS STARTED. AND YES, I KNOW MACHINE WELL. IF I REMEMBER RIGHT, I ALMOST LOST A HAND IN THE PROCESS. CRAZY THING—OR MAYBE IT WAS US WHO WERE CRAZY. LETTIE AND I WISHING YOU LUCK IN FINAL. MUTTLY TOO. BRING IT HOME.

Almost lost a hand? He can't be serious. Then again… He eyed Cranial Concusser suspiciously.

CHAPTER 43

The hour was closing in. Since that fifteen-minute warning knock came to the door, Cyrus paced Room 213 like a mad man held in solitary confinement. His heart, though stiffened for a fight, was working a hard, steady rhythm, crashing at his ribs despite his best attempts to temper it. Every so often he would stop, take a deep breath, wait for his pulse to lighten, then begin to pace some more; the beats per minutes, however, had the upper hand.

To abate his nerves, he focused on the strategy ahead. *OK, horizontal spinner that can reverse its polarity. Gotta send a message to Ray right away that if you come in close you'll get punished. Still, he can just ram through, regardless of any message. And those discs are a heavy lick to take, been working so far for him. What if I keep the flipper pumping, constant jabbing movements? That may work...there's plenty clearance below...but I've seen him flip over like a dozen of times...seems to love it. Playing on the other side and different disc...almost begs his opponents to flip him. Just gotta disable one of them, just like I did last year with the rototillers...that would be a start. But how? Timing, execution...that's how...just like you've been doing, Cy. But what about that saying "the best laid plans..."*

The clock in the room read 7:25. In five minutes—the witching hour.

The momentum towards the final showdown was evident on

Room 213's monitor. Cyrus watched the noiseless crowd, knowing very well they were anything but quiet in the cone of the volcano. The spider camera zipped across the top of the decagon, and below he caught a glimpse of Shon'dae Marquette talking animatedly into a camera with screaming fans behind her. The spotlights began their crisscrossing reverie. It all seemed surreal; he in an isolated room, everyone out there waiting for Cyrus Hamstead and his fighting robot.

The claustrophobia of Room 213 was getting to him. The confinement was making him near crazy. He decided an intake of oxygen in a non-suffocating room was the answer. He walked out into the hallway, and there he drew a deep breath. No officials or workers in sight. Eerily quiet, like an office building after hours. He looked at his phone: 7:28.

An ominous sound pealed throughout the corridor, like an air raid siren reverberating across the countryside. He realized that was the horn indicating match time.

Cyrus decided he'd walk to the end of the corridor, if only to reassure himself that someone was on the way.

Ahead at the corner, he heard footfalls followed by light banter. As the people approached, he saw in his periphery red-and-white stripes. *An official. About time.*

Seconds later he was face to face with the curmudgeonly, snubbed-nosed official. And behind him loomed Ray Dokestout, buttressed by two of his obedient soldiers. One pulled an industrial platform on which Doke-a-250 was covered. They stopped in their tracks. They all glared at Cyrus.

Ray cocked his head, his greasy onyx hair whipping with a quick jerk. His slate gray eyes appeared to be crossed, though maybe that was because Cyrus was so close to him. The closest, in fact, he'd ever been. On his black T-shirt was a schematical rendering of Doke-a-250 outlined in gold.

Cyrus muscles constricted. A trickle of sweat cascaded down his neck. He remained silent.

"Made it back, huh, sport?" Ray said rancidly, glowering at him.

"Made it back," said Cyrus cagily.

"Where's your stock-in-trade?" asked a crew member, the one with an affinity for Saguaro cacti.

"Waiting. Waiting back in the room." Cyrus noticed another official walking down the corridor to meet him. "Waiting for official word," he said, nodding toward the oncoming official.

"Lot of waiting," Ray said sarcastically.

"Yep. Lots. But why wait any longer. All this waiting and what we're really here for is action." Cyrus shook his head slowly. He stared dead-eye at Ray. "I mean, that's why we're here, right?"

Ray laughed. "Yeah, you better believe it. And no better time than the present. Let's stop all this waiting. Let's get your little project into the decagon. Then we'll see if your little project is worth me waiting for."

Cyrus gave him a half-smirk. "You'll get to see my 'little project' soon enough. Up and personal. Like you did before."

"Like I did before, huh? Sport, I think you've lost it a bit." His crew belted a laugh. The official grinned awkwardly, then echoed their laughter.

"I don't know," continued Cyrus, "maybe you'll remember. Maybe not. But I know one thing: it will remember."

"Good god," Ray said, tapping the official on the shoulder and whispering loudly in his ear, "been sucking on his CO_2 cylinder probably. Isn't that against the bylaws of this event?" The official snickered lightly. "Hey, save some of that gas for whatever thing you got attached to your little project. See you in the decagon, sport. If you can make it there."

The snubbed-nosed official walked past Cyrus. Ray, his crew, and Doke-a-250, strolled haughtily behind.

The other official suddenly appeared next to Cyrus. "What was that all about?" she asked.

"In the fight business I think they call it a stare-down," replied Cyrus. "And, yes, I'm ready."

CHAPTER 44

In his fighting pod, Cyrus' grip was nice and steady. Tight, not so much that his fingers would crimp and go numb, but just enough so that the physical was aligned with the mental. He tapped his thumb on the controller's motion knob, eagerly. Deft maneuvering was needed. He wanted to be ready.

Superior execution, that was is thinking. However, he had to not overthink it. *Just react, stay alert, anticipate as need be. Things change quickly out there.* He did his best to clear his head, stay focused, dial in to what was the biggest moment of his life. Keep psychological ramblings from taking root. Block out the frenzy, the lightshow, the decibels, the peppering of mayhem from the stands. And the vast financial reward. Anything which might cause him distraction.

Cranial Concusser was stationed on the other side of the clear walls, awaiting its commands. He could feel its energy seeping through the polycarbonate barrier, the very energy he felt harnessed inside it as he guided it through the decagon door. A rage that roiled beneath its metallic skin, a hurricane in a can. Yet, he remembered—*yes, distinctly, I'm sure of it*—its safety breaker had not yet been activated at that point. Which was...*strange.* Once he did flip that switch, the energy intensified, swelled, pulsed. But he was sure he felt some dormant energy. *I'm starting to imagine things. Just keep steady, Cy, stay focused.*

The monster on the opposite side of the decagon rambled into the center floor and maneuvered in circles. Doke-a-250: a drive train torque of four-hundred-and-thirty pounds; small quad wheels for pinpoint turning and lizard-like locomotion; two radial discs capable of twenty-one hundred RPM's, no matter which of its sides happened to be upright. Still, thought Cyrus, this is a single-weaponed beast with one straightforward weapon system. *I've seen those before. I can do this! We got this!*

Outside the decagon, the PA announcer took center spotlight. His voice squelched throughout the arena. "Who's ready?" A brief pause. "I repeat, whoooooo's ready!?" he belted out. The arena erupted. "Alright. That's more like it. It's time for the ultimate fight in the MegaBot division. Here and now, the showdown of all showdowns, the illustrious, highly exalted warfare of the heavy-weight robot class, in this twenty-eighth edition of the preeminent combat robotics competition known to both man and machine...ComBot." The laser lightshow crisscrossed the arena's interior comb. "With the winner to hold aloft the coveted Mega-Bot trophy, a challis which happens to be stuffed with fifty thousand bills, that's right, folks, fifty thousand wonderful American denominations with the great George Washington smirking on its front.

"On this side, Cyrus Hampstead has targeted his metal arrowhead at some of ComBot28's most fearsome of competitors. He aimed high, he aimed low, he aimed the mighty mallet, and he struck them all down with a force only vengeance could offer. One win shy from this spot last year, he remained undeterred, found renewed energy, and came into the decagon with a mechanized assemblage that packs one hell of a potent punch. Yes, vengeance and redemption, these are the ultimate rewards, and in turn, the rewards that come with ComBot's decagon. A notch older at seventeen, Cyrus is out to show the world that a meat hammer can be so hardcore, so badass, so lethal, that at its very sight, and this I've been truthfully told, folks, no lie, that a ribeye steak once got up from the butcher block and ran back to pasture. I reintroduce to you, Cyrus Hampstead and his carnal conquistador...Cranial Concusser."

Lights dizzied the crowd, sending them further into madness. Cyrus Hampstead waved his hand in appreciation of the support. He then pounded Cranial Concusser's hammer against the decagon floor. The announcer continued: "And over here is a mechanized menace for the ages, a bot looking to cap the last jewel on the crown on the greatest champion ever to grace the sport of combat robotics, a man who has two hundred and forty-nine victories under his belt, and before his long journey reaches its final conclusion, here tonight in this very decagon, he's looking to claim one last win, one last victory to earn the moniker of the very bot you see before you, see it folks, see it from any direction you like, a device as lethal from the view south as much from the view north, a dual disc, polarity defying spectacle from the one-and-only legend of our sport. For your enjoyment and primal pleasure, I offer you Ray Dokestout and his deleterious deal-with-the-devil...Doke-a-250."

Amidst the furor, Cyrus heard a voice ringing in his head. *Ride the mojo! Ride the mojo!*

At the sound of the buzzer, Cyrus sent Cranial Concusser's hammer into statuesque suspension. He drew his bot forward, weaved it around the decagon, passed tauntingly over the sawblade, which was stalled, but lying in wait. With his adrenaline in overdrive, he floated his thumb over the knob in anticipation of the oncoming assault.

In the opposite corner, Doke-a-250 moved not an inch. Its discs remained dormant. Its ferocity anything but.

Cyrus heard the jeers from the stands, the sharp whistles of impatience all around. He turned a side-eye glance to the opposing pod. There, Ray Dokestout stared calmly inside the decagon, his upper lip upturned a quarter inch. Cyrus looked behind Ray. His crew harbored sneaky smiles. Their arms were crossed with stubborn resolve.

Cyrus thumbed at the knob and Cranial Concusser danced a short jig. He jostled the knob some more and Cranial Concusser teased his opponent with a tail wiggle over the sawblade's open slot. He then realized: his balletic maneuvers were not poetic; the artistry in ComBot is in destruction, and destruction, or at least the promise of it, was all the people in the arena wanted. Obliteration, not ballet. Pure and simple. All his maneuvering felt empty. Like some empty promise.

But I'm not going to make the first move. So, he kept on goading, despite the hissing crowd.

Doke-a-250 just sat there like a comatose toad.

Cyrus analyzed the situation further. *Should I steamroll in? Go heavy with the mallet before Ray can make a move? Or wait for the obstacles to run, see how they come into play, game my decisions off them? He's toying this out for whatever reason. Should I do the same?*

The pit o' fire then flashed like an old-time camera bulb, waking up the sleepy decagon. The floor sawblade soon ripped to life, disrupting Cranial Concusser's dance with a nip of its dagger. A pulse of yellow-and-white. A squelch as startling as a bolt of lightning.

Cranial Concusser wobbled. Cyrus pirouetted his machine out from the sawblade. Doke-a-250 bore down full throttle on its backend, its twin discs coming in at high revolutions. Before Cyrus could turn his bot, yellow streaks of light arched over the decagon floor. Doke-a-250 had ripped a gouge midway up Cranial Concusser's hammer's sleeve. The laceration was minor; anything deeper might have dissected the arm, assuring defeat.

Cranial Concusser turned tight to the right and peeled in reverse. It circled the sawblade, keeping the obstacle between it and Doke-a-250. But Doke-a-250 was out-for-blood, on the chase. As it zeroed in, its lower disc revved inches from the side of the sawblade; its upper disc cleared the teeth by a few inches more.

Cyrus maneuvered Cranial Concusser to a sidewall and eased the throttle. Doke-a-250, now against an opposing wall, raced the perimeter of the decagon. Cranial Concusser kept its distance, mirroring its opponent's speed. When Doke-a-250 moved, Cranial Concusser moved; when Doke-a-250 stopped, Cranial Concusser stopped in kind—a hot and slow pursuit around the floor with a violent obstacle spinning at its center.

The game of cat and mouse went on for the better part of a minute—a ComBot eternity.

Cyrus heard the moans and shrieks from the stands, the amorphous cursing and calls for chaos. He knew this couldn't go on forever. Nor did he want it to. He was itching to hear his machine's hammer hit metal.

Still, he was careful not to fall for the "slam on the brakes" trick. Doke-a-250 would be on his heels in no time.

Then Cyrus saw things change.

Cranial Concusser stopped in its tracks. It drew the hammer to its apex, making it appear like the paw of a dumbstruck cat waiting for an ambushing bird.

Cyrus quickly looked to his controller. The throttle was forward, the hammer's button unpressed. He had given no signal, yet there it was, his bot going rogue. Once again. *Come on! I thought we worked through this already.* Cyrus was as confused as a cat. *No friggen' way!*

To hell with it! If that's what it wants. Cyrus thumbed hard at the controller lunching Cranial Concusser. It obeyed his commands by heading toward the sawblade, center floor. Doke-a-250 followed its tracks.

As the sawblade spat its fury and Doke-a-250 closing in, Cyrus crashed his finger at the controller. Cranial Concusser beat its hammer, a perfectly timed connection squarely upon the flat side of Doke-a-250's upper disc. The contusion lumbered Doke-a-250; its disc gouged the floor. A bloom of sparks shot the decagon.

The impact of the upper disc colliding with the hammer's head was too much. Both machines staggered.

Again, Cyrus punched the button. Again, the mallet coiled midway. *Shit! Jammed!*

Before Doke-a-250 recomposed, Cyrus pivoted Cranial Concusser one-hundred-and-eighty degrees and throttled in reverse. With full force, the tail dagger rammed into Doke-a-250's lower disc. An eerie, whining screech filled the arena. Cyrus squinted his eyes. A dilemma: Cranial Concusser's tail was lost within the recesses of Doke-a-250, in the slot of the disc.

Cyrus tried to pull out but the bots were entwined. Cyrus looked to Ray's pod. The furious, whip-like signals given to his machine produced a whimpering shrill.

Cyrus slammed his finger at the button to activate the hammer. Nothing doing. *Crap!*

Fierce strikes at the flipper switch. Wasted energy. *Fuck!*

The bots were hooked like angry rams, jostling with wasteful energy. Cyrus again shot a look to the opposing pod. Ray met his eyes with disdain—a look of evil.

Then a curious expression befell Ray's face. He was staring behind Cyrus in a state of shock, pure confusion in his eyes. *What's got into this asshole?*

"Where's the mojo?"

To Cyrus, the voice was as beautiful as there ever was one. Sweet, sonorous, a singsong of courage lifted from the depths of nowhere. It was if a guardian angel had swooped over a beleaguered foxhole to revive the battered troops.

Cyrus spun around. "Wait! What? How did…"

"Cyrus, look out!"

Leslie had seen it coming before Cyrus could. Doke-a-250 had rocked out from the embrace and was on the retreat. In its wake, a metallic nub was left to the floor. Cranial Concusser's tail had been dismembered from butt to tip.

Cyrus took one hand from the controller and reached behind him. He grabbed Leslie by the hand and pulled her in, gave her a quick hug and a quick kiss. She dropped what appeared to be a thin silver object. Cyrus paid little attention but had noticed it flash to the ground. Cyrus had no idea what it was, but given the circumstances, why would he care.

"Focus, Cy. Keep focus on taking that bastard out," Leslie yelled into his ear. Leslie quickly shut the pod door and reached down to retrieve the silver object. She stuffed it in her back pocket. "I'll explain everything later," she blurted.

"Got it. Thank God you're here," he yelled back. He throttled his bot to the far end of the decagon.

Doke-a-250 came headstrong at Cranial Concusser. Cyrus throttled his bot to meet it square. Right before impact, Cyrus launched the flipper. Doke-a-250 catapulted to a flare of sparks and crashed to its side, then immediately righted itself. Cyrus heard the crowd erupt.

Cyrus raced Cranial Concusser along a sidewall and stopped in front of the corkscrew. The obstacle gyrated at full speed. *OK, let's get composed, catch a short break.* He knew Dokestout wouldn't be barreling in, not with all that churning metal behind him. Leslie was on the exact same page.

"He's not going to risk it," she said. "If anything, he'll come in from the side, not straight on."

The corkscrew scrabbled hard at where Cranial Concusser's tail had once been. Doke-a-250 lingered across the decagon in "wait mode," shifting forward and backward with anticipatory intension.

"Be patient, Cy. If he eases in slow, you'll at least have an option out."

"Or he may come in hard on the side, attack along the wall. I'm not sure."

"Wow, this is fun," chirped Leslie.

Doke-a-250 navigated the sidewall, creeping steadily closer. Several feet away, the thwacker pounded, seeking a victim.

"And don't forget nerve-racking, Les," chimed Cyrus.

"Cyrus, something's off, something's not right."

"I know. My hammer's not working."

"What?"

"My hammer, it's barely moving. I think I lost it."

Doke-a-250 circumvented the thwacker, eased back along the sidewall. A slow, methodical advance.

"Crap! Seriously? Why didn't you say something?"

"I just did."

"OK, look, we'll deal with that as we go. But I meant Ray's upper disc. It's barely moving. Only the bottom one's at full force." She looked across his shoulder to the opposing pod. Cyrus briefly followed her glance. The crew behind Ray glared over with hateful venom and seething indictment. Cyrus wasn't quite sure why. *What's up with these shitbags?* After a second, he realized they weren't glaring at him, but at Leslie.

"Ray looks panicky, Cy", she murmured in his ear. "And those creeps, ugghh."

"You're right. And you're right about that disc. It's pretty much slowed to nothing." Once Doke-a-250 came within a wall's length away, its upper disc fully shut down. "It can't touch us with just the lower one." Cyrus seized on the advantage.

Doke-a-250 raced in at full speed but Cyrus pivoted Cranial Concusser out. On the chase, Doke-a-250 caught a hard edge on the corkscrew, propelling it a foot in the air and flipping it back over. "It reversed itself," screamed Leslie. "Damn it!"

"We're still good," replied Cyrus. "We just got to get it back to its other side. Because I'm down to only one weapon. My flipper."

"Do it," screeched Leslie.

Doke-a-250 took a sweeping arc around the floor's sawblade, then accelerated with all it had. Once in range, Cyrus depressed the flipper button. The collision—a cataclysmic explosion of flying sparks and wayward shards and splinters of metal and indeterminate robotic parts—left

Cyrus with one conclusion. He spun to Leslie. "Think my flipper's gone too."

"You kidding me?"

"Unfortunately, no."

Cyrus reversed Cranial Concusser from the fray. It lurched, staggered. Cyrus began to question how much his bot had left in the tank. And what he could really accomplish with a fizzled hammer, a missing tail, and a bunk flipper.

Leslie pointed at Doke-a-250. "Oh God, 250 flipped again! Look!" The bot treaded clumsily around the sawblade, unsure, shaky, nearly being nipped by the saw's teeth. Its upper disc came to life. It steadily gained RPM's.

"You're right," Cyrus said dejectedly.

Panic seized Cyrus. His brain stymied, his heart skipped several beats. He felt frozen, lost in a strange netherworld. It was like he was reliving the experience from a year ago, the moment when Spiral Cyclone was dragged into the pit o' fire. The moment when he became a cadaver propped by cardboard legs. It was de-ja' vu, only with different bots playing their parts in the decagon. He had no idea what to do, what he should do, how to do anything, really.

He peered at his controller. He then looked ruefully to Leslie.

"It's OK, Cy, just keep fighting," she cried over the baying arena.

Cyrus hands were pressed to the side of the controller, his fingers paralyzed. His thumb twitched uncontrollably over the throttle, unable to make a coherent move. His eyes became glassed, his face wane and distant. Leslie placed her hand on top of his.

"Cyrus, it's alright. Hey, you alright?"

Doke-a-250 staggered around the sawblade, closing the distance.

He looked up. Her lovely face and glowing emerald eyes melded into his vision. For a fleeting instant, they were back at the Chromiums game—front row, the taste the sweetness on her mouth, the softness of her lips, the touch of her hand on his arm. If not for the sight of Doke-a-250 marching towards his bot, he could have sworn they were both there, exploring the possibility of love for the first time. "I'm good," he said with a weak smile. He was far from good.

Doke-a-250 continued stalking, revved up like a demon.

He again shot a look to Ray's pod. The crew behind him were yelling at one another. *What's pissing them?* But he knew this was no time for silent questioning.

When fate wants its way, the only thing to do is surrender.

Beyond Leslie, the blurred decagon came into Cyrus' view. He adjusted his eyes. Cranial Concusser was slamming its hammer madly. A violent tantrum against the floor.

He looked at his fingers. They weren't touching the remote's buttons.

It's in your hands now!

Cyrus handed Leslie the controller. She stared back at him in shock. "Cy, what're doing? I don't have the slightest…"

Doke-a-250 closed within four short feet.

"Just steady the throttle," he said, pointing down, "it's got the rest."

Leslie did as Cyrus instructed.

Two feet separated Cranial Concusser and Doke-a-250—the ideal distance for weapon deployment. It was then that Cyrus' machine uncorked the most rage-fueled, fiercely wicked and exacting blow he had ever witnessed from his bot. He watched as his machine recoiled its hammer, fired off a clubbing, and another, and another, a succession of blows each more vicious than last. Cataclysmic thunderclaps reverberated across the arena.

Doke-a-250's upper disc caved into the shape of a crescent moon. Crippled, it stumbled over to the corkscrew. It tried to overturn and right itself, but the corkscrew kicked the edge of the disc, bouncing it over and over against the decagon floor. Cranial Concusser, meanwhile, stalked its prey.

"I'm not doing any of this, Cy. What the hell's going on?"

Cyrus looked to the opposing pod. Behind Ray, the crew were yelling at one another, pointing fingers accusingly. Ray whipped his head continuously from the decagon to his crew, barking orders. He appeared to be close to slinging his controller to the ground, or thought Cyrus, at his crew. Everything seemed to be lost.

"Not sure. But I think we have the upper hand."

Cyrus turned to Leslie. They smiled at each other. Cyrus thought he saw a deceitful turn of her lip, a shifty grin of self-satisfaction. The kind she exhibited after beating him at ro-sham-bo.

They looked inside the decagon.

Inside, Cranial Concusser finished what it had come here to do. What it was designed to do. What it was…programmed to do. It approached its opponent, now waylaid with the beaten curve of its disc jammed into the floor, and loomed over it. Leslie held the controller in the palm of hand. Her fingers outstretched. She had a wild look in her eyes. And her laugh, it matched her look. A beautiful, complex, slightly wicked laugh over the noisy cacophony of the crowd and the metal-on-metal assault still echoing throughout the arena.

CHAPTER 45

Leslie pulled Cyrus close and interlocked her fingers across his back to where his arms were locked tightly against his side. She squeezed his chest so hard his breath escaped in a gasp. A short wobble, then his legs found themselves. But she never let go. She wouldn't let go. Never mind his own euphoria being hindered, the crush of her embrace was enough for Cyrus. He could have stayed like this for hours.

But there was chaos and pandemonium around him, a thousand thoughts racing in his head, Leslie screaming in his ear and him not knowing exactly the words coming out of her. The world was muffled, distorted, electric. Still, Cyrus gave thanks to the heavens that this wonderful girl was with him, clutching him so tight his limbs barely moved an inch.

After a timeless moment, Leslie released her grip and began kissing him incessantly on the face, one cheek and then the other. Cyrus gave in to the smothering, even though he felt a little like he was pinned down by a puppy with all the love in the world to give—like Muttly.

"You won, Cy, you did it!"

"I think so, I think so," he screamed back. "But it looks like you did it. Because I know I didn't do it. What the hell just happened?"

"Concusser walloped that thing. Look!"

Inside the decagon, Cranial Concusser stood by idly like it was waiting for the next train to arrive. Next to it was a battered carcass.

"Oh yeah, I knew it had it in him," he yelled into her ear as the PA announcer's voice came to life. "You should've been here at the beginning. What a rush, the whole intro was awesome, the lead up and the crowd and the way…"

"Cyrus, I was here. I've been here the whole time."

"Wait…what? Why didn't you say anything about that. Why didn't you come into the pod earlier?"

"Why? Because of this." Leslie extracted the silver object from her back pocket. She placed it in his hand and produced a devious grin.

"I don't understand," he said, looking at the device confusingly.

Leslie looked over at the opposing pod, now emptied of contestants. Ray and his crew waited dejectedly outside the decagon door to claim their metallic victim. Since the announcer's baritone proclamations of victory filled the arena, Leslie had to speak directly into his ear.

"Look, here's the deal, I knew something was fishy, so I…hey, you never asked how I got here, or why."

"That was my next question, of course. I've been wondering that all along," he said into her ear.

"I told the camp folks, like the one's who make sure you're actually there, that I twisted my ankle and needed to go to urgent care, you know, to get an X-ray. Well, that was a lie, naturally, but it gave me an excuse to leave in a hurry and drive up here. You see, I needed to be here, Cy, I really did. And eventually, I'll have to drive back. But I had to come up with something. You proud?"

"More than you know. More...than...you...know. But," he held up the silver object, "what does this have to do with anything?"

"That, Cyrus Hampstead," she said levelly, holding his chin so he could see her words over the commotion, "has been their key to winning all along. It's what they've been using to jam the reception of Concusser's signal. You know how you get a dedicated wavelength assigned to you, to just your robot, before each tournament? Well, your friendly neighborhood greaseball and his loser gang over there somehow got hold of what that wavelength was and have been using this thing to kill your reception."

"You're telling me that Ray," he said with disbelief, "has basically been scrambling my frequency? At the right moment? From the get-go?"

"Along with the help of his crew. That's the truth. Painfully."

"Which means..."

"They did the same with Spiral Cyclone."

"And to Cranial Concusser, like ten years ago."

"But they didn't do it today. They tried, but the guy I noticed sneaking away from the group, sitting all nonchalant up in the stands, didn't count on one Leslie Borowski showing up and ripping it out of his mealy hands."

"I friggen' knew it. But how did, I mean, how you were you able to...?"

"I knew what those assholes were up to, I just didn't know how or who. So, I stood back, watched all the hoopla and stuff before the finals, which by the way was a blast, and kept my eyes on them. Just kept on looking. I just knew one of them would break free from the rest, because that person wouldn't do anything like that in the fighting pod. Too obvious. And that's what happened. I tracked him down."

"Wow, I've got to say," said Cyrus as a tournament official opened the pod door, "you are a badass. One hundred percent." The official held up Cyrus' arm in a claim of victory. The crowd sent a roar of salute. With his opposite hand, Cyrus held up Leslie's arm.

"Cyrus, watch out!" she pierced loudly, recoiling.

Cyrus laughed hysterically. "Les, that's just the spider cam. Trying to get a good shot of us, you know, for when we watch this in November."

"It better get my good side then," she teased, turning to her right and kissing his cheek.

Coming down the aisle in a formal parade was an official holding ComBot28's trophy. The other official, the surly slug-nosed man who escorted Ray Dokestout and Doke-a-250 into the decagon—the one he remembered from a year ago—followed behind with a giant-sized check. He looked beleaguered and distraught, as if he had just lost everything in a game of cards. Right then, it occurred to Cyrus.

"That's how they did it," he whispered to Leslie. "That official right there." He pointed up the aisle. "I'm almost positive about it."

Leslie looked up the aisle. She paused, reflected a moment, then spoke clearly into his ear. "What's done is done. That's the past and there's nothing more you can do about it. Let's just celebrate the win. Your win." Cyrus nodded in agreement.

Over the cheering, the lights, the PA announcer's sizzling voice, the orbiting spider cam, and the pomp and spoils heading their way, the world slowed down for Cyrus. One single voice rose in his head. A divine voice from above.

We finally did it, boy. But it was all you. And all those people who love you. I couldn't be prouder. Hella proud, my boy.

CHAPTER 46

The clouds arrayed over Cyrus Hampstead's back lawn, shadows of gray giving way to the occasional sunburst. As Cyrus sat on his back porch watching the hallucinatory display from above, Mongrel leapt onto his lap. The cat began to knead his legs, arranging himself for the optimal place to relax. With his Adirondack chair reclined three-quarters of the way back, Cyrus was in no position to give resistance to Mongrel's territorial claim. He felt the cat deserved a good rest, seeing that his hunting days were well behind him and all he had to look forward to in life was a steady course of two-a-day feedings and a shady place to settle. Soon enough, winter would force Mongrel back to his old basement sleeping spot. Back to where it all began. The cat, for all its slouching idleness, was the impetus to something great, and Cyrus felt the least he could do was provide his feline friend an offering of serenity. This was Mongrel's reward.

With Mongrel settled, Cyrus threw his head back and watched the parade of clouds. He thought about the events of the last year, thought about the future, thought about life.

If it was fate, then fate it was. God, how unpredictable life can be, how uncertain. But whatever comes my way from this point forward, I'm just going to roll with the punches, keep on rolling and hope for the best. He came to realize that nothing in life is set in stone; you set your sights on something, find a road to take you there and work hard, all the while knowing that whatever may happen, there will always be another fork that appears somewhere along the path. A different road altogether. *That's a given.* The more he came to understand this, the more at peace he felt. A year ago, that very notion would have pricked him into a full-blown anxious sweat. *What's the word: serendipity?*

He scratched behind Mongrel's ear. A few rubs later and not even the hardest of summer's winds could roust the cat from his purring nap.

"Hey, what's with all this lazing around?" Cyrus' head snapped. Mongrel, for his part, didn't twitch a whisker.

"I thought you were coming over later?" asked Cyrus. His surprise was a joyous one.

Leslie plopped down on the Adirondack chair next to him. "Finished babysitting early. I was gonna go home but, I don't know, I felt antsy." She reached over and stroked Mongrel's tail.

"Ahh, now look who's the antsy one."

"Hey, don't judge."

"Never. And I'd never complain about you showing up early. Anywhere."

"Timeliness," she said with a sly grin, "is one of my super traits. It certainly isn't solving for the area of an ellipse or figuring out the area of that cone thingy."

"School's two weeks away, Les, I don't wanna think about solving for anything. Seriously. Unless it's what movie we want to watch tonight. Something along those lines."

Leslie leaned back in her chair and raised her chin to the sky. Cyrus watched her emerald eyes capture the blue and morph into sapphire. But he could tell she wasn't relaxed. There was a hunger in there, something unfulfilled. He could see it in her eyes. Over the past year, he had developed a pretty good understanding of her harbored desires.

"Still antsy?" he asked casually.

"Little. Cyrus, I think's there's something we have to do," she said in a level tone.

Cyrus reached down and tried to cudgel Mongrel off his legs. The cat refused to budge. "Oh...oh, OK. Well, uh, you know my mother's upstairs."

Leslie lowered her head and tilted him a stare. "Not that, Cy. Well, maybe later, but not now. I've just, you know, been thinking."

She pulled herself up from the chair and rose to her feet. With one hand she grabbed Cyrus' arm, with the other she gently rubbed Mongrel's neck. "Sorry ole boy. Hate to disturb you, but there's something more important."

Cyrus split his legs and a mass of gray fur fumbled down. Mongrel stretched briefly on the ground, then went languidly back to his nap.

Leslie led Cyrus to the shed. There, she grabbed the shovel. She pointed to the object sitting just outside the shed's door, an object which had seen better days. An object which once housed wires and gears and rods and all sorts of manmade contrivances, but had been repurposed for another end.

"Got a burlap sack or something?" she asked.

"Yep, in the shed" he replied, a smile a foot wide.

They tramped along the neglected wooded path, kicking the thicket and hacking their way through rangy weeds and thorny vines which stretched over the trail. Eventually, they arrived at a small clearing. A trickle of sunlight poked through the trees, yet soon the area was grayed by a passing cloud. On the far side of the clearing was a stump, weathered by rot and reconfigured by termite channels. Cyrus stared at it for a long moment, then placed the burlap sack on the ground in front of him. "This looks like a good spot."

"Look there, Cy. It looks like a toothpick some fairytale giant would use." She pointed to a nearby tree branch.

Cyrus focused his eyes on the insect perched atop a broad leaf. It lay motionless, its rice paper wings flattened along the length of its back. Six needle-like legs supported its delicate frame. In the shade, its wings appeared sapphire; in a sunburst, aquamarine. It was as if an iridescent origami figure had somehow blown into the woods.

The insect fluttered away and became a ghost.

"Was that a dragonfly?" asked Leslie.

"No, that was a damselfly. They're related to dragonflies, but dragonflies have their wings sticking out from their sides."

"How do you know this?"

"Lot of time at the creek. That's where they breed. Are you sure you don't want to go there? I can take you afterwards. There's a lot of light left in the day. I know this cool spot."

She shifted her lips back and forth. "Maybe. Someday. Just not today. You see how it just took off like that. Flew away. I wouldn't mind, you know, doing that. Like maybe going to Europe."

"Huh, little farther than the creek. Probably somewhat more expensive too."

"I'm serious, Cyrus," she said, swiping leaves away from the ground with the shovel. "I need to have something to look forward to. I can't go through my senior year without having something on the horizon. And I've been thinking a lot about Europe next summer. You know, backpacking, staying at hostels, doing the train thing."

"That sounds awesome, really."

"That's what *I'm* saying," she reiterated spunkily.

With a thrust, she planted the shovel into the dirt and left it sticking upright. "Ro-sham-bo to dig."

"I'll do the digging, Les," he said, grabbing the shovel's handle.

She swiped his hand away. "I wouldn't think of doing this but fairly."

They beat fists to palms. They made their reveal; Cyrus emerged scissors, Leslie paper.

"Won," said Cyrus.

"You got me this time. Here you go," she said, pushing the handle at him.

He caught it in his hand. He tilted his head. "But I won."

"Yeah, you did. Congrats. And now you get digging rights."

Leslie released the opening of the burlap sack and eased the tree out to the ground. It had grown nearly two feet since they first planted it. She kneeled down and gingerly spread the roots.

"This isn't easy earth," said Cyrus, shaking out his hands. "These old roots are brutal. So, where are you thinking of going? You know, in Europe?"

"Not just me, Cy, I'm talking about *us* going to Europe. You deserve it, too."

"Oh, really? I mean, that would be great. I did do alright last year, from a financial standpoint," Cyrus said as he tossed aside some dirt.

"Yes, you did. But you know that has your college's name all over it. Good luck convincing you mom you'll be bouncing all over Europe with it."

"You forget, there's a machine called Brown Toro..."

"How could I forget..."

"Well, it made me a few grand last winter. When the snow falls again, as I know it will, there's my European money right there. Oh, and whatever commission I may get from Smitty's lighting promotion."

"My babysitting, your earnings. Oh, and once Uncle Carl sees his name in victory during ComBot's telecast, I'll be leaning heavy for some frequent flier points. There are our tickets to Madrid right there," said Leslie, bundling her silky hair into a bun.

"Madrid?" asked Cyrus. "Kinda thinking about Paris. Always

wanted to see the Eiffel Tower. All those triangles."

"Triangles?"

"Yeah, you know, just like they appear on that poster on the wall in class."

"What poster? What wall? Our class?"

Cyrus learned against the handle of the shovel, trying not to laugh. The edge of the shovel slipped, and a foot fell in the hole. "Never mind," he said, wiping the dirt from his shoe.

"Listen," she said seriously, "I don't know what's going to happen this next year, I don't even know...you know..." She looked up at him. "Sometimes one person may decide things aren't right for them."

Cyrus stopped shoveling. "Are you trying to tell me something, Leslie?"

"No, it's not me, Cyrus. Not at *all*. It's just that I've seen break-ups, lots of them in school, and I don't particularly want to get hurt."

He walked over to her, plucked a leaf from the elm, and held it between his fingers. He placed it in her hands. "Trust me, I couldn't imagine being with anyone else. That's the honest truth. And I understand. I understand things can change. I do. But if I ever feel anything different, and I really don't believe I will, then if that fork appears in the road, I will tell you. We'll talk about it."

"We had a great year, huh?"

"The best. A script flippen' year," he said. "I think the hole's big enough now."

"Yes, I think so."

Together they held the tree, Leslie by the roots, Cyrus by the trunk. They knelt down and eased the elm into the hole, covering it with rich country soil. They walked to the other side of the clearing. Cyrus checked for proper verticality. He nodded.

"Should rain tomorrow," said Cyrus, "so we should be good for now."

Just then, the damselfly returned and took up position atop the newly planted elm.

Cyrus stared at its beauty. He then had a idea. He took out his phone and launched his compass app. "Tell you what? We'll make this interesting. Depending on which direction the damselfly flies off, that will be the European country we go to first. Then from there, we can head out anywhere on the train. Deal? East is that way," he pointed easterly, "so that's London. North," he pointed in front of him, "would be Paris," he thumbed behind him, "south is Madrid, and that way is west so that is, uh, Munich."

"No more ro-sham-bos?" asked Leslie with a smirk.

"Please no."

"Deal."

They stood back and waited. The damselfly fluttered, briefly took a turn west, then came right at them, splitting them in a display of fleeting iridescent beauty.

"Ha. South. That's Madrid. Can't wait."

"You win again."

"Never thought I wouldn't," she laughed and gave him a kiss.

Cyrus saluted the new addition to the woods, a tear tickling his eye. He threw the burlap sack over his shoulder, and together they walked down that old spur path, towards their future.

EPILOGUE

From: Caroline Wythe
To: Cyrus Hampstead
Subject: Congratulations!
Hello Cyrus,

I just wanted to send you a quick note of congratulations on your second trip to the big robot event. Can't wait to find out how it went. I know you worked so hard this past year, in both geometry and your competitive sport. You should be a shining example of commitment and determination to the students at SEHS.

I'm really looking forward to being your instructor next fall for AP Calc. Senior year is always the best for students, but that doesn't mean you get to coast through. I'll make sure of that. You are such a bright student, so that's the least of my worries. And again, thank you for helping with tutoring. That was a huge help for some of the other students who were struggling.

Funny thing, my husband tells me when he's watching something in bed and I'm fast asleep, I'm somehow able to explain to him the next morning exactly what happened. If it was a mystery, like one of those whodunits, I'm able to tell him exactly who did do it. For whatever reason, the information just seeps in, despite me being knocked out cold. An amazing trait, isn't it Cyrus?

Well, I don't know why that just crossed my mind. This is about you, a wonderful, conscientious, considerate, respectful young man. And helpful, especially when it really counts, like when the chips are down. I'm sure there are some traits you need to develop more, we all have those, but I must say, I couldn't be prouder to have you as one of my students.

See you first day of class.
Regards,
Mrs. Wythe

ACKNOWLEDGEMENTS

This novel would not have gone the direction it did without the guiding influence of several people, especially my wonderful mentors at Antioch University, Los Angeles' MFA Writing Program.

Aditi Khorana was instrumental in helping lay out the roadmap and pushing me along the path. After spending a second semester under her guidance, I sent her a thank you note telling her she was like a witch in the woods who shows the confused traveler the right way. In no way was this indictment on her personality or temperament; she has a magically creative mind and without her I truly would have been lost.

For one term and in many workshops, I was under the mentorship of Francesca Lia Block, a master of the craft of writing. I was in awe of her knowledge of story plotting, arcs and beats, as well as character development, and with those concepts in mind I was able to grasp (hopefully) the workings of story. She is a great teacher and a better person.

Sarah Van Arsdale, another Antioch mentor, equally contributed to major parts of this story; with four succinct words she set me straight, and those words always reverberate in my head as I continue my writing journey.

A big thanks to Jamie Gallagher for adding her knowledge to one of the chapters, and Will Gallagher to another.

Lastly, and really the most important person in this entire endeavor (and my life), is my wife, Alison. She allowed me the space and time to create and has always been very supportive of all my follies. Thank you for your energy, guidance, love and all you do.

My kids, for whom this book is dedicated, I thank you all for inspiring my creativity and letting me into your teenage world – a necessary foray when one writes about young people. And now that this book is complete, I am happy to be released from that world, although I know I'll have to dip in now and again as my time on this earth passes by.

About the Author

Joe G. Becker lives in
Manhattan Beach, California with his family.

He has three children. Joe earned his MFA in Creative
Writing from Antioch University, Los Angeles.